# THE
# WITCH
## AND THE
# VAMPIRE

ALSO BY FRANCESCA FLORES

*Diamond City*
*Shadow City*

# THE
# WITCH
## AND THE
# VAMPIRE

A NOVEL

# FRANCESCA
# FLORES

WEDNESDAY BOOKS
NEW YORK

First published in the United States by Wednesday Books, an imprint of St. Martin's Publishing Group

THE WITCH AND THE VAMPIRE. Copyright © 2023 by Francesca Flores. All rights reserved. Printed in the United States of America. For information, address St. Martin's Publishing Group, 120 Broadway, New York, NY 10271.

www.wednesdaybooks.com

Designed by Devan Norman
Case stamp based off cover illustration by Colin Verdi

The Library of Congress Cataloging-in-Publication Data is available upon request.

ISBN 978-1-250-22051-6 (hardcover)
ISBN 978-1-250-22052-3 (ebook)

Our books may be purchased in bulk for promotional, educational, or business use. Please contact your local bookseller or the Macmillan Corporate and Premium Sales Department at 1-800-221-7945, extension 5442, or by email at MacmillanSpecialMarkets@macmillan.com.

First Edition: 2023

10  9  8  7  6  5  4  3  2  1

DEDICATED TO
M. L. S. AND N

# PART 1

## The Tower and the Wall

# CHAPTER 1

- AVA -

*Deep in the woods, darkness treads.*

*Her name is Casiopea, the queen of the undead with blood on their lips.*

*She leads them to prey, humans and witches who've lost their way.*

*She draws them to her waiting arms with anguished cries that never end.*

*Their blood spills, the shadows encroach,*

*but the thirst never dies.*

—JOURNAL, AUTHOR UNKNOWN

I slam the journal shut when a floorboard creaks downstairs, and listen closely for any more movement. Zenos must be awake now, which means he and my mother will come to my attic soon—and I'll have to play the part of the perfect, obedient daughter.

Standing on my bed, I push aside a loose tile on the ceiling. Dust falls onto my face as I place the book up there—a journal that tells of the vampire queen, Casiopea, and the history of vampires in Arborren. My fingers brush against my other hidden trinkets: a doll my mother gave me back when we loved each other, a ruby necklace she brought me from one of her trips. A woven scarf gifted to me by my old school friend Kaye.

If I manage to escape today, I'll have to leave most of it behind. I squeeze the doll's arm once, then replace the ceiling tile and jump down from my bed.

Soon, my mother will come up here to take from me again. She can say she's keeping me here to protect me all she wants, but I know the truth: she needs me more than I need her.

Grabbing a broom from the corner, I sweep the floor, and look out of my western window every few seconds. The silver bars crossing it block some of my view, but I can still see the forest stretching away to the horizon. My non-beating heart swells at the sight of it: the towering oak, the golden-green leaves lit by dawn, and the pale, shimmering barrier that wraps all around it. I imagine the smoke-sweet scent of those trees, and a deep urge to go to them tugs at me.

After sweeping the room, I straighten the stacks of scarves and gloves I've knitted to pass the time. I ignore the throbbing sensation in the back of my throat that tells me I need blood soon. My hair, which is long enough to nearly touch the floor on its own, gets caught on loose nails and stacks of books as I move around the room. But I'm so used to it, it doesn't bother me. I simply tug it free, suppressing a smile as strands of it fall to the floor. I'm not allowed to cut it, but I can still get rid of some of it like this.

Then I wipe the dust off the books on literature and mathematics that my mother gives me, the ones I never touch because the journal tells me all I need to know: that there's a whole world of vampires waiting in the trees.

A faintly shimmering barrier around the forest keeps humans safe by locking the vampires in, but the forest is also a vast territory where vampires roam free, ruled by a queen named Casiopea. She became their leader after they were locked inside, and shaped the forest into a haven where they are safe from the mortals who seek to destroy them. That barrier is the only thing keeping both the humans and the vampires safe.

At night, when all is quiet, whispers call me from the woods.

I've heard them for two years now. Thousands of voices coming from the direction of the trees. I can never make out what they say, but I remember the scary stories passed among children at school—that if you strayed too close to the trees and a vampire called out to you, it was already too late; your blood was theirs for the taking.

The whispers I hear at night must be the vampires calling me. They *have* to be.

I'll escape and join them. I'll use the information in the journal to reach the vampire queen and her territory. I'll follow the whispers.

The sounds of my mother collecting documents, writing letters, and packing clothes into a trunk for her trip reach me through the thin floors below. Like me, she never sleeps.

Footsteps pounding on the staircase below send a jolt of panic through me. The wooden stairs are weak and weathered, each step making them groan. It must be Zenos. My mother would never make that much noise. I force myself to remember my plan.

*Go in front of the armoire, Ava, and open it a crack.*

I dart to the armoire that stands between the door and my vanity table, nearly tripping over my hair as I do. Then I open the armoire just wide enough to fit my hand through.

The door opens and my stepfather shuffles inside, with his

ratlike nose and mouth, steel-gray eyes, salt-and-pepper hair, and rail-thin body that is much stronger than it looks. In one hand he carries a candle, the tiny flickering flame adding hollows under his eyes. In his other hand, a small clay cup.

"You waited by the door?" he asks me with a raised eyebrow. I stiffen as he closes the door behind him. "Greedy little thing."

His words sound like an insult, but I know he's just trying to rile me. He holds out the cup, which is filled to the brim with a deep red liquid that makes my mouth water and clouds my thoughts. A familiar, dull ache suffuses my gums as my fangs itch to sink into something. I've never liked the coppery smell of blood; something about the scent feels so sinister. Reminds me I'm actually drinking human blood.

I fight down a shudder, and remind myself I've never killed or hurt anyone. I was made into a vampire against my will. The fact that I have to drink this to survive is not my fault.

I shove aside the whispers of doubt and guilt, then reach out to take the cup from Zenos. He grips it for a second longer than he needs to, tugging on it at the same time I do. My eyes widen. He wouldn't keep my blood from me, would he? Is this a new experiment of his?

"No need to hide your thirst," he says with a taunting chuckle. His dirty fingers brush against mine as he relinquishes the cup. "It's fascinating how the blood fills your veins and makes your body function like a well-tuned machine."

Ignoring him, I drink from the cup. Once the blood touches my tongue, I savor it, how the mere taste wakes up every sense inside me, lights me up as if I've been wallowing in a dark cave since the last time I drank. The world becomes brighter; I feel every dust mote as it falls on my skin, see every ant that crawls on the floorboards of this attic, hear my mother scribbling something with a pen two floors down from here. Confidence floods every part of me, until escaping sounds not only possible, but easy.

I feel alive again.

Maybe drinking blood makes me evil in the eyes of humans, but it feels so good that for a moment I stop caring.

Zenos takes in every small change of my expression with a delighted glint in his gaze. I always avoid looking in mirrors when I drink, but I know what I look like now: veins showing under my eyes, pupils dilated, fangs growing past my lips. It will fade soon. It doesn't matter if Zenos stares now; as long as I'm smart and follow through with my plan, I'll get out of here and he'll never be able to look at me again.

"Is Mother almost ready for her trip?" I ask, keeping a friendly tone to my voice so he won't suspect me of anything.

"So eager for Eugenia to be gone?" Zenos asks, stepping toward me and the armoire. I try my hardest not to look at it and give myself away. "Once she leaves, we'll both be bored all day. I'll go into town, of course, but I know you won't have much to do. I'll invite you downstairs on occasion and you can sit with me there, all right?"

"That sounds wonderful," I say, forcing a smile onto my face. I'd rather stay locked in this attic for another two years than spend any time with him alone.

He turns to leave, but pauses at the door to say, "See you in four hours."

When he leaves, I only have seconds. I reach inside the armoire, under the thick paper I've painted to match the wooden bottom, and retrieve a length of cloth and a small hairpin. I dart to the door and catch it by the silver knob right before it closes. Gritting my teeth from the pain that shoots through me—silver is one of the only ways to debilitate a vampire—I shove the cloth inside the lock, then tap the hairpin on the doorknob to mimic the sound of the door locking. My mother always makes sure the door is locked before descending, but Zenos is far too confident in his power over me to bother checking.

I let the door close with the wadded cloth preventing it from locking. Once Zenos's footsteps have completely cleared the creaking stairs, I turn the knob. The door opens without a sound. Relief floods through me; my plan might work after all.

After I return the cloth and hairpin to the fake bottom of my armoire, I lock the door so my mother won't notice anything amiss.

There's nothing to be done about the searing pain on my hand, but my adrenaline is rushing so much I hardly care. My test went perfectly. All I need to do now is wait for my mother to leave.

A moment later it's her light footsteps on the stairs. I rush to the vanity and pick up a hairbrush before she enters, forcing myself to look calm. Through the mirror, I smile at her as she opens the door and walks toward me.

"Good morning, sweet girl." Her arms wrap around my shoulders and squeeze for a moment. Her touch feels like ants crawling on my skin—like she's searching for something.

We look so alike. Heart-shaped faces, tawny skin, and long, straight black hair parted down the middle, though hers stops at her elbows and mine trails to my ankles. Before I became a vampire, I had warm undertones to my skin, bright and full of life. Now it's dull and no pinch to my cheeks can bring any rosiness to them. My lips are bloodless as a corpse's. My mother, though . . . she's mastered it. Crushed berries to bring a tint to her lips and cheeks, and after the hours she spent practicing breathing patterns in front of a mirror, no one would guess her lungs no longer function. Even now, I see the steady rise and fall of her chest. Since she's leaving soon, she practices even in front of me. Her deep brown eyes soften as they meet mine in our reflections.

"I'll pick something beautiful for you to wear," she says.

I nod and begin brushing my hair, a task that usually takes a good half hour to complete. My mother starts rummaging through the armoire, and I almost drop the brush. If she finds the false floor . . .

But all she does is draw out a bell-sleeved white blouse with a high black collar and a long, pleated black skirt to match. She hands the clothes to me, and then removes one of her own rings to give me: a black one with a brilliant ruby at the center. The letter A, for my name, is engraved on the surface of the ruby.

"This will look lovely on you," she says, beaming at me as she passes me the ring.

My mouth twitches slightly. "No one will see me except you and Zenos."

"Yes, but . . ." Her eyes darken for a moment, but then she shakes her head. "Do it for me, please. Wearing neutral colors like this makes your skin look warm and alive. Go ahead, put it on."

I bite back my complaints and take the clothes from her. As I dress, she walks around the room humming to herself. Like Zenos, she would seem normal to anyone who doesn't know her. But every morning, when she walks around my attic, it's like watching a lion stalk a herd of deer and trying to guess when it will pounce.

She peers closely at the silver bars on my windows to check for loose nails. She lifts up the blankets on the bed, searches through the pillowcases for any weapons or tools I might have pilfered to help me break out of here. Then she goes to the stack of books in the corner and lifts a few, flipping through the pages.

Her eyes cut over to me sharply, but I look out the window before she can catch me staring.

Dawn light graces the town of Arborren, which I can see clearly from the fourth floor of our towering, narrow house. Burnt-orange tile roofs spread away over soft yellow and white buildings, the Clarity Council Hall and the Silver District of miners' homes, the market I went to every day after school because I didn't want to go home, the alleys I walked through with my friends Kaye and Tristan. Arborren is a large town in the east of Erlanis Empire. Humans and witches are mortals who can only see a few blocks ahead, only notice the bright colors and the morning songs of birds.

But with my vision, stronger than theirs, I see the stains on those pretty walls, the soot on the rooftops from the last time the townspeople set up a pyre for a vampire, and my stomach twists at the thought. They would never accept me here. There's only one place I can belong: the vampire haven in the forest with the queen, Casiopea.

And once I find her, I'll warn her about my mother and what she intends to do.

Finally finishing her search, my mother makes a satisfied *hmm* noise in the back of her throat. I try not to look too relieved.

"You look beautiful," she says once I've put on the blouse,

the skirt, and the ring, but my hair still needs brushing. "Finish your hair after I leave. It looks so beautiful when it's all brushed, just like when you were a little girl."

I hold back a grimace and the complaint at the tip of my tongue. I've asked to cut my hair a thousand times, but she insists on keeping it this length, and I don't have any way to cut it myself. I often wore it this long as a child, but I still cut it frequently to make it manageable. Now I can barely do anything with it, but my mother likes it this long to remind her of the child I used to be. Before I became a vampire.

I wonder if making me look presentable, innocent, and sweet helps her feel better about locking me inside this tower in the first place.

She steps forward to smooth out some wrinkles on my sleeves. She wraps her arms around me in a hug, and a lump builds in my throat. I hold on for a second longer than I normally would. I need to escape, but . . . this is still the only home I've ever known.

She pulls away from the embrace, then brushes my hair behind my ears with a contemplative expression. "I'll be gone for a week. Zenos will look out for you."

"I don't want Zenos to look out for me," I mutter under my breath. "I don't like him."

"He's just a human, Ava. He can't hurt you."

I gulp, pushing back my questions about their marriage once more. She met him three years ago, when I was fifteen and my mother was newly a vampire herself, and they married within a month. He keeps her secrets, and she lets him stick around— probably because he's the emperor's nephew and therefore a good connection to have. But she's never believed me when I tell her about Zenos's experiments and games that happen when she's out of town.

She places her hands on my shoulders, and I tense, knowing what's coming next. It starts with a burning sensation in my chest. Sweat breaks out on my forehead. I squeeze my hands into fists and bite my lower lip.

"Relax," my mother says in a hard voice. "You'll be fine."

Forcing my shoulders to loosen up, I let her do what she needs to do every week. She closes her eyes as a glowing light spreads outward from my chest, to my shoulders, and to her hands. Already, I feel weaker, like I'll collapse if she doesn't maintain her grip on me. I close my eyes and wait for it to pass.

Every witch's powers grow strongest once she turns fifteen; those are the hardest years of training for witches in Arborren, when our regular schooling ends, and we're trained to master our magical skills before the potency lessens to a steadier level—one that can still be incredibly strong, if we're trained enough in our youth. For the next few years of school, a witch's power is nearly uncontrollable, dangerous, but also dazzling when used. Other witches are strengthened when they're near young witches, and can pull on our energy to enhance their own powers, as long as they are the same type of witch we are. My mother is a Root witch like I am, so she can take mine.

If a witch is killed and turned into a vampire, she loses her powers—unless she is killed in these prime years.

Then, the power stays and she—or any older Root witch— can take it from me, no matter how much I wish she would stop.

My mother's arms and chest and face are all glowing with the light that passes through her, and she lets out a steady breath. When she opens her eyes, the brown color glitters with an inner fire and I recoil slightly. It's been three years since she was turned into a vampire, but some childish part of me still misses the loving way she used to be. Not this power-hungry woman who threatens the safety of humans and vampires.

The first few months Zenos was here, he would drink far too much mead every night, and spill secrets to me whenever my mother was out of the house.

Secrets like her plans to tear down the barrier that surrounds the forest.

Whenever I pressed him for more information, his words would slur together and he'd wave me off. I don't know how exactly she plans to break the barrier, but she has access to so many historical documents and tales in the Council Hall that I'm sure she's gathered the information.

My mother raises one hand, palm turned upward. A moment later, wind swirls above it, pulling in dirt from outside; it flies under the door to my room, probably from an open window downstairs. The dirt coalesces on her hand, spinning frantically. Moments later, a small white flower appears, with a yellow middle and a sweet, nutty scent—something only a Root witch could do, with our connection to the earth and everything in it: soil, rocks, plants, flowers, roots.

The berries on her lips, the breathing patterns . . . they help her keep up the ruse of being a mortal. But her witch power is what truly convinces them all she's still one of them. It allows her to stay on the Clarity, the local government body composed of several humans and witches—the next highest level of government after the emperor. It allows her to kill solitary humans and witches on the outskirts of Arborren without ever drawing suspicion to herself.

"Perfect," she whispers, not even looking at me. A warm satisfaction fills her eyes. She drops her other hand from my shoulder, and my knees buckle. My vision sways, and I have to catch myself on the back of my vanity chair. "Zenos will bring blood for you soon to recover. You'll practice while I'm gone, won't you?"

I nod immediately, knowing that's the answer she wants—she often brings plants to my room, or occasionally a tub of dirt and rocks, for me to practice my Root witch abilities with.

"Wouldn't want your powers to wane," she says softly. "They protect us, and soon we won't have to hide who we are anymore. When I return, we'll be safer than ever, Ava."

*When I return* . . . A chill sweeps through me. I thought she was going on a regular trip for Clarity-related business. But what if she's aiming to destroy the barrier and free the vampires this time? This *week*? Panic shoots through me.

If she succeeds, I know the humans and witches will keep fighting us, and countless lives will be lost. It won't give us freedom and power. Humans will take back the forest, and the vampires will have no home while mortals hunt us down.

If I take this information to Casiopea, she'll protect me. She'll stand up to my mother to stop the barrier from falling and destroying her queendom.

If there were some other way to convince my mother to stop . . . some way to return her to who she was before . . .

"While you're away . . ." I begin, my voice weakened and shaky. "Can I go outside, just for an hour or two? I'll even go with Zenos."

She stiffens, such a small movement that no mortal would notice it.

"Leaving this tower now will only get you killed, Ava," she says in a strained voice. "And I have fought too hard to give you a chance at life. You know that, don't you?" She gestures to the window behind her, a dismissive movement. "You don't know what it's like out there, where they hate people like us. You are too naive, too weak, and far too kind to survive in such a cruel world, where mortals claim that anyone different from them must be killed. You don't know what it's like to only be able to count on yourself. So count on me, and trust that I will provide a way for you to be safe."

Her voices rings with finality, and I open my mouth to— what? Argue, beg, rage at her? I don't know, but the words die in my throat and a moment later my mother leaves, her heels tapping against the wood floor in a determined stride. The door closes behind her, and she tugs on the handle twice to make sure it's locked. The other side isn't silver, so this causes her no pain.

Then she's gone. I wipe away the tears at the corners of my eyes, knowing this is the last time I'll see my mother.

I collapse into my vanity chair, limbs weak and mind hazy. More blood and sleep are the only things that will give me back my strength, but for now I must focus on breaking free of here.

From downstairs I hear a heavy trunk dragged across the floor. Doors open and close, my mother tells Zenos goodbye, and silence falls inside the house. From the window, I watch her walk down the street with a retinue of guards who are assigned to protect the councilors of the Clarity of Arborren. If she succeeds, they'll all die, and so will everyone in this town. And she'll continue to leach my powers.

As much as they hate me, I won't let that happen to them. As much as they have reason to fear me and other vampires who must drink blood to survive, I'm still the same Ava. I still care for these people and this place, even if they'll never love me back. Saving this town will prove that, even if only to me.

An hour later, after I've taken the journal and the scarf from my nook in the ceiling and stuffed them in a pillowcase that I sewed straps through, Zenos's footsteps ascend the stairs. I place the pillowcase lightly on the floor of the armoire and stand in one smooth movement.

The door opens and Zenos steps through, holding another tiny cup of blood.

"Is that enough for you?" he asks in a gruff tone.

"Thank you, Zenos," I say in a sweet tone that I hate, but it makes him light up. My stomach twists in disgust, but I remind myself this is necessary for my freedom. This single ounce of blood won't keep me satisfied for long, but if I make Zenos complacent enough, maybe he won't pay attention later. He won't notice me sneaking down to the bottom floor to take some of the sacks of blood stored in the cooler, and he won't notice me leaving the house. I need that blood so I won't have to worry about my thirst while traveling to Casiopea.

After I drink and hand him back the cup, he turns to leave. My pulse would be racing now if it could. I reach inside the armoire for the cloth and the pin. On light feet, I bound to the door, stick the cloth in the lock, and tap the silver knob with the pin. My hand sears in pain while holding the doorknob, but a rush of energy floods me until I barely notice the stinging. Every step I take now must be careful. Zenos's footsteps disappear downstairs, and I wait until I hear him riffling through papers in the office.

*I can do this,* I think, willing myself to be brave. *I'll escape this house. I'll follow the whispers and the journal wherever they lead me, and learn all I can to help stop my mother.*

*I'll save Arborren because I still have a heart even if it hasn't beaten in two years. And along the way, I'll find a new home, and freedom, with the vampire queen.*

I grab my pillowcase sack and swing it around my shoulders before leaving. The staircase spirals down the next three floors to the bottom floor. I try not to think about what else has happened down there. My vision narrows, tunnel-like, as I descend the stairs. I walk quietly, so the wood doesn't creak. Everything is going the way I imagined, exactly like I've dreamed about for so long.

My feet have touched the third-floor landing, exhilaration racing through me, when a hand wraps tightly around my elbow.

I'm jerked backward, stumbling into Zenos. Panic grips me and I know I've lost, all my chances vanishing like smoke from a pyre. His cold voice slithers through the air.

"Where do you think you're going, bloodsucker?"

He places a silver bar across my neck, and I scream.

# CHAPTER
## 2

·KAYE·

*The first thing a young Flame witch must learn is that we are strongest together,*
  *and must never abandon one another.*
  *A fire rages stronger with other flames to stoke it.*
  *A single flickering candle will only burn out.*
  —TRAINING ACADEMY FOR
  YOUNG WITCHES OF ARBORREN

As I step out of the courtyard's washroom, fireflies dart through the fog in front of me. The fog must have descended over Arborren while I was inside. I have half an hour before my shift of patrolling the forest barrier and checking for any cracks where vampires might slip through—just enough time to get ready and leave.

The courtyard is in the center of a large house shared by several families. There are many houses like this in the Silver District, each one the legacy of a silver-mining family. With the influx of Flame witches into town, hired by the emperor to annihilate vampires, they've opened rooms to us as well. My mother, pregnant at the time she moved here, made sure to get a good one for us, and stayed here even after she became an esteemed Clarity councilor.

Shivering, I hurry through a rickety wooden gate across the courtyard, and head upstairs to the second floor. Wind blows through the thin slatted walls to whistle in my ears. Wood-smoke and incense seep through the whole building. I enter my apartment at the end of the hall and step into a darkened front room. An unlit candle nearly melted to the stub sits on a small table near a sofa.

It's so quiet, I hear my own breath and the brush of my jacket sleeve against the doorknob. I walk through the room silently, reverently, like I'm somewhere sacred—a temple or ancient burial ground.

With each step toward my room, the ghosts of laughter and stories come back to me, drifting out of the dark, quiet corners. I hurry into my room and shut the door behind me. At least in this space, my mother's ghost isn't as loud.

After bringing a small flame to life on my fingers, I let it hover while I change clothes and stock my belt with freshly sharpened knives. I also put on the gold wrist cuff bracelets given to all Flame witches when we start training. They're the most beautiful things I own, and I wear them as often as I can. They're cut into the shapes of flickering flames. The face of the first Flame witch we know of, born a thousand years ago, is expertly engraved on the gold surface and shrouded by clouds of hair that look like puffs of smoke.

Before I leave, I catch sight of the mirror near the door that I've covered with a black sheet. At the top of the bronze frame, my name is engraved with long, swooping letters: *Kaye*. It was a gift from my mother when my powers came in, only a few months before she died. I wonder if she knew how relieved I was when it finally happened; but now she'll never see me graduate to hunt vampires on my own, like she did.

I will graduate, become the best Flame witch I possibly can, and find the vampire that killed her. My anger at what was done to her has carried me this far, and it will carry me further.

It has to. It's all I have left.

I leave my building and the Silver District, turning down a tree-lined street with fog sliding in between buildings and people. The Silver District gets quieter each year, families leaving for other parts of the empire when they no longer want to risk their lives entering the forest for the silver mines. Only the most desperate are left, and as they pass me, they give me silent nods: the respect shared between Flames and the humans who mine silver to fight vampires.

Then I take to the roofs. Most buildings in Arborren are only two stories high, so all I need to do is find the windowsills, the ledges, the broken bricks, and haul myself up.

Orange- and brown-clay-tiled, gabled roofs spread away for a few miles around me, pale under fog. The woods form a half-moon around the east and north of the town, while roads to other parts of the empire lead out from the west and south. The autumn air chills me, so I start running to warm up.

Flame witches are trained in physical skills—doing laps around the town, scaling buildings, hand-to-hand combat, different techniques with the power of fire, light, and shadow, traversing the forest, learning how to use our silver knives—as well as strategy, wilderness survival, and every bit of information about vampires we can learn. Anything to beat them.

Roofs and alleys vanish past my quick sprints toward the northern edge of the town. Soon I pass the larger homes that belong to the rich families—the ones who have been in the Clarity for generations, or are friends with the emperor. None of those houses were available for my mother when she got her Clarity position, but she hadn't wanted one anyway. She'd wanted to be closer to the rest of the town, not above and away from the people.

I look toward one of those houses, recognizing it instantly: it's the Serení home. It's unique: narrow and tall, the towering four-story building is wrapped in deep green ivy from trees planted around it. It stands in its own little square, the dark gray stone stark against the warmer colors of the buildings nearby. It twists and curves upward like a column, reminding me of the inescapable prison towers in old stories. The trees surrounding the Serení home cover nearly all the windows. But not the attic window.

My heart pounds faster and the world seems to darken around me as I look toward the attic window, wondering if I'll see her—Ava. My old friend.

I'd searched for Ava for hours the day my mother died. She'd always been there for me before, but she suddenly disappeared that same night.

Her mother told everyone she'd been sent to another province to study, but I know better. I learned the truth a few days after my mother's death by looking toward Ava's towering home.

She's not there now, but I see her sometimes, standing in that window, blood dripping down her chin.

A vampire in our midst.

My mother's body was found long after all the bloodsuckers

caught that night were set to flame, which means her killer is still free. I can't accept it as coincidence that Ava disappeared that same day and I saw her with blood on her chin a few days later.

If Ava truly was responsible for my mother's death, she'll be the first vampire I ever put to flame. I'll find out the truth, and get enough proof to accuse her of my mother's death and her powerful councilor mother, Eugenia, of harboring her.

"I will come for you, Ava Sereni," I say under my breath, the words lost in a gust of wind.

Soon, I reach the edge of town, drop off the corner of a low roof, and look up toward the trees. Every time I gaze into the depths of the trees, a chill stirs inside my bones, perhaps prompted by the ghost stories we used to tell as children about spirits that stalk the woods; or perhaps from my training, the two years of drilling my body to fight anything I might find in this forest, from dangerous animals to the weakest vampire to the fearsome queen, Casiopea, who rules their immortal kind.

A shimmering, nearly transparent barrier stands in front of the woods, rising up as far as I can see and creating a dome over the woods. The Bone Wall.

I wonder how many vampires are near the wall right now. They hide in the trees, waiting for any opportunity to slip through, attack, and drain our blood. I wrap my hand around the hilt of a silver dagger at my belt and squeeze.

Let them try.

"Kaye!" I tense up when Tristan calls my name. I turn to see the patrol I'm joining, approaching from about twenty feet away. There's Tristan, and three other boys from our class, all eighteen like me—all of us still in the peak of our power as trainee Flames.

"We checked this part of the wall for holes last week,"

Tristan says in his usual self-assured tone. The other boys congregate behind him like a pack of wolves following their alpha.

"Well, I'm checking it again." I already know he's going to keep badgering me, so it's hard to keep the annoyance out of my voice.

"All right," Tristan says slowly. "No need to outdo us all. You're still my father's favorite."

My ears burn, but as I'm about to turn back to the wall and ignore them, the whispers among the other boys carry over to me.

"Such a show-off."

"Has to overcompensate because of her mother."

I bite down a retort and glare at them out of the corner of my eye. Tristan avoids my gaze and shuffles his feet in the dirt. Just a couple of years ago, he would have told them off for all the comments they make; trying to mess me up in training, joking that I'll be labeled a traitor one day like my mother was, or whispering that there's no way a half-Sarenian girl could ever be a good Flame witch.

He used to stand with me.

Now, he looks over his shoulder and mutters that they should get back home soon, and my heart twists. *Why did you change so much, Tristan?*

I let out a sound that's half sigh, half growl. "This is our job, Tristan. If you actually did yours, maybe you could be his favorite, too." The words come out in a rush, surprising even me with how cutting they are. He winces, and for a moment I feel bad for him. I can't imagine what it's like to have to fight for the smallest bit of praise or support from my father, but I see it every day with Tristan.

Maybe if he hadn't pulled so far away from me, I'd apologize. But that's a softness I can't afford.

Tristan runs a hand through his sandy-blond hair. They all have the red or blond hair, light skin, and freckles that mark them as eastern Erlantian. My thicker, darker hair, my defined jaw and cheekbones are so different from theirs, even though I'm a blend of them with my green eyes and lighter skin. I'm similar enough that they won't kick me out of the patrol, but different enough that they've always doubted my abilities and don't fully trust me.

And ever since my mother was labeled a traitor, they've isolated me more, losing the bit of respect they had for me as her daughter. She'd always been praised as one of the best Flame witches Arborren had ever seen, until she began to show mercy to vampires. She still annihilated those who got into the town or killed a villager, but she didn't believe in seeking them out to destroy them and eliminate the threat of their existence, like we're taught to do. Up until her death, Tristan helped me stand up to those who questioned my and my mother's loyalty to the Flames. He hasn't helped me in a long time, though.

"Kaye, you don't have to try so hard," he mutters, taking a step toward me, but I pull back.

"If we get lazy and miss a hole in the wall, vampires get in, and people die, Tristan," I hiss, turning back to the Bone Wall. Trainees are considered too reckless and uncontrolled to go hunt vampires in the forest unsupervised; we could end up burning the whole forest down by mistake. So we're put on patrol duty until Liander—Tristan's father, Clarity councilor, and leader of the Flames—allows us to graduate.

But I know I can control my powers and destroy those bloodsuckers with the skill of a witch ten years older than me. Doing my job properly now will get me closer to graduating and becoming the strongest Flame witch I can be.

One step closer to annihilating the vampire that killed my mother.

I exhale slowly as I take in the Bone Wall; the floating bone shards and bone dust glitter in the weak sunlight. It surrounds the entire forest, from northern Arborren to the mountains and the sea and every small town in between.

From my Flame witch training, I know that the ancient witches of this land imbued their power in a great oak tree that lies deep in the woods. That tree's roots extend for miles and stop abruptly at the base of the Bone Wall, feeding it with their magic so the barrier will stand forever strong. While everyone can see the Bone Wall, the tree is not common knowledge; I only learned of it in my training. We're taught that the tree and the barrier are protected by ancient magic.

Humans and witches can pass through whenever we want, but only Flame witches and trained hunters have enough skill to survive in the forest, so no one else ever dares enter it.

Vampires, on the other hand, are always locked inside . . . except when they find cracks in the wall. It's the job of trainee Flame witches to search for any cracks.

I wonder where exactly the vampires entered town that fateful day two years ago. My throat tightens and my chest aches as the memories crash into me.

It was deep winter; snow covered the cobblestone roads, frost built up on windows, and icicles hung from eaves.

My mother's glass-like stare, blood from the wound on her neck forming a crimson halo around her head where she lay in the snow, the odd twist of her limbs.

At least, that's what Tristan and I heard of her death the night she died. We hid in a hallway of the Clarity Council Hall while she was brought in. Her body was draped in a blanket, but the harried whispers of the women carrying her in conveyed to me that since she was found so late after the captured vampires had been burned, her killer was likely still free.

I kneel in front of the wall, peering through the trees. Vampires have better vision than mortals, so they can find breaks in the wall with their eyes alone. It's hard to make out the small motes of bone dust shimmering in the air unless I'm standing right in front of the wall, so our patrols use another method.

I hold out my hands and then bring them toward me, palms pressed together, in one of the movement patterns passed down among witches over centuries. I focus on the area just beyond the Bone Wall. Not the trees, not the dirt, but the air itself; Flame witches command not only fire, but light and shadow.

I inhale deeply and the light fades away from the immediate area beyond the Bone Wall. Soon, the area is doused in darkness. If I looked up, I'd see the light halting in midair some thirty feet above me, as if it had been blocked and deflected elsewhere. But in front of me, all I see is the glittering bone dust, and a pall of deepest night beyond it. It's like staring into a deep cavern.

Stepping back, I stare into this well of darkness, checking for any gaps in the bone shards and floating dust. Behind me, the boys have started walking away.

Then I see it, and my breath catches in my throat.

There, near the bottom left of the darkness, a giant hole gapes in the Bone Wall. The bone shards cut off around it in jagged edges. It's big enough for at least two people to walk in, side by side.

*Not people,* I remind myself as a chill goes down my spine.

I have to tell Liander. Our official orders whenever we find a break are to inform Liander, rally the Flames to track down any vampires that got through, and then figure out a way to block the hole.

"Tristan," I say in a low voice, not bothering to turn around. A dead silence falls around me, and a second later, Tristan jogs back over.

"What's that?" Tristan's sharp voice cuts through my shock. His green eyes flash and he pushes me aside as the other boys approach.

"What's it look like?" I snap. "A break! They're going to get in. If we'd skipped this part of the wall like you wanted to, we would have missed it entirely."

For a moment, Tristan's hard facade breaks; fear flickers in his eyes and I remember how we used to comfort each other on training journeys through the woods when we feared a vampire would come out of the fog to devour us.

Then he rolls his shoulders back and I practically hear the flames crackle at his fingertips.

"This is our chance," he breathes, determination roaring to life in his eyes. When I say nothing, when the other boys look dumbfounded by his change in demeanor, he takes me by the shoulders and steers me away from them. I feel an odd mix of disgust and satisfaction. As much as he pretends to think nothing of me anymore, he knows I'm the only one here who can truly match his ambition; the only one who wants to impress Liander as much as he does. "If we tell my father . . . no. No. We have to annihilate them. Kaye—"

A fervor takes over his gaze and his hands drop from my shoulders. I try to keep my expression neutral.

Two years ago, when we'd still been friends, Tristan wanted

to help me find my mother's killer. But then he changed, drifting apart from me more every day—leaving just as much an absence as Ava and my mother.

I can't trust him. I can't trust anyone.

"What?" Tristan asks in a flat tone, his head tilted toward me. "You're planning something, Kaye. Going to chase all the big, scary bloodsuckers on your own?"

Lifting my chin, I fight to keep my expression unreadable. If he thinks I'm just as reckless as him, I'll be able to get to his father before he finds even one vampire.

"And what if I do, Tristan?" I ask, not caring what the other boys think of me. My anger flares and I bite out, "I found the break on my own, after all. Might as well keep up my winning streak."

He tilts his head slightly to the side, a spark of curiosity in his eyes. But I have no time to figure out what it means, because he gestures to the rest of the group to follow him.

"Come on," he calls to them, walking away from me and into the town. "Let's see how many we can get by sundown."

Once they leave, I face the wall again and let out a long breath that causes the shadows to lift into the sky. Light streams back in, and the trees and dirt are visible again. I don't want to make it any easier for vampires to find the gap by leaving a giant black shadow right in front of it, so it's best to leave it clear.

The holes usually heal on their own in a few days, and once I inform Liander and the rest of the Clarity, the metalworkers in the city will construct a silver blockade to work as a temporary barrier. The best thing I can do is warn them.

This will prove I belong, and that I'm ready to graduate and truly be one of the Flame witches. A sense of justice floods me, and for a moment, the knife I hold makes me feel as strong as my mother.

I'm about to walk away when glinting yellow eyes catch my attention from the trees. The deep emerald leaves are dark as shadows, with a thin fog passing through them. A set of eyes blinks from within the trees once more, slow and calculating.

My breath hitches and I stumble back a step. My shaking hand draws my knife from my belt, but I don't see the eyes anymore. There's just fog and trees and wind, and the sound of my own shallow breaths. My whole body tingles with nerves as I search for some sign of what I saw.

But there's nothing. I curse, tucking the knife back into my belt. I'm wasting time here, imagining things in the trees.

A real Flame witch fears nothing, least of all vampires.

# CHAPTER
3

- AVA -

*An everlasting oak tree stands in the center of the sacred forest.*
*From the tree's roots, witches crafted a barrier a thousand*
*years ago, to keep the vampires inside.*
—JOURNAL, AUTHOR UNKNOWN

Zenos's stubble scratches against my ear as he whispers, "I always tell your mother you need a sharper hand." One of his hands curls so tightly in my hair, it starts to rip from my skull, but that pain is nothing compared to the silver bar. A searing, throbbing heat spreads along my neck and collarbone, and I don't know if I'm imagining the way the bar begins to sink into my skin or if it is truly about to cut through my neck. My vision goes white and a weak cry leaves my lips.

He lets go and steps back from me. My knees buckle and I drop to the floor. Tears blur the wooden planks in front of me. The last time silver was placed on my neck was a punishment for trying to send a letter to a friend. My mother's cruel eyes flash in my memory now.

My fingers grip the grooves in the wooden floor, and I wish I could rip it apart. Vampires are supposed to be strong, but I've always been the weak one here.

"I only wanted more blood." I choke out the lie, hating the way my words catch around a sob. "That's all."

"I know," Zenos says in a scathing tone from somewhere behind me. "I've never met anyone as greedy as you, not even other bloodsuckers."

*Bloodsuckers*. He would never use that insulting term with my mother around. My hands go to my neck and I tense up at the feel of raw skin. I'll need sleep or blood to heal it.

Only fire or decapitation can kill a vampire, but silver can weaken us, the pain intense enough to make us black out if we're exposed to it long enough. In my head, I hear the screams of vampires who were burned after being caught entering the city, or in the forest by those who hunt them. My mother always brought me downstairs and opened the window on those nights, to let in the cloying smoke and remind me why I should stay inside.

Slowly, I turn around. Zenos stands a few feet back from me, his body blocking me from the third-floor sitting room. A glass window etched with geometric designs is on the eastern wall, but unlike my windows in the attic, there are no silver bars here. Old family paintings line the walls, while candelabras and wool-draped chairs take up the corners. There's an empty spot above the fireplace where a painting of my mother and father had hung before he died, before my mother and I were both undead—before everything changed. Flames crackle in the fireplace, with orange light and shadows dancing in Zenos's stonelike gaze.

In this very sitting room, my father used to read me stories from large books with sweeping, colored illustrations about the old gods, known as the Arkana. Whenever he finished a story about the ancient witches and the Arkana who gave them their power eons ago, he'd tell me one day I would grow up to be just as strong and magical as them. I try to embolden myself with the hope he had for me.

"Come." Zenos beckons me with one twitch of a bony finger, his gray eyes clear and piercing like glass, and my hope shrinks. I'd hoped to avoid him while getting out of here, and now I don't know if I can escape—he's always managed to overpower me before.

The smartest thing I can do now is make him think he has the upper hand until I find an opportunity to get away from him. I gulp and hunch my shoulders theatrically, then follow him to the window.

We stand silently for long minutes, watching the mortal people of Arborren go about their early-evening tasks. I wonder who among them is a human or a witch, and what kind of witches they are. Root witches who work with the earth have always been the most common here, but in recent decades Flame witches have come in droves, hired to kill vampires. There are other witches, some who can heal, some who work with metal, some who can compel humans to do their bidding—but I know most people I see below are either Root witch, Flame witch, or human. I place one hand on the window, feeling a pang of loss in my heart. I'll never walk through my home, among these people, ever again. And deep down, I know they have every right to fear me.

"There," Zenos whispers behind me, and he points out the window. Following the line of his finger, I stiffen.

A girl my age is perched on a roof a few blocks away. Zenos

might only be able to see basic details of her from here, but I can make out more: the wide green eyes that resemble the color of leaves just after dawn; the loose strands of chestnut hair falling away from her braid; how she tilts her head in the direction of our window, like she knows we're standing here watching her, and I wonder if that's even possible with mortal vision. Her sharp, calculating expression—it's a face I remember better than any other. A face I always search for on the streets below, and sometimes I see her, standing on the rooftops and looking toward my attic window.

My stomach plummets. I have to get out of here, if only for her sake.

"Did you go to school with her?" Zenos asks. I give a jerky nod. "What's her name?"

"Marie," I lie. No one around my age at school was named Marie.

But I say her real name to myself: *Kaye*. The same name I've said hundreds of times with a smile on my lips. The name I spoke with my last mortal breath, wishing she could come help me.

Kaye has disappeared from the roof now, and I truly hope Zenos didn't get a good look at her. He always asks for the names of former classmates. When they vanish and are found days later with their blood drained, it's easy enough for my mother and Zenos to blame it on the vampires who occasionally manage to break through the barrier into Arborren. Every time I hear them talk about it, or mention a specific person's name, I refuse to drink blood for as long as I can, terrified that I might have known the person it came from. But the thirst always wins.

I can't let anyone else die because of us.

Then Zenos touches the glass and traces lines along the etched designs. Each stroke of his finger outlines my reflection, like he's cutting me into pieces. "Funny how rumors spread," he whispers. "In the capital, where I'm from, they say vampires have no reflection. But the capital is well protected against vampires, so they don't really meet many of you." He rests his chin on my shoulder then, and I'm so grateful for the hair and the blouse between us, so I don't feel his skin. "You certainly have a reflection, but it's missing something, don't you think? A thousand panes of glass. Which one shows the blood at your lips"—he pauses to brush away a trail of crimson on my chin that I hadn't even realized was there—"and which one shows the thirst in your eyes? Which one finally convinces you you're evil?"

"I'm not," I say, the words coming out of me faster than I even think them. I remember the fear I felt whenever vampires broke into town, before I was one myself. I cowered under my bed here, or with Kaye at her house, and could barely breathe until the danger was clear. I remember feeling like the world dropped out from under my feet when my mother came home that first night, dripping in blood. I understand the people's fear. But I didn't choose this life, and I don't want to lose all of my humanity to become a bloodthirsty predator. I've never killed a human, and I never will.

He straightens and examines me as I continue staring out the window, avoiding his gaze. Goose bumps rise on my skin. He's probably been waiting for this moment—for my mother to be gone—for months now. It only happens a few times a year, after all.

"We've already determined how long it takes for small appendages, like your fingers, to regrow after being removed," he says, monotone. "With the help of blood, you regenerate. A living person's fluids help you resemble a living person and keep you from truly perishing—almost like an insect, caught in amber. But what happens if you don't have blood?"

I feel like I'm back in school again, because he already knows the answer and just wants to hear me say it.

"In three days, I'll be ravenous." My voice goes shallow and hollow; this has happened, the times that I tried to refuse drinking blood early on. All my mother had to do was wait until I lost any sense of reason, then slip a cup of blood in my room while Zenos stayed safely downstairs. "I'll attack any human around me."

He waves a hand dismissively. "The proper restraints will be employed. What happens after that?"

"In a week without blood, I'll start to disintegrate."

"Yes, yes, but will the regeneration process have begun? Will your finger be partially healed even as you begin to disintegrate? Will the regrowth begin by using the blood from the last time you drank, or does it only work with a new supply of blood? Does the amount of blood or the timing of its distribution matter at all? We'll need to test with different variables."

He asks all these questions rapidly and to himself, like I'm not even there. Like I'm not someone whose finger he's considering chopping off for the sake of curiosity. I've dealt with him for long enough that I shouldn't be surprised, but it still astonishes me how quickly he shows his true nature once my mother leaves the house.

Then he taps a finger on his chin. "I should finish paperwork for my uncle; the emperor doesn't like to be kept waiting. But I shouldn't leave you alone, after you just attempted something so foolish."

Urgency prickles through me—I don't have long to figure

out another way to escape before Zenos starts his games. I could try to fight him off, but he carries silver on him at all times. Vampires are supposed to be stronger than humans, but that's never applied to me.

The heat from the fireplace warms my cheeks even from a few feet away. I swallow and find my throat dry. I imagine the blood downstairs, neatly stored in burlap sacks and waiting for me to drink the sweet liquid inside. I need to go down there and escape this place, but first I have to get away from Zenos.

A scream rends the air somewhere outside, and birds shriek from rooftops before taking off. Voices shout at people to get inside and bar their doors. As Zenos peers out the window, I shoot a quick glance toward the vines trailing up the side of the house. I flex the fingers of one hand. I've tried to reach those vines with my Root magic before, but they were too far from my attic window, and whenever I tried to get them to come to me, they barely twitched in response. But now I'm much closer to them.

"What do you think is going on out there?" Zenos asks, and the sky beyond the window darkens after his words. Clouds gather and, though I'm inside, I imagine there's a chill in the air. "Think one of your bloodsucker friends broke through?"

I try not to show any reaction. What if they did? I could try to find one of them and ask for their help in reaching Casiopea—but that would waste precious time getting to the forest, time where I might be caught and burned.

Kaye's face flashes through my thoughts, and my chest tightens with fear for her. Is she safe? Does she know what's happening?

"A predator," Zenos breathes, and I feel his fingers in my hair again.

"What about you?" I snap. "You're just using my mother because you wanted a councilor for a wife. What happened? Got bored of being tenth in line for the throne?"

"You think you're better than me?" He laughs, and the sound is like rats scrabbling along the hardwood. "At least I chose to be here, made my own path in life. You've never made any decision for yourself, Ava. I know you're young, but . . . there's a point where it becomes pathetic."

I keep my gaze on the window as he creeps closer. I remember his face in all its twists and turns, the spark of satisfaction in his eyes every time my mother leaves and he comes up with a new experiment. If I were still alive, I would have stopped breathing now.

That's one good thing about being a vampire—he can't tell I'm nervous by a racing pulse or scattered breaths. Only if I show it in my eyes or my voice.

Completely controlled, I say, "It's funny you've convinced yourself she's not using you, too."

It happens in a split second—his hand closes around my hair and yanks back. I let out a sharp gasp and stare up into his face. Sweat drips from his forehead and lands on my cheek, and those stone-gray eyes are brighter than ever in the light of the flames.

He pushes me to my knees and turns my head to face the fireplace blazing in the corner. My throat goes dry. "Your mother trusts me with you while she's away. Better watch your tongue, or else we'll both get burned, won't we? Only for you, I'm afraid that would be a much worse punishment."

A thousand retorts rise to the tip of my tongue. *My mother wouldn't let you get away with that. She would never let you burn me.*

And then I gulp. He's already done so many terrible things, and she's never believed me when I tell her.

He shoves me forward and I catch myself on the dusty floorboards. The flames are sparking so close I'm afraid they'll catch my hair. Then I spot the coals in the fireplace. I dig my fingers into the grooves between the floorboards, pulling myself closer to the ground—closer to the earth, where my Root magic is strongest.

I wish I weren't afraid, and that I were as strong as they all think I am.

I wish I were as powerful, too.

It comes as easily as moving a finger, the movement so natural I barely have to think of it. The coals rise up from the fireplace and, with a twitch of my hand, I fling them toward Zenos's face.

One of them hits him across the cheek. He yelps as he dodges the rest, but a bright red welt is already forming on his skin. I move toward the window, but his hand yanks my hair again. We fall to the ground, dust filling my nostrils, and his face is the only thing I see.

I jerk forward, slam my head into his nose, and then dart away.

We face each other and I raise my shaking hands. Blood streams out of his nose and a low, steady growl rises in the back of my throat. My fangs ache as they push through my gums, begging to be used. My vision narrows on him and it's all I can do to keep myself from lunging for him.

Noticing my gaze, he lets out a snarl. "Greedy little thing. Go ahead. Do it, bloodsucker, and find out what happens to you after."

His taunting voice snaps me out of my trance. Forcing my thirst to the back of my mind, I look instead toward the window while Zenos and I circle each other.

I curl my left hand in a fist, like it's closing around a vine, and pull toward myself. Behind me, glass crashes, and a long, thick vine shoots into the room like a javelin. I push my hands forward and it changes direction, slamming into Zenos's chest. He's thrust into the wall behind him, head slamming against it. He slumps to his knees, then face-first onto the floor, unmoving.

I bite down on my fist to stop from screaming. I attacked him. Is he dead? I strain my ears to catch the faint beat of his pulse; then I sigh in relief. He's alive, but definitely injured.

Even while he lies unconscious and weaker than I've ever seen him . . . every nightmare I've ever had, every bad memory of him, sparks fear in my bones that he'll lurch to his feet and drag me toward him any second now.

He would tell me I wanted to attack him, that I crave human blood, and that I'm lucky I haven't been burned at the stake yet. . . . His voice drowns out my own thoughts until I want to scream.

*No.* I had to fight him. He would have burned me, or locked me back up in my attic, and I'd never get out of here. I repeat one thought over and over in my head: *I had to do it, I had to do it, I had to do it.* Another scream outside snaps me out of my shock. I run to the nearest chair, a wooden one gleaming bronze in the light of the flames. It's heavy, but I carry it to the window where the vine pierces through, glass cracking around it.

With all my strength, I hurl the chair through the window. Glass shatters everywhere and the screams outside grow louder. I wince when the chair smacks against the cobblestone three stories down.

A cool autumn breeze wafts in through the jagged, chair-sized hole in the window. I could still try to go down to the cooler downstairs to get more blood, but I'm scared Zenos will wake up. I have to get out of here right now.

I crouch on the windowsill, drawing my long hair in front of me, and try to ignore the screams in the distance.

And though I don't need to, I draw in a deep breath, inhaling the scents of grilled meat and fresh fruit and newly baked bread. I take in Arborren for the last time, feeling a strange tug in my heart as I do. It's the place where I ran down alleys and jumped in puddles and whispered secrets with Kaye in quiet stables, the moon above us, cedar-scented wind blowing past and colored stones beneath our feet. It's where I hid from loud fireworks in the summer and we found empty basements to sit in the dark and talk all night. It's my home, far more than this tower is.

I shake away the brief nostalgia. I have to get into the woods and find Casiopea, or else the humans and the vampires will all be in danger from my mother's plans to tear down the Bone Wall. The vampire queen will take me in and protect me as one of her own, and I'll have a new home—far away from this one.

I look toward those trees, vast and expansive, the vampire domain somewhere within. I know there are vampire hunters there, too, and that it will be a long, lonely journey. But I've come this far already.

Lightly gripping the vine, I slide out the window, my hair billowing around me like a cloud.

The air whistles past me as I drop, and it's the sweetest sound I've ever heard.

# CHAPTER
## 4

· KAYE ·

*The second rule a Flame witch must know is that we trust one another first.*

*If one among us strays too far, bring them back into the fold and remind them of our mission.*

*For the moment we fall apart is when our enemy succeeds, and when the beast overtakes the man.*

—TRAINING ACADEMY FOR
YOUNG WITCHES OF ARBORREN

I take to the rooftops and approach the Clarity Council Hall faster than I would below. It's a smooth, white sandstone building in the center of Arborren, with imposing columns at the front framing an oak door.

The treasury and town hall take up two other sides of the square. A grandiose stone fountain sits in the middle, decorated with a statue of the emperor, who rules from Erlanis City far to the west. The houses surrounding the square are mostly those of government employees, and this part of the town is noticeably quieter than the rest. But if vampires have gotten into the city already, it won't stay quiet for long.

A familiar voice reaches my ears, and I nearly tumble off the roof. Tristan and the other boys are striding across the square toward the Council Hall. I blink rapidly, like that will clear the image of them here.

They're supposed to be off somewhere hunting bloodsuckers and leaving me alone.

Tristan tilts his head up toward the sky then, and I feel like he's looking for me so he can gloat.

Letting out an irritated huff of air, I sprint toward the roof of the Council Hall. I know of a secret way inside that might help me reach Tristan's father before he can. In the central courtyard is a greenhouse where much of Arborren's food is grown. With the forest overrun by vampires, it's too dangerous to get food from there, so Root witches work around the clock in the greenhouse to feed us.

I'm halfway there by the time Tristan and the others reach the front door, waiting for security to let them in. Liander will be with the other Clarity councilors in the Broad Hall at the very center of the building—and right in front of the courtyard.

I'm over the roof in seconds, moving so fast it's a mystery how I haven't tripped yet. Sliding down the gabled roof to the other side, I catch myself by pressing my boots into the gutter. Now I'm inside. Exhilaration rushes through me, but I still need to reach the Broad Hall before Tristan.

The courtyard below is entirely taken up by the greenhouse. There are other open areas of the building—passages with sun roofs, a balcony on the third floor at the back of the building. I used to spend hours wandering around this building with Ava and Tristan. The thought places a bitter taste in the back of my mouth, and I shove away those memories.

The fog has finally reached the town and now passes over the glass roof of the greenhouse. Without the glare of the sun, it's easy to see inside now: plenty of Root witches checking tiny plots of vegetables and herbs, their beige uniforms rustling as they use the magic at their fingertips to make the plants grow faster.

If I had my mother's skill with Flame magic, I'd bend the light away from me so that no one could see me. She always used it while journeying through the forest when she didn't want to risk being seen.

But despite how often she tried to teach me, I could never quite get the hang of it. It's easier to bend light away from other objects and people if they stay still. On moving objects it's infinitely harder, and doing it on myself while sneaking into the Council Hall . . . nearly impossible. I don't even think Liander knows how to do it.

On light feet, I edge down the roof and hang from the burnt-orange eaves by my fingertips. It'll be a miracle if no one hears me, but I don't have time to find any other route if I want to beat Tristan. I drop and land soundlessly on the glass roof.

Hardly daring to breathe, I look below me, but the Root witches haven't reacted at all.

My shadow, though . . . that will catch attention, since the witches' eyes are always on the ground. I raise a hand and position it right at my feet where my shadow begins to extend. Then I make a swiping motion, cutting off the shadow so I can move without it. It will return on its own once the spell wears off.

With a wild grin, I dart across the roof of the greenhouse

and stop at the entrance to the Broad Hall. The doors of it open into the greenhouse, but there's a sliver of space where I'll be able to squeeze through and drop to the floor. Liander won't care that I broke into the Council Hall, since this is so important, and I know I can make up a good excuse for why I didn't go through the front door. The Broad Hall is a circular room with a marble floor and benches rising on two sides. A round table sits in the center of the room, and it's usually occupied by the nine Clarity councilors. The main door is open, showing the plaza ahead.

A moment later, voices and footsteps from within the Broad Hall reach me over the chatter of the witches in the greenhouse.

"Father, it's bigger than any break I've ever seen." Tristan's voice is inflected with awe, and my heart sinks. My eyes dart to the round table, where my mother used to sit, and that empty chair feels farther away than ever. "We have to seal it up."

"Thank you for telling me, Tristan," says Liander in a steady, calming voice. They come into my view now: Tristan, the other three boys from the patrol, Liander, a few security guards, and all of the councilors . . . except for Eugenia. "You'll show me the break at once. But where is Kaye? We need her here."

Tristan tenses up, annoyance rippling across his face.

"Kaye . . ." Tristan breathes out the word with a perfectly rehearsed tinge of regret. "She went to find them on her own, Father. She wants to impress you, but I knew you would want to know about the hole in the barrier before making any rash decisions."

"You little—"

My foot slips, and the very creative name I was about to call Tristan gets swallowed by the wind. I slip through the gap and land in a clump on the floor, right in plain sight of every councilor who's just rounded the corner.

Gasps rise up from the witches in the greenhouse behind me, and someone from my class snickers. The security guards run toward me, but stop when they realize I'm the same girl who wandered these halls for years, bothering them with bad jokes and asking for candy.

Liander's shadow falls over me as he approaches, disappointment etched in every line on his face. My stomach drops faster than I just did.

But before I can rise or sputter out an excuse, a shrill scream reaches us from the plaza. A woman is racing toward the guards at the entrance.

"Help, help!" she yells. "Vampires in the city!"

Everything happens in the span of a breath: Something streaks out of the shadows from the left—it looks vaguely human, but it's moving at an impossible speed, with mud and dried blood along its torso. A sickening crack echoes in the plaza as the vampire breaks the woman's neck, then whisks her body away over the nearest rooftop.

Chaos erupts in the Broad Hall. Guards run from every direction to spill into the plaza, but the vampire is already gone. Their heavy steps echo off the walls, clashing with the councilors shouting to bar the entrance. The only councilor who hasn't reacted is Liander.

I lurch to my feet, but my vision spins with a sudden lightheaded feeling. I'm in the past—the screams, the blood, hiding under my bed each time the vampires broke in and hoping my mother was safe. For a moment, I swear I see a ghost of her, standing next to Liander with a steady, calm expression. They were always the levelheaded ones, the Flame witch councilors who could round up vampires in a matter of hours.

As Liander moves to stand in front of the rest of the councilors, the ghost fades away, and I snap myself out of my fear.

. . . *the moment we fall apart is when our enemy succeeds, and when the beast overtakes the man.*

I repeat the words from my earliest Flame witch lessons, a mantra of sorts, as Liander raises one hand. Silence immediately falls among the other councilors as they turn to him.

"We will secure the town and seek out any intruders." His voice booms out across the Broad Hall. Then he nods at a human councilor who leads the town's smithing and manufacturing. She snaps to attention. "Doris, if you could ask a smith to forge a silver blockade for the gap in the Bone Wall. The rest of you, warn your people; tell them to get inside."

The councilors all run off in a flurry of movement toward the door, no hesitation among them, and their confidence reminds me how proud I am to help protect Arborren. We protect our people, and we always stand strong.

Liander turns to our patrol, and his carefully stoic features drop into a scowl.

"Liander, I came here to tell you about the break," I blurt out, ignoring how Tristan glares at me. "I wasn't going to look for them."

He raises one eyebrow, like he doesn't believe me, and my heart sinks. "I don't know what games all of you have been up to today, but now it is time to work." Tristan and I stand at full attention, while the rest of our patrol shuffles their feet awkwardly. "The Flames inside the city will take care of the vampires already here, but there will be more coming toward Arborren if they learn of the break in the Bone Wall. The emperor pays for every vampire caught, so now is the chance to capture a lot of them at once. I know you're all hungry to prove yourselves, and now I'm giving you a chance. Go to the forest, apprehend a vampire, and bring it to Chrysalis before the full moon; that's where they're rounded up. I will watch and see how you work, and whoever does the best will be permitted to graduate early and join the ranks of a regular forest patrol. The rest of you will continue training until your official graduation next spring."

Adrenaline rushes through me at his words. As far as I know, Liander has never offered a class a chance to graduate early; whenever vampires infiltrate the town, he'll go into the forest with the other adult Flame witches and tell the students to stay safe at home. But he knows our potential, and now . . .

If I succeed at this, I'll finally be able to prove myself as a real Flame witch who can protect Arborren from vampires. Not a traitor, not inferior in any way—just as good as any of them, maybe even better. This is the chance I've been waiting for.

*Ava.* She flits through my mind for a brief moment, long black hair and a sparkling smile, but then I snuff out the image. My old friend is no longer a friend. And if she is the vampire who killed my mother . . .

She's the one I'll capture.

"I accept this challenge, Father," Tristan says with a slight bow of the head. "I won't disappoint."

"I accept, too," I say quickly, shooting Tristan a dark look out of the corner of my eye. He grimaces back, his eyes blank, blocking me out as usual. But I don't care now. I have no time in my life for half friends, for people who claim to support you and then disappear—and certainly no time for traitors, like him and Ava. Fire burns through my veins at the thought.

Just like always, I'll do this alone.

My gaze trails westward, in the direction of the Serení home. The full moon is five days from now—I'll capture a vampire and bring it to the forest village of Chrysalis before any of the others even stumble upon one.

Liander dismisses the patrol. I begin to move toward the door with them, but he gestures for me to stop.

Tristan's already leaving with a silver dagger in hand. He shoots a smirk over his shoulder and calls out, "Good luck!"

"Liander, I—"

"Sit with me, Kaye," he says, ignoring my protest. I follow him to the large round table in the center of the Broad Hall and try not to let my frustration get the best of me. He worked side by side with my mother for years, and she was never one to lose her temper. I want to be like her, but knowing how she was killed, it's impossible to stay as calm as she was.

Once I'm graduated, I'll be able to speak to Liander as more of an equal. Right now, no one would trust the word of a trainee Flame witch over an esteemed Clarity councilor with the emperor's favor like Eugenia Serení. I need status to my name and I need proof that her daughter was involved in my mother's death.

He takes his seat at the table and pulls out the large wooden chair next to him. It squeaks on the tiled floor below, and all my thoughts about the challenge vanish. This is my mother's place at the table, the tenth seat. I pause, watching the gold flames of a candle on the table flicker back and forth. When I sit down, I inhale, hoping to find some trace of her in the air— maybe the scent of the pomegranates she loved to eat for breakfast, the lilac perfume she wore every day—but I only smell the incense from the altar in the corner.

"I know you weren't going to hunt them all down yourself,"

Liander says, folding his hands together and leaning toward me—his green eyes soft and kind, so similar to how Tristan's used to be. I relax a little under his understanding gaze; he's one of the few people who's never made me feel like I don't belong here. "You and Tristan are very obvious when you're trying to outdo one another." He sighs, and his gaze trails toward the chair I'm sitting in, and I know he's imagining—maybe wishing—that my mother were here instead. "Calluna used to challenge me, too, to be stronger and more astute, but also . . . more compassionate. I didn't always agree with her, especially when she grew soft toward bloodsuckers and argued against our mission here. It's discomfiting to think how much she advocated for us not to hunt them down anymore, only for her to die at their hands."

My whole body goes cold, and I feel numb when I say, "It's infuriating. We have to fear for our lives and can't even get food from the forest anymore because of them. The miners risk their lives just to get silver for our weapons. There's no bargaining with bloodsuckers that murder us and shouldn't exist—" My voice cuts off as flames spring to life at the tips of my fingers. I quickly pull them back from the wooden table and close my hands into fists to extinguish the small fire, my heartbeat racing.

"You remind me so much of her, but you have a certain fire in you that she didn't. Your anger is a gift," Liander says, resting a hand on my shoulder. "Use it. Hone it. They won't get the best of you as long as you stand strong."

"I won't let them," I whisper, wanting to prove how well I'd taken in all his lessons. Whenever I worry I'm not strong enough, it's always Liander who reminds me of the power in my hands; who always gives it back to me when I'm afraid. I'll give him no reason to doubt me now. "I'll bring a vampire to Chrysalis before anyone else."

Liander nods in approval, and just like that, I'm dismissed. I stand, wavering for a moment—if I go all the way home, who knows how much chaos could happen in that time? Ava might be on the loose right now. There are plenty of spare supplies for Flame witches in the Council Hall. Liander watches as I turn and head toward one of the hallways leading out of the Broad Hall, probably guessing what I'm about to do.

I bring a flame to life on my hands and head down two sets of stone stairs until I'm in a basement that seems permanently infused with a winter chill. Water drips from somewhere nearby, and all the walls look faintly damp. The farther I walk, the stronger the stench of unwashed bodies grows. Beyond a heavy oak door at the end of a hall is the pathway to Arborren's prison underneath the Council Hall. The four guards standing outside eye me carefully, relaxing when they realize who I am. Being the daughter of a Clarity councilor has had its perks. I wave to them and enter a side door so small I have to stoop to get inside.

It's an armory of sorts, shared by the Clarity's guards and Flame witches. I grab an empty pack and begin filling it with supplies to get me through the journey to Chrysalis, the only sounds my heartbeat pounding in my ears and a low, pained moan from the cells nearby. Any vampires rounded up tonight will be placed into those cells and interrogated on the location of any other vampires they entered the city with, then brought to the plaza to be burned in public.

I stuff dry food, spare clothes, a sleeping bag, and a silver-studded net into the pack, then adjust my belt of silver knives. Then I pack waterskins, prefilled since there aren't many water sources between here and Chrysalis—many of the streams in the forest have gone dry over the years. I stand and sling the pack over my shoulders, my breaths shallow with anticipation. I'll go to the Serení home, that four-story building in the north of Arborren, with vines covering its walls and a vampire who used to be a girl.

In minutes, I leave the Council Hall and the neighborhood of tall, austere homes, passing the streets of the market where people slam doors shut and shout to friends and family to get inside. The hair on the back of my neck rises as I turn down a dark, tree-lined street with fog sliding in between buildings and people.

Eugenia Serení must be away on one of her quarterly business trips, I realize as I move through the fog-choked streets. Liander often goes with her, but she must have gone alone this time. So her vampire daughter would be left with that creepy stepfather of hers. But he's just a human and no match for my flames. I've trained two years for this, in fighting, stealth, and tracking. I can take out anyone who crosses my path or tries to stop me.

Just three more blocks, and I'll reach the Serení home. I keep my eyes glued on the higher windows, running now and blotting out the screams I hear from nearby streets. Somewhere to my right, smoke rises into the sky and I catch the crackle of flames on the air. Orange sparks flit above a nearby house. Are pyres already being set up? My pulse races faster at the thought.

I skid to a stop at the end of this block as a figure steps into the intersection, sniffing the air like a dog. Flattening myself to a wall, I hardly dare to breathe. The vampire's fangs are bared. His eyes have darkened, pupils round like coins, and purple veins stretch under his eyes like cracked earth. He must be from the forest—mud coats his tattered clothes, and leaves and twigs mat his hair.

I've seen vampires in the forest before on training trips, but our instructors would always handle them and order the students to stay back so that we wouldn't be put at risk or accidentally burn down the forest. If we ever disobeyed or tried to be a hero, we would be banned from training indefinitely, so no one ever tried it. It wasn't unheard of for newly graduated Flames to die on their first trip into the forest from being overconfident, let alone students. But even knowing the risks, I'd always wanted to join in, the flames at my fingertips itching to be used.

But now, with one of them a mere thirty feet away, I freeze, my fingers numb atop the hilt of a dagger. I've never been so close to one without backup. Every nerve in my body yells at me to run, but I stand entirely still, the old fear of these creatures settling into my bones and reminding me of every dead, blood-drained body I've seen.

Before I can decide what to do, his bare feet slap against the pavement as he runs toward me, foaming at the mouth like a feral animal. I call Liander's lessons to mind—*your anger is a gift*.

I let out a fierce cry as I fling a silver dagger at one of the vampire's legs and roll out of the way. He skids past me on the cobblestones, blood spilling from his ankle, where the dagger sticks out.

Strategies flash through my mind so fast, I hardly know what I'm doing before I act; I bring my hands to my face, clasped together, then draw them down toward my chest as he runs at me. Ten feet away, five feet—

He lets out a sharp hiss as his vision is deflected; I'm using light and shadows to make him see the side street across from us rather than directly in front of him. He spins in confusion, clutching his head.

Flames roar to life on my hands. Is this really the first vampire I'm going to annihilate? All thoughts flee my mind except an image of my mother, telling me to be cautious and peaceful and exercise judgment.

*Well, I'm exercising judgment right now,* I think, then reach back to throw a wall of flames at the vampire.

His head whips toward me; his vision may be scattered but his hearing is still much stronger than mine. As my flames race toward him, he leaps out of the way so fast I lose sight of him. I try not to move, but he must hear my breath to find me; in the blink of an eye, he's behind me, and shoves me into the wall of flames I sent at him. I fly toward them so fast I can't catch my balance.

They sting, but they can't burn or kill me. I shove them away with a thrust, eyes searing from the light. By the time I stand up straight and look behind me, the vampire is gone, and I'm panting so fast, my breaths come in sharp bursts. He must have decided to abandon me to look for an easier target. I could give chase and try to capture him. But I don't want him.

I only want Ava.

My flames have scattered toward houses and shop fronts, and a shout from an open door nearby jolts me into action. I run toward the flames and put them out, then head to the next building, cursing myself for the lost time and not being able to stop the damage. This is why young Flames are almost always supervised. If Liander saw this, he'd never let me graduate early.

My heart sinks for a moment, but then I remind myself I fought a vampire alone and survived. I take that small success and use it to bolster my confidence. I'll need lots of it to capture Ava.

The windows of the bottom floor are dark when I approach. A large chair lies in the gravel, surrounded by broken glass. Looking up, I see a shattered window on the third floor and frown, not sure what to think of this. A long green vine trails from the window to the ground. Listening closely for a sign of anyone inside, I wait a moment before deciding this first floor must be empty. Then I take one of my blades and press it into the gap in the door, forcing the lock aside long enough to turn the knob.

It's pitch-black inside when I enter, and silence weighs heavily on the house like a pall. All around, I smell blood and decay. Nausea rises through me and I hold my breath as I step past an open door with white clouds of chilly air billowing out.

Pausing, I check the shadows of the room for anyone watching, then step toward the open door and nearly gag on a sharp, metallic smell. I'd expected to see food—but instead, burlap sacks line shelves on both walls of this giant cooler. And it all reeks of blood. With a small shudder, I push the cooler door closed.

Will I find more blood upstairs? More gruesome proof that this house holds a vampire inside? I've often wondered how Ava was turned into one, but it doesn't matter. Blood is all they care about. Destruction is all they cause. Whoever she was before no longer exists.

I head up the rickety stairs, cursing every time the wood creaks beneath my steps. The second floor has a dark, empty bedroom, but then I reach the third and see a parlor with a fireplace on the opposite side, flames blazing.

*Don't bloodsuckers hate fire?* Frowning, I continue, gripping my silver blade tighter.

The sharp copper scent of blood permeates the room. I shudder at the smell, trying to force back those memories—the night she was carried into the Council Hall, one pale hand hanging off the stretcher, the stench of blood—and then I trip.

When I see the man lying on the ground, I jerk away. The councilor's husband, Zenos. His chest slowly rises and falls. There's some dried blood on his chin, but he seems uninjured otherwise. He doesn't look like he'll be getting up anytime soon, though. And there, in front of him . . .

A long, thick green vine trails along the floor, away from Zenos and toward the broken window, which has a giant hole outlined in shattered glass. The vine leads out of it like a rope.

She escaped. I let out a small gasp as the realization hits me; her Root witch powers had just come in when she disappeared, and I'd forgotten about them until now. Since she was turned young, she kept those powers, and she'll be an even more formidable opponent than the vampire I just faced.

In the gravel below, a trail of footsteps leads north toward the edge of town. My curiosity is piqued. Has she gone into the forest?

I'll find that traitor, that once-friend of mine, and bring her to Chrysalis before the full moon. I'll trap her in my flames, steal her voice with my smoke, and hold a silver blade to her neck to get the truth out of her—*Did you kill my mother, Ava?* If she fights me, then I can truly make her burn, and there will be one less vampire in the world to tear families apart.

# CHAPTER
## 5

- AVA -

*The ancient gods first gifted mortals with magic that connected them with nature.*
*They imbued the forest with their new gifts, giving it sentience.*
*And only Root witches still feel this connection, as they are one with the woods.*

—ORAL HISTORIES OF ERLANIS EMPIRE

Everything in Arborren looks bigger from the ground, and my mouth gapes as I walk past shadowed alcoves and under clotheslines that blow in the breeze. My house is nearly at the edge of the town, but this feels like the longest journey.

So much of Arborren is the same as when I last walked through it, but some has changed; there are more businesses in this part of the town than before, shoemakers, bakeries, tailors, blacksmiths, fortune-tellers, clinics—most probably run by humans, but possibly some by witches as well.

I wonder where Kaye is now. Even when her mother was called a traitor and my mother forbade me from going to visit them in the Silver District, Kaye and I spent all our time after school together. Is she afraid of the screams, of the vampires who might have broken through the barrier? I hope she's safe, but I can't go to my old friend. I need to reach the forest before I'm caught and burned.

A group of boys runs past me at a crossroads and I flinch backward into an alley, stepping on my own hair as I do. I back into the wall with my hands covering my head.

Behind me, a steady growl rises from the darkness. I freeze, my eyes widening, but before I can turn around, something latches on to my shoulders.

With strength I didn't know I had, I shove them off, baring my fangs and leaping back with a hiss.

"A sister," says a voice from farther down the alley. Slamming my mouth shut and cursing myself for showing my fangs, I take in my attackers: two vampires, with dark purple veins showing under their eyes, pupils dilated and eyes bloodshot. There's a male vampire, the one who grabbed me, and a female vampire loping toward me from the shadows with blood coating her torso.

I breathe it in, stepping closer, the pure thirst at the back of my throat tugging me forward. In the recesses of the alley, a limp form lies on the ground. Black edges into the corners of my vision, and it takes all my effort to stay in place. A growl rises in my throat involuntarily.

*Greedy little thing.* Zenos's voice slides into my mind. I shut it down and rein in my thirst.

"Far from home, aren't you?" the male vampire asks with a raised eyebrow, and even though I haven't walked through Arborren in two years, I know exactly what he means.

"I was born here," I say, unable to keep the cutting edge from my voice. "I've never been to Saren."

The man shrugs, then gestures over his shoulder. "We left a body back there. You can see if there's anything left."

"She's certainly thirsty, but that's not all she is," says the woman now, placing her hands on her hips and peering closely at me. I cringe back from her, closer to the mouth of the alley. "That beacon of magic around you. You're still a witch. Turned young, still young now. You look like a lost puppy out here. Were you just turned this afternoon?"

Gulping, I look between the prone form at the back of the alley and the street beyond, my thoughts racing in panic. The scent of smoke catches my attention again, and I suppress a shudder. I can't let that happen to me. I push down the last of my cravings and stand up straight. *Focus, Ava.*

"I'm going to the forest," I say slowly. "I want to find Casiopea. Can you tell me where she is?"

The two vampires send each other a dark look, and then the woman says, "The vampire queen? Some of our kind do crave more guidance, and a leader, and she'll give that to you if you want it. We prefer to be on our own. Casiopea and her vampires live near an ancient oak they call the Heart Tree, about fifteen miles northeast of Chrysalis. But hunters and Flame witches roam those woods all day long. If you're going into the forest, you need to be careful, and you can't hesitate about drinking from these creatures. You never know when they'll have silver on them, or if they're a Flame witch."

They leave me then, slinking away like snakes. The Heart Tree . . . I remember it now from mentions of it in the journal. For a moment, I'm surprised these vampires even know it; I never heard of it until I read the journal. But it makes sense these vampires would, since they live in the forest.

The Heart Tree is the name of an ancient tree that holds

up the Bone Wall barrier, which was crafted by Root witches a thousand years ago. I've seen the Bone Wall my whole life, but the tree itself isn't common knowledge. I wonder why the vampire queen would stay near there, but I don't have time to think on it now.

I step out of the alley, wondering what I'll do for blood once I'm in the woods. The wind gusts and chills my arms through my blouse as I walk toward the trees. Roiling gray clouds above threaten a storm. I wince as little rocks cut into my feet with every step, but at the same time, I can't help but laugh. It's been so long since I've left the house, I forgot to bring shoes.

Leaves in every color swirl in front of me in the next gust of wind, and I reach out to catch one. It's sepia colored with tiny holes in it, and I'm reminded how much I love autumn— everything is dying; everything is a little closer to me. I died and I'm still here, so I should stop fearing my own shadow, and get out of this town before someone catches me.

I place the leaf in my sack, then I move faster through the dirty streets. People run past me in the opposite direction, screaming that there are vampires in the city. They're all blurs in my vision as I move, faster and faster, toward the Bone Wall and the forest. I can't blame the humans for being afraid, especially after seeing what those vampires did to that human back in the alley.

But I'm afraid, too. If they find me, they'll burn me to cinders or decapitate me—the only two ways to kill a vampire. They won't ask questions, they'll just kill me.

Peering around the edge of the last building, I spot of a group of five boys at the entrance to the woods, all of them strapped with silver weapons. They're either human vampire hunters or the Flame witches who also hunt us.

But then I notice the faint golden glow outlining their skin, and a sort of electricity that crackles in the air as they move—they're definitely witches. That glow is what the vampire woman saw on me, as well—only a vampire's eyesight is sharp enough to notice the magic emanating around young witches in the prime of their power, and even we have to be close to them to see it. Kaye came into her powers a few months before I was locked inside, and she has it, too.

"Tristan, we shouldn't split up," said a boy's voice with a tinge of panic, and my mouth falls open as I recognize another old friend of mine, Tristan. Since he, Kaye, and I all had parents in the Clarity, we often spent time together in the Council Hall.

"You all can go in pairs if you want, but I'm going alone. We've decided our rendezvous points, so what are we waiting for? Remember, we'll meet every night to check in with the vampires we catch."

My heart sinks at his words. He's ready to kill any vampire he comes across.

Quickly, I move a few blocks away from the Flame witches, checking over my shoulder every couple of seconds to make sure no one has seen me. Then I stop to take in the Bone Wall up close.

Tiny shards of bone and glimmering dust hang suspended in the air, rising high past the tallest tree. Thick roots protrude from the ground at the very edge of the forest, butting against the Bone Wall and then growing into the bottom of it, like they're fused together. The journal says the roots are from the Heart Tree itself.

The wall only stops vampires from coming into Arborren; I'll be able to leave, but I can't return. I take a deep breath, shove aside any remaining doubts and fears I have, and run through the barrier.

I expect to get bone dust on my hair or taste it in my mouth, but nothing like that happens. As I run through the Bone Wall, the world briefly darkens until I'm on the other side. It's like the sun winked at the world and now it's back again.

My bare feet touch dirt and grass and roots for the first time in two years, and exhilaration sweeps through me.

Everything seems quieter in here, beyond the chaos of the town. Trees tower over me as I step over roots, under branches, and into the woods. I turn around to look at Arborren once more. It's still so close, but all sounds beyond the wall are muted. There are still screams, but muffled somehow. The people and buildings are blurred around the edges, colors running together. My home disappearing . . . fading away behind me.

I reach out toward the wall, wondering what will happen if I touch it; but even half a foot away, my hand won't go any farther. There's an invisible wall that my palm rests on.

Tearing my gaze away, I turn and look at the roots that lead away from the Bone Wall; the ones that supposedly lead to the Heart Tree. Kneeling in the dirt, I place my palms on the edge of a root, right before it goes underground. With my Root magic, I can sense that the root is long and very old, but I can't tell the direction it goes belowground; it gets tangled with other roots going in all sorts of directions. It's a complex web down there, impossible to make any sense of.

But I won't let this discourage me. I'll find the Heart Tree no matter what it takes. I stand, brush the dirt off my skirt, and plunge deeper into the trees.

The sky soon clears to reveal a cool autumn afternoon. The sun gilds the topmost leaves so they're light greens, reds, and yellows, while the ones closer to the ground are emerald, ruby, gold. I breathe in, catching so many scents at once. Wet, loamy earth and moss. I touch my hands to every tree trunk, relishing the rough feel of them and the twigs and rocks that prick my feet as I walk. The wind sounds like an alluring whisper as it glides past my ears, and I pay attention to it, wondering when I'll hear the voices that called to me every night in my attic.

I begin to run, wanting to see more of this endless place. Sunlight flashes on the ground, beaming through breaks in the branches and leaves above. I trip over my hair and my long black skirt a hundred times. But every time I see strands of my hair along the ground, I feel freer, farther away from my prison than before.

Finally, after I've run far enough that I can no longer say if Arborren is north, south, east, or west of me, I grab on to a tree trunk to steady myself. The bark cutting into my palms is a relief. It proves I'm here and that my freedom isn't just a dream. It's not a dusty attic. It's not silver bars, false words from my mother's lips, and the sour stench of Zenos's breath.

I'm here. I escaped. I made it.

A giddy laugh escapes me, loud enough that a bird nearby flies away with a sharp caw.

"Sorry," I whisper, but still can't contain my smile.

Just by touching the trees again, I feel like I'm tapping into the ancient magic of the forest and hearing my father's voice telling me the story of magic's origin. I'm connecting to the earth in the way all Root witches should. The Arkana used to walk through this forest, every step and touch of theirs commanding great magic.

*That beacon of magic around you* . . . A chill goes down my spine as I remember the stray vampire's words. Will some of them who used to be witches try to drain my power, like my mother does? I gulp, not having thought of that before. When

I find Casiopea and tell her of my mother's plans, I'll have to make sure she'll protect me.

I know one thing—I won't stop using these powers and my connection to the forest. They're the only part of my old life I can keep, and I won't let them go.

I'll travel for a few miles, then climb the trees and search for the Heart Tree and the valley where it stands. I can do this.

I draw my hand away from the tree then and a strange, sticky substance comes with it. It's white and gooey and smells like rot. With a grimace, I wipe it off on a leaf hanging near my head.

As I walk away, I notice similar patches on almost every tree I pass, and can't get the stench out of my nostrils. A wild thought hits me. Are the woods sick?

Not just one tree, but all of them?

Before I was turned, I'd been training to become one of the Root witches who worked in the greenhouses. The forest is too dangerous to get food from, so Root witches are essential—but I'd never had a reason to think there was actually something wrong with the forest. This strange growth on the trees, the rotting scent . . . I can't remember learning about this in school, and my mother and Zenos have never talked about it. But a foreboding feeling burrows inside me. This isn't how a healthy forest is supposed to be. Before I can think much on it, leaves nearby rustle and I dart behind the nearest tree. What was that noise? Maybe a bird, or a rabbit.

But it sounded bigger than that.

Fear twinges through me as clouds drift above to block the sun. The chill of autumn descends, and I know I'll regret not having brought anything warmer to wear once night falls. I can't freeze to death, but my fingers and toes can still fall off from frostbite. They'd grow back, but it would take time and blood for them to do so.

I'm thirsty, and I need to fix that problem before I actually lose control. I've never heard of vampires drinking from animals before, but I'll have to try. So far, all I've seen are insects on trees and birds flying too high to catch. I really hope the sickness in these trees hasn't caused the other animals to leave, or else I'll be in trouble. The thought of killing an innocent creature makes my stomach roil, but at least it will stop me from attacking a human. If I want to avoid ever hurting a human, this is what I must do.

A small, insidious whisper rises in the back of my thoughts: *But you have drunk human blood.*

I shut it down quickly. I only drank what my mother gave me because there was no alternative. Now, the choice is in my hands, and once I have control over my own blood sources, I'll have control over my cravings as well.

Before I go any farther, I should make sure I'm headed in the right direction. I withdraw the journal from my sack and begin to read. A gentle wind flaps the corner of the page I've opened to, one that shows a map of the empire. Far west is my parents' homeland, Saren. They were invited to the empire's capital to study, and the emperor offered them Clarity positions to forge a connection between the two nations. Then, twenty years ago, they moved east to Arborren. . . . I trace a line along their path and stop at the beginning of the forest. Whoever made the map colored the forest a deep emerald, almost black. It's dense, thick, wide, and impossible to master. It stretches toward the edge of the sea far to the north, with hundreds of acres in between. The only thing of note that's marked inside it is Chrysalis. I draw a line slightly up and away from it, thinking of the vampire I met in Arborren who told me the Heart Tree was fifteen miles northeast of Chrysalis.

I wonder where my mother is now, and if she's already begun trying to destroy the Bone Wall. Once I'm a safe distance away from any hunters or witches, I'll need to look over the journal more for some hint of how my mother plans to bring down the barrier. It has over a hundred pages of tiny, cramped writing, and every time I look at it, I find something new. It must have *some* information about the Bone Wall.

When I close the journal and look through the trees again, I spot someone fifty feet away. A man carrying a silver blade, his eyes expertly tracking every movement in the trees around me. I stiffen at the sight of the blade, reminded of Zenos pressing the bar to my throat. My hand goes to my neck now, finding the skin rough and mottled.

If I move quietly enough . . .

I manage a few feet backward before I trip again. A voice calls out from deeper within the trees.

"You hear that, Yann? Something's there."

I jolt upward and run. I slip between trees, still tripping over every gnarled root that sticks up from the ground, making so much noise I'm sure those men will find me. My mother said vampires are faster than mortals, stronger than them, but I don't know what was true and what was a lie. Zenos was always able to catch me.

If I could have run, back then, would I have escaped him? There hadn't been far to go.

Here, I can run forever. Here, they'll never get their hands on me. I'll find a safe place. I'll find my new family and we'll protect this forest together.

It still feels like I cannot run fast enough.

Night sets in fast, and I can see clearly, but it's frightening. The whole world looks different at night. New animals awaken, tiny lights and eyes flitting through the trees. Every flutter of leaves above and every crunch of a twig nearby sends me into a panic.

As I walk under one tree with great sweeping branches, I notice something sparkling in the higher reaches of it. Craning my head back, I take in a trap . . . a large one, used by vampire hunters from Arborren and Chrysalis. My skin goes clammy at the sight of the silver bars and the sharp, nail-like edges. On the ground, thin, brown, snakelike lines loop around tree trunks and toward the cage above.

I know how that thing works; it's the same kind of trap that killed my father, catching him unawares and leaving him suspended in the trees for days until he starved. The memory of his body being brought back, of my mother breaking down afterward, flashes through my mind. I clench my jaw and shove those memories into the back of my mind. That was the last time my family was whole, and I'll never get it back. There's no use thinking of it.

Giving the area with the trap a wide berth, I move through the trees more carefully, searching overhead for any sign of silver. The whole forest is turning out to be a deathtrap.

My path through the closely pressed trees grows tighter. I try to rein in my rising panic and the memories clawing at me. The forest is too similar to the dark, winding stairwells and cramped rooms of my towering home.

Without wanting to, I hear my mother's voice in my head, telling me to be still as she drains more Root magic from me. I tense up as I narrowly avoid another silver trap, remembering the many tools and weapons Zenos used on me.

A small breeze chills my skin, and I catch the shadow of a voice: *Help us.*

I freeze in my tracks. It's just like the whispers I'd heard in my attic, but for the first time, I actually heard the words.

"What are you?" I breathe, my throat dry as I speak. "Why are you calling me?"

And then, far ahead, at least one hundred feet from here, a small light flickers in the forest. Flame, hovering in midair, or . . . no, not in midair, but above someone's hand, throwing the rest of them into shadow.

My head spins and I feel like I'm going to pass out. The Flame witches must be close.

My mother would kill them all. She'd shield me and battle any witch who came against us; then she'd drain them of their blood. She'd pour some into her hands and have me drink from them, since she knows the idea of putting my fangs to someone's throat terrifies me. She'd keep us safe.

If I die in this forest, will she ever know what happened to me? I impulsively twist the black ring she gave me, its ruby still shining even in the darkness. For a moment, I miss my mother. Regret tugs at my heart, telling me I've made a mistake. *You're safest with me, Ava.*

I shake the thought away. I no longer need her. I will find my way through these trees, to Casiopea, and stop my mother's plans to destroy the Bone Wall. That's the only way I'll be able to live freely, away from the mortals who would kill me and safe from my mother and Zenos.

The flame in the distance draws closer, and my skin prickles with fear before I sink deeper into the woods.

# CHAPTER 6

## · KAYE ·

*The third law a Flame witch must follow is to never take a vampire's word as truth.*

*As they steal blood and life from those they kill, so too do they speak falsely of their own humanity.*

*Never real, never just.*

—TRAINING ACADEMY FOR
YOUNG WITCHES OF ARBORREN

The bone-dust barrier glimmers and shines in front of me, but my eyes turn to the forest beyond it. I breathe in shallowly, like I'm afraid something in it will hear me. I have to go through the barrier, something I've never done alone, to find Ava.

It was easy enough to follow Ava's tracks through the gravel and to the closest path into the forest from her home. Now all I have to do is track her in the trees, something I've never actually done, but have been trained to do.

Shaking away any final hesitation, I run through the barrier. The world briefly darkens, and then I'm inside. Pine scent envelops me the first time I breathe in. Bird chirps and rustling leaves fill the air. I glance over my shoulder once. Clouds hover over the roofs of Arborren, giving the town an ominous cast. I can't even hear the screams anymore, and it all looks blurred.

I bend down to examine the fallen leaves, twigs, and mud. Vampires move quicker than mortals, so their steps are lighter than ours. Liander taught us well, because I find Ava's steps—narrow feet that barely leave an indent in the mud—quite fast. Even with those light steps, she's tripped over plenty of roots on her way through the woods, leaving scattered rocks and twigs in her wake, as well as many fallen strands of black hair.

I set off, keeping my eyes and ears sharp. The forest is hundreds of acres large, with the sea at one end and mountains at another. Chrysalis waits in the middle, and while there are trails, I'm trying to avoid people. Flames patrol the forest weekly, bringing trainees along once per month. Human vampire hunters follow their own schedule, coming from both Arborren and Chrysalis. But with the break in the Bone Wall, Flames will be storming the forest to round up any bloodsucker near the wall so they don't stand a chance at getting inside. The trails will be very busy.

But if I keep a northeastern pace and check that I'm not too far off the trail every so often, I should be able to reach Chrysalis without running into any Flames or hunters.

If I can convince Ava to come with me. And if no vampires try to kill me along the way.

As a dusky light touches the trees ahead, I wonder if Tristan has caught a vampire yet. He's my only competition among the other trainees. After Liander gets the situation in Arborren under control, he'll enter the forest along with the older Flame witches, and there are always human vampire hunters in the woods. The ones from Chrysalis are skilled at catching vampires, too. Some do it for payment from the emperor to supplement their work in the mines, some do it to protect their homes . . . but others, they cut out vampire fangs and sell them as charms, on necklaces or set into rings. A shiver passes through me at the thought.

I exhale sharply, shoving a branch aside—and regretting it when it flings back at my face and I have to duck. I cut through a rough patch of undergrowth with one of my silver blades, wincing at how loud the sound is.

The journey to Chrysalis will be difficult, especially if we come across other vampires who will fight me to help her escape. For a brief moment, I wish Tristan were here, working alongside me.

I remember playing hide-and-seek in the Council Hall with him and Ava, losing track of the hours and days as we played. Childish things that don't serve me now. If I want to capture Ava, I can't feel nostalgic for who she was in her mortal life. And I can't use my mother's kindheartedness to survive in these woods; I need Liander's brutality instead.

My mother always tried to protect me from the people who thought I didn't belong here.

Most Flames are from the east of Erlanis Empire—the desert province Sunshore, or the bustling city of Solem, my mother's home. She was sent to work as a spy in Saren, a nation west of Erlanis, and met my father there. She began supporting Saren, and fed our emperor false information to slow his attempts to conquer the country—a secret she made me vow to keep for the rest of my life. My Sarenian father doesn't know I exist, as my mother had already been contracted to come work in Arborren, and she knew that the tensions between our nations would make life difficult for me if she gave birth outside Erlanis.

She'd thought the part of me that is East Erlantian would make me fit in here easily. But with the emperor's propaganda to justify invading Saren, he'd popularized so many misconceptions: that Sarenians were headstrong, violent, irrational, rude, and impure; that they focused far too much on strange technology like steam and gas rather than Erlanis's traditional industries of forestry and mining; that they didn't believe in the same old gods who first brought magic into this world, and therefore they needed guidance from Erlantians. These beliefs rubbed off on everyone, even here, so far from the capital.

She used to tell me to embrace every part of me, even the parts other people said didn't fit. She'd tell me to be myself, and to never be who anyone else wants me to become.

And I won't. I'll be the Flame witch I'm destined to be, even if no one thinks I deserve it.

While squeezing through tight clusters of trees, I try out different conversations in my head for when I find Ava to get her to come with me. I could pretend to be nice and offer her an escort through the woods as an old friend; it would be difficult, after all, to drag her kicking and screaming all the way to Chrysalis. I would get exhausted if I used my powers too much, and then she would break away. I'll avoid confronting her about my mother's death until we're close enough to Chrysalis that it'll be easy to drag her the rest of the way.

Hoots of owls rise around me, and cold fog seeps deep between the trees. The forest grows darker, not just with the fall of night, but the mud beneath my feet blackening and hardening, the trees turning umber, the leaves above deep green and bloodred and rich brown. I bring a small flame to my palm to see better. Hanging vines brush against my shoulders, then curl around my neck before falling away all on their own—a shiver goes down my spine every time they do. I smell rot and wonder if there's a dead animal nearby. I hear only my breaths and the crunch of dying leaves under my boots, and it's easy to think I'm the only person here.

In these woods, I'm no one. Even with the risk of encountering a vampire, I love every minute inside these woods—I feel a buoying freedom, like I'm floating along this eerie path. There are no mirrors to show my face. There are no whispers, no one staring at me and trying to solve me like I'm some kind of mystery. There's no doubt about who I am.

I am Kaye Mentara, Flame witch and hunter of vampires.

Friendship, a connection, forgiveness—that all ceased to exist two years ago, and I've needed none of it since. Nothing like that matters, not when I feel like a cloud drifting through these woods, with no body, no identity, and no one at my side. Nothing is real except the flames at my fingertips and the justice they'll bring.

I stop between two towering trees. Dappled moonlight shines through the leaves and gaps in the fog. The moon is more than half full now, a silver glow along its curve—five more days.

The tracks lead into tight-packed foliage, and something moves ahead, rustling the leaves. I hold my breath, douse my flames, and approach with the quietest steps I can manage. There's no sound of breathing or panicked gasps, only movement in the trees.

But vampires have no reason to breathe.

Ducking under a branch, I see her. Long black hair twirls around her, down to her ankles, as she searches for an opening in this enclosure of trees. And though she can't pant or have a racing pulse to give away her fear, I see it easily enough. A thin shaft of moonlight shines on those oak-brown eyes that glisten with unshed tears.

My heart beats faster, and I lean back into the shadows. Her face is as familiar as if I saw it up close yesterday, everything about her just like the girl I used to know. The girl who'd spent hours in empty classrooms with me, the girl whose laugh is etched in my memory.

I remember screaming her name in a courtyard that night, my voice hoarse and aching. I remember pounding on her door and getting no answer. I remember her empty seat at school the next day. My heart hardens and all I want to do right now is confront her. I forget all my plans of subterfuge, all my rehearsed lines, and step through the trees with my lips curled back in a snarl.

She pauses, then whips around to face me.

Raising my hands that glow gold with the flames waiting to be unleashed, I whisper, "Hello, bloodsucker."

# CHAPTER
## 7

- AVA -

*The queen holds court near the Heart Tree day and night,*
*at constant tension with the ancient magic*
*that binds the tree and the Bone Wall,*
*and keeps them all inside.*

—JOURNAL, AUTHOR UNKNOWN

The flames latch on to me before I can move, before I can blink. They wrap themselves like ropes around my wrists and up the length of my arms. I jerk backward to fling them off, but they don't leave. Then more appear around my ankles, and I'm too nervous to try to move. It'll burn my skin right off. The mark at my neck smarts with pain. My mind spirals back to being strapped to a chair by Zenos, a silver bar pressing into my skin, and I feel like I'm about to retch.

The only light between me and my attacker, who'd stepped out of the trees soundless as a ghost, is these flames. Their sparks rise and catch in my hair, making me cringe back from them. Far too close to flesh. But then, I notice that the fiery bands around my wrists and ankles don't actually touch my skin; they hover a half inch above. If they were touching me, I'd already be dead. I gulp at the sight, tracking the tiny flames and sparks with my eyes.

Then my attacker steps slightly closer, and I let out a small breath of recognition.

"Kaye," I whisper, so low I'm not sure she can hear me over the crackle of the flames. Then I brighten, the barest smile flickering across my lips. "It's me; Ava. It's been so long, I—"

Kaye steps closer, but she does not smile. Her jaw hardens and her eyes turn to flint. She angles herself to the side, both feet pressed into the ground and hands raised in a fighting stance.

The last time I saw her, we braided each other's hair after school, in an empty classroom where we sat on the desks with sunlight streaming in.

"Kaye," I say again, my voice shaking over the name as I try to make sense of the person in front of me. It's been years now, and I look over her face a thousand times as if that will make up for the lost years. That deep brown hair that turns copper in the sun. Big green eyes set deep, her features different from those of anyone else I've ever met. Light beige skin that glows in the light of her own flames, and the soft golden light that limns her skin—the magic that marks her as a young witch.

My stomach plummets and my mother's voice whispers in my thoughts: *Their entire purpose is to kill us. You cannot trust them.*

And that's exactly what she thinks about me, too. A heavy, desperate feeling sinks into my skin. Our friendship, our memories turn into ashes and disappear on the wind. All that's left is her fire at my wrists.

She lifts her hands, eyes narrowed to a dagger point. That's not simply mistrust or caution in her eyes. That's hatred, and it stings through me sharper than poison.

All the times I looked for her, the times I saw her on those rooftops . . . I'd hoped to meet her again. Does she simply hope to burn me?

"I'm still me, Kaye." My voice is so low, I'm surprised she hears me, but she lets out a bitter laugh and shakes her head.

The tips of her fingers turn molten red, and I react instinctively, thrusting my arms upward in an X. Roots shoot up from the ground and wrap around her torso. She lets out a snarl as they squeeze tighter, but her hands begin to shake.

"I'm sorry," I say quickly. "Kaye, take the flames off me, and I'll let you go."

The roots curl up toward her neck, and she sputters, the first hint of fear entering her eyes.

I almost relinquish my grip—I don't want to see her in pain— but the flames still burn near my skin. I squeeze my hands tighter and Kaye grunts in discomfort. One swipe, and I'd crush her ribs. One gesture from her, and her flames would devour me.

After a long, tense moment, the flames around my wrists and ankles begin to falter, light flickering out. I slowly let go of the roots. They slide back to the ground, limp once more.

Kaye stumbles back, trying to catch her breath. One of her hands curls into a fist, like she's preparing to wrap more flames around me, but then she loosens up. She seems shocked I've let her go.

In the distance, more voices rise, along with thunderous footsteps. Tiny lights appear between the trees a few hundred feet away. It could be hunters, it could be more Flames, it could be . . . Zenos, recovered and come to drag me back. My throat tightens and my vision wavers. I'd rather let Kaye turn me to ash than go back to Zenos.

"Are they coming here?" I ask, stepping backward. "Did you tell them where to find me?"

Kaye lifts her gaze to mine. Then she brings a small flame to life on her palm.

"Oh, they know where to look for you, and you've made it so much easier by leaving your Clarity mother's protection," she says in a low, sinister voice as the flickering flame lights her face from beneath. "One of them found out the truth; they saw you standing in your window with blood on your face one day. I couldn't believe it. I thought you were studying in some distant province, like your mother told everyone. How was I to know the truth?"

She pauses, her eyes hardening as she takes in my surprise. I didn't expect anyone to have known I was a vampire—if they knew that, why wasn't I hunted down before? Is it simply because of how powerful my mother is? I'd only ever seen Kaye look up at my window. But maybe . . . maybe she was the only person I paid attention to. Maybe other people saw me, too, and would track me down now that I've left my mother's protection.

"Look, I have no love for vampires, unlike my mother," Kaye continues. "But I will honor her wishes to protect those of you who may deserve a second chance. You are running away, I assume?"

The impersonal way she speaks with me feels like she's punching me in the gut several times over. She's so different from before.

"You were going to kill me, too," I say, the words coming out of me in a flustered rush.

Her green eyes flash in the light of the flames, but she doesn't reply. I've spent years reading lies and half-truths from my mother and Zenos. This doesn't seem like a lie, yet doubt still tugs at me.

The sounds of underbrush being hacked down nearby and a triumphant *whoop* cut through the air. I shrink away, my back hitting the closest tree.

"Do you want them to find you or not?" Kaye asks, sending a panicked glance over her shoulder toward the source of the sound. "Look, it's obvious you're running away, you don't even have any shoes. I will escort you to the nearest town—Chrysalis—and if any witches come across us, I will explain that you are mine; I cannot have any of them think I'm turning against my own kind. Likewise, if we come across any vampires, you will tell them I'm yours. You will help protect me from any vampires we cross paths with, and I will get you to Chrysalis. Do not expect anything more: this is a transaction . . . in honor of my mother." Her voice hardens as she finishes speaking and she stares me down, her gaze something fierce—and, vaguely, demanding.

For a moment, I'm too panicked to think clearly, but then what she said trickles in. She would escort me to Chrysalis. . . .

The vampire I'd met in Arborren told me the Heart Tree is fifteen miles northeast of Chrysalis. It would be a good place for me to start out from, but getting there would be nearly impossible on my own. I'd be caught and burned in a day, at the rate things are going. They kill vampires for sport in that village, so I won't actually go inside it. But if Kaye can escort me to within a mile or two of it . . . then I can go off on my own. Having someone else to travel alongside will also give me time to listen to the whispers in the trees to find out why they're calling me, and to read the journal and find out more about the

connection between the Heart Tree and the Bone Wall. If my
mother truly is planning to destroy the wall on her trip, then
I need to figure out how and warn Casiopea as fast as possible.
Someone offering to help is more than I expected, but might be
just what I need.

Maybe Kaye hates me now, but a sense of duty to her mother
means she will keep her word. I remember Calluna fondly; she's
like an aunt to me, and always slipped me candy and little po-
etry books before I went home in the evenings. She's so kind, I
can't imagine how Kaye became so cruel.

"Make a decision," she hisses.

Ice slides down my spine at her words, and I peel away from
the tree with a hard grimace. If she takes me to Chrysalis . . .
she doesn't need to know my destination beyond that. I won't
put the other vampires at risk by leading a Flame there.

She's breathing heavily like she just ran a mile, sweat making a loose wave of hair stick to her face. I feel a pang of remorse
and wonder what's happened to her. If she had gotten the letter
I'd tried to send her two years ago, would she have helped me?

There's a faint tug inside me that wants to prove to Kaye I'm
still me. Even though I know it's useless. I'll be with Casiopea soon
enough, and it won't matter what Kaye thinks of me. It won't matter what any mortal thinks . . . which is the way it should be.

As the movements of other witches and hunters in the trees
draw ever closer, Kaye exhales sharply and snaps her palm shut.
The flames disappear with the faintest hint of smoke, plunging
us into deeper darkness. But I can still see her face.

"Look." Kaye levels her gaze at me, with an urgent cut to her
voice. "Either we go together now, or I leave you for the hunters
to find."

# PART 2

## Blood and Water

# CHAPTER
# 8

## · KAYE ·

*Flame witches are not made for this land of trees; we are anathema to it.*
  *But nonetheless, we have been called to protect it.*
  —TRAINING ACADEMY FOR
  YOUNG WITCHES OF ARBORREN

*I can't believe she fell for it,* I think as we leave the clearing, trying to conceal any shock on my face.

Guilt squirms through me at how I'd used my mother to convince Ava she'd be safe with me. And I should only use fire in these woods when truly necessary; Flames are taught to fight with silver first, to avoid letting our anger get the best of us. When I saw Ava, it was like all my lessons dropped out of my mind. But I got her to come with me in the end, and that's what matters.

I'll keep up this charade, and slowly pull the truth out of her about my mother's death. Once we're close enough to Chrysalis, I'll confront her and incapacitate her, drag her to the village so Liander can see I've caught a vampire, then annihilate the traitor.

But right now, we need to find a place to rest for the night and plot our path to Chrysalis. There's always a chance that human hunters are in these woods, but they tend to stick to the trails and only veer off when they want to set a trap. Flames will cut their own paths most often. With all of us headed toward Chrysalis, I won't be surprised if we encounter my fellow Flames on the way. But the forest is vast, and if I'm careful in avoiding common paths and checking if anyone is near us, perhaps I can get Ava all the way to Chrysalis without running into anyone.

Vampires, though . . . that's a different matter. They travel by the forest canopy, sliding along the branches to search for prey below. If they attack, I won't even see them until they're right on top of me; I trust my reflexes and my skills, but I don't trust Ava not to turn on me and help one of her fellows kill me.

Her footsteps behind me are nearly inaudible, so I keep checking to make sure she's still there. She's staring up at the moon, silver reflected in her dark eyes like starlight on the sea. I sigh and turn back around. It's unnerving, how human vampires can look.

Night has settled deeply, my breath fogging in front of me. As we step through a narrow patch of trees, there's a rustle of leaves nearby. I hold out a hand behind me to stop Ava moving forward, heart pounding in my ears.

"No one is there," says a soft voice, and I nearly jump out of my skin as Ava steps next to me.

"I can see that," I snap.

Ava raises an eyebrow and points west. "Then do you see that?"

Everything in that direction is a black abyss. Whenever Liander led our class through the woods, he recommended finding a type of berry that improves night vision. But I can't remember what the berry looks like, and a vampire is right next to me with sharper vision than I'll ever have.

"Is there an animal?" I finally ask in a begrudging tone.

"A witch, with a flame on their hand, about three hundred feet away. One of your kind. Look, you lead the way to Chrysalis and I'll watch out for anyone approaching—vampires and mortals alike."

Instead of replying, I give her a stiff nod. We begin walking, and I keep track of a northeast direction through snatches of stars above, as Flame witches are trained to do. Occasionally, Ava gestures for us to pause or change direction, whispering that we're not alone.

For a long time, our footsteps trudging through the mud and undergrowth, the leaves whistling in the wind above, and scattered birdcalls are the only sounds. Midnight has seeped through it all and holds the forest with captive breath.

"It's been a long time since we've seen each other, Kaye," Ava says from beside me, and the sudden sound makes me jump.

"Why are you talking to me as if we're friends?" She winces at the harshness of my voice. I roll my eyes; she's not the one walking alone next to a bloodthirsty vampire, so what could she have to fear?

I glare at her out of the corner of my eye as she bites her lip, deep in thought. She seems more anxious than she used to. More hesitant. More cautious. A brief spark of curiosity flits through me, but I snuff it out. I have to keep her convinced I'm leading her to safety, but I don't have to pretend to like her.

"I just . . ." she begins, her hands twisting together in front of her. "I know we're both different now, but—"

"Different?" I can't help scoffing. "That's some understatement, bloodsucker."

"Don't call me that," Ava says with a low hiss.

"Simply by choosing to exist in this world, you've chosen to be a killer," I say, my voice too loud. In one side of my head, I hear my mother's voice begging for temperance and kindness, but on the other side I have Liander reminding me what I've lost and how hard I need to fight these vampires that shouldn't exist. I can't hold both of them inside me at once, and right now, the anger wins out. "You require blood to fake being alive, but that's all it is—faking."

In a cutting tone, she says, "Mortals kill other mortals all the time and you still call them people."

I want to rage at her, but bite down on my fury and try to rein it back. If I keep going like this, I might make her suspicious of me, and we're still quite a long way from Chrysalis; it will be infinitely more difficult to take her there if she realizes I intend to betray her.

"My mother would want me to guide you safely through these woods," I say through gritted teeth. I watch her face for even the smallest reaction to me talking about my mother, but she remains stoic. "That's why I'm doing it. But don't mistake that for me giving any leniency to vampires. Even ones I used to know."

I let out a heavy sigh—from exhaustion after everything that's happened today, from the effort I'll have to exert to keep up this ruse—and Ava meets my gaze as I do. I wonder if she misses breathing.

*Why am I even thinking that?*

A wave of loneliness crashes into me then. Suddenly I'm nine years old again and sitting on a desk in an empty classroom. She found me in there, hiding from the other children who were playing outside. They wouldn't want me with them anyway—their parents had all told them I was half Sarenian, half not good enough to be their friend. Tristan was with his father, who often pulled him out of school to spend the day at the Council Hall. But Ava had shown up, and stood in the doorway watching me in a black silk school dress, her head tilted to the side. Even though she was Sarenian, I assumed she wouldn't want anything to do with me because she lived in one of the big, nice houses in the north of Arborren, and her family was close to the emperor. Even though both our mothers were Clarity councilors, she'd always seemed so much more impressive than me. But she often kept to herself at school, too.

"Why are you here?" she asked then. Her voice was like a bell in that dusty room.

A long silence passed before I said anything, and I expected her to lose interest and leave. But she didn't.

Finally, I said, "I don't know."

She wrinkled her nose, but not at me—at the unused classroom. "Well, it smells in here. Come on, I want to show you something."

As she turned to exit, I stood up slowly, hesitant. What if this was all a trick?

But once she reached the door, Ava looked over her shoulder at me with a glittering smile, and my heart softened for the first time all day. Holding back tears of gratitude, I followed her—and continued following her for years, until she left.

I shake the memory away; there's no need for it here.

When I look up, Ava is standing in front of a tree with

low-hanging, bell-shaped flowers. Her long black hair tumbles down her back like a waterfall made of night. With wide eyes, she holds one of the flowers between two fingers and stares at it like it's the most wondrous thing in the world. I cornered her only an hour ago, my flames around her wrists and ankles as she breathed my name like a prayer, then as the hope in her eyes shattered. She looked so disappointed in me.

But I know vampires play tricks like this to mess with your mind. I won't fall for it.

Brushing away a vine that has snaked onto my neck, I snap, "We don't have time to look at flowers."

She barely reacts, just keeps running her finger over that flower. In a low voice, she whispers, "It's dying."

Then I notice the brown edges of the flower she holds, the yellow pus that seeps from the center. In an uncertain voice, I blurt out, "It's autumn. Of course things are dying."

"Not like that." She bites her lip, looking as unsure as I feel. "Don't you feel it? Like these woods are alive, but barely? Gasping for breath?"

A chill passes over me as she speaks. Of course I feel it; there's something wrong with these woods. When I was younger, I used to overhear conversations between my mother and Liander about dwindling water sources in the forest. All Flames know to bring enough water from home and not rely on finding any out here. But I've never seen anything like this flower Ava is holding.

"The last time I came here," I begin slowly, looking into the distance, "it was early morning. We could barely see because of the fog, which is what we were training for—how to travel through here with limited visibility. But even in the fog, I saw sparks of light sometimes, green and yellow, swirling in patterns.

At the time, I told myself it was just because I was thirsty and seeing things. But now, I'm not so sure. We all know the stories. When the old gods gifted magic to mortals for the first time, they spread it to the land around them, including this forest."

My mother had so many old books about these woods and the history of vampires in the area, written by Flames who came before us. As a child, I never got more than a few chapters in before slamming the books closed; the stories about vampires had always given me nightmares.

There are countless scary stories told to keep children away from the woods—about bloodsuckers that move through the trees so stealthily you'd never see them coming, and ghosts of ancient witches that drag you to their graves. And of course, tales of the vampire queen, and her army of vampires that stalks these woods for prey.

But there's also the feel of it. Like something is always watching and waiting, counting my breaths and reading my thoughts and fears.

Then I notice Ava's feet, covered in mud and scratches with blood welling up. She winces a little as she shifts her weight from side to side. That's not even her blood; vampires are only kept in a state resembling life by drinking others' blood. It keeps them functioning and makes them resemble us, on a surface level, so that we never see them coming when they hunt us. When they bleed, it's the blood of their victims seeping out, not their own. The very sight of it is infuriating and repulsive and . . . it reminds me that my old friend no longer exists. That she is long dead.

It also proves she's not innocent. But it still seems to hurt her. I remember a cold night we'd walked home from school together, with a hailstorm that had come out of nowhere. She'd held her jacket over both of us, and when I insisted she didn't have to, she'd rolled her eyes and pressed closer to me.

With a heavy sigh, I pull my pack from my shoulders, then withdraw a second pair of boots I'd packed in case mine give me blisters. I grimace as I toss them on the ground in front of her. We'll move much faster if she isn't bleeding all over the place, and the nearest campsite I know of is still an hour away.

"Thank you," she whispers, sliding them onto her damaged feet. Her eyes spark as she looks at me to lead, and my breath briefly catches. She bites her lower lip, which is chapped, and her fangs peek out from under her lips. I stiffen, watching her. Are the veins under her eyes growing more prominent or am I imagining it? The thirstier vampires get, the more terrifying they become.

Did she look like this the night she killed my mother? The sole vampire that escaped punishment that night, hidden by her Clarity mother, an excuse ready for her absence the next day. I don't know how she was changed; perhaps she met a vampire that day too and attacked the first person she saw when she became undead.

Only hours before, after school, she'd been mortal, her skin warm, her eyes full of life.

I tear my gaze away and keep walking, imagining all the ways I'll get her to reveal the truth about my mother. No innocent smile or kind eyes will save her then.

# CHAPTER 9

## - AVA -

*The sorrow of Casiopea, the first vampire, has lasted a thousand years.*
  *The death of her vampire son at the hands of humans.*
  *The imprisonment in the forest.*
  *Her reign is never-ending, as is her pain.*
  —JOURNAL, AUTHOR UNKNOWN

All I can think about is blood.

Kaye is slightly ahead of me, turning around every few minutes to hiss at me to keep up. I start stumbling into trees, my vision blurring as an ache builds at the back of my throat.

I continue searching the trees for sign of an animal to drink from. Night birds flit through branches, but nothing else, as if all life has been stamped out of these woods. The idea of leaping up a tree and wrenching a bird out of the air like a true predator disturbs me, but I know I'll have to do something about this thirst before it takes me over completely.

Ahead of me, Kaye walks steadily, light steps finding every soft patch of mud and leaves while I blunder away behind her.

She's only a few steps away, her braid swaying across her back. I could lunge at her and put my fangs to her throat in seconds. But the moment I think that, a pit of shame opens up in me, and I recoil in disgust. I'll never hurt Kaye. She's still important to me, even if she hates me. I'll only fight her if she strikes first.

I'm thirsty, but I'm controlling it, and I'll continue to find ways to sate the thirst without attacking mortals. I understand why Kaye hates the fearsome vampires who hunt and kill mortals like true predators, but I'm not as strong or brutal as them. I wouldn't stand a chance in these woods without her help. And so, despite her hurtful words, I won't leave her yet.

An ache tugs at my non-beating heart. Only two years have passed, but it could have been twenty, with how much has changed.

I shouldn't want to break the silence between us now. I shouldn't want to patch things up with a girl who easily calls me "bloodsucker" and throws away all our memories like they're nothing. She's just one of the many things I lost when I was turned, and I have to get used to that if I'm to make a new life for myself, with other immortals—where I belong.

This arrangement is only temporary.

My gaze goes to the dark spots between the trees and I imagine them extending all the way to the Heart Tree, the great oak deep in the center of the woods, limned in silver light from low-hanging fog. I'll travel with Kaye until I'm close to Chrysalis, then go on my own the rest of the way to find Casiopea at the Heart Tree.

Kaye slows, waiting for me to catch up to her, and I notice the dark circles under her eyes.

"There's a campsite nearby. Maybe you don't need sleep, but if I'm going to be an effective guide, I'll have to rest."

"Sleep helps me heal, actually," I say in a hoarse voice, touching the scarred skin on my neck. My hand still has wounds from this morning, too, when I'd held on to the silver doorknob of my attic. It feels like a million years ago already.

We walk for another twenty minutes before stepping through a gap in the trees and entering a tiny clearing. Kaye lets out a sigh of relief, her shoulders slumping. There are some overturned logs, flat patches of grass that had clearly been lain on, and a scorched pile of wood in the center over a bed of dried leaves. The stench of rotting trees still hangs in the air, but the wood-smoke here helps diminish it.

"Are you sure this is safe?" I ask, and another owl hoot punctures my question. I settle onto one of the logs and my dizziness slowly subsides. "It looks like people have been here recently. Some of your friends, I suppose?"

Bitterness leaks into my voice when speaking of the Flame witches, but Kaye doesn't seem to mind. Her forehead creases a little, but then smooths out, and she says, "No, why would we need twigs and wood to start a fire? This is probably human vampire hunters, either from Arborren or Chrysalis. My guess is Chrysalis though; they already live in the middle of the woods, so they're comfortable with it. No one from Arborren wants to stay here overnight."

For some reason, that makes me laugh. "Yet here we are."

"Yet here we are," Kaye repeats in a whisper. Her eyes are unreadable as she spreads meager supplies on the ground. "I don't know if they'll come back tonight. This is my first time being in this part of the woods."

"Your first time?" I ask, too loudly. The owl hoots again and lifts away, wings illuminated by moonlight as it soars over the trees. But I don't care if anyone heard me. "How much do you really know about these woods? Do you even know how to get to Chrysalis?"

Sharp green eyes cut to me. She holds out a hand, and flames rise underneath. Watching me the whole time, she coaxes a small cooking fire into being above the wood left by the hunters. Finally, when the fire is stable, she leans toward me and the flames light her cheeks, leaving the hollows of her eyes in shadows.

"I've been in the woods plenty of times, just not to Chrysalis nor on this exact path. But I know these trees like I know the way to school, or my house, or the market. They teach us, hour after hour, how to master these woods, so that we're better able to fight bloodsuckers." Her voice cuts off in one breath and I lean back, a chill sweeping through me at her cold, callous words. "I knew where to find this clearing, didn't I? Trust me, if I wanted to kill you, I could have done so ten times already."

*And I could have done the same to you,* I want to bite out at her, but instead, I grumble under my breath and stare into the fire. As much as it's a source of fear for me, I can't deny I like the warmth.

We both go quiet for a while, Kaye eating and shooting me quick glances from the corners of her eyes every few minutes like I'll attack her if she looks away for too long.

*Bloodsucker. Greedy little thing.*

The words Zenos called me were insults, but he always said them with a purr in his voice, like he secretly approved. Taunting me pleased him. My throat closes up as I remember him resting his chin on my shoulder, his grimy fingers wiping away the blood from the corner of my lips, his contemplation of cutting off my fingers and denying me blood.

I pull my hair in front of me and sigh at how tangled it is, with dirt and twigs nested inside it. I've never gone this long without brushing it, and it's never been this dirty before. The thought makes a small smile twitch at the corner of my lips; my mother would be furious to see me like this.

Kaye has finished eating and her eyes take me in like I'm a curious find at a museum. This is probably the first time she's ever seen a vampire up close. I watch her unabashedly, trying to find some remnant of the girl she used to be. Can she see that in me at all, her old friend, or does she only see a dead girl now?

My thirst prickles painfully at the back of my throat again, but I don't want Kaye to see how desperate I am. I swallow it down and grit my teeth. As night wears on, Kaye prepares to sleep. She withdraws a long net from her backpack and throws it over herself. When I notice the tiny silver spokes embedded all over it, I scoff in disbelief. She raises an eyebrow. If I wanted to attack her, that net wouldn't stop me. Although it would deter me enough that she'd wake up and be able to fight.

I reach for my pillowcase sack and pull out the crinkled leaf I caught earlier, back in Arborren. After jostling around in the sack for hours, it's more broken and dead than ever. I spread it over one of my knees and take in all the little torn spots.

I can't just let this leaf break apart. I spread the fingers of my palm and let a steady, calming feeling rush through me. Slowly, the tears in it begin to restitch themselves, and the dull leaf becomes vibrant yellow.

I settle the leaf on the ground softly, then withdraw the journal from my sack again to trace the path from Arborren, to Chrysalis, to roughly where the Heart Tree should be. Flipping through the pages, I search for more mentions of the Heart Tree, but I only see it referred to in a historical sense as the place where the vampires' imprisonment began; an invincible artifact from another time, imbued with magic to protect mortals. The vampire queen, locked inside the forest, took the chance to build a home and domain for her fellow prisoners.

It's sometimes hard to read the journal, which has cramped writing and jumps from topic to topic, as if the author could hardly write fast enough to get all their thoughts out. Every time I read it, I find something new.

My fingers brush over a page with fading ink, as if the author's quill was running out but they were writing too urgently to fill it.

. . . *the great oak is a beacon around which the vampire queendom gathers, and it is believed to be invincible* . . .

Believed? Does *believed to be invincible* mean there's a chance it's not? And what would that mean for the Bone Wall? I frown, the dizziness from my thirst coming back and making it hard to think properly.

As I close the journal, I notice Kaye is fast asleep. She must have been more tired than she was letting on. She's drooling all over the wadded-up cloth she's using as a pillow. In one hand she grips a silver knife, though her fingers have become loose around it. She removed her braid before sleeping, so now soft chestnut waves fall above her head, looking oddly like a pool of blood leaking out of her. The angle of her head while she sleeps exposes her neck, lit up by the fire. Focusing and straining my ears to hear over the crackle of flames, I catch the steady beat of her pulse, and my stomach twists at the sound.

Before I know what I'm doing, I slip off the log I'm sitting on and move closer to her, one hand stretched toward the net.

*No,* says a voice rising in the back of my thoughts. I yank my hand back, and a new wave of dizziness washes over me.

My body is heavy, weighed down with my injuries, the need for blood making me weaker.

My wounds will heal by morning. Then I'll fix my blood problem. I can hold out until then.

Tearing my gaze away from Kaye's neck, I close my eyes.

When I wake in the morning, the damaged skin on my neck and hands is smooth again, but the thirst is back stronger than ever. It sears, like tiny needles prickling my throat. My stomach feels like a stone weighing me down as I stand and sway on my feet. Kaye isn't here, but her belongings are still strewn next to the ashes of the fire, so she must be close. Dawn light bathes the clearing in a pale gray glow.

My head spins, and bile rises in my throat. I need blood now.

Forcing myself to focus, I stumble through trees, tripping over every root like I did yesterday. I hear voices whispering between the branches, their words panicked but indistinct. There's movement around me, something big that rustles leaves with every step. A sinister feeling grips my chest, sending fear down my spine in a cold sweep. If one of those hunters from yesterday slid out of the trees right now with a silver blade in hand, I'm not sure I could fend them off. I scan the ground and the branches, searching for any living thing with blood in its veins.

I stumble upon another clearing, this one overgrown with weeds. A fallen tree cuts the space in half. Vines hang down from the trees, and maybe I'm delusional with thirst, but it looks like they're reaching toward the ground, swaying and searching for something on the dry, dead forest floor.

There—a squirrel, nearly blending in with the brown bark

of the fallen tree. It makes little chomping sounds as it eats acorns fallen from the oak trees nearby.

This is my only option, then. I'll have to stomach it. It's still killing, but at least it's not a human.

Approaching with as quiet steps as I can manage, I lift my hands and focus on the squirrel. Its jaw moves so fast while eating the acorns.

The back of my throat itches and stings, and my vision briefly blackens before returning. All I need to do is snap the squirrel's neck in one swift strike to make it as painless as possible. I could run forward and do it with my hands, but the squirrel will end up suffering if I can't do it properly.

I gulp and lift my hand, which shakes terribly. I remember sitting in my attic for two years, vowing to never become a killer like my mother, vowing to not lose who I am or the humanity that was taken from me far too early. How do I justify what I'm doing now, as I raise a long root out of the ground and it sways like a snake, ready to do my bidding?

I remind myself I'm doing this *for* my humanity; if I kill this squirrel now, that will spare a human from my thirst. It's the only way I can . . .

Kaye's words stab through my thoughts. *Simply by choosing to exist in this world, you've chosen to be a killer.*

Tears stream down my cheeks as I wrap the root around the squirrel's throat and then tug, so fast it has no idea what happened. The animal makes one horrible sound as it falls, and in the silence that follows, I feel only the wind on my shoulders.

*Find us. Help us.*

I jump in place. There go the voices again. Mist has seeped into the clearing, shrouding it like a blanket, and with it comes the stench of carrion on the air.

On stiff legs, I stand. The mist clears to reveal a small field of rich brown, loamy earth.

With dead bodies spread across it, and a spark of green light dancing ahead.

# CHAPTER
## 10

### · KAYE ·

*A Flame is made of air, energy, fire, and light,*
   *all things wild and pure.*
   *But the greatest skill we can learn is self-control,*
   *for our own survival,*
   *and to protect the integrity of the Flames as a whole.*
                                —TRAINING ACADEMY FOR
                        YOUNG WITCHES OF ARBORREN

Midmorning sunlight spills into the clearing when I wake. I smell woodsmoke from the fire I made, and Ava sleeps a few feet away. She took her shoes off before resting last night, and I marvel at how all the cuts are now gone, the skin smoothed over. There's still a mark on her neck, and some damage to her hands, but even these have faded from yesterday. With a few more hours of rest, I bet they'll be gone, too.

The thought sends a quiet simmer of fury through me. She can heal in a matter of hours, while my mother didn't get a second chance. She'd died alone in a snow-coated alley.

The image of her body being carried into the Council Hall comes back to me in a rush and my breath shortens, my chest contracting and my whole body tensing up like a taut bowstring.

The old me would have lain next to Ava until she woke, told her my nightmares and fears, and listened to her comforting voice until the pain went away. I can't be around her—and the memories of how we used to be.

I leave the clearing and walk a ways north. As I do, the back of my throat aches, my tongue like sandpaper—I have water at our campsite, but I need to be careful with how much I drink. Chrysalis is still thirty miles away through vast stretches of wild, difficult-to-traverse woods with very few clear paths; plenty of time to encounter vampires. I can't risk running out of water before reaching our destination.

When Ava wakes up, we'll keep moving, and I'll have to do a better job of holding my temper in check today to keep up this ruse.

When I breathe in, the scent of rot clings to the air, the tree trunks appear gray in the dawn light, and a strange white substance leaks from the branches—that must be part of the sickness Ava pointed out last night. I wonder if this has anything to do with the dwindling water sources in the woods.

My mother and I used to take trips into these woods, escorted by Flames and hunters. The streams were already beginning to dry up back then, but there were still some hints of water between the trees. We'd go to a glistening lake where we'd swim for hours with a few other families. Whenever they'd successfully cleared out vampires from that part of the forest, they would bring their families on a vacation of sorts to prove their strength and that the forest didn't really belong to the vampires. Clarity councilors would often come, too, but one of my favorite memories was just with me, my mother, and Tristan. Except the chill of the water unnerved me, and I'd always been afraid to put my head under.

"Just hold your breath and put your head under water," Tristan had said on one of these trips in a cheerful voice, his sandy hair glistening with water drops as he trod water next to me. "You won't feel cold anymore."

"I'm scared," I'd said in a whisper. "What if I drown, or if there's a bloodsucker under the water?"

He frowned at the water, then joked, "My legs are longer. They'll catch me first and then you can get away."

"That's not funny!" I'd said, my arms flailing in the water and splashing it back at him.

Laughing, he said, "I won't let anything happen to you, Kaye. I'm right here."

That lake is probably dry now. The last time we went on one of those trips was years ago, before that part of the forest was overrun by vampires, too.

I drum my fingers on the handle of one of my daggers, a nervous gesture. Fear had always felt like a myth before, a locked-away thing that rarely ever spoke up and could be dispelled with a few kind words. A deep pain tugs at my heart, like tiny silver blades reaching into my chest. My mother's gone, Ava's no longer who she was, and Tristan forgets that we were friends once, too. Fear laughs at me now and makes sure I know I'm not good enough. Everyone always leaves, and then you're on your own against the world. I squeeze my eyes shut harder, but all I see is turned backs, hands on doorknobs, unspoken goodbyes.

A wave of loneliness washes over me, and I struggle to turn it into anything more useful.

A rustling ahead catches my attention, something big moving through a cluster of trees. Heart shooting into my throat, I lift my dagger.

When Tristan steps out of the thicket a moment later, I let out a stream of curses. "Tristan, you scared the hell out of me!"

He turns and waves, a triumphant grin lighting up his face. "Kaye! Didn't think I'd run into you before Chrysalis. Haven't caught any bloodsuckers, I see."

I really want to correct him, but before I can bite out a retort, I wonder where the rest of our classmates are. What if they're searching the woods and capture Ava for themselves?

"Where are the others, Tristan?" I ask, trying to stay calm so I can get out of here without making him suspicious.

"There were some dead hunters, fang marks on their necks, blood all around them." His eyes glisten with the thrill of the hunt. "I tracked the two vampires who did it and bound them myself; I check in with the others every night, and we watch over the vampires in shifts to keep them bound and unconscious. I'm looking for more now; my dad didn't say we had to stop at one." He pauses, twirls a dagger in the air, and then asks without looking at me, "What about you, Kaye? How's it been, going at it alone?"

*Alone.* The word's bitter tone sinks into me. Has he forgotten everything, how we used to work together on these trips through the woods? How he wanted to help me after my mother's death? Something got to him, and I suspect it had to do with how he never thought he was good enough, how he always tried to impress his father, who never seemed to acknowledge him.

In that way, we're the same—I'm never good enough for any of them, no matter how well I do. Only Liander notices my skill, and if that's because he sees my mother in me, I take that as a compliment.

"It's going fine," I finally bite out. "I'll see you in Chrysalis, okay?"

He nods and vanishes into the trees without a backward glance.

I let out a sharp breath and head back toward the clearing. We can't waste any more time resting; the full moon is only four days away, and that's when Liander expects me in Chrysalis.

But when I reach the camp, Ava's gone. So are the shoes I gave her. My belongings are still strewn next to the extinguished campfire, which looks sad and dead in the middle of it all.

"That lying—" I'm about to say, "lying witch," but stop myself before I can be too much of a hypocrite.

She did an excellent job of looking so innocent and helpless, but clearly she was plotting something else. That's what vampires do; they're made of lies and trickery.

But what she's terrible at is hiding her tracks. I can already see them—light, small steps heading east.

I quickly throw my belongings back into my pack and swing it over one shoulder. As I stand, the hair on the back of my neck rises, as if something is watching me. A cool mist brushes against my skin, almost like soft fingers. The forest is silent around me, without even the chirp of birds to accompany me.

I whip around, one hand at a knife, my breaths coming hard and fast. Then I catch the glint of eyes, bright specks up in the trees, and my heart shoots into my throat. The eyes of a predator. I'd think it was an animal if it weren't for the pale hand I spot gripping onto a branch.

The hand disappears. I search the trees for some sign of it, but there's nothing. The only sound is my own rapid pulse. Leaving the clearing, I try to calm the fear that a vampire will descend on me from the trees any moment now.

I follow Ava's tracks into a thicket of trees, one of them fallen across the center of an overgrown clearing. Ava stands in front of the fallen tree. Her back and shoulders are taut through the thin silk of her shirt. And then I see the lifeless squirrel she clutches in one of her hands.

"What did you do?" I ask, my voice high-pitched.

No answer. Then I hear the sobs—her whole body is racked with them. When I look more closely, my stomach twists at the sight of the broken squirrel.

She whips around, tears streaking down her cheeks, and my breathing slows. She lifts her other hand and points. Following the line of her hand, I see a small field up ahead, with . . .

My stomach drops and I feel like I'm going to faint. Bile rises in the back of my throat, and it takes all my effort to not vomit right here. Approaching on stiff legs, my shoes squishing into the mud below, I stop a few feet away from her and stare out at the dead bodies strewn across the earth. Mostly animal, but some human, their limbs scattered haphazardly. Rot and decay hang thick in the air, and I pull my shirt over my nose to avoid smelling it.

And then, a deep whining sound rises up from the earth. We both step back, transfixed as the soil shifts back and forth over the dead bodies, and small pits open in the earth to suck them in. The earth rocks hard enough that I have to catch my balance, but I can't tear my eyes away as the ground continues pulling those bodies into it. Roots from deep in the earth pull the creatures down below like the reaching arms of a giant.

In seconds, the bodies are gone, and the earth stops moving.

"What the hell was that?" I breathe, taking a step backward. As I do, something tightens around my ankle and pulls me back.

Pulling a silver dagger from my belt, I twist around, prepared to face a vampire. But then I see that a tree root is wrapped around my ankle instead.

"Let her go!" Ava says then, running up in front of me, squirrel still gripped in one hand. With her other hand, she slashes through the air, and the root breaks in half, falling to the ground on either side of my foot. I scramble upward and nearly fall into Ava; her back bangs into a tree and I stop right before slamming into her. My hands catch the bark above her head with the dagger still held tightly between them. The sun shines blindingly on my gold wrist cuffs, but I'm not looking at them. I'm looking at Ava.

My breath comes in quick, shallow gasps, and her wide, frightened brown eyes are all I see. The sunlight sparkles on them, and there's a strange fluttering sensation in my chest. I pull back from her and shake my head to clear it.

That was far too similar to how I used to feel about her—the way her eyes always drew me in, how we could stay up all night talking, how I used to rest my hand next to hers and wish she would take it.

All useless things that ceased to matter the moment she became a vampire.

I force myself back to the present and ask, "What is wrong with this forest? Why did the ground suck up those bodies? Why did that root grab me?"

"I don't know, I . . . I heard a voice near here, asking for help, and then . . . this happened." Her hands shake so badly she drops the squirrel.

As much as I think we should get out of here and away from whatever just happened in that field, Ava needs blood to move on. Better she take it from an already dead creature than from me.

I approach the squirrel and pick it up, curious for a moment. I didn't even know vampires could drink from animals.

Usually I passed this ugly task off to someone else in my class whenever we trained in the woods. But I've seen it done before.

Silently, my breaths shallow the whole time, I skin the squirrel with my dagger. As I'm about to hand it back to Ava, her hand strikes out and grabs it. She sinks her fangs into it without looking at me. It's like she's forgotten I'm here.

I lean slightly back on my heels, watching as crimson blood trickles down her jaw and then her neck. Purple veins stick out on the skin under her eyes and on her forearms, her muscles taut as she drinks. It's terrifying. It's unnatural. But for some reason, I can't look away.

She sighs in relief after she drinks, her head tilted back so hazy morning sunlight shines on her face. Her mouth hangs open, her lips and teeth red. She grimaces at the squirrel, her eyes deepening with regret, before she places it on the ground again. Then she starts shoveling dirt over the squirrel's corpse, like she's burying it.

"I don't get it," I say suddenly, hating how my voice shakes as I do. "You drink from humans. Why do you feel bad about this?"

She cuts me a sharp look. "I don't drink from humans."

"Liar," I say through gritted teeth, my fury rising so fast it surprises even me. "I've seen you in that window, I've seen the blood on you, I've heard about the bodies left in the woods just outside the city, their blood drained—"

"I thought you said it was a different Flame witch who saw me in the window," she says in a low voice, her umber eyes pinning me in place.

"Does it matter?" I snap, my voice far too loud, but I don't care right now. All I see, when I look at her, is red—blood from the deaths she's caused. "You're a killer. The only honorable thing you can do is admit it." I'm seething as I stare her down, the real accusation I want to hurl at her right at the tip of my tongue.

Maybe I should. Could I keep her unconscious and bound all the way to Chrysalis with no one to help me? I doubt it, and that's the only thing that makes me bite my tongue to keep my anger in check for now.

"Kaye, we used to be friends. The best of friends." Her voice cracks, and a desperation fills her eyes. I take a step back in response. "Do you remember? You're not acting like yourself."

Of course I remember what it felt like to lose my best friend, to have her disappear when I needed her the most and turn into an immortal being whose sole desire is to kill. Her words only make the loss hurt more.

"Don't talk to me like you know anything about me," I bite out, blinking to clear the tears at the corners of my eyes.

"I do know you, Kaye." She reaches a hand toward one of mine, but I yank it back. "This isn't you."

Just then, a loud rustle comes from the trees, and branches creak under a heavy weight. Far too loud to be a bird.

"They're coming," Ava whispers. In a frantic movement, she stands and shoves me behind her.

"What? Who?" I ask, but then my blood goes cold. If these were hunters or Flame witches, she wouldn't be pushing me behind her for protection. Fear flits through me, and I ask, "Bloodsuckers?"

She barely has time to nod before they slink from the trees like shadows peeling off trunks and branches. They're like fog, passing unseen until suddenly it's upon you. Even from here, I spot the rust-colored stains on their clothes, and their fangs, which protrude over their drawn-back lips. Leaves and twigs are twisted in their hair, and mud is smeared across their clothes. I exhale sharply and wonder if it's my last breath.

*No,* I think to myself. *I am Calluna Mentara's daughter. I am stronger than that.*

Ava straightens at my side, her gaze fierce, and I wonder if she plans to forsake me now that her own kind are here. A desperate feeling reaches up inside me. She can't leave. Not before I get the truth out of her.

Three bloodsuckers take loping strides toward us, but I draw air to my palm and a moment later, more flames spark to life. If I have to fight all of them alone, so be it.

Then Ava lifts her own hands and bares her fangs—at the other vampires.

There are two male vampires and one female vampire, all of them circling us. I recognize the bright green eyes of one of the men, who sniffs the air as he approaches us—he's the one I saw in the clearing earlier.

"I only hear one heartbeat here." He pauses, taking us both in before moving to Ava in the blink of an eye, faster than I've ever seen Ava move. She glares up at him without a shred of fear on her face. When he bares his fangs at her, she doesn't even flinch.

"I saw you in Arborren, remember?" she asks in a steady voice. "You leave me to my business, and I'll leave you to yours."

He tilts his head at me, a curious glint in his eyes. "You don't share your meals? We offered the same to you, back in Arbor-ren."

Ava lifts her chin in defiance. "This one is mine."

My eyes dart to her. I didn't expect her to actually uphold our agreement to help each other in the forest.

But I look away a breath too long. The female vampire races behind me in the blink of an eye.

Her cold hands graze my neck right before I whip around. My knife slashes across her collarbone. She hisses at the silver and jumps back.

"Not one step closer," Ava says to the other vampires, raising her hands with fear flashing in her eyes. The two males laugh at the challenge as the woman straightens, swipes through the blood I drew on her chest, and licks it from her fingers with a spark in her eyes.

Liander always said to move two steps ahead of them.

I duck before she charges again, and swing my knife across the backs of her ankles. She falters for a moment before lunging toward me. I stand my ground, bringing flames to my hands at the last second. She lands with her head next to mine and I wrap my hands around her neck, leaving the flames a hair's breadth from her skin. She pauses with her fangs brushing my neck, her matted blond hair falling into my face. I stop breathing, and she tenses in my grip.

Any second now, one of us will die.

"Don't think I won't do it," I hiss in her ear. We're supposed to use silver to subdue the vampires, since the fire is too dangerous in these woods. I don't know if I could contain a forest fire, so I hold back now—but if she reaches for me with those fangs, I'll have to risk it.

Then I hear panicked cries from the other two vampires. They're pinned to trees with long, thick roots holding them in place like chains, and I nearly laugh at the sight. Ava might scare easily, but she's more than a match for these vampires.

"Why are you alone?" one of the vampires near Ava chokes out. "You could have an army at your command, with those powers. You could have feasts of humans every day, yet you keep one around like a guard dog."

A sharp crack rends the air and the bloodsucker screams as the roots crack his ribs.

"Get off her," Ava calls over her shoulder.

The vampire pinning me down nods, but leans toward me to whisper, "I've never drunk from a witch before, with that golden glow around you. I wonder if your blood tastes any different. I'll be watching . . . the moment your little protector looks away . . ."

She lifts her hands off me, a glint in her eyes, and I try not to show any reaction to what she just said. Vampires can see a faint glow around young witches; I've never seen it myself, because mortal eyesight isn't good enough. But it usually scares them, since they know we're powerful. This vampire, however . . . doesn't seem scared at all.

Slowly, I remove the flames from my hands so she can move. She lurches to her feet, brushing off the dirt, and glares at me as I stand, too.

"There are plenty of other humans in these woods," Ava says. The two male vampires gasp in relief, but one of them struggles more than his companion to stand up. By the way he's holding his ribs, I guess that Ava's broken more than one. "Go feed on them."

Silence passes between us all for a moment, but eventually one of the vampires says, "We're leaving," to the other two.

With a glare at Ava over his shoulder, he mutters, "That witch will only get you killed."

A chill passes down my spine as Ava meets my eyes. The woman vampire continues to watch me with a steely glare.

"Come, Nuira," one of the men says. "The traitor is right; we passed that group of human hunters on the way here. We can drag a few of them away."

As they approach the tree line, Ava turns back to face the field where the animals had sunk into the earth. But I keep my eyes on the vampires.

Quick as blinking, they turn back around, charging toward us so fast I barely have time to move. I sprint toward the field, leaping over the fallen tree, and Ava is quick to follow. I send a bolt of flame behind me and one of the vampires yells out.

"Go up," I hiss at Ava, hoping she knows what I mean.

Then, after I close my hand in a fist and open it one finger at a time, a burst of light explodes behind me; not fire that would burn down the forest, but a bright white flash to distract the vampires.

In the same moment, I grab on to the nearest tree and haul myself up to perch on a thick branch. Something yanks on my shoulder, but I shove it off and keep climbing.

When I look down, the vampires are still chasing Ava, but she leaps in the air and grabs on to a hanging vine. It pulls her higher, responding to her Root witch powers, as the vampires careen to a stop below. Frantically, I try to push the light away from me to make myself invisible, sweat pouring down my brow. I remember my mother's concentrated expression as she tried to teach me the skill, my own frustration every time it failed, her insistence that I would need it one day. My heart pounds so loudly, it'll give me away before I ever get this to work.

Then, the whining noise rises up from the earth again. The ground begins to roil, pulling everything on it into a deep pit. Inside the pit, I spot white bones and limbs getting sucked farther in. Two of the vampires lose their footing and let out sharp screams as the roots pull them under. The woman vampire, Nuira, leaps away just in time.

And that's when I spot my pack of supplies, gripped in her hand. The vampire locks eyes with me with a smirk on her lips. Then she tosses the pack into the pit before racing away into the trees.

She must have grabbed it when I leaped onto the tree. A wave of dread washes over me and I feel like I'm going to faint. I grip harder to the tree branch to stay steady and hardly notice as the sharp bark cuts into my skin. In a breath, my pack is swallowed by the earth.

Along with all my clothes. All my food.

And all my water.

# CHAPTER 11

## - AVA -

*Not all vampires align with Casiopea.*
*Some travel and feed on their own,*
*and feel no loyalty to their kind,*
*while others seek the protection and guidance of their queen.*
——Journal, author unknown

I hang from the vine for a long moment, mouth open at the sight of the vampires getting sucked into the earth. I'm surprised I didn't collapse in fear in front of them; the rust-like stains on their teeth, the leaves in their hair and mud on their bodies. They were so willing to do anything for blood, and I . . . was nearly at that point myself an hour ago.

I reach out a hand and call another vine to me. The ground where the vampires were swallowed is deeper and darker, like freshly tilled land, so when I swing on the vine, I make sure to land outside of the field. I slide down the vine while Kaye moves behind me, traveling swiftly over the branches like a cat would.

I drop to the muddy ground and reach for a few dewy leaves

to wipe the blood from the squirrel off my face. Once I finish, Kaye lands behind me—along with the sharp copper scent of blood.

With a stiff neck, I turn slowly to see Kaye clutching her elbow. Blood glistens on her skin, lit by dappled sunlight from above. A deep growl builds in my throat, and my gums ache, fangs piercing through at the sight of blood. I take two quick steps forward, but then the image of the other vampires about to attack Kaye comes back to me. I force myself to drop to my knees.

"Go," I bite out. "Take care of that, bandage it or something, I—" Then my eyes catch on some wildflowers. There's one with long red leaves in the shape of triangles and a creamy gold center: red star flowers. I read about them in one of the books on plants and flowers my mother gave me.

I walk over to rip it from the ground, and inhale the strong scent of persimmon and cinnamon. Keeping my back turned, I hold it out behind me.

"Wrap this around your elbow."

"Done," she whispers after a few seconds, and I finally turn around.

She's wiped off the blood on a leaf hanging from a nearby branch, and the wound is covered with the flower, the stem wrapping around the back of her elbow. There's still a faint copper tinge in the air, but the strong scent of the flower is dousing it. I hold myself as still as I can, but my fingers shake.

I just drank from a squirrel, and I'd felt sated at the time. But the moment I saw Kaye's blood, the thirst came back so strongly I could barely stop myself from lunging at her. Is there a chance drinking from animals doesn't fulfill thirst as well as drinking from humans would? Once I find Casiopea, I could seek guidance on this . . . but all the stories mention her drinking from humans. She—and all the vampires who follow her—will be devouring humans in front of me once I join them. How will I control myself then?

*You could have an army at your command, with those powers,* those vampires had said. I feel like I'm going to pass out. I don't want an army, I don't want to turn bloodthirsty and lose all sense of myself, I don't want to be like the vampires who kill without a thought.

If I can't hold on to anything else from my life, the least I can do is fight to keep my humanity. Even once I join Casiopea, I won't lose myself.

"You could have joined them," Kaye says in a low, accusing tone. "Made me into your next meal."

"That's not who I am, Kaye," I snap. "I never asked for this life. I didn't choose to lose my real—my . . . old life."

After a few seconds of silence, Kaye whispers, "A vampire is still a killer even if it didn't choose to be one."

I take in the deep mistrust in her eyes, and I wonder if, when I drank from that squirrel, she saw me as exactly the same as those vampires that attacked us. In a softer tone, I ask, "I could have joined them, but I didn't. We promised to lead each other safely to Chrysalis, didn't we?"

She gives a jerky nod, and my heart sinks. Nothing of our old friendship, nothing of who we used to be, ties her to me. Even when I protected her just now, even when I stopped my urge to drink from her multiple times. The only thing that keeps her here is this sense of duty she has to follow her mother's wishes. I wish Calluna were here now to talk some more sense into her.

But I shouldn't care either way. I'm supposed to be leav-

ing humans behind, joining Casiopea to help protect this forest
and the Bone Wall that separates the mortal from the immortal. Distance, not understanding. It doesn't matter if Kaye never
changes her mind about me.

So why does it hurt so much?

"Look." Kaye points with her chin to a spot behind me. "It's
an old burial ground."

This patch of the forest is filled with wildflowers, but embedded in the ground are rocks that jut upward, like spades
stuck in the dirt.

"There are inscriptions," I say, kneeling in front of them.
"In the old writing system, like those texts in the archive room
at the Council Hall."

Kaye briefly meets my gaze and nods. I feel a spark of memory dashing between us of all the days we spent in the back
rooms of the Council Hall, sometimes alone, sometimes with
Tristan. One day, in the library, while she'd sat by a window,
cross-legged and reading a book, was the first time I noticed
how pretty her hair looked in the sun. It was the first time I'd
ever wanted to reach out and run my hands through it.

"I wonder how long this has been here," Kaye murmurs,
and a loose strand of hair falls from her braid. I feel a sudden
urge to push it back for her, then scold myself—I shouldn't
have any thoughts like these. She doesn't want me in her life,
and I need to push her from mine.

No more thinking about how pretty her hair is. Or the daring spark in her eyes. Or the soft, pensive expression on her face
as she stares at the inscriptions.

Shaking my head, I focus on the burial ground instead.

"Before you came to the clearing, I saw a green light over
here," I say then. "You told me about that time you came here

with the other Flames and saw sparks of light in the morning. I think it was something similar."

"Is it something to do with the ancient gods, do you think?" Kaye asks, trepidation tingeing her voice. "I remember the stories you used to tell me and Tristan, from your dad, about how this forest is full of the Arkana's magic. Teachers taught us the same thing in school, but it was boring the way they told it." I look up at her, surprised she's even acknowledging our friendship. "The Arkana live in another plane, but they wanted to gift their magic to mortals. So they took on the bodies of mortals and had mortal children who inherited some of their gifts. They taught the children how to use their magic, and when their human bodies were ready to die, they took on a new form, and spread more magic elsewhere. Those children of the Arkana became the first witches, separating them from humans, and all their descendants passed the magic on. Eventually the Arkana left and returned to their plane."

I was only five years old when I heard this tale for the first time. I'd sat on my mother's lap while my father gestured with his hands to show the movement patterns that the gods originally taught their witch descendants—the same patterns that summon our magic now. He'd been a Storm witch, highly valued in Saren for harnessing electricity, which I've never seen but my parents told me about. There weren't many Storm witches in Erlanis Empire, so his skill was coveted, and put to use stopping mudslides and floods. He'd used those same skilled hands to weave ancient tales that I can still hear as if it were yesterday. My mother told me he used to read hundreds of books a year when they lived in the capital and that I didn't have to try to remember all of it.

"You have something in common with the old gods and the

first witches, Ava," she'd said at the end of a story, her eyes sparkling. "You're just as strong and dazzling as they are. You'll see one day."

The magic of this forest, the magic in me, the magic that holds the Heart Tree and the Bone Wall in place . . . my connection to it as a Root witch and to the vampires who call it home . . . all of it ties me to this place.

What if this is what's been calling me to the forest? What if it's connected to the Arkana somehow?

Then an even wilder thought comes to mind. What if the voices calling me are actually the Arkana? They communicated with mortals centuries ago to pass on their magic and create witches. There's nothing stopping them from doing it again, but why would they? And why communicate with me?

Biting my lower lip, I hesitate for a moment, and then reach out to place a hand atop one of the burial stones. I close my eyes.

Immediately, I feel a heartbeat, a pounding drum beating through my chest—no, below me, in the earth, reaching down through soil and rock and root and bone. My Root magic has never done anything like this before; is this something to do with the magic in the forest?

Then, it's as if my hand is stretching wider, fingers reaching through the earth to distant ends of the forest, and a vision overtakes my senses. There's Arborren, another town that must be Chrysalis, mountains and sea, a lake of pure fresh water that glitters in the sun, and a deep valley tinged in gray with fog hanging over it like an oppressive, heavy shroud. It weighs down on me, pushing me farther into the earth. The fog wavers, showing ruby leaves and silver bark. From deep within, a chorus of voices calls out to me again.

*Help us. Come to us.*

I gasp, pulling my hand back from the rock, and the world bounces back into focus in front of me. The green leaves and vines swaying above, the sunlight glinting on the burial stones, and Kaye next to me, one eyebrow raised in confusion.

"What was that? You went really still and you didn't hear anything I said to you."

I shake my head, unsure how much to tell her. But whatever that vision was, it showed me a majestic tree deep in a valley, cloaked in fog. It must have been the Heart Tree. And the voices I've been hearing . . . they came from that tree.

Slowly, I say, "There's another reason I wanted to come to this forest, not just to run away. I've heard voices calling me here for over a year now, all the way in my attic when I'm alone at night. This is the clearest they've ever been, in this burial ground. It just showed me the forest."

"It showed you where Chrysalis is? Like a vision?"

I shrug. "It showed me the town, and I know it's northeast of here." I don't want to divulge any more. If I can somehow have more visions like that, I might be able to find the Heart Tree, and Casiopea, all on my own.

But . . . I'm not ready to leave Kaye. We've just started talking again, and even though she seems to hate me, part of me still wants to prove to her that I'm the same friend she used to have.

Besides, this journey will only continue to grow more dangerous. A shudder goes through me as I think of the Flames and hunters we narrowly avoided yesterday.

"I do need a guide," I say. "If you're still willing to be mine."

Kaye goes silent for a moment, her hands clenching into fists over her knees. Finally, Kaye nods. "But there's a problem. That vampire woman grabbed my pack and threw it into the pit. I don't have any water. All I have is what's on my belt. Daggers, a compass. That's it."

"Oh, Kaye, I'm sorry." I take in the small changes in her expression—fury changing to fear. "How long do you think it will take us to get to Chrysalis?"

She gulps and wipes sweat from her forehead. "More than a day. Less than two, if nothing else attacks us on the way."

"I saw water, but it was north of Chrysalis," I say slowly. "I'm sure we'll find a stream somewhere."

She gives a dismissive shake of her head. "Chrysalis has wells in the town; that's the closest source of water," she mutters. The panic settling in her expression reminds me all too much of the times Zenos deprived me of blood, and my hands curl into fists at my sides.

"Conserve your energy, and don't panic," I say. "You'll be fine."

She doesn't say anything but starts walking anyway. The fog has lifted and bright sun warms my shoulders as we trek for miles over roughly cut paths.

I lose track of time while busy looking out for silver traps and vampires. I also notice more of the strange-smelling sap I saw on the trees when I first entered the woods yesterday.

Hours later, we've passed three dry streambeds. Kaye's lips are chapped and I catch her swallowing multiple times. A worried crease forms on her brow when we crouch at the edge of a dry stream.

The gully is strewn with yellow and brown weeds. As I watch, a pebble sinks into the earth. Humans ears wouldn't catch it, but I hear a strange, bone-chilling moan. On the opposite side of the bank, gnarled tree roots stick out, pale-colored, like they're petrified. The twisting of them, how they reach deeper into the earth . . . it reminds me of veins.

"The forest is . . ." I let out a long breath, taking in every leaf around me, the rotten stench just barely underneath the fragrant pine. "Isn't it a bit like a vampire?"

Kaye shifts her feet closer to herself like she's trying to curl into a ball. "What do you mean?"

"It's hungry." The realization hits me like a gust of icy wind. I touch the roots closest to me, imagining them reaching up and choking me. "It's like something is leeching off of them and they need to make up for it."

The root lays itself gently over my finger as if confirming my words, and a deep unease stirs in me. Something is desperately wrong with these woods. I wonder how it affects Casiopea and the other vampires, or if they have any connection to it. I close my eyes and try to sense something of the magic here again, or trigger another vision; I can feel this root burrowing into the earth, and that it's dry and in need of water. But no vision comes to me like before. I sigh and open my eyes.

Kaye speaks up then. "I know this forest has magic in it, but I still don't get why the ground sucked up those bodies all on its own, as if it *wants* to. None of it makes sense."

I shrug, running one finger down a gnarled root. Her voice is hoarser than I expected it to be; it'll be best if we stop talking.

In a few moments, we're up and walking again. My own thirst starts to agitate me again, and I know it's exacerbated by Kaye's rapid pulse, how she's growing more panicked and moving faster without water of her own.

As we walk, my gaze trails a bird hopping from branch to branch above. I wonder how much blood it has inside, and lick my lips.

"You drink really often," Kaye remarks, her tone more confused than harsh.

I shrug, uncomfortable at the question. I don't know how often other vampires drink.

"It's always been like this for me. I get one ounce at a time, four times per day."

Kaye frowns. "I thought your kind only needed blood a couple of times a week. That's what we were taught."

I bite my lip, wondering what she thinks of this. She knows I disappeared two years ago and that I'm a vampire, but does she know my mother is, too? That she locked me inside to leach my powers and fool them all?

My mother's lessons come to me at once: *Lie, spin a story, make them believe your tale. It's all to keep you safe.*

No, it was to keep *her* safe.

Telling the truth, telling your story, is a sort of freedom, isn't it? My mouth opens slightly, and I want to tell Kaye everything, even if she won't believe me. I could afford to crack open the locked drawer in my mind where I keep these memories, air them out a little to Kaye, my old friend. . . .

I clamp my mouth shut. The locked drawer slams shut, and my memories scatter into the back of my mind.

I'm not ready. I'm not ready to tell Kaye about the past two years of my life, or about my mother's involvement. And if I explain that my mother is a vampire, too, she won't be safe in Arborren anymore. As desperately as I wanted to get away from her, I don't want her to become a target of the Flame witches.

Kaye has started walking again and is slightly ahead of me. I notice the soft glow surrounding her, and the way the sun shines on the chestnut color of her hair, creating little streaks of gold that look like flower sprigs. My own hair trails to my ankles, has twigs in it, and is flying in different directions. It's completely matted and unmanageable, and will only slow us down. I'm also covered in sweat and I must have tripped over my hair and my long skirt a thousand times already.

Kaye has noticed that I stopped walking and turns back around, an eyebrow raised. Still holding my hair, I contemplate what I'm about to say. I think of my mother picking out dresses and jewelry for me to wear even though she locked me inside, always expecting me to look presentable, my hair long and brushed. And Zenos, his fingers snagging in my hair, his grip tight around it to pull me back . . .

I'll cut off everything that made me theirs. I'll give them no chance to drag me back.

Finally turning to Kaye, I ask, "Can I have your help with something?"

From the way I'm holding my hair, she's already guessed what I want to do.

"We should do your clothes, too," she says, approaching me and palming one of her silver blades. I gulp at the sight; her grip doesn't look as steady as it did before. "That long skirt and the draping sleeves keep getting caught on branches and roots, which is probably why you're tripping so much. Or maybe you're just the clumsiest vampire in the world."

She moves toward me then, and if I were alive, I'm sure I'd stop breathing now. Kaye's long fingers lift my sleeve to check where would be good to cut.

From the corner of my eye, I notice the dried blood on her arm, which must have leaked from the wound hidden under the red star flower. At least it's dry now. But I still have to fight down the thirst that rises up at the thought of it.

Instead, I focus on her touch: it's so much softer than Zenos's, with no hidden threat behind it like my mother's. She's warm, like a moving source of light. As she stands behind me, I feel her breath on my neck and have the sudden urge to lean into it.

"Be careful," I whisper as she lifts the silver blade near the top of the sleeve.

"I'll try, but it'll have to be quick. We can't waste time here." Each word is a little breath against my neck, like she's just a finger's breadth away. She's shorter than me and I know if she leaned forward, her lips would touch my shoulder.

I swallow hard, wondering why I'm thinking of these things. Then I grit my teeth, expecting the bite of silver against my skin. But a moment later, fabric rips, and the sleeve flutters to the ground like a white bird. Kaye removes the other sleeve and then cuts the black skirt up to my knees.

When she straightens, her face flushed for some reason, I hold out my hair with my fingers at chin length.

"That short?" she sputters, her green eyes wide. "Why would you—"

"Kaye, if every single thing about you, from the way you look down to the way you move and even talk to other people, was decided by someone else . . . wouldn't you want to just cut it all off?"

She goes quiet for a long moment, her eyes trailing down the sparkling, sunlit black of my hair. "There's a lot of me that I wish I could just cut off." She shakes her head then and holds up the silver blade. "If you want it off, it's gone. Your choice."

*Your choice.* Nothing has ever been my choice until recently; fighting Zenos, fleeing my house, running into these woods, heading on a path to the Heart Tree, Casiopea, and my new family. Choice. What a beautiful thing. I want to clutch it to me forever, prevent anyone from taking it from me again.

Kaye's warm fingers brush the back of my neck as she takes my hair. She pulls it taut and I stiffen, remembering all the times Zenos did the same. But then there's the sound of a smooth cut, and her grip on my hair falls away.

She shakes her head at the long length of hair that's fallen to the ground. It looks like someone abandoned a thick black blanket in the middle of the forest.

There's a brief pang in my heart, but then I smile. My sleeves are cut up to my shoulders with frayed ends tickling my arms. The breeze sweeps the black skirt around my knees and my head feels lighter, cooler, freer already.

When we start walking again, I lead this time, Kaye giving me simple directions as we move on. As the hours pass and night approaches, I spot a flicker of orange light a few hundred feet ahead. Flames, close to the ground—likely a campfire.

"Kaye?" I ask, and she looks toward me slowly, her eyes a little unfocused. Not a good sign. "There's a campsite up ahead. You should see if they'll give you some water."

Her eyes tighten with worry, but then she licks her dry, chapped lips. "I'll try. You should stay out of sight."

I nod, relief flooding me that she wants to help me hide. "I'll go closer with you, but I'll stand back far enough that they won't see me."

As we approach the campsite, laughter and clinking glasses reach my ears. It's a group of about twenty men, all armed with silver, and . . .

I stop abruptly, my whole body turning to ice. I know that ratlike face, those glinting eyes. That smug smirk.

"Zenos," I whisper. "He's here to find me."

# CHAPTER 12

## · KAYE ·

*If a Flame witch ever turns their back on their own kind,*
*then they were never truly worthy of our heritage.*
—TRAINING ACADEMY FOR
YOUNG WITCHES OF ARBORREN

Fear is written all over Ava's face, and she digs her hands into the bark of a tree as I leave her to walk toward the campsite. I've never had a good feeling about her stepfather, and the way her whole body tensed up at the sight of him makes my skin prickle uneasily. It also makes me want to knock Zenos out cold and tie him to a tree for a bloodsucker to find as punishment for whatever he's done to make Ava so scared of him.

I shake off that thought like it's an irritating gnat. I shouldn't feel protective of her. She saved me earlier, so I'll help her stay out of sight of Zenos now—and that's it.

As I approach the camp, I watch Zenos through the trees.

"Don't you worry, we'll find your daughter by tomorrow," one of the hunters, with bloodshot eyes, says to Zenos. "She can't have gone far all by herself."

Zenos gives the man a conciliatory grin, confidence oozing off him. "Thank you. She may not be my blood, but I care for her just the same."

I grimace at his words, then lift my hands. I failed at making myself invisible when the vampires attacked us, but that was a dangerous, fast-paced situation. If I can do it now, to mask my movements . . . I could simply steal water from them and not even need to draw attention to myself. Gulping, I slowly begin to push the light away from me.

Like a streak of paint being washed away by water, the tips of my fingers fade away. But then they flicker back into view just as quickly. I curse under my breath and will it to work.

*I'm the best student Liander's had in years,* I think, straining with the effort of pushing the light away. *I will master this, just like I've mastered everything else. I will succeed.*

The nocking of an arrow shocks me out of my concentration, and I pivot to face a sentry who's stepped out of the trees ten feet from the group. He levels his bow and arrow at me.

"I'm a Flame witch from Arborren," I stutter out, raising my hands to show I'm not a threat. The chatter at the campfire falls silent. "I got separated from my group on the way to Chrysalis. I wanted to ask if you have some water to share?"

I try to make myself sound confident despite the unease settling in my bones, but one of the men from the group speaks up with false pity lacing his voice.

"Oh, one of the Flames finally needs our help? Join us, girl. There's an empty seat right here." He slaps his thigh and laughs at his own joke, which is quickly picked up by the rest of the group, including Zenos. When I say nothing, he scoffs, "Suit yourself, then. Die of thirst out there. There are better-looking girls in Chrysalis, anyway."

I grit my teeth to hold back a barrage of insults I want to throw at him, then turn back in to the trees, tightly gripping a dagger at my belt. If only I could have gotten my mother's invisibility skill to work . . .

A hundred feet away from the camp, Ava steps out of the trees to join me, biting her lip with a worried expression.

"They're useless." I exhale harshly. "Let's go."

My thoughts and footsteps become more sluggish as we walk. Even so, I grip my silver dagger tightly and scan the trees; there's a constant feeling of being watched in these trees, and I never know if it's real or imagined. The woman vampire Nuira's words slither through my thoughts as we walk: *The moment your little protector looks away . . .*

We pause once to rest, and I lean against a tree to catch my breath. If I were alone, I don't know if I'd ever make it out of these woods. Having someone keeping a steady pace beside me helps me stay upright. As she waits for me to gather my energy, Ava carefully checks the trees above us for any sign of a threat, and I'm grateful for that, since I can hardly think straight.

Her newly short hair blows back in the wind, distracting me from thinking about the journey. At first, I was shocked Ava had wanted to cut her hair off. It was beautiful; I used to like watching it drape over her shoulder during class. But the short hair suits her, and she looks light as air, like a huge weight has been lifted off her.

I remember my fingers brushing the back of her neck, the spark that went through me at standing so close to her. It must be because of how long it's been since we've last seen one another up close; anyone would feel electrified standing next to someone you've gone from caring about to hating in the span of a couple of years.

"Earlier, when you cut my hair," she says in a pensive tone, "what did you mean when you said there are parts of you that you wish you could cut off?"

The question catches me off guard, and heat flushes my cheeks. "You wouldn't understand."

"Try me. Not like anyone's around to overhear."

I can hear the blood pounding in my ears at the pressure to speak. No one's ever asked me to explain this before. I've never met anyone even slightly interested in what it's like to be no one. Even old, human Ava had never asked me this—and it was something I liked about her, back then. She was the only one who didn't stare at my face like it was a puzzle she was trying to solve. But as the years went by and I grew lonelier, I only felt my separation from the rest of the world even more poignantly.

"I don't look like anyone," I say, shrugging and shaking my head at the same time. "Not the Flame witches, who are all from the eastern provinces, close enough to Arborren that they fit in here. My father is from Saren, but my mother was from around here. They . . . no one understands it. It's not common, having children with someone from outside your land, and people just don't get it. They don't think I should be here, or that I should even exist. When they look at my face, it's like they're trying to figure out what's wrong with it. They're angry they can't put a name to what I am or who I am. It's like, putting me into a box they already know will give them greater control over me. I don't want to give them that control and I don't care how angry they get about it, I'm just sick of being looked at like I'm not even a person."

We both go silent for a long moment. A group of fireflies hovers near one of the branches above us, lending light to both our faces.

"People looking at you like you're not even a person?" Ava asks softly. My breath catches and we lock eyes then, and I can already tell what she's going to say. "Looks like we have something in common, then."

I avert my gaze, not trusting myself to reply in a civil manner.

"Do you remember I'm Sarenian, too, Kaye?" She gestures at herself, her eyes wide and challenging. "Our situations aren't exactly the same, but I do understand. We first became friends because no one else wanted to talk to us, remember?" She scoffs and turns away before I can say anything. I follow after her, my face heating—first with shame for assuming she wouldn't understand, then with anger at her for bringing up our past friendship. I don't want to think about that at all. Not when I'll be turning her over to Liander the minute we arrive in Chrysalis.

We walk for another hour, and I start to worry we'll come across more hunters and Flames now that we're approaching Chrysalis. Which means we both need enough sustenance to stay sharp—and we'll need it soon.

Once midnight blankets us in darkness, we stop at the edge of a dry stream. Ava sits cross-legged against a tree while I crouch at the shore, searching for water that I know isn't there. All I can do is hope that more fog will come by morning. At least there's water in the droplets of mist.

"I didn't see any animals on the way here apart from spiders," Ava says, wrinkling her nose. "I'm getting thirsty, too. I wonder if I can find out more about the vision I had in here."

She starts rustling in the pillowcase she wears strapped to her back, and withdraws a journal with a yellow tassel. A familiar ache tugs at me when I see it. As she opens the journal, the table of contents—and tiny drawings near the page numbers—catches my eye.

I lunge for the journal and stumble into Ava. She catches me by the shoulder and helps me sit down—my knees shake and my head spins with thirst, but I ignore all that.

With a trembling finger, I trail the drawings of flowers next to the page numbers, then flick back to the title page. A stunned breath leaves me. Right underneath the title, a name was written, but it's been crossed out with ink pressed so hard into the page, it's nearly ripped. But I know what it said, and I remember the handwriting as clearly as if it were yesterday. A sob rises to the back of my throat. Even with the words crossed out, the curve of the letter "C" is still visible, and the small "a" at the end of the name.

*Calluna Mentara.*

"This was hers." I breathe out. I try to force myself to calm down, to remember my plan of pretending to help her. But seeing this journal breaks something in me.

I'm tired of waiting, being careful, holding back my anger. I snap out of my thirst and my lethargy, the rage whipping through me like a storm. "It was you, wasn't it? You killed her. I know you did."

Her eyes widen like she's been slapped, and I let out a yell of frustration. Vampires will do anything to convince us they're innocent. Flames are at my fingers before I even know what's happening. She says my name, but I barely hear her—I raise my hands and shoot fire toward her arms.

She dodges with a yelp, moving faster than I expected.

With one hand, I grab a silver dagger, and with the other,

I bring more flames to life. If there's any vampire I'm ready to fight, it's this one.

As she moves to the side again, I charge toward her, bringing flames along the ground like a snake. She dodges my strike with the knife and tries to push me back but misses. The flames nearly reach her, but she throws herself backward and digs her hands into the ground. A moment later, roots lurch out of the earth and wrap around my ankle and tug. I trip forward but manage to burn the roots away and swing around to face Ava again.

"Kaye, I didn't even know Calluna died!" she shouts. "How could I? I've been locked inside for two years."

"I'm not stupid," I snarl at her. "She had bite marks on her neck, and the vampire who killed her was never caught. You were changed that same day and hidden away. If you were innocent, why hide you?"

She lets out a peal of laughter. "As if anyone would believe me. You don't think any of us could ever be innocent. Don't be a hypocrite now, Kaye."

Before she's done speaking, I weave my hands in a quick pattern to bend shadows and light in front of her to blur her vision. She gasps, and I draw a silver dagger from my belt, but then I hesitate, not sure what I even want to do with Ava right now.

That hesitation buys her all the time she needs. She flits away from me, faster than I can even blink; she nearly runs into a tree and feels along the trunk to orient herself, then swipes a hand through the air in my direction.

There's a loud creaking sound above me, and I barely dodge out of the way in time when a heavy branch falls from the nearest tree. It crashes to the ground, and the sound sends birds flying away into the night with sharp caws.

Ava's blinking rapidly to try to clear her vision, and my own breaths are labored, too. I feel my thirst more acutely than ever after fighting with her. My whole body is heavy, and all I want to do is pass out on the ground. I rest my hands on my knees and glare up at her. Her vision must be back now, because she focuses on me with something like pity in her eyes.

"Why do you have her journal?" I spit out. "Why did you disappear that day?"

"I found it one day," Ava says in a rush, and the fact that she's not out of breath like I am infuriates me. "In my backpack, after a festival near school, a few weeks before I was turned. Someone slipped it in there. If I knew it was your mother, I would have told you about it earlier, but I didn't know."

"I can't trust a word you say." My voice breaks a little as I speak, from thirst and exhaustion. Not just physical exhaustion, but the past two years of wanting to confront Ava, mourning my mother alone, and Tristan turning on me, too . . . all of it weighs on me, and I find there's some deep part of me that wants to believe her.

But I can't. I've come this far trying to find my mother's killer. It's all that's driven me these past two years.

And Ava . . . she left me. She became the same kind of predator that killed my mother. I cannot trust her, even if a part of me wants to. Everything they do is in an effort to feed and kill.

Except when she saved me earlier today. She could have easily turned on me, but didn't.

The traitor's soft voice reaches me through the maelstrom of my thoughts. "My mother is a vampire, too."

At those words, I'm jolted out of my shock at seeing my mother's old journal. Eugenia Serení, the councilor who works so closely with Liander and all the other witches and humans every day . . . is a vampire? If that's true, she could be working against Arborren and sneaking in vampires whenever she wants and no one would notice. But someone has to have noticed, haven't they?

"But she . . . I've seen her use magic, and—"

"She steals mine," Ava says through gritted teeth, looking toward the ground. "Two years ago, she—"

Her voice cuts off then, like her breath has been robbed. Her eyes are wide and fearful in a way that makes me want to comfort her, but I quickly shut down that thought. Not until I get real answers from her—her real story.

"What did she do, two years ago?"

A long silence passes before Ava says in a monotone voice, "Two years ago, she turned me into a vampire, and she's kept me locked in that attic ever since."

Her words hit me like a rock, and it takes a few moments for the reality of what she just said to sink in. For someone to become a vampire, they have to die with vampire blood in their body. It's the only way.

"Your mother . . ." I begin in a tense, choppy voice. "She killed you." Ava winces and begins to pull away, but this time I reach for her. My hand rests on her shoulder, and I wait for her to look me in the eyes; her own are filled with tears. "You said you only get a small serving of blood every few hours. That's why you can't go long without blood, and you're not as physically strong as the others. She trained you to need it every day, to keep you close . . . so you would stay in that attic."

My thoughts race with this realization, and I remember the broken window and the chair on the ground outside Ava's house. I'd assumed Ava ran away, but I never considered that she was locked inside fully against her will.

"And so she could take Root witch powers from me, to convince the rest of you she's still a mortal." Her words come out sharp and unforgiving. "I know, Kaye. I've lived with this for two years, while everyone continued their lives without ever questioning what happened to me. No one came. No one asked." She pulls back, shaking my hand off her shoulder. "I know how it must have looked when I vanished that day, and I'm sorry I wasn't there when you needed me, Kaye. But no one's been there for me, either."

I pull back from her, stung by her words, but then my own anger rushes forward again. "So you've been locked away for two years with no idea of anything that's happened. Completely clueless. Sure, I believe you." She scoffs, but I barrel on. "Your mother still kept you alive, didn't she? Where did the blood come from, Ava?"

She leans back on her heels, a guarded expression coming over her face. "I tried to starve myself once. She waited until I nearly lost my mind and then slipped blood into the room. It was all her and Zenos. Yes, I drank the blood, and yes, I'm a vampire now—but I didn't want this. All I want is to live my life, yet I'm being hunted while my mother and stepfather roam freely and get away with killing as many people as they want."

"So you think it's perfectly all right that she killed people for your survival?"

"What? No. I left, didn't I?"

"That's not why you left. You wanted your freedom, that's why you left. You didn't care who she was killing."

Ava opens her mouth to speak, then closes it again. Her eyes darken. "She already killed me, Kaye. What sympathy did I have to spread around for anyone else?"

"So you never knew whose blood you were drinking," I spit out as another somber thought comes to me. "And you were turned the same day my mother died. The blood you drank that day . . . do you know where it came from? If Eugenia killed her . . . put it together, Ava."

I finally break through to her. She looks like she's about to be sick, horror rising on her face.

Maybe she didn't kill my mother, but her mother likely did. Eugenia is powerful, and it will be difficult to confront her or take her down. But a new, steady fury builds up inside me.

"Kaye, I didn't know about your mother's death." Ava breaks the silence after a long minute, waiting for me to meet her eyes. I finally do. "But maybe my own mother does. She's the one who chose to change me that night, and . . . what if your mother gave me this journal for a reason?"

I bite my lip as I consider her words. I'm now convinced Eugenia had something to do with my mother's death, but I'm not sure what the journal has to do with it.

"Why would she want you to have it, and not me?" I whisper, my throat aching unpleasantly. But I'm nowhere near ready to stop talking.

"I don't know. Maybe . . . maybe she figured out what my mother was, and wanted to warn me. Or maybe there's something important in here about the forest. That's mostly what she wrote about. Calluna went into the forest on patrols frequently, didn't she?"

I nod, and reach forward to take the journal from her, turning each page carefully. The very first page is about some flowers my mother discovered with healing properties. But as I flip through more of the pages, the contents change; the writing becomes more frantic, some words written so fiercely the paper has almost ripped. Memories float back to me of my mother scribbling away at the table after dinner, her eyes red and strained. When I'd asked what she was doing, she simply said she was writing about her experience in the forest, and brushed off any questions I had. What was she hiding from me?

In the margin of a page I've flipped to is a handwritten note in print so small I have to squint to read it: *Every day, I'm afraid. But I already have enough regrets in my life. I won't let this be one also.*

With a lump in my throat, I murmur, "Maybe she found out about this strange sickness in the trees, or the forest devouring people. But she only started to write in this one about a year before she died."

I grip the journal so hard, there's a slight ripping sound in the spine. Ava gasps and reaches over, but stops just short of grabbing the journal.

She stiffens, her gaze fixed on something in the distance behind me.

"I see fire approaching. . . . Can't tell if it's a Flame or a hunter yet. We should move."

Ava takes the journal and stuffs it back in her sack. I stand, swaying slightly, and fling out my arms to catch my balance. I definitely couldn't fight off anyone who attacked us right now. And I'm not letting Ava out of my sight until I get a better look at that journal and find out more about what Eugenia has done.

We begin walking again, and I move faster than I probably should, my head spinning and the ground beneath me wobbling. But only twenty minutes later, there's a rustling in the trees nearby.

Ava whispers my name. I draw my blade, willing myself to stay alert.

Then Ava shoves me to the ground as a whistling sound cuts through the air. I land on my back, the breath knocked out of me, as a dagger slams into the trunk of a tree right where my head was a moment ago.

"Show yourself," I try to shout, but my voice cracks and fades away. Animals skitter away in every direction as I stumble to my feet.

"Kaye—" Ava calls out, but when she takes one step back, a trip wire triggers a silver-studded net to snap up from the ground and close around her, locking her inside like a cocoon. With a yelp, she's ripped off the ground and into the air. I dart forward to try to grab her, but then someone from behind yanks my arms and pulls them behind my back in a painful twist. A meaty hand clamps over my mouth. I struggle against my captor, trying to call flames to my fingers, but he's pinning my hands down so I can't use them.

More shapes coalesce in the dark spaces between trees—men with silver-tipped arrows notched in bows and others holding torches. Ava's thirty feet in the air, peering down at me from a net she's trapped inside. I yell out Ava's name right before I'm dragged back into the trees.

# CHAPTER 13

## - AVA -

*The forest knows a great wrong has been done.*
*The trees have eyes, the water hears.*
*The roots will grab you and make you theirs.*
*The forest will always listen to you,*
*although it doesn't always have your best interests at heart.*
—ORAL HISTORIES OF ERLANIS EMPIRE

I reach out to the net holding me, but as soon as I touch it, my hands burn. Kaye was just dragged into the trees below, and her muffled scream still rings in my ears.

Twisting around inside the net, I look down at the forest floor some thirty feet away and feel dizzy at the sheer height; it's like I'm back in my attic, watching the world go on. The threads of the net have tiny shards of silver embedded in them, sparkling in the moonlight. I try to cover my skin with my skirt, but since Kaye cut it, it's too short to do much good, as are my sleeves. And even through the fabric of my skirt and blouse, I feel the tiny pricks of silver. It's almost like my thirst pricking at the back of my throat, but all over my body.

Zenos. What if this is him? My torturer. My nightmare. My head spins and I feel like I'm going to faint.

Forcing myself to ignore it and focus on what's happening below, I search for some sign of Kaye, but there are only the hunters who captured us, staring up at me with triumphant expressions. They've caught me, but what on earth are they doing with Kaye?

I start tugging at the netting, but the silver makes me flinch back. The mechanism holding the net together at the top of it is also made of silver. A deep panic settles in my chest. The ache for blood intensifies, and it's like someone has stuck a hot poker down my throat.

How long has it been since I drank? Like Kaye said, I drink more frequently than other vampires because of my mother's conditioning. Does that mean I'll lose control faster than others? Disintegrate faster than others?

What if it makes me more desperate for blood, and more of the killer Kaye already sees me as? My heart breaks at the way she accused me of killing her mother. She thought something so terrible of me for two years, I can't imagine how much resentment she built up in that time. Calluna . . . she was always kind to me, practically like a second mother. I never would have hurt her.

*You wanted your freedom, that's why you left. You didn't care who she was killing.*

Kaye's words sear into me, even more painful than the thirst. Whenever I thought about the blood I was given, I hated it and I hated myself, and then I would try to abstain. My mother would let me play at rebellion for a few days and then slip a cup of blood into my room once I reached the brink.

At that point, I couldn't care less where it had come from. In those moments, there was no control.

No humanity.

I grip the net and tug; the silver still sears my skin, but the net begins to rip in my hands. This is the same kind of trap that killed my father years ago, yet he was only a witch. I should be able to rip through it, but maybe my mother weakened me so much I can't even do this.

Voices reach my ears from below. Tensing, I look down, and my eyes narrow to slits at the humans.

Hunters with silver-studded leashes and daggers at their belts, with hard eyes and grime-slick faces. I take them in, trying to figure out if these are the men from Zenos's group or not. If they drag me back to Arborren, my mother will lock me up even more securely, and drain my powers forever.

My fangs grow, piercing through my gums, and I imagine the taste of their blood. All of them, not just one. I hope Zenos is nearby, his throat exposed so I can hold him down and take from him instead.

Then I come back to my senses. I shake those thoughts away; that's what a predator would think. And I'm not like that. Kaye is who I need to go to now, because she's in danger. And after we reach Chrysalis, I'm headed to meet Casiopea and stop my mother's plans to tear down the Bone Wall. I'll protect both vampires and mortals.

But a small part of me—a part that terrifies me—wonders why I'm bothering to help them at all.

"It had a friend," one of the men says in a gruff tone. "Lewis and his boy are taking care of her. Scope the area for any others; they don't often travel alone. Once the place is secure, we'll deliver the bloodsuckers."

I try not to imagine what could be happening with Kaye. Panicking won't help either of us now. They seem to think Kaye is a vampire, too, which means they're not Zenos's group—she'd told them she was a Flame witch and asked for water, after all. But *deliver the bloodsuckers*? Why would they bother taking us anywhere at all instead of just killing us?

Reaching a hand through one of the holes in the net and gritting my teeth as my wrist begins to burn, I try to grab on to the roots below, but nothing happens. Is it too far for my powers to work? Some of the hunters begin to leak back into the trees, their weapons lit green in the light of the fireflies still encircling trees below.

Wind gusts through these higher branches as the men stare up at me with a stark hatred in their eyes. I bare my fangs at them, but they might not even be able to see with their pathetic mortal eyes.

And then it comes—a deep, whining sound, like something is moving far down in the earth. I gape as the men still standing there look around for the source of the noise.

The ground shakes beneath them, roiling and bucking up and down. I freeze, unable to look away. The ground begins to sink below the men, a dark pit opening up. They scream as bone-white roots from the nearest trees wrap around their ankles, and they're tugged into the deep, dark hole as their shouts for help rise up and shake the leaves on the trees.

A moment later, the hole closes. The men are gone, their screams a distant memory. Fireflies glint emerald above the smoothed-over dirt. My mouth has fallen open, but I can't seem to close it. I was right about the forest being a predator, but I'm still no closer to learning why.

Fog wraps around the tree trunks in tendrils even though it was a clear night just moments ago. I shiver at its touch. And then another scream rings out from nearby, this time a girl's.

"Kaye!" I shout, and grab the top of the net. It's all silver, and my fingers blister, my palms turn red and welted, as I try to force the net to relinquish me.

I promised Kaye I'd protect her until we reach Chrysalis. I can't abandon her. We promised each other we'd journey to Chrysalis together, and I won't break that promise. If there's any part of my humanity I'll fight to hold on to, it's this—being Kaye's friend.

Finally, the material rips apart in my hands, and a moment later, I'm falling. Air whooshes past and then I slam into the earth, the net falling open to either side of me in tattered threads. The pain is sharp enough that I almost black out. But I don't want the ground to open up again and swallow me whole, so I force myself to stand and walk into the trees ahead.

"Kaye!" I yell, my throat searing with how loud my voice is. Then I drop it to a whisper. "Where are you?"

Straining my ears, I hear labored breaths and quick footsteps—a fight. Darting through the narrow trees, I slip between them much faster than when I first entered the forest, my focus solely on the sounds of humans fighting nearby.

I come to a stop when I see them—Kaye, her hands bound behind her back, dodges the attempts of one older man and a boy around my age who are trying to capture her. In the trees just beyond them are two people hanging in silver nets like I was—two vampires, I think, recognizing one of them as the woman who attacked Kaye. Nuira.

I jump into the fight, and Kaye's eyes shine with relief when she sees me. She narrowly dodges a knife strike from the older man, while the younger one turns to me. I bare my fangs at him and he stumbles backward.

"Please don't hurt me," he begins whispering over and over,

and I falter for a moment. I probably look like one of the vampires from his nightmares right now. But they captured me and are trying to hurt Kaye. They deserve to be scared.

I reach for his neck and slam him into the tree. He cries out in fear. Two desires war inside me: punish him for trying to hurt us, or let him see a vampire with mercy in her heart.

I can't choose.

Next to me, the older man lunges for Kaye, but she strikes back. Her blade clips his arm, and blood gushes down.

All other thoughts vanish. My thirst rises with a roar that rips out of my throat. My vision clouds; Kaye disappears, the forest disappears, the only thing left is the bleeding person in front of me.

Before he can even stumble away, I lunge toward the man and force him to his knees.

# CHAPTER 14

## · KAYE ·

*While many witches receive their power from nature, or minerals and elements,*
*    Flames receive ours from light itself.*
*    Everything we see,*
*    and everything that is hidden.*

—TRAINING ACADEMY FOR
YOUNG WITCHES OF ARBORREN

I raise my shaking hands in the air, hoping Ava will see me. She crouches over the man she just tackled, black hair covering one side of her face. Her lips are pulled back over sharp fangs that rest only a few inches from the man's throat.

"Ava, listen to me," I say slowly. I feel Nuira's eyes on me from the net she's trapped in, and my heart pounds fast. If she gets free, she'll kill me right here. *The moment your little protector looks away . . .*

No. I need Ava to come back to me now, not disappear into her thirst.

"Remember what you've been saying?" I ask Ava. "That you don't want to drink from humans. You came back to help me, didn't you? You don't have to drink from him."

I don't even know if I believe what I'm saying. Of course she wants to drink from humans; she wouldn't have pushed this bleeding man to the ground otherwise.

But I'm the reason he's bleeding now. And she hasn't drunk from him yet.

Slowly, her eyes rise to meet mine, and I see the pain and indecision swirling in hers. Her grip on the man's shoulders relaxes, but he looks too petrified to move. I need to give him and the boy a chance to run.

Stepping forward, I wrap my arms around Ava and pull her close. The man below scrambles away, along with the boy. Ava hugs me back and I breathe in her scent, which is earthy and woodsy and alive.

I don't let go until I hear more movement nearby, heavy footsteps on the ground and urgent voices.

Ava pulls back and peers over my shoulder. "More hunters are coming." She sends one glance up at the vampires in the silver nets. "I'm not going to give them a chance to hurt you, and there's no time. We need to go."

Ava tugs at me to follow her, and as we leave, I look over my shoulder at the captive vampires once more. Nuira slams herself against her net and hisses at me. As the footsteps of hunters draw closer, Ava and I vanish into the trees just in time. The hunters' voices rise behind us, demanding the vampires tell them what happened to the other men.

Ava and I keep running. We go for at least a mile before coming to a stop in front of yet another dry streambed. I let out a groan at the sight of it as I catch my breath, wishing more than anything that water would appear, or that the sky would crack open and rain would fall.

We kneel in the dirt, me trying to catch my breath and Ava trying to still the shaking of silver-damaged hands. Cricket chirps fill the air around us, and fireflies skim lazily over the dry stream in front of us.

"I almost . . . I can't believe I almost killed—" Ava's voice cuts off, and she clasps her trembling hands in her lap.

"But you didn't," I say, reaching over to take one of her hands, careful not to touch the damaged parts. After a short time, I ask, "What happened to the hunters who captured you? How did you escape?"

"They got swallowed by the earth," she chokes out. "Like the bodies we saw in the field."

I gulp, wondering what this could mean. I never saw this on training trips through the woods, but then again, we never went this far in. But my mother certainly did in her time.

"My mother's journal . . ." I say slowly. "I know she used to write notes in it about what she saw in the forest while she traveled here. Does it have anything that explains why the forest is devouring people?"

"It talks about the Heart Tree and its connection to the Bone Wall, how Casiopea is the queen of vampires and protects them here, but some of them don't follow her. And it talks about the magic of the forest, and how it built the Bone Wall to keep the vampires in—" She pauses, then says slowly, "It says that the forest knows a great wrong has been done. I wonder if that has something to do with the sick trees we've seen, and the forest sucking people underground. But it doesn't tell everything. Like she was being careful when she wrote it."

"She wrote it in the last year of her life," I say in a hoarse voice. "I think she was afraid of something being found out, so she was vague in the journal, even while giving it to you. My mother was considered a traitor because she wanted the Flame witches to stop trying to stamp out vampires. She might have realized what she was doing was risky, and maybe those pages had something in there that would get her ostracized. Something that went against Flame witch beliefs."

"Like what?" Ava asks, her brow furrowed.

"I don't know," I say, a sad tone entering my voice as it trails off.

I know the forest has always been dangerous because of the vampires who live here, but what about this sickness? Is that because of them, too? The forest is full of magic and life, but there are dead things roaming through it and killing everything in their paths. That doesn't seem like a harmonious combination, so I'd be unsurprised if they have something to do with the sickness.

Out of the corner of my eye, I watch this vampire girl I'm traveling with. Something deep inside me aches at the sight of her, and I feel an impulse to take her hands now and hold them to comfort her while her wounds heal, but I'm in enough control of myself to rein that in. Nothing good would come of that.

But she's saved me twice now. And I sensed truth in her words when she told me she had no idea my mother had even died. What if I've been hating my friend for two years for something she didn't do? My thoughts race, trying to reconcile the image of this vulnerable girl in front of me with the memory of her lunging for that hunter.

She did stop herself from drinking from him. I never thought vampires had that type of control.

But she's still a vampire who must kill to live, and it's still my job to annihilate vampires. That's what Flame witches do, and if I go against that, I'll just prove to them all that I've never really been one of them. That they were all right about me from the start.

*Vampires lie, trick, and kill to get what they want.* Liander's voice rises in the back of my head, repeating everything I've been told for years. *They can never be trusted.*

When she winces in pain, I tell that inner voice to be quiet. She's avoiding looking at her scarred hands, staring off into the distance like she can't rid her mind of the net whisking her into the air.

"You should rest," I whisper. "You'll heal faster that way."

She lets out a small laugh, but there's no amusement in it. "I keep telling you I'm not that different from mortals, trying to prove that I deserve to live. But if a mortal were injured, they wouldn't heal like I do. What I do is unnatural."

"I can't be burned," I say, not sure why I'm trying to reassure her, but some part of me is beginning to realize that the scared, innocent girl act isn't a farce. The panic in Ava's eyes is real, the way she's staring at her own body as if it's foreign to her. I know all too well what that feels like. "Witches aren't human either. But we were given our power by the Arkana. If that's not natural, what is? And if a human were injured, they'd go to a witch who can heal, or a human curer. It's still healing, just in a different way."

We both fall silent and I can tell that my words haven't helped at all. For long moments, we watch her injuries heal, the skin smoothing over, the rawness fading by the second. As we do, I remove the red star flower wrapped around my elbow. The blood is dry, the wound starting to heal. Ava has gone tense at the sight, but she doesn't react otherwise. She has so much more self-control than I ever thought a vampire would.

A feeling of dread settles into me. I've been telling her she doesn't deserve life for days, and now that she finally seems to believe it herself, I feel sick.

A silence falls over us, broken only by crickets chirping nearby. The mark on her neck has mostly healed, and I wonder if it was from her mother or her stepfather.

"Can I ask how your mother became a vampire?" I ask, my throat aching with thirst, as the buzz of fireflies fills the air around us, their small lights adding a soft glow to this dry, dying wood.

Ava looks off into the trees, twisting the black-and-ruby ring around her finger absentmindedly. I'm reminded so much of when we were younger, when we planned to skip classes together or when we were contemplating which food stall at the market we wanted to try that day, that a brief smile touches my lips.

"My parents were from Saren, as you know," Ava says finally. "They studied in Erlanis City, and the emperor liked them enough to give them Clarity positions in Arborren. For a long time, they were happy. But when I was ten . . ."

The memory comes back to me then, like a boat bobbing along soft waves back to shore. "Your father . . . he got caught in a trap meant for vampires."

She nods once. "He couldn't get out, and the hunters didn't come back for days. He died there. My mother changed after that, but she was still a regular witch for a long time. Three years ago, she was on a trip for Clarity business, and when she returned through the forest, her carriage was attacked by vampires. The guards who were with her were killed, and she was on the brink of death, but a vampire there offered her a new life. She took the chance. She didn't want to leave me, she said."

I gulp at the grim story. "You sound like you don't believe that."

She gives a half nod, half shrug. "I just don't think that's the only reason. Now I believe that it's the power of being a vampire that she covets most. But she hated that she lost her Root witch abilities, too. I kept her secret for a year. Once I was old enough that my powers were coming in, she changed me . . . so she could always have that power close at hand."

Her voice takes on a hard edge by the end of her sentence. I know there's nothing I can do to change what's happened to her. The very thought of it makes me feel sick. While she was keeping her mother's secret of being a vampire, my mother was being accused of sympathizing with vampires.

I frown at the thought. That seems like too much of a coincidence. How exactly are our mothers connected?

"Zenos is just as bad as her," she mutters then. "I think he moved here to be closer to the forest and vampires. He has odd tastes. He likes to experiment on me."

"Experiment?" My blood goes cold with what she said, and I can't help imagining the worst: scalpels, test tubes, injections. "Your mother allowed that? What was he trying to find out?"

"She doesn't kn—" Ava's voice falters, and then she shakes her head sharply and says, "Tests to see how vampires work, what kind of pain we can withstand, how we heal . . . all of that. Like how the old emperors used to do to witches. He does the tests whenever my mother is out of town."

"I always thought something was off about him, but I didn't

know what." I let out a long, shaky breath. "What do you mean, 'like how the old emperors used to do to witches'?"

Her eyes widen in shock. "I forgot they didn't teach us that in the regular classes. But I assumed they would have taught you once you moved on to your Flame witch training. . . . Your mother's journal goes into detail about how the witches used to be hated in this land and seen as a threat to humanity, something too unnatural. Humans craved to harness their power as a weapon, and did experiments on them to try to figure out how to take the magic. It was a long time ago, before vampires existed. When vampires came around, I suppose the empire found a new enemy to hate, and needed witches to fight them."

My mind races with what she just said. My first instinct is to say the journal is lying. My mother had to be wrong. Witches have always been a valued part of the empire.

But what if my teachers were wrong instead?

Ava's watching me now, and I feel my cheeks warm under her gaze. We're so close, much closer than I ever expected to be with her again, and a deep part of me wants to know what the past two years would have been like if she hadn't been turned. Would we still be close, would Tristan still be with us, too? I hold the image of the three of us, friends working together, at the front of my mind, wishing desperately it could be true.

On impulse, I reach out to take one of her hands, holding it by the wrist so as not to aggravate the newly healed skin. *What on earth am I doing?* She tenses for a moment, then relaxes in my grip.

An ache presses down on my chest, and I imagine Ava in that attic, every time I saw her there, not knowing she was locked inside against her will. Was she just as lonely as I've been these past two years? My heart swells as I remember the nights I'd stayed awake in my empty home, staring at the moon and wishing things could go back to the way they'd been. Had she stared at the same moon those long nights and wished to be with me, too?

"Do you see why I'm in the woods?" Ava mutters. "Nowhere else is safe for me. This place is important for vampires, especially ones like me who were turned against our will."

"It was unfair to you," I say, acknowledging that what her mother did was wrong. "But it's also unfair to everyone who dies because vampires need blood. Everyone dies at their time, fair or not. You died when your mother changed you. That's when things stopped being fair. And I . . ." My voice chokes up for a moment and I look away from her. "I hate it. You think I didn't miss you when you went away? Do you think I didn't want my friend back? And now, to think you're not even the same anymore . . ."

"I want my friend back, too, Kaye," Ava says then, squeezing my hand. "I don't want to fight just because they told us to hate each other. You see that, don't you? That I'm still me?"

I give a noncommittal grunt and stare at the ground. Neither of us is the person we were two years ago. But I sense that this would only hurt her to hear, so I keep quiet. Instead, I think of her mother, and what kind of woman would turn her own daughter into a vampire.

Someone who's probably killed plenty of others. Someone who is not safe to have in a position of power in Arborren. I'll need to find a way to show Liander what she really is, confront her about my mother's death, and figure out what her plans are.

"I'm here for you now, Kaye."

"Thank you." Without thinking, I begin tracing a circle over her palm. It's soft, and warm somehow—the blood she drinks becomes her blood, fueling her body for whatever functions it needs to pretend it's alive. I stare down at the outline of her veins on her inner wrist, wondering whose blood that is. My heart beats faster, and I wonder if she can hear it.

Ava's eyes, which have been so bright and full of light every time she's looked at me so far, now have this lost, empty cast to them. I don't know what kind of comfort she needs, but silence, just sitting here under this tree, its low-hanging leaves touching our faces and shrouding us from whatever might be watching, seems to be enough for her. As time passes and night deepens, her eyes regain a little life.

*Life,* I think, as a firefly passes between us and adds warmth to her skin. How could she regain what isn't there?

Ava stands up, a stony expression on her face, then walks toward the edge of the streambed and stares off into the trees with her arms crossed. Already I feel colder without her near.

I let out a long, shaky breath and look toward the stream. Ava's black hair skirts her chin—I did a terrible job of cutting it. Something about her looks so . . . tired.

An urge fills me to go to her, ask her to rest so we can run if we need to, but something holds me back.

Who knows when will be the last time that I see her?

I shake my head, swallowing hard. She's not a mortal like me. She's dead. What use is there in thinking anything else? Even if she could fool me into thinking she's living, that she deserves to kill for her own nourishment, that she's the same as she was back then . . . the truth would remain. She's a vampire, and I'm not. That will always stand between us.

And so my only choice is to stay here and watch her, as she

pushes her hair behind her ears with both hands and stares up at the moonlight as if she's searching the sky for something.

"We should rest," I say after a while. "It's too dangerous in the forest, but you need to heal, and I need to get at least a few hours of sleep before we move on."

She nods and, after I bring a small fire to life atop a bed of twigs, we lie down with our backs to each other. I feel more vulnerable without my silver-studded net, but I'm too tired to try to protect myself in some other way. Darkness surrounds us here, spilling into the world like ink even with the moonlight above. I look up at the sky and feel calmed by the endless expanse of stars, and I realize now why the sight of Ava staring up at the sky had affected me so strongly.

"My mother loved the stars and the moon," I say, my voice muffled by my knees, which I've drawn up to my face to curl into a ball. Ava says nothing, but it doesn't matter. I don't want a response from her. Just wanted to get out the thought. Speak it into existence.

The spaces between the trees grow darker and deeper as night wears on. I twirl a blade of grass in my fingers as I begin to slip off to sleep.

"What was her favorite constellation?" says a soft voice, and I stiffen, not having expected her to say anything at all.

A swarm of guilt rises up inside me. Had my mother ever mentioned a favorite constellation? Did she even know their names? I should know the answer to this. But I remember that on nights when the moon was full, she would point up at the sky, smile widely, and say, "Look how beautiful the night is, Kaye."

I remember she always did that on the full moon.

"She loved the full moon," I finally say. "It always seemed to give her more energy, on those nights."

My voice grows thick and cuts off near the end. A tear drips onto the grass beneath me, and I stay completely still, not wanting to show someone I'm supposed to be holding captive that I'm crying.

"That makes sense," Ava says, her voice nearby yet somehow filtering into the air above us like a cloud, soft and wont to disappear. "I like the sunrise."

I make a sound that might be a grunt or some sign of approval. If I speak, I know it'll be obvious I'm still choked up.

"It signals a new day," Ava continues. "A new chance. Hours and hours where you might be able to live the life you couldn't the day before."

Something about those words calms me, makes my breathing come more easily. My tears stop falling.

A breath later, she turns over, and her arm drapes over me. I tense slightly before leaning into her warmth. Something I used to dream about doing. She feels so real, so alive, even if I know she's not. She feels warm, when the night is so cold. Then she holds up a strip of cloth in her long fingers; she must have ripped a piece from her blouse.

After a moment of hesitation, I take the cloth from her to dry my tears and whisper, "Thank you."

"Kaye," she says, her arm still draped over me, her chin resting above my head. "Every time you saw me staring out of my attic window . . . I was looking for you."

My heart clenches, but I don't say anything. I don't know what to think anymore. I know she didn't kill my mother, but she's still a vampire.

In the morning, I wake to find myself staring directly at Ava. Somehow, in the night, we've rolled over to face each other. I stop breathing for a moment, taking in her calm features. Her hair falls to one side, and for one wild moment I'm tempted to touch it. Shadows cover half her face, her skin amber where the morning light hits and sienna where it doesn't.

Ava yawns, waking up, and she meets my gaze with a soft smile. Her eyes brighten, and it feels like the sun is shining on me.

And then I see the tip of one of her fangs, and I shrink slightly away.

We got far too close last night. Shame creeps up on me now, and I imagine Liander's disappointed face, Tristan's knowing shake of the head as he watches me crumble, my mother's memory fading away until all that's left is a daughter who moved on too fast.

I can't turn over Ava to be burned, like I planned. But I can't turn my back on the Flames, either.

All Ava wants is to be free somewhere her mother and humans won't hurt her. I should let her go and do that, even if . . . that leaves her alive to hunt.

I won't gleefully march her to her death when she's tried so hard to avoid hurting humans. As long as she remains this clearheaded about it, I don't see any reason she needs to be annihilated.

When we stand up, a wave of dizziness passes through me. Ava catches my shoulders and helps me stand straight. I meet her eyes blearily.

"Once we're closer to Chrysalis . . ." I mutter, voice hoarse and scratching against the dryness in my throat. "Don't go into the village. Stay at the borders, and let me go in alone. We'll part there."

She nods, biting her lip. She knows Chrysalis would be dangerous for her. They're so used to vampires in that town, they'll recognize her for what she is much faster than most people in Arborren would. I may not know what to do with her, but as long as she stays out of Chrysalis, I won't have to decide. As long as I can keep her out of there . . . I'll go back to my life, and she'll go on with hers. As it should be.

She rises, brushes the dirt off her skirt, and gives me a smile that I can't bring myself to return.

Resting with her like this, talking long into the night, means more time to share secrets with each other, more time to notice the way the moon sparkles in her eyes and how there's almost always a smile quirking at her lips, even when she speaks of dreadful things. More time to question everything I'm doing with my life.

# CHAPTER
## 15

- AVA -

*The rampion flower grows in unexpected places,*
    *and is a cure for those who are gravely injured,*
    *much like the blood of vampires can heal a human,*
    *as long as it's not too late.*
    *Given to a human on the verge of death, the blood will trans-*
*form them.*
    *So it follows that when Casiopea created another vampire for*
*the first time,*
    *she was likely trying to save their life.*
                    —JOURNAL BY CALLUNA MENTARA

As we walk onward, I take in Kaye's face from the corner of my eye, remembering what she told me last night, and I wonder what other people see when they look at her, why they try to put her in boxes and tell her who she is and who she isn't. Her face is perfect, and I'm glad that it makes people mad. Let them be angry.

Telling Kaye my truths about Zenos and my mother makes me feel like a weight has been lifted from my shoulders. I feel close to her once more, even though I know we must separate so I can join Casiopea and she can continue her life. I'm still a vampire, and she's still a witch.

A few hours into the day's journey, Kaye mutters something in a voice so low I barely hear it. She sways in place for a moment, and I reach out to steady her. My own thirst has turned into a dull ache at the back of my throat, making it difficult to speak or focus on anything. But I force myself to for Kaye's sake, and it takes all my effort to ignore her pulse, the flush of her cheeks, and the sight of the veins on her forearms. She needs me to focus right now.

"You need water," I say, then bite my lower lip as I think what to do. "How close are we to Chrysalis?"

At that moment, Kaye sways and stumbles toward me.

I catch her around the shoulders, and her hair tickles my chin, sending a fluttering feeling through me. We stay like that for exactly ten heartbeats—I know because I'm counting hers. Then she looks up in surprise, but doesn't pull away immediately like I expect her to. For a long minute, I'm lost in the green depths of her eyes, her heartbeat, and our memories—a night so similar to this at an outdoor theater performance. We'd left our mothers in the audience and gone behind the stage to talk, sitting on the cerulean and marigold cobblestones covering the streets of the town center. Our heads leaned toward each other, the world around us disappearing, before fireworks went up behind us and we'd jolted apart. Only a week or two later, my mother changed me.

I wonder what would have happened then if we'd kissed. I haven't allowed myself to think about that night since I was turned. But I'm next to her right now, still lost in her eyes.

*Not for long, though,* I remind myself.

"Kaye?" I whisper, coming back to the present. She straightens and shakes her head to wake herself up more.

She opens her mouth to answer, but only a small sigh escapes her lips. I can go three days without blood before suffering, but I forget how long humans can go without water. Not long, if Kaye's sickly pallor is anything to judge by. I can't go into Chrysalis, but what will she do? Crawl to the village from wherever I leave her?

We move onward, and soon my throat feels like it's going to close up. Kaye's eyes grow heavy, and her steps are getting more careless. I fight against my thirst, knowing I can't risk losing myself now. We can't both fall apart, or we're dead.

Well, she'll be dead. I'll just be deader.

Glancing around us, I pick a tree with low-hanging branches. The trees are still too thick around us for me to see far ahead, but if I'm high up, I can see how far we are from the town.

"I'll be right back, Kaye," I tell her, gesturing her to sit on a soft patch of fallen leaves near the base of the tree she's currently leaning against. "Rest for a few minutes."

She drops down without a word and leans her head against the trunk. My heart clenches at how gray her skin looks, the sweat beading on her forehead and neck even though the sky is cloudy today. The faster we get to Chrysalis, the better.

It's been years since I've climbed a tree, but the skill comes back quickly, and I pull myself up the branches with startling ease. I've never truly tested my strength as a vampire like this.

*You could have an army at your command, with those powers.*

I pause near the highest branches of the tree. I press my hands into the bark, imagining ripping the tree in half with my hands. Is that something I could do?

I think of the vampires who attacked us in the trees. At the time, I was frightened for Kaye, but . . . Their graceful limbs. The lionlike way they'd slid from the trees and stalked toward us, confidence glowing on their undead skin. No one would look at them and think they're powerless.

All I want right now is to fly to the Heart Tree and join the vampires there, meet Casiopea and help her protect the forest. No one would ever take advantage of me again.

If I had drunk from that hunter, how strong would I be now?

I shove all these thoughts far down, scared of how easily they rise up in me.

In minutes, I reach the top of the tree and choose a branch to perch on. The forest spreads away before me, umber and burnt-orange leaves extending for miles in all directions. Black birds swoop over the trees ahead in a V pattern. There are mountains to the east, with fog already building against them, pooling in the foothills before it will sweep back down to swallow the forest. To the west, the trees fall away, and the horizon is tinged with the soft green of the narrow sea separating Arborren and the capital. Islands dot the water between, but I can't make any of them out from here. Beyond that still lies Saren, the sun-soaked land where my parents came from years before I was born.

I breathe in the fresh air even if I don't need it, simply because it's so much nicer than the rot-tinged forest below me. The view here is almost exactly like what I saw through my vision in the burial grounds.

From up here, Chrysalis is easy to spot among the trees. The town is a collection of ramshackle houses with woodsmoke rising above in gray puffs of air, just a little north of here. We're close now.

We'll have to split up, Kaye to the village and me onward to the Heart Tree. I wonder who will leave whom first.

My heart clenches at the thought, and I think of the girl below, waiting for me. The girl who's been alone and afraid and angry the past two years, much like me. The girl who lost her mother because of vampires. The girl whom I held all last night. I think of the emerald glow of her eyes in the sun, her light touch on my neck, her heartbeats as she fell asleep. My best friend, Kaye. When we'd first met in these woods, the differences between us had seemed insurmountable. But now it's like we're the same two girls who'd find empty classrooms or basements or stairwells, spend the whole night talking under the stars till our voices grew hoarse, and still not want to leave each other's side. That hasn't changed, even though everything else has.

I descend the tree again, moving even quicker than I did on the way up. Most of the leaves and fruit hanging from it are dead. But halfway down, I find a patch of violet-colored berries that spark something in my memory. Calluna's journal said this kind of berry helps with night vision.

The first night we'd traveled together, I'd had to guide us numerous times because Kaye couldn't see far in the dark. I pluck some of the berries before climbing down the rest of the way.

"These are for you," I say, approaching Kaye, where she still sits in front of the tree with her head resting on her knees.

Her eyes widen when she sees the berries I'm holding out to her.

"These are the ones for night vision," she says in a scratchy voice.

"I figured you could . . . use them." She frowns, like she's not sure what I mean. In a rush, I add, "The town is close. We'll reach it within an hour."

She nods and uses the tree to help herself stand, then pulls a dagger from her belt and hands it to me by the hilt.

"You take this. I know you can protect yourself, but just . . . I want you to have another weapon."

Her words are so low I have to lean close to hear them. Wrapping my arm around her waist, I help her stay upright for the rest of our walk, and try to remember what I can about Chrysalis.

It's mostly silver miners there who built their village in the middle of the woods, daring to live where vampires tread in order to be closer to the mines. As such, they've grown skilled at defending themselves from vampires, and collect money from the emperor for each kill, much like the Flame witches in Arborren. But without the Bone Wall protecting them the way it does Arborren, they live in constant danger. They're more than happy to kill any vampire, if it gets them closer to claiming the forest— and the mines—as their own.

Twenty minutes later, Kaye's eyes drift shut, but she's still moving. Kaye told me not to go into the village, but I can't leave her like this. I have to go in with her, even if it's dangerous. I shove aside the fear prickling my skin and whisper encouragement to Kaye.

Soon, the trees begin to thin. A large wooden fence encircles the village, and a gate manned by two guards with silver weapons strapped to their bodies stands ahead. More silver cages and nets hang from the tree branches above.

The guards wave in a few villagers approaching the gate, but put up their hands when they spot us.

I'm nearly trembling under their glare. I can't give myself away now.

All my mother's methods to trick humans into thinking she's one of them come to mind. If I want to survive this village,

I'll have to use them. I start panting to make myself look exhausted, and stumble along with Kaye until we're right in front of the guards.

"Where are you two from?" one of the guards asks, one hand resting on the hilt of a dagger.

"Arborren," I gasp out. "She got separated from the other Flame witches, and I . . . I was here foraging for seeds for our greenhouses." Raising one hand, I coax the grass below to break and lift into the air. The blades of grass hover for a few moments, and when I relax my hand, they fall back to the earth. "I ran into her and we decided to travel together, but we're out of water. Please, let us in. We've had too many close calls with bloodsuckers, and I can't fight them off myself."

They're already nodding and waving us inside the gate. Exhilaration floods me. I can't believe it worked. Vampires who retain their witch abilities are so rare that all I have to do is show them my magic once and they're convinced I'm mortal.

But it's not over yet. Squat thatch buildings surround us as we stumble into the village. People eye us curiously as I help Kaye walk down a narrow dirt road, with dust kicked up from a wagon ahead of us. The houses create a shadowed tunnel we pass through to reach the center of the village.

A few women stand together, hanging sheets from a clothesline that runs between their windows. They pause in their work to watch us with furrowed brows. Some of them push their children behind them. My skin prickles with the feel of their stares. Is it because we're both clearly Sarenian, or because we're girls who just walked out of the forest with mud all over us and twigs in our hair? Probably both.

I keep my head down as we reach the center. Chrysalis is

much smaller than Arborren, but is still crowded with people. We cross two streets filled with the scents of fresh-baking bread, carts full of medicinal herbs and flowers like milk thistle and rampion, and wagons full of logs and tinder. We approach an inn with oil lamps hanging outside, already lit in the dusk of early evening.

I'm afraid to go inside, because what if something I do gives away that I'm not a mortal? There's an engraved sign hanging from the doorknob that says there are vacancies.

I prop Kaye against a wall and walk toward the back of the inn. An outdoor staircase leads up to the rooms on the second floor. I check to make sure no one's watching, then help Kaye up the creaking stairs. We only need somewhere to rest for a few hours.

Once we're up the stairs, we walk down the rickety walkway and I listen at each door for voices on the other side. At the very end of the walkway is one last door. When I lean against it and hear nothing, I use Kaye's dagger to shove aside the lock.

The room is empty apart from a cot in the corner, a window looking out of the side of the building, and a dresser. I sigh with relief and ease Kaye onto the bed.

"I'll be right back," I whisper to her, but she doesn't even respond. Her heart is beating slower than before, sending panic through me. I need to get water for her now.

As fast as I dare to move without drawing attention to myself, I leave the room and make my way back toward the center of the village. Outside of a school building is a water fountain. People hold out their hands or small wooden cups to catch the water tumbling out. I ease my way around the students and spot a waterskin leaning against the side of the fountain. A human girl stands next to it, but she's busy chatting with her friend and not paying attention.

"Excuse me," I mutter, stepping behind her to act as if I'm reaching for the streaming water. She's close—too close. Her skin is flushed from the sun, and I can almost smell the blood running through her veins. Involuntarily, I begin to lean toward her, but then I remember Kaye. She's waiting for me, weak and desperate for water. She needs me. Carefully, I slip the girl's waterskin—which is already full—under my arm, and dart away as quickly as I can.

As I step away from the fountain, my senses are on high alert. I nervously twist the ring my mother gave me around my finger as I walk, careful not to show any reaction when the human girl starts asking if anyone saw where her water went. I'm almost to the other side of the square when I spot a man in an alley watching me with a smirk on his face. He looks familiar, but I can't figure out how I recognize him. I slip down another street and look behind me to check if anyone's following, but no one's there.

In minutes, I'm back at the inn, and forcing Kaye to sit upright so she can drink. She takes a few sips, and her eyes slowly come back to life.

"Thank you," she murmurs. She leans her head on my shoulder, and I catch the lemon and woodsmoke scent of her hair.

I make out the sound of her heartbeat, louder than I've ever heard it before. I hear it, but I also feel it through her body pressed against mine. I want to memorize the beats of it and count it out to her while she sleeps.

In minutes, I fall asleep, too.

When I wake up, it's because of loud noises outside. But the first thing I notice is that Kaye is gone.

The loud voices outside draw closer, and I look out the window to see what's happening. Villagers scatter out of the way of five men charging down the alley. I recognize two of them: the man who watched me at the fountain, and Zenos.

It's some of his group that Kaye and I saw in the forest. I jolt away from the window, my hands shaking.

He knows I'm here.

They're coming straight for the inn, and Zenos's beady eyes are fixed on the building like he's staring through the walls to find me. They pass under my room and walk toward the staircase at the other end of the building.

I only have seconds. I grab the silver knife Kaye gave me and run to the window.

Heavy boots sound on the stairs outside, so much like Zenos coming up to my attic every morning. Crouching in the windowsill, I examine the hard ground below. I might twist my ankle with this fall, but unlike any mortal, I won't be gravely injured. I'll go on, an undead being that only exists by killing others, like how I almost killed that man in the forest.

Maybe everyone is right that I'm unnatural, that I don't deserve to live.

Lucky for them, I'm already dead.

And as Zenos's footsteps stop right outside the door, I remember that there are scarier things than death, and I leap.

# CHAPTER 16

## · KAYE ·

*A Flame witch never hesitates,*
*especially when confronted with a killer that only exists to*
*destroy us all.*

—TRAINING ACADEMY FOR
YOUNG WITCHES OF ARBORREN

As soon as I'm outside in Chrysalis, I see signs of other Flame witches here; older ones who've caught vampires are gathered in a courtyard near a school. My heart races at the sight of vampires on their knees in silver binds, with silver-studded collars at their necks. When I'd woken up next to Ava at the inn, I chugged the water she'd brought, and then left to see if the Flames were here already. She needs to stay in the room until they're gone.

I pause near the entrance to the courtyard, at a fountain where I refill the waterskin. Tristan and the rest of my classmates stand nearby. Half of them look forlorn and disappointed with themselves; the other half gaze up at Tristan in awe as he laughs at something, his voice booming and echoing in the courtyard. I consider going up to them, sharing stories of our journeys through the woods and how good it is to be back as a team. . . . My heart swells for a brief moment, thinking we might be able to revert to the early days of our witch training, when everything was new, and we were so happy to finally have our powers.

My body tingles with nerves as I approach them. Something about this day, the stark gray clouds in the sky, the captive vampires in the courtyard . . . it all makes me want to hide. That's the last thing a strong Flame witch should do. I try to shake off the uneasiness I feel, but it clings to me like a heavy fog.

I think of Ava, waiting for me at the inn, and my head spins with indecision and guilt. All my thoughts about vampires, about Ava, about what we do as Flames, are becoming jumbled. They defy nature and everything good in the world. They killed my mother with no shred of remorse, all so they could continue on in their cursed existence. They deserve annihilation. It's not killing when they're already dead.

As I walk across the courtyard toward my team, I think of Ava and try to apply everything I think about vampires to her.

*They're cursed.* I think of the girl who looked at every tree like it was a gift.

*They're evil.* I remember the girl who gave me a cloth to wipe away my tears.

*They shouldn't exist. They are not living beings.* Ava's laugh rings through my ears; the sparkle of her eyes comes back to me in a way that tugs at my heart and draws me short of breath by the time I reach my classmates.

She's not like the rest of them. She dragged me to Chrysalis half dead, after all, when she could have killed me instead. I've made the right choice not bringing her in . . . haven't I?

My classmates notice me approaching, and Tristan's eyes widen in surprise. He calls over, "Hey, Kaye. So you didn't—"

"When did you arrive?" I interrupt in a rush.

"Yesterday." Tristan shrugs. "Walk with me, I'll show you where we're keeping the rest of them."

He leads me out of the courtyard to an empty stable. Next to it is a silver door leading to a basement. The hair on the back of my neck rises and a sudden chill goes through me. Tristan says quietly, "This is it. My father is going to send some Flames to retrieve them all soon." He takes a deep breath before adding, "I'm sorry you didn't catch any. I know we were sort of . . . going up against each other. But I was still rooting for you."

Tristan heads back to the courtyard before I can think of a response to that. If he was rooting for me, why didn't he ask me to travel with him in the first place? Why isolate me for the past two years? Nothing he does makes any sense.

I walk on stiff, numb legs down the road, taking a long route back to the inn where I left Ava. I need time to think about how I'm going to face Liander and tell him I failed. My heart squeezes tight like a bowstring at the thought. It will prove I'm not good enough, just like most of the Flames already think. They know Liander always praises my skill, so the fact that I haven't turned in a vampire might make them think I'm becoming a traitor like my mother. They'll find a way to turn on me, too.

Unbidden, the image of Ava leaping toward that hunter's blood comes back to me, and I know I might be making a mistake letting her go free. If I hadn't been there, she would have drunk from him.

Squeezing my fists, I try to focus on my new goals. I'll prove myself to Liander some other way, and I'll expose Eugenia Serení for being a vampire and accuse her of killing my mother. I let Liander's words the last time I saw him infuse me: *Your anger is a gift.*

I draw it up around me like a shield and sword. I will prove myself to the other witches no matter what it takes.

Once I'm a few blocks away from the courtyard, a loud, rhythmic chanting builds up from the center of the town, raising the hair on the back of my neck. Then I hear screams, and the crackle of flames. My breath catches in my throat.

It's coming from the courtyard—have they already started the annihilation?

A loud boom echoes through the village and I'm nearly thrown backward into a cart. Swinging my arms out to catch myself, I stand upright at the same time a bloodsucker hurtles around the edge of the wall, closely followed by a companion. Screams rise up from the villagers as more bloodsuckers break loose.

I look over my shoulder toward the inn. As long as Ava stays inside, she's safe. I need to do my duty and help round up the escaping vampires.

Running toward the courtyard, I join the other witches streaming out. Liander charges forward, flames already at both of his hands and a deadly focus in his eyes.

Ten feet from me, a vampire has grabbed a human man near the fountain and cracks his neck. I flinch as the vampire places his fangs at the man's throat, and begin to run toward them, but Liander gets there first. He sends a wall of flame at the vampire, who lurches back, screaming as the fire devours him.

I've seen enough burnings that it shouldn't shock me. But the annihilations in Arborren are more orderly, done with a pyre, the vampire prisoners led out one by one. This is pure carnage, and I can't tear my eyes away as the stench of burning flesh makes me want to retch.

"Kaye!" Liander shouts at me, and I snap out of it. "What are you waiting for? Fight with us! Capture as many as you can."

I nod and run down the nearest street as the closest Flames and hunters subdue the vampires in the courtyard. There are more running down a side street, leaping over the walls of the courtyard and sending humans fleeing. The hunters from Chrysalis are always armed, though, and send silver-tipped arrows at the vampires. The street is soon bathed in blood, and I'm dodging arrows left and right.

A shadow leaps over me then, and my heart shoots into my throat. A male vampire lands and grabs a woman from Chrysalis who's standing too close to the wall. I reach for a silver dagger just as the vampire's fangs latch on to the woman's throat.

"Let her go!" I shout as I hurl the dagger. It lands in the middle of the vampire's back and he lets out a howl, his eyes fixing on me with murderous rage. He tosses the bleeding woman to the ground and rips the blade out of his back.

Then we're fighting, his fast reflexes and strength against my skill. He dodges every flame I send at him, but that doesn't deter me. Liander told me to fight, and I will—for every person lost senselessly to these killers, for every child left without a mother or father because of a vampire.

This, being locked in a fierce battle with a vampire, my skill and rage driving my every move, is what makes sense to me. This is where I'm in control, strong and capable and where I belong, fighting alongside the other Flames.

I blind the vampire with shadows, and sink another silver blade into his chest. His knees buckle, blood spilling from his lips. Liander said to capture them, didn't he? Why not annihilate them? He burned the one in the courtyard. I should show this vampire no mercy, either. I could cut through his neck. I could try to use light and shadow to kill him—one of the more advanced techniques I haven't mastered yet, creating weapons out of light that are just as effective as any blade.

Or . . . I raise my hands, flames roaring to life on my palms. Hatred for this creature, for all of them, floods through me.

I lift my hand back, preparing to fling the fire at this vampire, when a familiar voice makes me falter.

"Hurry! This way!"

It's Ava's voice.

I stop, abandoning the vampire as he pulls the knife out of his chest again and stumbles back.

There, at the back wall of the courtyard: Ava crouches on the edge of the wall and gestures for the vampires to climb over. They leap past her to race out of the town and toward the forest.

Including . . . Nuira. The vampire who attacked me in the woods, threw away my pack, and threatened to come after me. My whole body goes numb as Ava takes her hand to help her over the wall.

Everything around me fades away except Ava. She's helping them escape.

# CHAPTER 17

## - AVA -

*When vampire hunters killed Casiopea's son,*
*she did not know what to do.*
*But years of being a test subject of the empire*
*gave her some ideas.*
—JOURNAL BY CALLUNA MENTARA

My ankle twists sharply when I land on the stone ground outside of the inn. Gritting my teeth against the pain, I step into the shadows cast by the side of the building, and then I hop on one foot alongside the wall as quietly as I can.

A loud crash sounds above me in the room I've just left, and then Zenos's voice rings out, "She knew we were coming. Spread out and find her; if she disappears again, her mother will lock up all of us—even me."

A chill spreads down my spine and I feel numb as I run to the nearest alley, putting weight on my twisted ankle and wincing through the pain.

I run, turning onto random streets and moving as fast as I can. People gasp as I sprint past them, and for a moment I wonder if I'm moving as fast as other vampires and giving myself away right now. But using this speed, this strength, is the only way I'll get away from him.

As I careen down the next street and nearly twist my ankle again, I spot two people at the end of it whom I recognize, from all the hours I'd spent staring out of my attic window. Two Flame witches from Arborren walking toward me. I slow my pace immediately. I may be faster, but these witches have been taught to catch vampires, and I don't know yet if I'm a match for their flames and silver.

But also, I wonder why they're here. Chrysalis relies on its own people to control the vampires in their immediate area, not Flame witches. The only reason I can imagine Flames coming here is if there are more vampires than the human hunters can handle.

The thought makes me slow as the witches pass me, my thoughts racing. They're too absorbed in their own conversation to pay attention to me.

"Come here, girl," says a voice to my left, and I stiffen, expecting one of Zenos's men to have found me. But when I turn my head to the side, I see a wizened old man behind a cart of trinkets. A sign hanging in front of the cart is etched with the words CHARMS AGAINST EVIL. "No one should be wandering without protection, especially this time of year. Can I interest you in a necklace? Or earrings, mine are getting more popular these days."

All the jewelry laid out is adorned with glistening white fangs. Necklaces, rings, earrings, bracelets—they all have fangs set into them, some simply polished so the ivory color shines under the sun, and others doused with colorful dust or paint to give them a different, fashionable color.

"I—I'm fine, thank you," I stutter out before turning to follow the two Flame witches.

As I do, a cold hard determination settles in my bones. If they have vampire captives here, I'll do whatever I can to save them. I know not all of them are good and many have likely killed humans. I don't blame the humans for fearing them. But I also don't want to watch them be slaughtered.

I follow them at a steady pace, wincing at every step on my injured ankle, and checking every corner for a sign of Zenos. We reach the main roads of Chrysalis, near the school I'd seen earlier, and the witches step into a stone courtyard with an arched entryway.

When I reach the arch, I stand at the side of it and peer around the corner. There are at least twenty Flame witches, as well as human hunters with gleaming silver weapons at their belts. There's a line of prisoners with their ankles and wrists tied together by silver chains. But separate from them, in the center of the courtyard, five vampires kneel with their hands tied behind their backs. A hunter stands behind each of them with a long, curved silver blade at their neck, and my heart shoots into my throat. My mother told me about those particular blades, used for decapitation, but I've never seen one up close until now.

Then I recognize Nuira and the other vampire I saw caught in those silver nets when the hunters attacked me and Kaye. As I consider what to do, one of the Flame witches—the Clarity councilor Liander, who trained Kaye—paces in front of the vampires. Small flames spark at his fingers, and the vampires flinch whenever he passes them.

"I'll ask you once more: How did you kill so many of the hunters who were in charge of capturing you? What did you do with their bodies? Do you have an accomplice who's still free?" Liander's voice booms out across the courtyard, and the rest of the Flames and hunters seem to hold their breath in antici- pation. He must be talking about how the forest swallowed all those hunters who captured Kaye and me, but he thinks Nuira had something to do with it.

He comes to a dead stop in front of Nuira. Withdrawing a silver blade, Liander places it under her chin and forces her gaze up. She grits her teeth against the pain of the silver, but manages to shake her hair away from her face and glare at Liander.

"If I knew, what makes you think I'd tell you?" Then she spits in his face. "Put the toy away and fight me with your hands. Let's see who's stronger then."

A cold silence settles upon the courtyard as Liander stares at the vampire with a spark of amusement in his eyes. My stomach twists at the sight; it's far too similar to Zenos's face whenever he comes up with new experiments for me. I waver for a mo- ment, part of me inclined to leave Nuira—she tried to attack me and Kaye, after all. But on the other hand, I want to help the vampires. And she could have told Liander about me, but she didn't.

I search the courtyard quickly for something—anything—to help them escape. It's a square courtyard made of stone walls, and this is the only main entrance from the street. There's a walk- way around the perimeter of the courtyard, with more arched entrances leading into it. Around the walkway are small crates filled with mulch, vegetables, and herbs. In the courtyard itself, there are wagons, some filled with hay, others with stone and bricks . . . I can use those.

Liander's voice breaks through my thoughts. "I have a better idea, bloodsucker," he tells Nuira in a low, deadly voice. "You will fight one of your fellow captives. Whoever wins will go free."

Nuira rises to the challenge as Liander points at one of the other vampires. The hunters move to undo their bindings, but Liander holds up a hand.

"Have you lost your minds? No, they fight with their hands still bound. Spread out and guard the exit."

Before he finishes his sentence, I move, running toward the side of the courtyard, which is close to the fountain I retrieved water from earlier. I begin climbing the wall, briefly touching my hands and feet to the grooves between stones, and in seconds I reach the roof and drop to a crouch. Behind me, I hear a gasp, and turn quickly to see a little girl staring up at me.

"Vampire," she whispers, her voice tinged with fear and awe. Before she can yell for help, I move farther into the courtyard along the roof; I'm on top of the walkways now on the eastern side, with the setting sun in my eyes. Too visible. I'll have to get around to the other side.

The hunters and Flames have formed a circle surrounding the two vampires, who now pace around each other with murder in their eyes. Below, I hear heartbeats thudding in anticipation and whispered bets between hunters.

Nuira's eyes seem to glitter in the setting sun, and she flashes the other vampire a taunting grin. He lets out a sinister growl that makes the hair on the back of my neck rise.

They lunge back and forth, trying to shove or trip one another. The man is growing more and more frustrated that he can't use his hands, but Nuira is getting too confident. She shouts taunts at him and he replies with fiercer attacks, moving so quickly they become a blur. At one point, she shoves him hard enough that he flies across the stone ground, and when he hits it, the earth cracks. He rolls to his feet, hardly noticing the broken stone he's left in his wake, and races toward her again. She dodges him, but he bares his fangs and rips a chunk of her flesh off her shoulder.

I'm so entranced by their speed and ferocity I nearly lose track of what I'm doing. Tearing my gaze away, I move the rest of the way around the courtyard and reach the shadowed part of the roof.

I'll incapacitate the guards closest to the three vampires still kneeling on the ground with their arms bound, then get the vampires' attention to tell them to follow me up the roof. There's a Flame witch directly below where I crouch, but I can take care of him, too.

I raise a hand, focusing on the lumps of stone and the bricks I saw in the wagon earlier, but then there's a shattering boom across the courtyard, and a cloud of dust rises in its wake.

The male vampire caught the upper hand at some point and pushed Nuira so forcefully, she flew across the courtyard and slammed into the stone wall. It buckled under the force of her crash, and rocks topple down to cover her. She doesn't get back up.

The other vampire lets out a triumphant shout. The hunters grumble to each other, some of them having lost their bets. As they do, I lift one of the stones in the wagon and fling it toward the guard's head. He drops with a small *oomph* sound as the breath is knocked out of him. The vampires next to him perk up at the sight, and I raise my other hand to take out the Flame witch below me.

Liander claps, the sound echoing in the silent courtyard—he's so distracted by the fight, he hasn't noticed anything I'm doing over here. With a smug smile, he walks up to the vampire who won the fight. As he does, I knock out the next Flame witch. The bound vampires have started shifting slightly, and one of them spots me crouched on the roof.

"Congratulations," Liander says to the winning vampire, and reaches for the man's bound hands behind his back. "You are free."

His hands light up in flames. The vampire doesn't notice at first. I freeze, watching the flames gleam against the silver bindings on his hands. The flames crackle as they finally reach the vampire's arms, and Liander holds on tight. The vampire tries to throw him off, but the flames travel quickly and Liander wraps his arms around the vampire's torso like an embrace. The vampire's screams pierce my ears, growing more strangled by the second.

The scent of burning flesh rises up, and my stomach churns. I let go of my grip on the rocks below as the flames reach the vampire's skull and his screams turn wildly high-pitched, his body writhing and bucking under Liander's iron hold.

*Stay with me, where it's safe,* my mother's voice whispers in my thoughts. *You are no match for them.*

With my vision that's much stronger than theirs, I see what these mortals would never have to witness themselves. The charred flesh below the flames, the bones protruding from—

A moment later, I vomit over the wall. It lands directly on the Flame witch's head. He whips his head around with a disgusted snarl and spots me on the wall.

I scramble backward, but one of the vampires slams his body into the witch, then digs his fangs into the witch's throat. He draws blood for a long second before the witch falls, then bends to grab the loop of keys at her belt with his fangs. This vampire and another, who just killed the hunter guarding them, race toward me and jump onto the roof. The one with the keys drops them into my palm, and I use them to quickly unlock their binds.

"What about the others?" I ask, nodding at the pile of rocks where Nuira is beginning to stir.

"Make your own choice," hisses one of the vampires on the roof with me.

The two of them disappear over the roof a moment later, and I'm tempted for a moment to follow them, but the burning vampire's final scream fills the air with a piercing finality, and I know I can't leave any of my kind to suffer the flame alone. The smoke filters into the sky, and he drops to the ground as a charred husk.

Without hesitation, I lift heavy rocks near the three Flame witches that stand closest to Nuira. Nuira has broken out of her pile of rocks and is racing toward the wall. As she does, I knock out the three Flame witches. As Nuira runs toward me, more Flames and hunters attack, hurling silver blades at her.

"Hurry! This way!" I shout, and I briefly wonder why the witches haven't burned her like they did the other vampires.

Nuira reaches the wall a moment later and I stretch out a hand to help her over.

"I see you've decided where your loyalties lie," she says, flashing me a wicked grin before jumping into the shadowed alley behind the courtyard. "Join us."

She doesn't wait for me to answer before sprinting down the road. After a brief pause, I follow, not knowing what else to do; the Flames and hunters will be after us in seconds, and Zenos is looking for me, too; it's a small enough town that he'll find me soon.

I have no idea where Kaye is, but I didn't see her in the courtyard. All I can do is hope she's safe.

*Her people are here, after all,* I think with a pang in my heart. *She'll be fine.*

I race after the two other vampires, pushing past the pain in my ankle and not caring when townspeople shriek at the sight of me. They would burn me to ash and not even blink. I didn't know the vampire who died back there, but it felt like I was him, my limbs burning to nothing, too, and his final moments are all I see and hear as I sprint across the stone roads. Another vampire grabs a man standing on his front steps and tears out his throat in one smooth gesture, drinking for a few long seconds. Nuira speeds onward, laughing as her blond hair whips behind her in the wind.

As we sprint past an intersection, I spot Zenos. He and a few men with him are striding down this road with silver daggers in their hands. I stumble back out of sight. I don't know if he saw me, but he'll find me soon enough. The fences around the village are well guarded; unless we kill every human, we won't get out of here.

There was never any escape from Zenos. He's always caught me. No matter how good I've tried to be, he is always my nightmare.

And the people I race past now while the other vampires around me wreak carnage . . . they'll always see me as *their* nightmare.

Tears streak my cheeks now as I remember every cup of blood brought to me, how carefully rationed it was. The way my mother checked the bars on my windows every day. The press of silver against my neck, inches away from decapitation. The way she begged me to keep her secret of being a vampire, and then turned on me once I did.

Everything she did was on purpose, like the day she told

me to lie still and had me drink from her bleeding hand before killing me an hour later. With her vampire's blood in my body at the time of death, I became this.

I'd made excuses for her for so long, kept her secret for a whole year before she turned me. I'd felt bad for her, losing my father and then nearly being killed herself—of course she had to pretend to be alive, of course she had to drain powers from me, it was the only way she could be there for me.

But she didn't have to turn me, too. She didn't have to shut me inside the top floor of our tower and purposefully keep me weak.

The locked drawer of memories in my mind slides open, and suddenly I feel the phantom touch of the silver-studded straps around my wrists and ankles in a chair in the dusty basement, cold and damp and far from any light.

The freezer stands open across from me and the scent of blood wafts out, but I can't have it, because Zenos stands in front of me making notes, checking my temperature, and examining me for any sign of disintegration.

The first time, I screamed and cried. The second time, I tried to tell my mother, and she thought I was lying. I begged her to make him leave.

But his experiments left no marks on me, so she thought they weren't real. His words were spoken only in my ears, so she ignored them.

The third time, I stopped screaming and braced myself.

Maybe I could have tried to tell her again or fought back harder against Zenos. But it only happened a few times a year. I'd convinced myself nothing bad had happened at all, and that even if it did, I had no proof. He always made sure I was healed before she came home. I'd told myself over and over again it wasn't really that bad, and if it was, better me than my mother—she'd already suffered enough.

Red still clouds my vision, but it no longer feels like blood; it feels like rage. Vampires are supposed to be stronger than mortals, but I've been kept weak with my mother's small rations of blood.

Touch me with silver and I crumble. Place a fire near me and I freeze. There is no power when everyone knows your weaknesses.

That thought used to make me despair. But now it sends fury through me, a sense of justice I can't contain.

Why does everyone try to control me? Why does everyone think they have a say in what I do? Is it because I'm a young girl who could be powerful if she only knew how to wield her weapons, her voice? Kaye's young and underestimated, too, but she's had freedom she takes for granted, a life I'll never know.

I want to take that power, my weapons, my voice, for myself.

Someone screams up ahead, and I flick my gaze over in time to see that Nuira has slammed a human woman's head into the wall. As she drops, Nuira immediately sinks her fangs into the woman's neck.

Then the familiar scent of copper reaches me, and I breathe it in deeply. For the first time in my life, the scent draws me in rather than disturbs me. I look to the right and see a bleeding man halfway down the shadows of this alley. There are silver weapons strapped to his belt; he must be a hunter, but an injured one. He's bleeding from the neck, but slowly, and now he's trying to crawl away. One of the other vampires must have gotten to him and not stuck around before finishing the job.

"Greedy little thing, where are you now?" yells Zenos from

nearby, and I slam back into the alley wall, my whole body shaking.

Breathing in, I catch the scent of blood on the air again. My fangs ache to be used. Pushing off from the wall, I stalk toward the bleeding man like I'm a shadow myself. My vision goes red, the thirst tugs me forward, and my mind goes blank.

He snarls at me and charges forward with his silver blade. I fling my arm up and the silver cuts into me, but I shove back harder and the man flies ten feet down the alley. His blood streaks the stones beneath him. I reach him in two strides.

I force both arms behind his back, the way my mother told me she does it. I use one hand to hold his arms in place, and the other to shove his neck to the side. He struggles, but somehow I'm able to hold him down. I hesitate for the briefest second, my fangs inches from his throat, the scent of his sweat and blood blocking out everything else around me except a whisper in the back of my mind: *Drink.*

I pierce his artery with a simple clutch of my fangs. Blood streams out, into my throat where it belongs.

I don't care who or what he is; he would think I'm evil no matter what I do, and as long as I still live, blood is what I need. It gushes into my mouth, warm and fresh, and soothes the burning sensation in my throat. I've never tasted anything better. This, as terrible as it is, is still my choice, is a part of who I am, and there's freedom in this choice to drink from someone. Suddenly, I know why the other vampires attacked in the way they did. Rather than be burned alive, they've turned on these people and taken what they deserve: life. That's what blood is, life on my lips, spilling down my throat and promising to make me real.

They're so convinced I'm a killer I see no reason to prove them wrong.

I keep drinking even once the man goes still and footsteps pound behind me. A familiar sound comes with them, the steady rushing of a heartbeat I know so well, one that's lulled me to sleep in the forest every night—and then I catch the lemon and woodsmoke scent of her on the air.

I come back to my senses. I drop the body, which is no longer moving. No breath, no pulse.

*What have I done?*

"Kaye," I whisper, spinning to face her with blood coating my chin and torso.

There's a group of Flame witches, fire raging at their fingertips. Before I can move, flames shoot out to wrap around my wrists and ankles like bindings.

Kaye stands at the front of the group, with an utterly blank expression on her face as she raises one hand to point at me and says, "Make sure to bind her hands. This vampire has been responsible for deaths in Arborren for years. Her name was Ava Sereni."

# CHAPTER 18

## · KAYE ·

*A bloodsucker always expects the obvious attack.*
*Outsmarting them is what separates man from predator.*
*And sometimes, fear is the greatest weapon.*
—TRAINING ACADEMY FOR
YOUNG WITCHES OF ARBORREN

The moment Ava is in chains, her searing gaze on me the last thing I see of her, Liander places a hand on my shoulder. I shiver involuntarily, but then turn to him with what I hope looks like a triumphant smile.

She ran through the streets with the other vampires, including that blond one who attacked me in the woods. She mercilessly drank from that hunter, killing him, and only stopped when I showed up.

*Remember they're the enemy,* I think vehemently. *Don't let her turn you into a traitor.*

"You've done so well, Kaye," Liander says then, and his doting smile brings me back to the present. I lock eyes with my patrolmates. There are scratches and bruises on their faces, and a haunted look to their eyes. "You may join the other victors for a drink tonight; Tristan will be there, too." He waves away the Flames closest to us with a quick command to them to round up the other vampires. "He reached Arborren first with blood-sucker captives, Kaye, so he did well, but . . . you have the bigger prize; Eugenia has been searching for her daughter and just arrived in Chrysalis. She'll want to reward you, too, and you'll be the winner of the task I set; once the vampires are annihilated and we return to Arborren, you'll have a formal graduation and join regular forest patrols soon."

My breath catches at that. Why would Eugenia reward me for capturing her daughter and setting her up to be annihilated? She'd been hiding Ava to protect her from exactly this fate.

Then, the rest of what Liander said hits me.

"Me?" I ask, my heart feeling lighter than air. "Thank you, Liander. I . . . this means the world to me."

Once I've graduated, no one will tell me I don't belong. As an adult, graduated Flame witch, I'll bring back honor to my mother's name. I'll be able to make a real difference in protecting Arborren from vampires.

I have a spring in my step as I return to the inn to collect my things; I assume we'll head to Arborren directly after the annihilation.

I take the stairs on the outside of the building two at a time and reach our room. The window is open, and a chill permeates the air. Ava hates the cold, so why would the window be open? My breath slows, and I feel her presence here, tense, accusatory, and . . . afraid. An odd sensation prickles at the corners of my senses, like I'm being watched, and I feel like I'm back in the forest again.

I wonder if the other Flames have seen what the trees do, how the forest floor swallows men whole, how the roots and vines grab and claw at limbs. And why was it never taught to me in training?

At least we're all Flames, I reassure myself. It'll be much easier traveling with my people through this forest than alone with a bloodsucker.

*Don't call me that,* says Ava's voice in my head, like a specter, and then I feel like it's her eyes on me, calculating everything and reading who I am by a mere glance.

I pick up her sack from the bed, peeking inside to see my mother's journal, nestled in a soft, woven blue fabric. I sling the sack's straps over my shoulders and leave the room.

Soon, I'm back in the courtyard, and the chaos in the town has died down. A line of vampires has been rounded up, silver cuffs around their ankles and tying their hands behind their backs, chains connecting them all. Ava is in the middle of the group, her whole body stiff and tense.

Instead of looking at her, which makes my stomach churn uneasily, I look toward Eugenia Serení. She wears a long black dress with white lace embroidery and gloves, along with a ruby choker at her neck.

*She's a vampire, too,* I think, a chill spreading down my spine. I take her in from here, looking for the telltale signs, but Ava was right that her mother covers up well. She breathes like a human, doesn't show any sign of having superior senses, and her cheeks are even flushed under the high sun. Does Liander have any idea? He must not, or else she'd be locked in silver binds, too.

How am I going to get the truth out of her about what happened to my mother? If I can find a way to expose what she is,

Liander will turn against her. I imagine turning her over to Liander, and a sense of justice floods me. It would serve her right for forcefully turning her daughter into a vampire and locking her up with that despicable man Zenos. He's here, too, walking up and down along the line of vampires and making notes on a sheaf of papers, muttering under his breath as he goes. I want to burn him where he stands. He sends Ava a condescending smile as he passes her, and she shrinks away from him. I bite my lip and tear my gaze away from her.

The pull I felt toward her in the forest . . . the warmth when she was near . . . my thirst must have left me delusional. I'm grateful she brought me to Chrysalis, but I can't let myself feel anything more for her.

For a moment, I'm so distracted that I barely notice Tristan has walked over to me until he's right at my side.

"We did it, Kaye." He places a hand on my shoulder, and when I meet his eyes, it's all triumph there. A long gash crosses his eyebrow and there are specks of dried blood on his neck and collarbone. "I didn't know you caught one, too. Dad just told me he'll let us both graduate. That'll be nice, won't it? I wonder if they'll put us on a patrol together."

That is certainly not what his father told me. My eyes trail toward Liander, who stands with his hands clasped behind his back and speaking to Eugenia. A twinge of regret for Tristan passes through me. All he wanted was to impress his father, and now his father might be lying to him. I don't know why he wouldn't allow us both to graduate, unless he simply wanted to make us fight harder for the chance.

"Those two are mine," Tristan says, and he points out two of the vampires, who both have gruesome scars along the sides of their faces, likely from silver. The sight makes my stomach roil.

Tristan caught two vampires *and* arrived in Chrysalis with them before me, but Liander is letting me graduate simply because of who Ava is? I want this as much as Tristan does, but right now I don't know if Liander is making a fair choice.

I nod toward the middle of the line and whisper to Tristan, "Ava Serení is—"

My voice catches and I can't finish the sentence.

Ava Serení is mine? *They think they control me, they think they own me.*

Ava Serení is my catch? *I'll fight them for locking me away and taking away all my choices.*

Tristan straightens, his brow furrowed with sweat beading on his forehead. "Wait a minute. That's Ava?"

My hands tremble when he says her name, so I clasp them in front of me and nod.

"I thought she went to Erlanis City to study," he says slowly, taking one step toward our old friend. I grab his elbow to stop him from moving any closer.

"She's been in Arborren the whole—" I stop midsentence when I feel a prickle on the back of my neck. Carefully, I look out of the corner of my eye and spot Eugenia, who's staring in the opposite direction. But I know in my gut she was listening in, so I hold back my next words. "Stop talking, Tristan. Don't say anything."

"But she was our friend before," he says, and I roll my eyes at his obstinacy. "And you two were really close. Did you travel with her the whole way here?"

Through gritted teeth, I say, "I captured her and brought her here." The words feel wrong on my tongue, but I can't show any sentiment toward Ava. For one, if Eugenia overheard me, she might guess that I know about her being a vampire, too, and I wouldn't put it past her to get rid of me like she did my mother. And the other Flames are nearby, as well. I won't give them a reason to doubt me.

Tristan's shock at seeing Ava fades and his face turns back to hard stone.

"Just be careful, Kaye," he says in a measured tone, one hand resting on the hilt of a silver dagger as he stares out at the line of vampires. "Remember they're not mortal anymore. They'll do anything to trick you into thinking they are. That's what makes a traitor."

"I have been careful," I snap, my ears going hot at his words. Was that how my mother became one? Did a vampire trick her into thinking it was human? The image of Ava covered in that hunter's blood comes back to me in a rush. I turned her over for a reason. I can't let her twist my mind.

The sun peeks out from behind clouds, turning everything into a starker shade: the grime and scars on the vampires' bodies, the cuts and dried blood on the Flame witches around me. Ava's Clarity mother leaves Liander's side then, and her shoes click across the stone ground. I hold my breath as she reaches Ava, tightens the silver binds around her wrists so that Ava winces, then pushes her hair aside to whisper something. A soft yellow glow appears around Eugenia's hands, and she closes her eyes briefly. I stiffen, wondering if anyone else just witnessed this— Eugenia stealing her daughter's powers because she lost her own. She walks away a moment later, and Ava's shoulders slump, defeated. Her hair slides in front of her face.

As Eugenia returns to Liander's side, her face tilted slightly downward, I notice that Liander hasn't reacted to this at all. Will Eugenia be punished somehow for harboring a vampire in Arborren? Maybe he has to get approval from the other Clarity councilors before acting against one of them. But he doesn't look surprised or angry, just . . . neutral.

The Flame witches and hunters with them begin prodding the vampires forward to walk in a line. I frown, wondering why we would move them. The courtyard would be the best place for an annihilation—lots of space, far enough from the trees that a fire won't be triggered. Since vampires can't enter Arborren unless there's a break in the Bone Wall, the ones found in the forest are always brought to Chrysalis for burning.

"Do you know where we're headed?" I ask Tristan over my shoulder as we pass through the quiet streets.

"There's a line of cages just on the outskirts of the town. We'll use them to transport the vampires."

"Where to?" I prod.

He shrugs and mutters uneasily, "I dunno."

Residents of Chrysalis have come out to see us off, some giving solemn waves or nods, others standing in doorways with their arms crossed, other spitting on the vampires as they pass. As one of them shouts at Ava, my hand goes to a silver knife at my waist. I remember her leaping in front of me when the vampires found us in the woods, fierce and brave even with three enemies against us.

Slowly, I remove my hand from the knife. Our alliance was only temporary. Any partnership, connection . . . tenderness that I might have felt toward her must now fade away, into the past, like everything else.

I avert my gaze from her and follow the other Flames and our vampire prisoners out of the town.

# PART 3

*Caged*

# CHAPTER 19

## - AVA -

*Three hundred years after the first vampire was created,*
*the empire released the witches it had chained,*
*for there was a fiercer enemy to face, and the empire knew*
*they could not do it alone.*

—JOURNAL BY CALLUNA MENTARA

Two years ago, standing in a cold, dark room, I whispered, "Mom, is that you?"

It was the middle of winter, yet she hadn't lit the fireplace. We used to spend hours in front of it, reading books and braiding each other's hair. Tonight only a flickering candle stood on an end table.

A faint sound reached my ears. Something shifted in the corner. I took one small step toward it and the creature spun around, with wild red eyes, and blood coating its mouth and jaw.

Only it wasn't a creature. It was my mother.

"Ava," she said, and then as an afterthought brushed the

blood off her face. It left a smear. "You're supposed to be in your room."

I gulped, not taking my eyes off the jumbled shape my mother had left twitching there. Zenos must have gone out somewhere, likely to a tavern.

"Nothing is happening yet," I replied.

She reached me in one swift stride, cupping my cheek with her bloodstained hand. "I told you, my sweet, it takes a day to settle in. You'll want to be somewhere secure when that happens."

"I don't want it to happen," I choked out, flinching slightly away from her touch. One hand went to the bruise on my neck. A painting of us and my father stood on the mantelpiece, and in the flickering light of a candle, I could swear his eyes were watching us.

"It is our only choice." Her voice rang with finality, a sharpness to it that was never present before. "Unless you want to go out there . . ." She gestured vaguely toward the window, a flicker of a sad smile on her lips. "You've seen what happens. You've heard it."

She was right. If anyone learned what we'd become, they'd burn us alive.

But I'd done so well at keeping her secret for the past year. Why did she have to change me, too? Tears stung the corners of my eyes. Just a few hours ago, I was with Kaye at school.

"They'll notice I'm missing from school," I say in a choked voice. "They'll look for me and find out. You'll have to keep pretending with the Clarity, and I won't be there to back you up."

As a response, my mother knelt next to the trembling body shrouded in shadows and touched it briefly. When she turned to face me, she dotted her lips with glistening blood, then her cheeks. It was some nightmare version of a clown's makeup.

"They will never know." Her voice glided toward me like snow cascading from the sky. "I will protect us both for as long as I live."

Now, in Chrysalis, my mother approaches me in the line of captives, her face hard and emotionless. I tense up as she leans close and checks the cuffs at my wrists. Then her eyes land on my hair and narrow in distaste. She yanks it back, making me wince, and whispers in my ear, "I told you it was safer inside."

She presses down hard on my hands and I feel the heat of Root witch magic rise up in me, sending an ache through my whole body. As the pain rushes through me, all I can think is one thing: I killed a man. I drank from a human until he collapsed. And I wanted more.

The heat reaches my hands, and my mother lets out a contented sigh, the tension fading from her eyes. She whispers, "Thank you," then vanishes from my side in one light step back to the line of Flame witches.

My knees nearly buckle, and it takes all my energy just to stand upright and focus. I try to remember if she's ever mentioned working with the Flames to keep up her ruse of being a mortal. But our conversations have always been limited, and about me rather than her. I stare at the ground and wonder if she has a plan to save me from this.

Peeking out from the curtain of black hair on my right, I look for my mother and spot her speaking in a low voice with Liander.

And there *she* is. At the sight of Kaye, the first thing I feel is the searing cut of betrayal. I should have known better than to trust her—or anyone.

She stands there with a stoic expression, hands held behind her back, like this is exactly how she expected everything to go and she feels no remorse at all. Her jaw is set tense as she stares at my mother, her eyes calculating. Some deep part of me wants to know whether she's had a chance to figure out if my mother is truly Calluna's killer, and wants to comfort her if it's true. Then I shove it down and turn away. There's no point in wondering; she's just like everyone else who wants to control me, own me, and use me. She is nothing.

I keep my hair in front of my face so she can't tell I'm looking at her, but I stare daggers at her as the group begins to move. That story about her mother and wanting to honor her memory, the tears, the shading of her eyes whenever she spoke of her loss . . . all of it was a lie. Turning on me must have been her plan all along. There was never a chance to win her trust. The betrayal stings and cuts deep, far deeper than I ever expected it could go—the girl I'd looked for from my window, the girl I'd shared all my secrets with, the girl I'd always gone to when I was scared or afraid. Something heavy weighs on my heart and pushes me down until I feel like I'm mired in a pit of grief. Like I've lost someone dear to me, too; like I've finally, finally stopped expecting my old friend to come back.

And now I don't even want her back.

The chains at our feet clink together as we exit the court-yard and proceed down the road. My ankle is healed now because of the blood I drank, but I feel weakened and slow from my mother draining me. The residents of Chrysalis come out to jeer at us as we're led out of the village, and I wonder if any of them is a relative of the man I drank from.

*The man I killed.* My head spins. In the moments I drank from him, it felt like I wasn't even entirely in control of my body. The thirst guided me where it wanted me to go, and my desperation to finally fight back helped it along.

My legs are shaky and my thoughts scattered. In the past hour, I've overheard rumors and guesses of where we might be going from the other prisoners: to Arborren to be burned; to an underground cell deep in the heart of the woods; to the capital, where we'll be experimented on to figure out a way to destroy our species forever. I need to find a way out of here, to get to Casiopea, who will protect me.

Or maybe the vampire queen will come for us instead, to free us from these traitors and thieves and make us a part of her family.

These hopes keep my head high on the last few blocks out of Chrysalis. In the distance, at the tree line, I make out a group of cages on wheels, and I stiffen. Those are entirely silver.

Someone walks into me from behind and grunts; another prisoner.

"Sorry," I whisper. Behind me, they take a deep breath and step back into place, waiting for me to move.

We're in the trees now, lined up in front of the cages. Without the sounds and smells of the town, I notice all the different sensations around me and pick out something strange. The prisoner who was behind me . . . I look to my right to see that it's a boy a few years younger than me, his chest rising and falling with breath.

I do a double take. He has no reason to pretend to be human. I strain my ears, and there it is . . . the rapid beat of a pulse. The boy is terrified.

The boy is human.

My mouth falls open, and I look at the line of prisoners. I quickly find the four vampires who escaped and then were rounded up by the fire witches, including the ones Kaye and I had met in the woods a few days ago. But there are around twenty prisoners total. Are there any other humans here, like the boy next to me?

My mind races with wondering why he's here, but I don't have time to think on it, nor do I have time to parse out the different scents and sounds around me to figure out who else might be human. The cage doors swing open with a creak of metal, and two Flame witches stand at each one, gesturing people inside. I search for Kaye immediately; she's at the next cage over, waving for prisoners to enter. Four cages, five of us in each.

I grit my teeth as I walk inside, as if I'm expecting the silver doors to close over me like the maw of a great beast. It's as if I'm stepping back into my attic, and the feel of it presses over me like a shroud.

I walk to one corner, careful not to touch the silver bars behind me while making space for the other prisoners. If I sit on that floor, I'll have scars for days—if they even plan on keeping me alive that long, of course. The sensation of silver prickles through my boots like tiny needles along my feet, but I do my best to ignore it. I'm grateful for the boots, even though Kaye gave them to me, because they help dull the pain of the silver. The human boy now leans against the bars with his arms crossed, head down. Another human enters and stands next to the boy, shrinking away from the rest of us: me, Nuira, and her companion.

The cages start moving then, pulled by a pair of horses at the front of the line. The pale green leaves, vines, and hanging branches brush against the bars of the cage as we move forward, and I find myself hoping the vines will reach down and pull our captors away, that the ground will open up and swallow them and let us go free. The Flames and hunters march alongside the cages, armed with silver.

My mother and Liander walk at the front, while Zenos trails behind with a dutiful expression. I cringe as I remember how he slithered past me when we were still in Chrysalis, a gloating smile on his face. If my mother manages to save me, I would be stuck with her and Zenos again . . . my mind shuts down, not wanting to imagine the punishments.

But is she planning to save me or let me die? I have no idea what she's up to, nor why she's traveling with the Flames. None of them seems surprised about her presence, or this journey with vampire captives. All this time, I thought they'd simply kill us if they caught us.

Unless this has something to do with my mother's plan to destroy the Bone Wall. She'll keep me in this cage if it's convenient for her somehow.

So either she's lying to the Flames about her goals, or they're also in on it. Perhaps if I expose her plans to the Flames, I can escape in the ensuing confrontation. But first I'd need to be sure of where the Flames stand.

Once we're deeper in the trees, the scent of rot fills the air, and all goes quiet around us except the trundling of the cage wheels. . . . A snarl comes from the male vampire.

I turn just in time to see him leap for the boy, knocking his head back to the bars. Nuira follows to attack the human woman. I lunge toward them both and try to shove them aside, but it's difficult with my hands still bound.

"Leave them alone!" I hiss. "They're not our enemies."

The male vampire shoves me off, hard enough that I fly back

into the bars behind me. His fangs flash right before Liander's voice rings out. "Light them up."

A burst of light sears my vision as one of the witches sends flames at our cage. I drop to the floor, not caring how much the silver stings as long as I'm away from the flames. Heat rages around me, and I expect death at any moment. A sob breaks out of my throat, and I curl myself tighter against the silver floor.

It takes me a long time to come out of it, when I realize I'm not being burned alive. Tears streak down my face as I sit up. The walls and roof of the cage are lit up with flames in a way that reminds me of when Kaye first found me in the woods and wrapped fire around my ankles and wrists. Those flames hadn't actually touched my skin, but I suspect these ones definitely would. The other two vampires huddle next to me, while the humans press closer to the fire just to get away from us.

Pulling my knees to my chest to keep as much of my body away from the silver floor as possible, I settle in for what will be a long day.

We travel for hours, and the Flames reignite the fire every so often to keep it going. My thirst grows sharper, searing the back of my throat. My vision feels hazy, and my muscles are slow and lethargic with the need for blood. Why would the Flame witches put us all in one cage, unless they're hoping for us to attack the humans? I breathe in, catching the scent of blood coursing inside their veins, and it takes all my self-control to not think about how sweet it would taste.

I don't recognize this part of me that truly wants to drink from humans, that actually liked drinking from that man earlier, but it is strong. I remind myself we're all prisoners and I don't want to hurt them.

A darker part of me wonders why I should care about the humans at all. I try to shake the thought away, but it clings to the back of my mind, persistent and venomous, just like the memory of how satisfying that man's blood was.

I killed a human, no matter how lost and confused I was when it happened. I'm not innocent. The realization hits me like an anvil. For all my efforts, they might have been right about me all along.

Once night falls, the cages pull to a stop in a wide clearing. A witch who'd set our cage aflame lifts his hand and then slowly closes it in a fist. The flames ebb away, and I blink to adjust to the new darkness. The first thing I see is my mother standing some twenty feet away, looking over her shoulder toward the cage I'm in. She averts her gaze the moment I meet her eyes.

Ahead of us, the hunters and witches begin setting up camp in a place where there are logs spread out around an extinguished fire. The campsite is large, comfortably fitting these four cages, the horse, and all the witches and hunters. My mother and Zenos set up a tent for themselves and whisper furtively to each other, but even I can't hear them over all the noise of camp.

Kaye and one of the hunters are going to each cage with gourds. Sniffing the air, I catch the scent of blood and it pulls me to the edge of the cage. I try to reach an arm through the bars as if that will get me closer to the blood, gritting my teeth against the bite of the silver. But I can only fit up to my elbow through; it's too narrow for anything wider.

Kaye comes to our cage and tends to one of the other vampires first. She withdraws a glass tube from her pocket and fills it with blood from the gourd, then places it on the cage floor in front of one of the other vampires, who immediately lunges for it. I keep my eyes on her as the hunter gives me my serving of blood. It reminds me so much of my mother's rationed servings, and how Kaye had realized the sinister purpose of it, that I squeeze hard enough to nearly break the tube. I throw it back in one swallow, closing my eyes to savor the taste. It has the gamy scent of an animal's blood, but I don't mind at this point.

When I open my eyes, my vision is brighter, energy floods through me, and I can think more clearly than before. I toss the glass tube out of the cage, ignoring how the hunter scoffs at me. Kaye's hands and lips tremble as she passes a tube of blood to the human boy.

The boy makes a disgusted face at the blood, and then, in a hoarse voice, says, "Water."

It takes a moment for Kaye to realize he's not taking the blood; she seems lost in her own thoughts, still hasn't even looked at any of us. The hunter comes up next to her and draws a separate flask from his belt to give to the human boy. The boy drinks the water, some of it spilling down his neck, then hands the rest of the flask to the woman next to him. Kaye finally looks up and her mouth drops open.

It hits me then: she had no idea there are human prisoners. Satisfaction surges through me at the thought; if these humans die with us, will she finally feel like the killer she is?

She gathers herself a moment later, wiping all signs of shock from her face, as she and the hunter move away. I lunge across the cage, slamming into the silver bars, but I don't care about the pain. They both whip around.

"Hey, traitor," I whisper, and Kaye stiffens at my words. "Liar. Killer. You know I'm talking to you, so look at me. Have you realized you're a hypocrite yet?"

Slowly, Kaye's eyes meet mine for the first time since she turned me over. They're a glassy green, filled with a hundred emotions. I search them, trying to find remorse, guilt, doubt, anything of the sort. She draws her mouth into a tight line as someone shouts her name; one of the other Flames, calling her to join their celebration.

"How will you do it then?" I ask in a flat voice. "Take a silver blade to my throat while I rest? Fling fire at me with my back turned?"

"Never while your back is turned." She gulps, and I can practically hear her trembling where she stands. "Never with your eyes closed, Ava."

"Does the way you kill me even matter? I'll be in a cage no matter what."

After a pause, with tears in the corners of her eyes, Kaye says in a thick voice, "If I were to annihilate you, I'd do it in a way that you knew exactly what was happening. I owe you at least that much."

"Annihilate," I scoff. "The word is 'kill.' Giving it a different word doesn't make you innocent."

Her gaze goes to the ground again, and she walks away without another word.

I know I must look like a true monster now to the humans and witches watching me, but I no longer care. That's all they'll ever see me as anyway.

At least a monster fights back.

# CHAPTER 20

## · KAYE ·

*A flame needs air to survive,*
*and all fires die eventually.*
*All Flames must learn sacrifice,*
*and how to act without hesitation.*

—TRAINING ACADEMY FOR
YOUNG WITCHES OF ARBORREN

The rest of the boys from Tristan's and my patrol were sent home; this final trip, deeper into the woods, is only to be made by Flame witches who succeeded. The victors include me, Tristan, Liander, and three other Flame witches. I join them in a circle around a campfire, and Liander passes me a mug of ale. Tristan sits next to me, but instead of trying to join the older witches' conversation like he usually does, he leans toward me with a concerned expression.

"Av—the bloodsucker jumped at you," he whispers, his brow furrowed. "Does she have a grudge against you?"

I give a jerky nod, still shaken by my confrontation with Ava, and the human boy in there with her. Why is there a human in that cage? We have no reason to be capturing a human, yet I'm the only Flame here who seems to be bothered by what's happening. Tristan seems lost, too, but I don't know how much I can trust him.

We trekked north for hours. What even is north? Arborren is south, the mountains lie east, so tall and impenetrable that the land beyond is untouched by the empire. West is the archipelago connecting the eastern provinces with the capital. The sea sweeps north as well, but how far? I remember the lake I used to go to with my mother and Tristan; it was north as well, even though it's likely dried up now. I know the Flames and hunters used to have outposts spread all over the forest, but those have dwindled. So where are we going?

Nothing makes sense, but I'm afraid to ask Liander or the other Flames. As much as Liander praised me earlier, I know any sign of questioning the Flames will mark me as a traitor. I've already spent my whole life tiptoeing around them and what's expected of me, working hard to fit the image of a perfect Flame so they'd believe I belong with them. Yet I know, deep down, that even one mistake would ruin all of that.

Gripping the mug between my hands just to have something to hold on to, I lean toward Tristan and say, "Meet me behind the tents after this is over, all right? I want to talk."

If he notices how unsettled I look, he doesn't mention it. He nods and turns back to the rest of the group to join their conversation. As Eugenia Serení and her husband Zenos join us, Liander introduces her to me.

"Eugenia, I'd like you to meet Kaye Mentara, our witch who found your daughter."

Eugenia's eyes spark as they meet mine, and Zenos looks at me with a hint of curiosity in his gaze. It takes all my self-control to smile at them. Zenos's slimy gaze seems to crawl along my skin, and I want to hurl this mug at him.

"Kaye Mentara? I remember you. Calluna's daughter." The name seems to send a ripple through the circle of gathered witches—shuttered eyes, averted gazes. A stab of irritation hits me; every single one of them wishes we would stop talking about her, like her death is something shameful that should just be brushed aside. Eugenia continues, "She'd be so proud to see you now. You'll be very well appointed once we return to Arborren, Miss Mentara."

Tristan tenses up next to me, and I can tell he's confused by her words—why praise me and not him? He looks toward his father, but Liander is in conversation with another Flame witch and doesn't seem to have heard.

"Thank you, Eugenia." And then, before I can stop them, the words come out: "My mother always wanted me to have great opportunities. She thought it would be a shame if I were kept inside all day."

Eugenia's smile flickers briefly, but she hitches it back up, probably convincing herself my words were a mere coincidence.

Whatever I choose to do next, however I choose to confront her about my mother, I know I can't act rashly. My thoughts have been too distracted, my emotions weak, ever since I entered the woods and began traveling with Ava.

Traitor. Liar. Killer.

Each word she called me hits me like a punch to the chest. All the things I'd seen her as for so long, she now sees in me. But I can't afford to linger on this, to have any more contradictions or wavering. Everything I do now must be carefully calculated, especially where Eugenia is concerned.

"I admit I was surprised," I say in a low tone so only Eugenia and Tristan can hear me. "I thought your daughter went to Erlanis City two years ago to study."

Eugenia lets out a perfectly rehearsed sigh. "Once she was turned, I sent her to live in the forest with the other vampires. I know I should have turned her over, but . . . can you blame me for wanting to give her a chance? She was my daughter for so long, after all. I was just as surprised to find her here as you. I'm grateful that Liander here understands how difficult it was for me."

It takes all my effort not to yell at her that she's lying. Squeezing my hands into fists over my knees, I say slowly, "Yes, I know that most people in Arborren would not be as understanding. My mother—"

Tristan delivers a sharp elbow to my ribs and I grunt. Eugenia turns away to speak with Zenos and I snap, "What?" to Tristan out of the corner of my mouth.

In a low hiss of a voice, he says, "Whatever questions you have, keep quiet. For now."

Just then, his father stands, beaming, and raises a glass toward us.

"Congratulations to our two young Flame witches, Tristan and Kaye. Tonight, we celebrate their individual successes."

I bow my head in gratitude as cheers rise up from the hunters and witches gathered. Tristan sits up straighter next to me, smiling broadly, but it doesn't quite reach his eyes.

As the applause dies down, Eugenia lets out a soft sigh. "I wish I could join, but I'll need to scout ahead."

It's an offhand comment, one that no one in our circle seems surprised by, but my ears perk up. Scout ahead for what?

My curiosity only rises as I see her and Liander whisper to each other, with occasional interjections from Zenos, as the evening continues. An hour goes by before I take even one sip of my ale, having forgotten it was there, but Tristan has already finished his, and he's as quiet as me.

In the smoke curling upward from the fire, in the dark spots beyond our small circle, in the quiet breaths of the forest around us, I feel my mother's ghost again, and imagine a disappointed expression on her face. If she saw me now . . . would she see a hero, or a killer?

"Follow me in a few minutes," I whisper to Tristan, then rise and walk toward the darkened trees at the outskirts of the clearing, behind the tents. I feel Liander's eyes on me as I do and hope he just assumes I'm heading off to sleep early.

I breathe in the scent of the trees, crinkling my nose against the rot. The deeper we go, the more poignant it becomes. If these woods aren't already dead, they're certainly dying. None of the other Flames has even said anything about it, and only Tristan seems the slightest bit disturbed by it. I'd noticed his confused expression while we'd walked here all day, the way his eyes lingered on the bone-white trees and the sinister sway of vines near our necks and arms.

Footsteps crunch in the leaves behind me and I turn, expecting to see Tristan, but it's Zenos standing there, beady eyes fixed on me from where he stands in the shadows. Everything Ava had said he'd done comes back to me, and I feel myself freeze where I'm standing. I wonder how many people he's dragged into the woods and drained of blood so he could stay close to Eugenia and Ava; I wonder if he's thinking about doing the same to me.

"Kaye." He says my name softly, like he's tasting it. He takes a step toward me, and I hold my ground, wanting to burn him where he stands; he's a human, not a vampire, but he's worse than any of those locked up in the cages here. "You should be proud of yourself, becoming a full Flame witch now. But you're still young, still in need of guidance. I know you'll graduate once we return to Arborren. Have you considered you might benefit from a contact with the emperor? I am, after all, his relation."

He holds out a small card to me, a twisted smile still in place as he waits for me to take it. From here, I can see it's a business card.

*I'll take it and then leave,* I think quickly, then reach up to grab the card.

When I tug on it, though, his hand slides up my wrist and forearm—a tight grip, but he traces light circles on my arm with his thumb.

I flinch back, everything in me recoiling from him, and the card drops to the ground between us.

"You're disgusting," I whisper. All I can think of is Ava, the halting in her voice as she spoke of him.

More footsteps approach the tents, crunching in the leaves, and Tristan comes up to us both. He places a hand on Zenos's shoulder and gives him a tense smile.

"Good evening, Zenos, I'm here to speak with Kaye. She's been waiting for me." He gives Zenos a look I remember—the one he used to use when he defended me from bullying at school, or reminded me to be careful when we were in the forest, though he never held me back from doing what I wanted. My heart aches at the thought, and as Zenos walks away with a grimace, I stare at Tristan for a long moment—imagining he's still my friend who will listen and be there for me.

"Thank you, Tristan," I breathe out, hating how much my voice shakes.

Tristan gives me a tense nod. "I've noticed the way he follows students home from the school. I always follow after him, too, and he usually notices me and then gives up." His eyes narrow at me, and a tic goes off in his jaw. "What did Eugenia mean back there, Kaye?"

Twisting my fingers together uncomfortably, I find it hard to meet his eyes for a moment. What if I share my concerns with him and he exposes me as a traitor? But I have no one else to tell. My familiar, deep loneliness tugs at my chest. I want to tell him, even though it terrifies me.

In a low voice, I say, "You should talk to your father, Tristan. He said he would give me the prize of graduation, and that Eugenia would support him because I'd helped find her daughter." A deep, dark pain flashes in Tristan's eyes, and any bravado he'd had begins to fall away. I step toward him, taking his hands and squeezing them. "I'm sorry, Tristan. I don't know why he'd pick me over you, when you came first and caught two vampires. But isn't that strange? That Eugenia wants to congratulate me for catching her daughter, and that your father bought her lie about sending Ava to the forest? Tristan, there are humans here in those cages, not just vampires, and I don't know—"

He scoffs at me, and when he speaks next, each word is broken, like he's trying to hold back tears the whole while. "My father lied to my face about giving me a fair chance for graduation when he wanted you to take it all along. What makes you think he'd tell me what we're doing here? I don't know where we're going, and I don't know why humans are in those cages. But I do know that traitors get themselves killed, Kaye." He runs a hand over his eyes and his voice grows more panicked as he says, "How do you think I felt when I saw Ava in that courtyard in Chrysalis? I can't watch anything bad happen to you, too. I've been trying so hard for the last two years to just—do the right thing, but nothing I ever do is good enough for him."

Without a backward glance, he storms off, back toward the campfire, his fists clenched the whole time with flames sparking at his knuckles. I stand here for a few moments as my shock fades. I understand his fear, but . . . like my mother, I can't stop myself from asking questions. I can't stop myself from wanting to find the truth.

My gaze trails back toward the cages with the vampires and humans.

Ava would have drunk from more humans if I hadn't been in the forest with her. She needed to be stopped, like all the others.

*But she was desperately thirsty,* the traitorous voice whispers. *She carried me into Chrysalis while her own thirst worsened.*

As my eyes find Ava in the cage, her gaze tilted toward the sky, eyes bright, her hands still locked behind her so she can't use her Root magic, I once again doubt everything I know.

I need to be alone for a while. I walk into the tent that I'm sharing with an older woman Flame witch, and roll out my sleeping bag. But after tossing and turning in it for a good twenty minutes, I know I won't be able to sleep. Sitting up, I brush my hair back from my face, which is covered in sweat even with the chill outside. I pick up the sack Ava carried and dump everything out. There really isn't much. Just my mother's journal, and . . . My breath catches in my throat.

That woven blue material I noticed at the inn . . . I didn't realize it was the scarf I gave Ava as a gift a few years ago. I'd seen it on a vendor's cart in the market and, knowing that Ava was always feeling cold, I bought it for her. She loved it and wore it to an outdoor theater performance that evening, where we sneaked away halfway through the show and talked behind the stage. For one wild moment, our heads had leaned toward each other, and I'd desperately wanted to kiss her. But we didn't.

My heart sinks. I had no idea she kept the scarf. With trembling hands, I place the scarf back in the bottom of the sack along with the journal. Then I gather more spare supplies from the tent. Some food rations, two full waterskins, a slingshot, a rope, a whistle, a compass, and a few more silver daggers.

I freeze, remembering the knife I gave Ava. That's not here, and it wasn't on the bed in the inn either.

Ava was there, too, and she . . . I inhale sharply. I remember when I first went to her house to capture her, but she'd escaped out of the window and left Zenos bleeding. He'd probably tried to stop her escaping. And we saw him in the forest recently. What if he came for her now, and she escaped through the window at the inn?

Maybe the knife was the only thing she could grab before leaping out of the window. If he hadn't shown up, she would have stayed in the inn, and would be safe now.

I move toward the entrance of the tent and pull back one of the flaps. The cages' silver bars shine in the light of the flames. Ava is resting now, her eyes closed with her knees pulled up to her chest. I grimace, knowing it can't be comfortable to have so much silver around her. She's smart to rest so that she can heal from whatever pain she feels now, but the moment she wakes, the pain will return. It's a futile effort, but it's all she has.

That, and my knife. I gulp, not knowing what to do, but . . . I feel no need to report her. I know any good Flame witch would prevent a vampire from having any weapons at all, but . . .

if having my knife gives her some form of comfort, then she should keep it. It's the least I can do.

*Traitor.* The word springs up from my thoughts, sharp and insidious, and my breath cuts short.

In the Flames' mission of ridding this world of vampires, we're taught that unity is key. Work together or else the vampires will win. Never doubt yourself or your team.

But what's so wrong with asking questions?

If more people had asked questions when my mother died, maybe I wouldn't be alone in finding her killer.

If more people had asked questions when Ava disappeared, maybe her suffering wouldn't have gone ignored.

My mother asked questions and wrote a whole journal full of them that she had to slip to Ava without even telling me about it. She knew what she did was dangerous, and maybe even then she could tell how dedicated I was to the Flames. It would have been too risky to confide in me.

As I peer out from the tent, Eugenia and Zenos rise from the campfire, and Liander wishes them luck. I don't trust anything those two are up to. I move behind the row of tents where no one can see me, then watch as Eugenia and Zenos enter their own tent.

Liander wouldn't want me to question and criticize them, but that goes against all his lessons of staying focused and vigilant. How much, exactly, does he know about Eugenia, her plans, and what she's done?

For a moment, I feel like my mother's ghost is standing beside me, waiting for me to do something: to bring justice for her; to restore her name; to be the kind and intelligent daughter she taught me to be instead of the fury-driven girl I've become. To listen to her voice instead of Liander's.

A moment later, Eugenia and Zenos come out of their tent with packs strapped to their backs. Without a backward glance to the rest of the camp, they turn and disappear into the woods.

I wait only two breaths before following.

# CHAPTER 21

## - AVA -

*Casiopea became the vampire queen because she was the first, the matron of a species,*
*and all vampires feel kinship with the one who turned them.*
*But not all of them choose to follow.*
—JOURNAL BY CALLUNA MENTARA

Night falls deeper, and my fellow prisoners shuffle around one another, trying to find space in this confinement. The other two vampires regard me warily, like they're trying to figure out whose side I'm on. I'm not ready to speak to them yet, but I know I will soon—at least to try planning an escape. The humans look like they're about to pass out from exhaustion.

I'll keep these two humans safe while I can, since they're prisoners as well, but the Flame witches? When I get out of here, they'll meet the same fate as that man I drank from in Chrysalis. I straighten slightly, feeling a surge of confidence. Drinking from a human was something I'd never thought I would do, but here I am, with stains of that man's blood still on my clothes, and my guilt ebbs away more by the second. These witches, these hunters, they still convince themselves they're better than us. We're all killers; they're just allowed to get away with it.

When I get out of this cage, I'll show them how dangerous I can really be. Starting with Kaye.

I watch as she slips through the trees after my mother and Zenos. I don't know what they're up to, but Kaye could be following them to confront my mother about Calluna's death—or perhaps because she saw the human boy in the cage and wanted to find out more about where we were going, and couldn't get a clear answer from the Flames, so she seeks one from my mother instead. I scoff under my breath. Of course she would put in that effort for a human boy she'd never met, but not me. If these humans weren't in the cages with us, she'd gladly burn us all.

The air feels colder, and I rub my hands along my arms to try to bring them warmth, remembering with a pang how Kaye used her fire to bring us both comfort in the cold autumn nights.

"You're from Arborren, aren't you?" says a cold voice from behind me. I give a stiff nod, looking over my shoulder at the two vampires and two humans I've been ignoring for most of the evening.

"How did you get away with living in that town?" asks the other vampire, Nuira, leaning toward me with her chin balanced on her hands.

With a long sigh that blows hair out of my face, I turn to them. I don't feel like telling them everything about me, but I understand their curiosity.

"I was kept there, by someone who didn't want to see me thrown in a cage like this. So they kept me in a cage of their own." Silence falls, and the humans have turned to me, too, their ears perked to listen. With all the attention, nerves prickle through me, and I change the subject. "Do any of you know where we're going?"

Nuira shakes her head slowly. "All I know is this isn't the first time that cages full of vampires and humans have been brought through the woods. I've seen it before, from a distance; with the same group of Flame witches leading them, and that vampire who's pretending to be mortal."

My mother. I try not to show any reaction.

"It's always around fifteen or twenty captives total, and they're taken a few times per year." Nuira turns to the humans. "Where are you two from?"

"Arborren," the boy mutters, his voice shaking over the simple word.

"Solem," says the woman with unshed tears in her eyes.

A chill goes down my spine at their words, and I feel sick. Whatever my mother is up to, I'd bet my own fangs it has something to do with her plans to tear down the Bone Wall, and she's roped the Flame witches into it somehow. It's imperative I get out of here, find Casiopea, and stop my mother.

Night deepens and silence falls in the cage again. The witches and hunters rest for a few hours before resuming our journey. With a jerk, the cages start moving, trundling through deep grooves in the earth that have clearly been made by similar journeys in the past.

I think my vision is playing tricks on me, because as we travel in the predawn hours and fog roils thickly through the trees, I see eyes blinking down at me from above. Deeper in the woods, hands reach out from the fog like they're grasping for these cages, and eyes glint with hunger, like those of the vampires who attacked Kaye and me.

The whispers come back to me then, calling for help once more from within the trees, but I hear anger in their voices now. *Help us. Help us.* Their calls take on a far more demanding, urgent voice than before. I wonder if it really is the old gods—the Arkana—calling me. If they are, what would they want with a vampire? Maybe Calluna's journal has more information, but I lost it when I fled from the inn in Chrysalis.

Through the bars of the cage, I stare at the hunters and the witches, imagining the earth swallowing each of them, the roots choking away their lives. And then I imagine their blood on my tongue.

The vines hanging down brush against the cage bars, sometimes wrapping around them briefly before letting go. They're sinister, lurking, waiting for a chance to strike. I look down at the hilt of the knife Kaye gave me, tucked in my boot. As long as my hands are tied behind my back and I can't use my powers, that knife is the only weapon I have.

When dawn light breaks through the fog with a pale silver glow, I beckon to the others in my cage. The two vampires lean close, but the humans watch me with wary eyes.

In a low voice, I say, "If you want to get out of here . . . I have a plan."

# CHAPTER 22

## · KAYE ·

*Tales of mortals who fall in love with bloodsuckers abound in our history.*
*Something alluring exists in the immortal, dangerous predator.*
*But all of these stories end the same:*
*with blood spilled, trust broken, and a life lost.*
—ORAL HISTORIES OF ERLANIS EMPIRE

The fog grows thicker, providing me with cover as midnight falls. The fog seems more insidious at night, its cold fingers drawing me in. I keep my steps light over the roots and twigs, grateful for the mud and fallen leaves that cover the sound of my steps. I time my breaths with Zenos's wheezing as he tries to keep up with Eugenia's quick pace.

After a good twenty minutes, Eugenia comes to an abrupt stop and hisses to Zenos over her shoulder, "I know you're a human, but try a little harder to walk quietly."

He mumbles an apology, and I smirk a little. I don't like Eugenia, but I enjoy watching her boss around Zenos.

More time passes, and we venture deeper into the woods.

Eugenia must be distracted—her gaze flicks to the tree branches above, and she stops at random points to look into moonlit clearings, like she's searching for something.

"Where is the queen? Is she all the way at the tree?" Zenos asks, his voice the only sound in the dead night.

Eugenia's hands curl into fists and she looks like she's seconds away from slapping him for making so much noise.

"Yes, she's likely at the tree—it's where she can protect it. If you learn to walk quieter, maybe we can reach it before she even knows we're here."

With that, she turns and walks along the path at a quicker pace, with Zenos right behind her. On stiff legs, I follow after Eugenia and Zenos, taking great care not to trip over anything in the dark.

Then I remember the berries Ava gave me. Reaching into a pouch at my waist, I pull one out and place it in my mouth. It has a slightly bitter taste, but isn't unpleasant.

As I swallow, a twig cracks behind me.

My entire body freezes. I jerk my head around, searching for what could have made the sound, but I see nothing. The night vision isn't working yet. I flex the fingers of one hand, wishing I could use my flames to light the path ahead, but that would only draw attention to me. I might try to use shadows and light to make myself invisible, but that didn't work for me when Ava and I ran from the vampires a few days ago, so I don't want to waste time trying now.

I follow Eugenia and Zenos for a long stretch of time in utter silence, and my vision grows clearer, almost like it's a gray dawn rather than the dead of night. I feel eyes watching me from everywhere, but I don't dare look up, fearful I'll miss a vampire right next to me waiting to sink their fangs into my neck. I grip my knives tighter, and part of me wishes Tristan or Ava were here to help—but I know I have to do this alone. I have to find out what's going on with Eugenia, the forest, and the Flame witches, even if it makes me question every truth I know.

The path ahead widens, and I expect us to come into a clearing, but instead, a dirt road opens up in the trees. Fog settles over it all. I can't see the sky, or what we're headed toward. The path slopes slightly upward, trees rising like soldiers standing sentinel at each side as Eugenia and Zenos walk along the path. I keep to the trees, skirting the edges. Mist glitters in the air around me and leaves droplets on my skin.

Eugenia and Zenos disappear over the lip of the path, and I rush to it, not wanting to lose sight of them. When I come to the crest, my eyes widen at the sight before me.

The path has dipped into a valley, but it's not a valley of plains and fields; there's a singular, massive tree, boughs laden with heavy, silver leaves. Its roots protrude from the earth and skate toward the edges of the valley, up the hills and into the forest, like veins.

"The Heart Tree," I whisper, my whole body going cold for a reason I don't understand. They taught us about this in training, the center of the vampire queen Casiopea's domain.

Above the tree, faint white slivers float upward like tiny stars. But they fade into the gray sky above, invisible to me down here. That must be the specks of bone dust and shards that make up the Bone Wall.

The mist rolling down into the valley, seeping through gaps in the branches and leaves of the Heart Tree, almost seems to breathe. The forest feels more alive here than ever before.

After a moment, I resume following Eugenia and Zenos, who

clings to his wife's side like he expects to be mauled by a vampire at any second.

They come into the shadows of the tree, and I crouch deep into the wild grass that covers the valley. It all smells like rot and dried blood. The scents make me dizzy and nauseous, but I force myself to focus. Vines swing down from the great oak tree and touch Zenos's neck and shoulders. He tenses, eyes nearly bugging out of his head.

"Leave him be," calls out Eugenia in a clear, bell-like voice. "He is not yours to take."

A rattling whisper rises from the depths of the fog, like it's coming from all sides of the valley at once.

"I'll be watching your progress, with my spies in the trees. I'll know if you try anything. You are getting greedy, Eugenia."

The voice is gravel and wind and rustling leaves at once. It raises the hair on the back of my neck, and I know it can be none other than Casiopea herself.

The tone that Casiopea uses with Eugenia reminds me of a mother trying to teach her child a lesson, and a suspicion sparks in me: Did Casiopea turn Eugenia into a vampire herself? I suck in a sharp breath, remembering Ava telling me that a vampire had saved Eugenia in the woods and then changed her.

"It is all part of a greater effort," Eugenia bites out. "One that you and I both benefit from."

"If it threatens my tree, I don't—"

"Do you want the sacrifices or not? There are fifteen, as well as five vampires for your army."

Eugenia's words send a shudder through me, and I think of the humans in the cages. I don't know why Casiopea needs Eugenia to bring her humans, let alone vampires, but that's clearly what's happening.

As Eugenia waits for Casiopea's reply, Zenos begins to wander. With his hands held behind his back, he gazes out at the valley as he walks. Keeping low and hardly daring to breathe, I move backward in a crouch, hoping the grass will cover me until I reach the trees. But I'll be exposed as soon as the valley starts to slope upward.

The moment Zenos turns and walks in another direction, I'll run for it. I've already gotten some information—Eugenia is bringing sacrifices to Casiopea, Eugenia might be planning something that hurts the Heart Tree, and Casiopea even considers her a threat. But if they're a threat to each other, why work together?

If Liander already knows this and is willingly handing over humans to the vampire queen . . . I gulp, not wanting to believe it. But everything about the past few days, how Liander and Eugenia are constantly plotting together, the mystery surrounding this journey into the deep woods . . . Liander must already know.

And if he does . . . what did my mother find out about it?

If Eugenia is a threat to the tree . . . and the tree's roots hold up the Bone Wall . . . does that mean she's trying to tear down the Bone Wall and set vampires free? My breath catches at the realization and my heartbeat slows. I didn't even know that was possible. But of course my mother would want to stop that; it would unleash a flood of vampires into the human world.

I'm so lost in my thoughts, I hardly notice that Zenos has gotten closer. I fling my hands up, hardly thinking of what I'm about to do. Moving my hands quickly, I will the light to hide me. Instead of pushing it away, I draw the light in different paths around me, reflecting light so the only thing Zenos can see is the grass behind me.

I stop breathing. Zenos is five feet away.

I'm in his line of sight, but . . . he doesn't react at all. He stares straight ahead into the valley, and I'm right in front of him.

Slowly, I step backward up the valley and into the trees until I'm alone once more. Dropping the invisibility, I place my hands on my knees and try to catch my breath. I let out an exhausted laugh.

I finally got the invisibility to work. I have no idea if I'll be able to do it again, or what exactly clicked for me this time, but . . . I did it. My mother would be so proud to see me now.

My vision blurs as I stare at the Heart Tree and remember my mother's kind heart, her smile, her laugh. Did she know about these orchestrated sacrifices and Eugenia's plans to tear down the Bone Wall? Did Eugenia kill her to cover it up?

Or did Liander?

It feels like something has grabbed my heart and is squeezing it until I'm nearly gasping for breath. I see spots and stars in front of my eyes. I feel like I'm going to fall over, and I grab on to a tree at the last second.

*Traitors get killed, Kaye,* Tristan had said, repeating a Flame witch mantra. But what if that's just a cover-up so Liander and Eugenia can get rid of anyone who speaks against their plans? Once someone is named a traitor, they're a pariah to society. No one would ask questions about their death.

I begin trekking back through the woods, so shaken I nearly trip several times, like Ava did her first days in the forest.

Once I'm far enough from the valley, I drop down and reach into the sack for my mother's journal. With trembling fingers, my heart aching at the sight of her handwriting, I flip through the pages and try to take in as much as I can.

There are more passages about how afraid she was, but she also described long nights in the forest watching her "old friend." That must be Liander.

*Things have gotten worse since this last trip he and the vampire woman took. He limits the number of graduates who can join, and I worry for them. I see the fear in their eyes and wonder if anyone else, like me, has doubts when they show up dead.*

I put the journal away and swing the sack back around my shoulders. A chill passes down my spine as I do. My mother's words were vague, and I suppose that's on purpose. She wanted to write down the truth, but she was terrified at the same time.

*He limits the number of graduates who can join. . . .*

That reminds me of Liander's competition to see who among my classmates could graduate early. And now only Tristan and I are on this trip. But in recent years, plenty of new graduates have died, caught by vampires in the woods and found later on.

But what if they weren't caught by vampires? What if they, like my mother, found out what was happening and questioned Liander? The answer is clear as day. He's been killing Flame witches who disapprove of what he's doing, and blaming it on vampires. Only the Flames who choose to follow him get to survive.

My mother must have used her invisibility skill to follow him and figure this all out, but Liander found out she was turning on him at some point.

But why is Liander doing this? What does he get out of an arrangement with Eugenia to deliver sacrifices to Casiopea and plot to tear down the Bone Wall?

Whatever is happening, I need to know the truth.

Ava's words come back to me then: *Mortals kill other mortals all the time and you still call them people.*

I thought we were better because it's not in a mortal's nature to kill, like it is for a vampire. But then, doesn't that make us worse when we choose to kill anyway? None of it is good. All of us, mortal and immortal, become brutal and broken the more we fight, and destroy everything around us.

*I'm sorry, Mom,* I think as darkness and silence surround me like a cloak. *You tried to do the right thing, and you died for it.*

For so long, Liander encouraged me to move on from my mother's death and focus on destroying vampires. He wanted me to use my anger and forget everything else—all the kindness and forgiveness my mother taught me.

*I'm sorry, Ava,* I think, with a pang hitting my heart. I know nothing I do will make up for betraying her. But I can still save her from the mess I put her into when all she wanted was to be free.

Maybe I couldn't save my mother, but I can save someone else who strives, against all odds, to be good.

# CHAPTER 23

## - AVA -

*The first few hundred years of vampires' existence were pure bloodshed*
    *until the mortals learned how to fight back.*
                    —ORAL HISTORIES OF ERLANIS EMPIRE

My thirst is starting to return, sharp and poignant. As I lick my dry lips, I notice that one of the Flame witches is watching our cage too closely, and then I do a double take. It's Tristan. I hadn't noticed he was with the group before.

Soon, he walks up to our cage and beckons for me to come closer. I'm wary, but curious to see what he has to say, especially after watching Kaye follow my mother and Zenos into the woods last night. I lean toward my old friend, inches away from the bars of the cage, and wait for him to speak.

"It's been a long time," Tristan says, his jaw held taut. "I can't believe you're . . . you know. Look, I don't know what happened with you and Kaye in the woods. But my father knows you used to be friends." His green eyes fix unerringly on me. "If you've swayed her somehow, or convinced her to follow in her mother's footsteps . . . it's not good for her. I don't know if any of the old Ava is still in there or if becoming a vampire has completely changed you, but . . . Kaye is putting a lot on the line for you. I hope you know that."

I'd tensed up while he spoke, taking in his words and try-ing to make sense of them. Even if Kaye is growing suspicious of what's happening, it's only out of concern for the humans in these cages. A cold certainty forms in my chest like a solid block of ice. Even if her concern extended to me, it would only be a matter of time until she turned on me again. I don't need false promises and lying smiles; I've had enough of that. I shut out any thought of her and scowl at Tristan. He clearly thinks the same as Kaye.

"Kaye only cares about her own twisted sense of justice" is what I finally say to Tristan, nearly spitting the words out. "And with any luck, justice will be served to all of you as well."

The shadows on Tristan's face darken as he peels away, but I push him from my mind the moment he leaves.

Smit, the human boy, lets out a nervous sigh and leans back on the cage bars. The other human, Dorothea, stares out at the trees with a tense expression. She's probably the one who least believes our plan will work. But the two vampires, Tairos and Nuira, look just as ready to break out of here as I am.

The wind has grown colder here, and as the humans breathe, their breath fogs in front of them. I wish I could run my hands along my arms to warm them, but my hands are still caged be-hind my back. For now.

Our group takes an upward slope, steep enough that the fog rolls down in waves. It will cover us in moments.

As the slope grows steeper, I purposely slide inside the cage, stopping myself when I bump into Smit.

"Sorry," I mutter, so the Flames nearby will think it was an accident, then shift slightly so I'm in front of him. In a low hiss, I say, "Cover me."

He and Dorothea both turn away from me to watch the patrols on either side of us, their bodies blocking me from view. I crane my neck to search for the guard who'd led us into this cage and would still have the keys to it. He's a hunter on the left side of the procession, but a bit farther back, trailing behind the rest of the group.

Once I'm free of my bindings, I need to get the keys, then cause a distraction.

Smit begins working behind me. The boy had worked for a silversmith in Arborren and when the man died was left penniless, his parents already dead from a mining accident years ago caused by a Clarity oversight. He suspected he'd been taken as a sacrifice because no one would miss him.

Kaye's silver knife is now in Smit's hands. In minutes, he takes out the screws that hold my bindings in place. The metal clicks open and he coughs at exactly the right moment to cover the sound.

I shift away from Smit, but still face in the same direction so none of the witches and hunters on this side of the cage can see what we've done. I keep my hands within their bindings, but I test them briefly. They're loose. If I thrust my hands to the side, the bindings will fall and I'll be free of them.

Mist fills the air, leaving droplets of water on my skin. I tilt my head back and catch sight of the long, hanging vines among the trees. With a curl of my fist, one of the vines stiffens, connected to me through my Root witch powers. Even as the cages trundle on, I keep my grasp on the vine firm until the hunter with the keys walks past it. Then, as carefully as I can, I direct the vine to reach for the set of keys hooked around his belt.

They jangle as they lift, and the man looks around. Panicking, I shove the vine forward, smacking him in the face. Nuira snorts a laugh behind me as the hunter falls on his backside, and the keys are whisked over to the next vine and up to the branches above our cage, then fall soundlessly into Smit's hands.

We all go still for a moment, waiting to see if anyone noticed what we just did. The ever-present stench of rot fills the air as I think over the next part of the plan: build a cover for us so the Flames won't see what we're doing. Behind me, Tairos and Nuira shift restlessly.

"Almost," I whisper.

I give a stiff nod, then look over my shoulder. Dorothea gulps as she shifts to face Smit, and in one quick slash, he cuts the skin at her collarbone with Kaye's knife. She bites down on her lips to hold back a gasp. In the next moment, Tairos lunges for her. He gently shoves her toward the cage bars, and Dorothea slides toward them, yelling out when she bumps her head on the bars.

"Help!" she cries out as Tairos places his head in the crook of her neck. Her hair covers Tairos's face, so none of the witches or hunters will see that he's not actually drinking from her.

But they can see the blood trickling down her chest, and the dramatic way she rolls her eyes back into her head. I stifle a laugh as the cages creak to a stop halfway up the hill; Dorothea used to be an actress in the city of Solem.

"Get back!" yells one of the hunters, running up to the cage with a silver rod in his hand. He pokes Tairos in the neck with it, and though Tairos tenses up against the burn of the silver, he stays glued to Dorothea.

"Move," Liander barks at the hunter, then raises his hands. I shrink back as flames shoot at the bars, wrapping around them in an instant. Tairos lets go of Dorothea and backs away, but as predicted, Liander doesn't lower the flames. We'll be punished for at least a few hours, like last time.

The sear of the flames makes sweat bead along my forehead, but I fight past the fear and wait until the cages start trundling up the hill once more. The Flames and hunters turn their attention back to the road. The rising orange flames on our cage cover us from view. Once I'm certain no one is looking, Smit uses Kaye's knife to undo everyone else's cuffs. We keep them around our wrists still, but loose and easy to fling off when the time comes.

"Now we wait until the flames come down and their backs are turned," I say in a low voice. "Smit, which key is it?"

"It'll be one of these two," he mutters, pointing out which of the hunter's keys are silver, like the cage itself. I take the keys from him with shaking fingers. I wince every time the silver brushes against my skin; but I have to do this task. A human would be too slow, and this was my idea in the first place.

Minutes later, the cages roll to a stop in a wide, muddy glade. There's a stark chill in the air. As the Flames and the hunters set up this camping ground, one of the Flame witches lowers the flames surrounding our cage. I hold his gaze, glaring at him, and he juts out his chin as if daring me to say something. Keeping the keys carefully concealed behind my back, I bare my fangs at the Flame and let a low hiss slide out of my throat.

Kaye springs into my thoughts for a moment, the look on

her face when I'd nearly drunk from that hunter in the woods. I shove the memory away like an irritating gnat. But there's still a traitorous pang in my heart as I hope she's safe right now.

Nuira nudges me from behind. The Flame is gone now, and the rest of the witches and hunters are busy setting up camp.

My hands are sweating and nearly fumble the keys, but I manage to push one inside the lock and try to turn it.

It doesn't work. Swearing, I grab the other key and push it in. I turn and it clicks.

"Eugenia!" Liander calls from near the trees. He waves as my mother and Zenos reenter the camp from the tree line. My mind goes blank and I drop the keys to the ground.

"Move!" Tairos hisses behind me, shoving me to the side to push the cage door open.

The four of them flood out past me, and as they do, Zenos looks at me from across the camp. His cold gaze jerks me out of my shock. I leap out of the cage behind the rest.

The Flames turn to us, but before they can even lift their hands, Tairos, Nuira, and I each grab one. I hold the woman Flame in my grasp, and she struggles to break free, but I really have gotten stronger since drinking human blood. Her eyes are wide and fearful, and they're the same green as Kaye's. I force her arm down and bring my fangs to her neck.

I pause, hesitating a breath away, every fiber in my body telling me to drink like I'm supposed to, like I deserve, but something in the back of my mind stalls me.

I'm holding down a human, on the verge of drinking from them, but I can't do it. What is wrong with me?

Then I lock eyes with Zenos as he and my mother stride toward us. A growl rises in the back of my throat and I push the witch away from me. I stalk toward Zenos, but Nuira grabs my shoulders and shoves me in the opposite direction. We run into the trees, with Smit and Dorothea behind us.

Smit yells out in pain and drops to his knees not ten feet into the forest. I swing back around to help him up, not sure how he could have fallen, and then Tairos drops, too. A moment later, a hunter is on him, pinning him to the ground with a silver bar at the back of his neck.

The fog behind us clears and my mother steps into the trees, her unblinking gaze on me. With a wave of her hand, Dorothea falls to the ground as well, and then I spot the root wrapping around her ankle. I fight down my shock; I've never seen my mother use the magic she takes from me to actually fight people.

I turn to run, but slam into Liander behind me. His hands wrap around my wrists like steel bindings, and I remember the vampire he burned to ash in Chrysalis. My whole body goes cold, and I hardly notice that my mother has reached me. She stands at my side, a sad smile spreading across her features, then brushes loose strands of hair behind my ears. I snap my fangs at her, but she doesn't even blink.

My mother makes a *tsk*ing noise. "You've ruined your hair, Ava. Do you see what happens when you run off on your own and ignore my warnings? You've completely fallen apart without my help. Come with me, we need to have a chat."

Liander spins me around and prods me back in the direction of the camp. Hunters and Flames line up on either side of me, like a tunnel closing in. My mother and Zenos each grab one of my arms and force me forward.

Nausea rises through me as we reenter the cold, gray camp. My mother whispers something to Liander, but before I can listen, I'm distracted by the shouts and snarls of Dorothea, Smit, Nuira, and Tairos as they're shoved back into our cage by the

Flames. My mother rejoins us, and she and Zenos guide me toward their large tent.

The opening of the tent flaps in a cold gust of wind, and the interior is so dark that fear grips my throat, makes it impossible to even whimper in fear as I'm thrust inside. I land on my knees.

Then my mother steps in front of me and places her hands on my head. A searing heat rises up my chest. For a moment I think she's setting me on fire, and I gasp, but then I notice the familiar golden light that rises off me when she steals my powers. A relieved smile lights up her face, and she closes her eyes, like she's at peace.

When it's done, I fall forward, catching myself just before my face hits the ground. Someone lights a candle on the floor behind me. Zenos spins me around to face my mother, and hooks more silver bindings on my arms—these ones attached to chains held down by heavy locks on either side of the tent floor. He winds them tight so my arms stretch out to both sides. I yank at them and try to rip them out of the earth, but my mother's siphoning has left me weak again. A pit of despair opens in me. Even while I'm fighting and standing up to them, they've still overpowered me.

My whole body feels numb. The burning from the silver cuffs is like a soft prickling pain now, I've grown so used to it.

The wind blows fiercely outside the tent. There's a faint whistling sound to it, and underneath that, a sinister whisper that places fear in my bones.

"I told you, daughter," my mother says as Zenos settles next to her. "You are safest with me."

My mind goes blank except for one thought: *I'm their prisoner again.*

# CHAPTER 24

## · KAYE ·

*When the old emperors paid witches to go after the vampires,*
*all manner of witches attempted to kill them.*
*Storms tried to drown them in hurricanes and floods.*
*Healers attempted to draw the blood out of them and force them*
*to disintegrate.*
*But only Flames could kill them quickly, efficiently, and per-*
*manently.*

—TRAINING ACADEMY FOR
YOUNG WITCHES OF ARBORREN

By midday, I reach the fringe of the trees and the muddy field where the Flames have camped. I squint, searching for Ava within the cages, but she's not inside the one from before. I suck in a sharp breath.

"Where are you?" I whisper, my mind racing. Did Zenos take her somewhere? The thought sends a jolt of fear through me, and I fight the urge to storm into the camp right now. That won't help either of us.

What I need to do is find the hunter with the master set of keys. Wherever she is, I'll be able to break her out.

Then, in front of the cage, a gleam catches my eye: the silver bindings that had held Ava's hands in place are abandoned on the ground. Did they find out about the knife she has? Did they take her for questioning somewhere? There's an old building up ahead that used to be Flame witch barracks in the forest before the vampire population started overwhelming them, and from my lessons, I know there are cells in the basement.

Tristan stands near one of the cages, handing cups of water to the human prisoners while a hunter next to him passes blood to the vampires. I bite my lip at the sight. None of those people deserves to be here, ready to be sacrificed to Casiopea. I've spent far too long believing whatever Liander told me, goaded by a desire for justice for what had happened to my mother. But now I can face the truth, and do something to reverse the wrongs I've committed.

I enter the campsite from the edge of the forest. My skin tingles as I cross the open field, feeling so exposed here after a night shielded by trees and fog. I could attempt to use the invisibility again, but I'll need to talk to them and show myself. To get the keys and find out where Ava is, I have to get information; I have to pretend I'm still on their side.

When I reach Tristan, I whisper his name to catch his attention. His eyes are unreadable as he meets mine, but I can tell he's still hurting from yesterday. A pang hits my heart at the thought; he doesn't even know what his father is truly capable of.

"Where did you go last night, Kaye?" His voice is flat and emotionless. He hands water to the next human and then faces me. "Some vampires almost broke out this morning. They might have caught you alone somewhere."

I look toward the cage where Ava was, my heart clenching

at her absence. If she was one of the vampires that tried to escape, the Flames are likely punishing her now.

"The . . . bloodsucker that I caught, she kept taunting me every time I walked by her cage. I couldn't stand it, I was going to light her up, but I know she's meant for Casiopea." I shake my head while the back of my throat tastes bitter with those words. Then, meeting Tristan's eyes again, I ask, "Did you know that? These people are being taken as sacrifices for her. She's taking the vampires, too, which means none left over for us."

He frowns, his eyes widening at what I just said. "What do you mean, Casiopea? The vampire queen?"

"Before Casiopea comes, would you want to go practice with one of them? We don't have to kill them yet, we could just scare them a little in the woods. Who has the keys, anyway?" I add it as an offhand comment, looking around the campsite with a raised chin, like I'm better than all the hunters here who just wanted to do their job and not have a little sport while they're at it.

"The lead hunter does," Tristan replies. "Kaye, are you sure you're—"

I leave before he can finish speaking, heading toward the hunters' tents on the northern side of the camp. Their leader has the biggest tent, an orange and brown one at the very edge of the field. Tristan is still loyal to his father and might rat me out at any second, but I can't waste any time if Ava is being punished somewhere.

Uneasiness prickles down my spine as I cross the muddy field, feeling eyes on me as I go. With shallow breaths, I spot Liander standing outside another tent. He's speaking to an older Flame witch, but I swear his eyes dart to me a few times.

In ten minutes, I've crossed the length of the camp and arrive outside the final tent. I double-check that no one is around me or watching my progress, then lean toward the tent.

"Hello?" I call, slightly lifting the tent flap. It's completely dark inside. Would he have left his keys in here or is he walking around the camp with them on him?

Footsteps crunch in the dirt behind me. I straighten and turn around—Liander stands in front of me like a brick wall, and I stop myself from yelping. Where did he come from? In seconds, two of his closest Flame witches approach from nearby and flank him, staring me down in a way that reminds me of how people looked at my mother when she was called a traitor.

In the distance, Tristan grips the side of a cage, and he shakes his head at me in a silent warning. My mother's journal entries scream back at me, reminding me of all Liander has done.

"There you are," Liander says in a slow, satisfied voice, and all my hope to get past him vanishes like smoke. "You gave yourself away when you ran away last night, foolish girl. A traitor just like your mother. You never really were one of us after all, were you?"

His words hit hard, twisting my heart in my chest, but then I exhale, feeling the need to prove myself fade away like smoke.

Beyond Liander and the Flames closing in on me, Tristan begins approaching us, his footsteps hesitant. He shakes his head again like he's telling me to stand down, but that only makes me angrier. Liander settles his stone-cold glare on me, waiting for me to speak.

"You killed her," I spit out.

"I had hoped you would learn your place, Kaye," Liander says in a patronizing tone. "But you are just like Calluna. Of course I killed her. She couldn't simply keep to herself, and she didn't approve of our greater mission. There is no other fate for a traitor like that."

He lifts his hands, and I tense up, everything in me screaming to run for my life right now. But instead I raise flames to my own hands, and he's the only thing I see. I imagine the light behind him cascading down like blades; I've read about witches doing that in the past, turning light into weapons, but I don't know if I can do it. A slow, cold breath leaves me. As I'm about to fight Liander, this feels like a tipping point, one that will forever take me away from the Flames and the only life I've ever known. But instead of being terrified, I feel empowered.

As Liander thrusts both his hands forward and a wall of searing flame rushes toward me, I drop my hands and run directly toward the flames. Then I bring my arms up in an X, flinging shadows and smoke through them. The flames swirl around me, sparks singeing my hair and clothes as I cough on the smoke.

I run toward Liander, bringing flames to my hands again. Then I see my mother's ghost beyond him, an inquisitive glint in her eyes. She doesn't move, she doesn't help; she watches, then fades away to show Tristan behind her, one hand outstretched but his feet staying in place.

Liander's men push me to the ground, one of them pinning my arms and legs down. I glare poison up at Liander, black edging the corners of my vision.

When one of them slams the hilt of a silver dagger into my forehead, the last thing I think of is Ava, and how I'm too late to save her, too.

# CHAPTER 25

## - AVA -

*The first vampire attacked mortals due to pure, blind thirst.*
*The first vampire tried to heal mortals, driven by guilt for what*
*she could not control.*
*The first vampire learned how to make new life, out of a need*
*not to be alone.*

——JOURNAL BY CALLUNA MENTARA

The walls of the tent seem to narrow around me, until darkness is everywhere except the faces of my mother and Zenos illuminated by the singular candle. My head throbs, and the domed roof of the tent makes me feel like I'm back in my attic, chained in place with these two keeping me there.

"How could you try to abandon me like that, Ava?" she asks, her voice trailing across the room toward me like a shadow. "After everything I've done to keep you safe."

I want to scream at her, but the words won't come out. There is no point; she caught me again. And in a way . . . she's right. She's the only one who ever fought to protect me. Not like Kaye, who gave me up so easily. I squeeze my eyes shut to hold back tears as my mother continues.

"But I am not angry with you. How could I be? You want our freedom, too. It's time I tell you what we've been working toward. Zenos, give me that."

Zenos hands my mother a vial filled with deep red liquid. She takes the stopper out, and the scent of blood permeates the air. As she gives it a small swirl inside the vial, my throat aches. If I had some blood, it would make me stronger, maybe strong enough to break out of these chains and escape again.

But I give the small chains a tug and hiss in pain when the silver chafes my wrists. My mother lifts the vial in my direction, and it reminds me so much of the small rations of blood she gave me each day that I shake my head violently at the sight. She sighs and downs the blood in one gulp.

"Where did you get it from?" I bite out, then jerk my head in Zenos's direction. "Did he kill another child for you?"

My mother's face pinches, like the blood is sour.

"Everything I have done, Ava . . . everything has been for you." My mother swallows hard, and I notice tears in her eyes that make my heart clench. "When your father died, I lost everything except you. I was away from my family in Saren, stuck in this land that only tolerated me as long as I worked for the emperor. He would have me killed if I tried to leave, with everything I know about the empire. I was terrified for both of us. When I was nearly killed, and a vampire appeared to offer me a second chance . . . of course I took it. That vampire was Casiopea. I died there to be here for you now, Ava."

My thoughts jumble together. I remember when she came back that day. It had been raining hard, a late spring evening, and she'd come home dripping both water and blood. Her voices chokes up for a moment.

"I knew it would be a difficult life for us from then on, but I did what I had to do to protect you."

*You call killing me protection?* I want to yell at her, but again, I find it hard to speak. Every time I want to rage and yell, my voice dies in my throat. It's like she's choking me before I can even say anything, and I don't know how to break through it. I don't know how to make her hear me when she's never listened before.

"I know your plans," I finally say instead. "You want to tear down the tree and the wall to free the vampires. I'm going to stop you."

After a moment of silence, my mother asks, "Do you know who Casiopea really is?"

I shrug and nod at the same time, as well as I can within these chains. "She's the first vampire. She's been guarding the vampires who live here for centuries, giving them a home."

"Hmm, you're missing some parts of the story," she says. "As you know, witches were not always so loved in this land. They were tortured and experimented on in the capital; royalty's efforts to try to gain some of their power for themselves."

*Experiments.* A chill sweeps through me and I meet Zenos's steel gaze over my mother's shoulder.

"Casiopea was one of them—a Root witch, one of the first of our kind, who could manipulate the earth to grow living things. She was caught by the empire when she was young. She broke out of her confinement in the palace and set to work trying to enhance her powers; she used the same experiments the emperors of old did on her to try to make herself, and other witches, strong enough to stand against the humans. But these experiments changed her—she became the vampire she is today."

"She was a Root witch, too?" I ask, shocked. "Like the one who made the—"

"Don't interrupt, dear." My mother's voice cuts through the chill in the tent. "As the first vampire, she had no self-control, no awareness of what was happening to her. She changed her own son, and he in turn became more bloodthirsty than her."

I close my eyes again at her last words, my heart aching at this mention of Casiopea's son. He was born a thousand years ago, but I feel his pain and fear. I feel the betrayal he must have felt, pounding against my undead heart like a drum.

"He was killed by people who lived in a forest village, which didn't have a name at the time, but is now Arborren. But his mother, you see . . . she was changed when he was a child; people gave birth very young back then. And she was young enough to keep her powers." Here, she pauses and twirls her fingers in an upward spiraling motion to coax weeds out of the ground. They twist around each other like writhing snakes, vibrant and eerie in the candlelight. She snaps her fingers and the weeds fall flat. "Do you think she wanted to be around humans? What would a Root witch do, when the entire world has ostracized her, and then took her son from her?"

The answer comes to me so clearly, I'm astounded I never saw it before. In an awestruck voice, I say, "She's the one who made the Bone Wall. She trapped the vampires in the forest . . . t-to protect them." My voice stutters over the last words. All this time, I'd thought Casiopea was trapped here with the rest of the vampires and then took it upon herself to make this land a proper home for them. I had no idea she'd also created it.

"Yes. Because that's how you keep family safe, isn't it? By keeping them close."

Irritation spikes through me at her words, but I try my best to focus.

"Ever since then, the empire has had a new enemy, and never stops at trying to expand its bounds, taking over new lands and gaining new power for itself. Witches suddenly became valued protectors of the land and aides in expanding the empire. If I were Casiopea, I'd feel a little cheated by the whole situation. Wouldn't you?"

My mind races at this. Of course I'd feel angry. I'd hate humans. I'd . . . want to hurt them.

The thought jabs through me like lightning, and I swallow the dryness in my throat, trying to quell the sudden rush of anger. Of course Casiopea hasn't been contentedly sitting in the forest for a thousand years. She would want to get revenge on the humans. And maybe on the witches as well.

Quietly, I say, "The people in the cages. Are you taking them to her for some reason?"

"Sacrifices, yes. The humans for their blood. The vampires to join her army; she'll take some of the stronger humans and transform them as well. Ava, why would a queen need an army?"

I gulp. "To fight." It slowly dawns on me, puzzle pieces flying together. "She wants to escape the forest, too, and lead them to kill."

The thought weighs on me, and I feel a tight sob in my chest wanting to break out. I escaped my mother to join Casiopea, but they both want the same thing. I was epically foolish for thinking Casiopea would value my information about my mother's plans. For thinking she'd protect me, and we'd live peacefully in these trees forever.

A child's idealism. I have no hope for protection. Even though I'm chained to the floor, I suddenly feel like I'm adrift at sea with nothing to hold on to. The path I imagined for myself loses clarity, fading into the mist. I have nothing. No plan, no place to escape to, and no one to run with.

As despair settles on me, I hear the whispering again, the sinister voice that seems to come from deep below the earth. The hair rises on the back of my neck. A harsh wind gusts against the tent, and I shiver uncontrollably, like we've suddenly been doused in the cold of winter.

I choke out, "Why are you telling me any of this? I told you I'm going to stop you." I hate the way my voice shakes when I speak, but I barrel on. "What you and Casiopea want is wrong. Do you crave pain and suffering? What do you and this useless rat get out of it?" I jerk my head at Zenos, who's now peering through the tent flap with a tense expression.

After a beat of silence, she reaches out to place a hand under my chin, and when she speaks next, her voice is so impassioned I almost feel myself drawn to her.

"When nearly everything is taken from you, Ava . . . you will fight to protect what you have left. I became the thing this empire fears and I am in the perfect position to strike. I made you into something stronger as well—something that can stand against all who aim to hurt us. You have the powers of a witch and a vampire; nothing can stop you if you take hold of that, and I gave that to you. Together we can make a new world where we don't have to fear anymore. But not while so many of our kind are loyal to their queen. She has powerful magic that holds them in her thrall."

She lets out a bitter laugh, her hand tightening on my chin. I jerk away, and her hand hangs in the air for a moment. Her voice drops to a dangerous purr as she continues, "The only way to bring down the Bone Wall is by destroying the Heart Tree, but only a Root witch can do so. Vampires have tried in the past—hacking at the roots, attacking the tree, but nothing they do ever works. Casiopea is a Root witch—she could have brought down the Bone Wall herself all along. But the tree is precious to Casiopea, and she ordered me to discover some other way to bring down the barrier. But there is no other way. I've brought her these sacrifices for three years now to get her to trust me, but she refuses to hurt the tree. If she's too weak to lead her army to freedom, then we will take it from her, and we will get rid of her as well. Once the vampires are set loose on Arborren, everyone wins: the humans will get back the forest and the mines they want so badly, the Flames will remain vital to the empire instead of being discarded like they would if the vampire threat didn't exist, and . . . you and I will save the vampires from the vicious Flame witches attacking them, and become their new queens. We'll lead our army wherever we please. The rest of the eastern provinces, Erlanis City, Saren . . . all of it. It is time for a change in who holds power, and who is afraid."

Zenos clears his throat in the corner, staring at my mother expectantly.

"Him, too," she adds begrudgingly, then grimaces at me. "The old emperors wanted the witches' power. It's no different now with vampires."

"Is that why you've been here the past three years?" I ask him, disgust seeping into my voice. "You want to become a vampire? Have you lost your mind?"

"I know the ways into the capital, I know all their secrets," Zenos snaps. "We could bring these humans to their knees."

My mother sighs and holds up her hand to make him stop talking. "First step is to bring down the barrier. In a way, your escaping and getting caught in Chrysalis was a stroke of genius, Ava. Casiopea is wary of me, but she doesn't know you. If you pretended to join her, you could take down that tree yourself before she even knows what's happening. So I thank you for breaking out and truly embracing this side of you. It will grant us both the future we deserve."

I don't move or react at all. My mother wants power, Casiopea wants revenge. I know neither of those will work. I've tried to be the innocent, I've tried to be the killer, and neither of those was right either, because they're both equally a part of me. It all makes me who I am.

I have to choose my own way. The idea lifts my heart, but I'm scared to go with it. Maybe I'm not so unlike my mother— I've spent so long craving protection and fighting to hold on to any chance at safety. So long molding myself into visions of who I should be, without realizing I could simply be what I already am.

A girl who's hurt, but pushes along no matter what. A girl who makes mistakes, but refuses to live with them forever. A girl who doesn't love the life she's been given, but chooses to make the best of it anyway.

Maybe my mother is right about one thing. Maybe I am stronger than I know.

"I will never follow you or your plans," I finally say.

"Hmmm," my mother says, looking toward Zenos with an amused glint in her eyes and shrugging. "Maybe your friend can help you with your decision, dear. You know, the one who turned you over. What was her name—Kaye? I remember how close you used to be, how you thought you could trust her. She thought she was being so sneaky and smart last night, I decided to be kind and let her think she had the upper hand. But the Flames don't like traitors—she should have learned that after seeing what happened to her mother. I wonder if Liander will get rid of her himself or hand her over to Casiopea. Would you like to watch and find out?"

"She betrayed me," I snap. "Do what you want with her."

I know the words are a lie as soon as I utter them. I think of Kaye slipping into the forest after my mother, the tug of sorrow in her voice when she told me her mother loved the moon, her soft touch on my skin.

I swallow hard, fighting down a hot rush of tears. She betrayed me and I miss her. She turned her back on me and left me and abandoned me.

After she was abandoned. After she was turned on, too. That doesn't make it right, but still, I know her heart. I know her pain, and I want to save her from any more of it. Right now, that hope is all that keeps me from falling apart. The realization crashes into me like a wave, the knowledge that I need to save her—that maybe only we can still save each other. That maybe the thin line between love and hate that we keep crossing will carry us through the storm ahead if we just take hold of it.

Then, as if someone else is inside the room with us, there's a great sigh, followed by a whistling in the air. Everything becomes colder in a way that makes my teeth chatter together, and whispers rise up from the darkest depths of the tent. I hang my head as the wind gusts harder, nearly caving in the tent on one side.

"Casiopea has arrived," my mother says simply. My head jerks up. Outside, screams rise up, blending in with the sharp wind.

My mother stands, brushes dirt off her cloak, and says to Zenos, "Stay."

Zenos shifts toward me, kneeling, then brushes back my hair from my face like my mother did. I spit at him, but he doesn't even flinch. Behind him, my mother raises an eyebrow at me, and his gray eyes spark with mirth.

"Look at you, finally becoming the vampire you were destined to be. Once I am one of you, things will be much more even between us. I look forward to our games, greedy little thing."

My mother's expression falters slightly, and the barest spark of regret flashes in her eyes before vanishing. She departs the tent with a flutter of her cloak. With a crushing feeling in my heart, I realize she's always known the truth about what Zenos did to me.

And she doesn't care.

# CHAPTER 26

## · KAYE ·

*Flame witches are the most valued, prized warriors in our empire.*
*Any young witch should be proud to join them.*
—TRAINING ACADEMY FOR
YOUNG WITCHES OF ARBORREN

Liander's men haul me to my feet and tie my hands together behind my back before shoving me forward. I walk with my head down, my whole body shaking.

I send a poisonous glare at Tristan, who walks next to us but isn't even looking at me, then shout back at Liander, "Is that how you killed my mom, too? Snuck up behind her because you knew you'd fail if you faced her yourself?"

He's silent, but the corners of his mouth twitch, like he's found my statement amusing. I yell out, bucking against my captors, but they push me to my knees and slam my face into the mud. The fog seems to wrap around my limbs as they hold me there, and when they haul me upward again and force me to walk, I swear it's gotten as cold as a deep winter night. The sky is pale ice above us.

The witches lead me toward the barracks I saw earlier and shove me inside the dusty foyer. There are no lights, but Liander and Tristan provide small flames on their palms to guide us. Everything is covered in cobwebs, but there are round tables in the center and a narrow staircase at the back of the room that leads to a loft with beds. I wonder how long it's been since anyone has comfortably slept here, with Casiopea's shadow falling over the woods.

Instead of going upstairs to the loft, we take a metal staircase down to a basement, where the air grows so cold, my breath fogs in front of me.

When we reach the bottom, the witches' flames light up a line of cells against a wall. My legs tremble as the witches behind me loosen their grip on my arms and Liander takes their place. His cold hand touches my shoulder and the back of my neck as he steers me toward the open doors of a rusted cell. He shoves me so hard, I slam into the wall.

"And to answer your question about how she died, no, I did not sneak up on her from behind." A twisted smile crosses his lips as Liander closes the cell door and locks it with a key. "She wanted to believe the best of everyone, never wanted to see any differences or trials between people. I suppose that explains you." His eyes trail over me in a way that makes my blood boil. "She knew I was growing displeased with her, but she thought she could talk to me and come to an agreement. Sliding a knife into her neck and making it look like a vampire attack was as simple as putting a bloodsucker to flame."

By the time he finishes speaking, I imagine sliding a knife into his neck. He grips the cell bars, shakes them to make sure they are locked, then turns to leave.

Tristan's eyes are bloodshot and his hands are curled into

fists. I want to spit a thousand curses at him, this boy who's never learned to think for himself. This boy who used to be my friend before his father got to him. He opens his mouth as if to say something, then jerks back around and follows his father. They leave, the doors above lock, and everything falls into darkness before I finally shed tears.

I imagine my mother, trying to make Liander see sense before he took her life. Did she think of me in her last moments? Did she wish she'd fled with me the moment she found out what Liander and Eugenia were doing? For a moment, bitterness sweeps through me, and I wish she had.

But then I never would have reunited with Ava, a vampire who takes my breath away and makes me feel full and alive rather than hollow and dead. Ava, who's more vibrant than any living person I know.

As my eyes adjust to the darkness, I make out the cell bars in front of me and remember Ava insisting on how human she was, and how much I'd told her she wasn't. They cut me now, like I used to wish I could cut and shape myself into an image that makes sense for people. All I ever wanted was for them to stop telling me who or what I am. Tears stream down my face as I realize what a hypocrite I've been.

It must have been so easy for Liander to string me along, never questioning or doubting him, because he knew how much I wanted to belong. Just like my mother's and Ava's kindness was used against them, my grief and desperation were used against me.

I've spent far too long making myself into what other people want, removing or adding parts of myself whenever I need to fit a certain image. Wishing they would simply accept my differences and judge me for my heart and actions. I don't know who I'll even be anymore if I cut away the parts of me that I've constructed for other people's sake.

*You never really were one of us,* Liander had said before his men attacked me outside.

Maybe I shouldn't be—and maybe I never should have wanted to be.

I slump on the cell floor with exhaustion, my eyes falling closed, my face splotchy with tears as the wind roars above.

I don't know how much time passes, but a rattling at my cage soon wakes me. I jerk away from the door, squeezing myself into a corner in case it's Liander here to finish me off.

A face blinks down at me in the darkness, and it takes me a minute to realize who's here.

"Tristan," I whisper, and I can't find any more words to say, because his face is twisted in agony, his hair standing on end like he's been running his hands through it. He's gasping for breath like he just ran here.

My first instinct is to yell at him to leave me alone. The words are on the tip of my tongue, but I bite them back. My shoulders slump and I feel deflated as I look up at one of my oldest friends. He grips the bars of the cage, his knuckles straining.

"Kaye, I didn't know he would turn on you like that," he says, his voice choking up. "I could tell he was growing angry with you, but I had no idea what he was doing here. One of the older Flames told me we're taking these humans and vampires to be sacrificed to Casiopea. They're planning to tear down the Bone Wall."

"I know, Tristan," I mutter, my eyes finding his in the darkness. Tears fall onto his cheeks as he grips the cell bars and leans his head against them. Then, a question I've been wanting to ask for two years spills out of me. "Why did you leave me?

Ever since . . . that day, nothing has been the same between us. You promised you'd help me find my mother's killer, and then you changed. Like you didn't want to be friends with me anymore."

He shakes his head slowly, eyes widening. "Kaye, I . . . after your mom died, I came to your house every day. You yelled at me to leave. In training sessions, you always stood apart from everyone. I know the others didn't make it easy on you, but I still tried to help you. I still tried to give you advice, be there for you, push you to become stronger. I guess eventually I started being angry with you, too, and I stopped trying."

Heat flushes my cheeks as he speaks, and I'm plunged back into the past. I remember yelling at him to leave. I didn't want him to see my empty house and how I hadn't cleaned in months and slept in my mother's bed the whole time. I didn't want him to see the long pages I'd written in my notebooks, nearly tearing the paper with my pencil, describing how I would rise in Flame witch ranks and take out hundreds of vampires myself. I didn't want him to see me staring out of my window wondering why Ava left and then beginning to hate her, too. A sob rises up my throat and I hold it back, just barely.

I thought Ava had left and betrayed me, so I pushed away everyone else. Did my mother do that, too? I bite my lip as I think of her life: leaving the man she loved in Saren to continue working as a Flame witch here, secretly supporting Saren's independence and passing along false information to the emperor, then hiding the truths she discovered about what Liander and Eugenia are doing. Just like her, I've kept all my pain to myself and pushed people away—Ava and Tristan. I accepted their betrayals as truth and shut them out of my life.

Maybe, if I'd been a real friend, I would have tried harder

to find out what happened to Ava. I would have beat her door down and fought her mother and Zenos until I got her out of there, vampire or not. I would have sought out Tristan instead of shutting him out.

Hot tears fall down my cheeks before I can stop them. Who really left whom?

"You were grieving, Kaye," Tristan says then, wiping his own eyes. "No one could have expected you to do better. I should have tried harder, too. But that day changed everything for me, also. Ava disappeared. You were heartbroken. My father became harder than ever on me in training and I was never good enough for him. I've been so lonely since then. My father . . . he told me he was afraid you would become a traitor one day. I didn't know he killed your mother for finding out the truth. All I knew was that I had to steer you away from that. If you seemed too interested in vampires, or were seen talking to any of them, I knew it would be bad for you. I wanted to go back to being your friend, but I didn't know how anymore. When I saw Ava in that line of vampires, I . . . started to come to my senses a bit. I want to make my own choices now, not just follow my father's."

"You could have come back anytime," I say with a lump in the back of my throat. "But I don't blame you. I was afraid to try to talk to you, too. Everything changed then. All that matters now is that we fix it. Remember those days at the lake when we were little? You were always there for me when I was afraid to swim. We were there for each other while training in the woods, too. We can protect each other again."

Tristan gives me a cautious smile, then inserts a key into the lock. The cell door swings open with a creak.

"I know you care about Ava. I spoke to her earlier, and . . . she was mad at you, Kaye, but I could see through her. She's still our friend, and I know she's important to you. I'll help you break her out, but we have to be careful the Flames don't see us. Give me another chance, Kaye. I won't let you down."

The old me would have told him no, attacked him to get out of here, and left him to suffer the consequences of my escape. But that bitter part of me falls away like a cloak sliding down my shoulders, and I step forward to embrace my old friend. He hugs me back, cautious at first, but then relaxing and letting out a sigh that ruffles my hair.

As he undoes the binding on my wrists, a lightened, hopeful feeling stirs awake in my chest, and I feel like I can breathe easily for the first time in two years. It feels like I have a piece of my heart back.

And now it's time to save another piece of it.

"Let's go," I say, and Tristan and I run up the stairs together.

# CHAPTER 27

## - AVA -

*Although the ancient ones are gone,*
*their touch remains on this world,*
*their magic imbuing everything around us, to give us strength*
*when we forget what we've come from.*
—ORAL HISTORIES OF ERLANIS EMPIRE

After Zenos finished taunting me, he moved back to the tent entrance to peer out at whatever was happening in the field. I strain against the chains holding me. While Casiopea wants the Bone Wall to come down, she doesn't want her tree to get hurt in the process. If I can convince her that there is no other way, maybe she'll still stand with me to protect the tree.

Yet even if I do, I doubt she'll give up trying to find another way. And I doubt she'll see me as an equal or let me go; she'll strive to keep me in her army, doing her bidding. My mother said Casiopea has a powerful magic that keeps her vampires tied to her. I've never heard of something like that.

The wind gusts even harder outside the tent. Panicked screams rise up from the prisoners out there, and my heart clenches when I think of Dorothea, Smit, Tairos, Nuira. They're about to lose either their freedom or their lives, while I sit trapped in this tent.

I close my eyes briefly, trying to catch the whispers I heard in the forest before, and the signs of the ancient gods at the burial ground. If they hate the presence of vampires in this forest, then why do they try to contact me? They asked for help—is it because I'm a Root witch? But according to what my mother said, Casiopea is, too. Maybe they tried asking her for help and she denied them.

But she's not just any Root witch. She's one of the first. And the very first witches . . . *were* the old gods.

The realization hits me like a cold gust of wind. The Arkana took the forms of humans and their descendants passed on the magic inherited from their Arkana parents. Our mythology says the Arkana returned to their plane after they had spread their powers all over the world, leaving behind their mortal families.

But what if one of them didn't leave? And if Casiopea really is Arkana, why are the other gods trying to speak to me about her? If I can make it to the forest, maybe I'll have a chance to figure it out.

Zenos is distracted by what's happening outside of the tent, his shoes pressing into the mud. I focus on that, curling my fingers to mold the mud and solidify it around Zenos's shoes and ankles. A satisfied smirk crosses my face.

"What are you so happy about?" he asks as he turns around. He tries to step toward me, but can't—his feet are trapped. "What have you done to me? Remove this curse at once!"

I yank as hard as I can on the chains, feeling metal grinding on their bases. Zenos's eyes widen as the bases begin to pull out of the ground. Maybe I can't get the chains themselves off me, but I can take them with me.

"You think your mother won't see you?" Zenos asks, sweat beading on his forehead as the wind grows stronger outside.

"Give me the key," I say in a low voice, "and I won't kill you."

He opens his mouth with a taunting glint in his eyes, but a moment later, he jerks forward, gasping like the breath has been knocked out of him. I look toward the ground to see if it's opening up to swallow him, but then Zenos grunts again. He drops to his knees, then falls face-first to the floor, unconscious, his feet still locked in place.

There's nothing there.

Then there's a clinking noise as his keys unhook themselves from his belt and float in the air. A moment later, the scene in front of me ripples like water, and new colors and shapes appear. Kaye and Tristan stand there, Tristan holding the keys.

"Hi, Ava," Kaye says cautiously.

My mouth falls open, but I can't bring myself to meet her eyes. Hope burns in my heart, but I'm afraid to let it grow too bright. I'm afraid to let her in again.

"Ava, I'm sorry. I was wrong, in everything I did. You can hate me once we get you out of here, but we need to leave first."

"Why are you helping me?" I ask in a small voice. "Figured out your leader was sacrificing precious humans as well and that was finally too much for you?"

Her face flushes with shame and she averts her eyes.

"There's more than that." Tristan speaks up behind her. "Liander is the one who killed Kaye's mother. When Kaye confronted him, he nearly killed her, too. We both want to leave this all behind."

My head jerks up at that and I search Kaye's face for how she's taking this news, but her jaw is clenched tight and her eyes reveal nothing. My heart aches for her as Tristan unlocks the chains from my wrists. Rubbing away the marks left by them, I still feel hesitant. Maybe she's learned not to trust Liander, but that doesn't mean she has any reason to care about me.

"You don't have to come with us afterward," Tristan says, his forehead crinkling in concern as he takes me in—and it's the way he speaks to me, like I'm just as human as he is, that convinces me to believe his words. "You can do whatever you want—flee to another land, make a life for yourself in the woods or the mountains. Anything. But you deserve to be free, and you won't get out of this campsite without help. Neither will we."

I know I can't trust Kaye, not after what she did—even if a burning part of me wants to. Even if all I want in the world is to put everything that happened behind us. For now, I have to be strong and focused for whatever happens once we leave this tent.

"Let's get out of here," I say, and Kaye's hopeful, answering smile is infectious. Even though we're about to run into chaos, I smile back. This chance to escape actually feels real.

"Hold on to me, and I can make us all disappear," Kaye whispers as we approach the edge of the tent. We pass Zenos and I give him a good kick to the ribs before placing a hand on Kaye's elbow. Tristan does the same on her other side.

For a moment, the world swims in front of me, like I'm staring at it through a bowl of water. Then it settles and I gasp when I look down at myself. I can't see anything; even when I wave my hand in front of my face, all I see is the tent behind it. To my right, Kaye has disappeared also, even though I still feel her arm under my hand, tense with how hard she's concentrating.

"You're really good at this," I murmur, and her arm relaxes under my touch.

We step out of the tent together, staying close so we don't get separated. My mouth falls open at the scene before me.

Even though it's midday, all the light seems to have been leached from the world, and we're left with a smoky gray haze. In the trees ahead, vampires hang from the branches like bats. Casiopea's soldiers. Their eyes glitter in the darkness, and their arms stretch down the tree trunks to wrap around their captives— about half of the human prisoners who were transported here with me, along with the vampires. My heart stutters when I see Smit held there with a vampire's arm pressing his torso into the tree and his face going pale above it. Nuira and Tairos struggle against their captors to no avail. The vampires who hold them have eerily bright eyes that look glazed over, as if in a trance.

I freeze when I spot the other humans, and bite down hard on my lip to stop from screaming when I notice Dorothea among them. Eight of them are spread out like chess pieces around the field and frozen in place, their mouths half open in screams that will never be heard. Bone-white roots have burst through the ground: Some wrap around the humans' arms and legs and chests, squeezing like snakes. Others have pierced through the humans like bayonets, and blood pools beneath them on the mud.

A gust of wind slams into us with a sharp whistling sound, and the earth bucks beneath our feet. Gasping, I clutch Kaye's arm so I don't lose her, and try to find my balance. Slowly, we move across the field. Every inch of me wants to go save those humans from my mother's and Casiopea's plans, but I know it's too late for the humans. If I want to do anything to stop the remaining ones from being killed and the other vampires from being taken forever, first I need to get out of this field. I can't face both my mother and Casiopea now; my only chance is to get Casiopea alone and convince her to side with me.

Most of the witches and hunters have retreated into their tents to wait this out. But some stand guard around the perimeter of the camp, gripping silver daggers and gritting their teeth against the harsh thrust of the wind.

In the distance, a pall of mist falls away and spreads along the ground toward the human sacrifices like fast-moving clouds. A woman approaches in its wake, but she glides along the earth rather than walks. Her hair is made of gray, dry leaves that fall down her back. Her skin is smooth and unblemished, but with sharp features and hardened, deep-set eyes that stand out to me immediately. She looks so young, even from here, that for a moment I forget Casiopea is a thousand years old. But as she glides over the land in our direction, she raises her hands slowly to the side and the earth rises, cracking apart at her merest gesture. When she opens her mouth, fangs extend past her lips and glint in the gray light. Roots crawl out of the earth like spiders and gather around her as she comes to a stop near my mother—who stares up at Casiopea with her arms crossed, like she's not impressed in the slightest.

With a lazy arm, my mother points toward the prisoners held against the trees by the vampires. Casiopea lifts one hand, and vines fall from the canopy of the forest to wrap around the prisoners and bind them in place. The vampires relax their grips and, when Casiopea lowers her hand, they charge for the human sacrifices pinned to the field.

"Move!" I hiss at Kaye and Tristan, and together we duck out of the way of the vampires. They flit across the earth like shadows, their gazes fixed on the blood falling from the prisoners. I tear my gaze away as one of them latches on to Dorothea and forces her head to the side.

One of the vampires barreling toward us, while we're invisible, smashes into Kaye next to me. She cries out and falls backward, while my and Tristan's grips on her are ripped away. In the span of a breath, all three of us are left visible on the field.

A hunter nearby has spotted Kaye and shouts for her to stop. Ten feet away from me, her heartbeat pounds frantically.

Kaye doesn't hesitate; embers flicker to life in her hand and then grow to a roaring flame that pierces through the gray light. She flings it toward the hunter, who narrowly avoids it by leaping to one side. The flames streak across the grass, and the vampires screech as it approaches them. Kaye's hair blazes in the light of the flames as she runs. If Casiopea or my mother sees what's happening, we'll never get out of here.

I race toward Kaye, Tristan at my side again, as a Flame witch corners Kaye at the very fringe of the trees.

A sharp whistling pierces the air and a silver dagger flies toward her. She cries out and falls to the ground. I reach the witch who attacked her and push him so hard he flies backward twenty feet before landing in a heap.

The vampires are still running from the fire, but some are coming toward us. At the same time, the roots slowly begin to retreat into the earth, pulling the human sacrifices with them like the ground is made of quicksand. I glance over my shoulder once to see Kaye falling forward, a gash of red along her thigh. Tristan scoops her up from the ground a moment later, and they both vanish from sight.

"Ava!" Tristan calls and I race toward the sound, my fingers grazing Kaye's. She squeezes mine, and I wish I could see her face right now and tell her she'll be okay.

But as the rippling effect of invisibility falls over me again, my mother finally spots me, and I draw in a sharp breath. Her eyes narrow to a deadly glare, and I sense her last bit of hope for me to join her slipping away, just as I disappear. Whenever I see her again, she will not help me. It's like the earth between us is breaking, separating us into different worlds where we are no longer mother and daughter. Where far too much damage has been done.

It feels like freedom, far more than escaping my house ever did.

Kaye squeezes my hand again as the invisibility completely covers me. I turn to run into the trees, with Tristan carrying Kaye next to me, her faint heartbeat louder than any other sound.

# PART

# 4

*Root and Wick*

# CHAPTER 28

## · KAYE ·

*As poisoned as the forest is,*
    *we mortals still hope to one day wrest control of it from the*
*undead,*
        *and return it to its proper owners: the living.*
                            —TRAINING ACADEMY FOR
                    YOUNG WITCHES OF ARBORREN

My vision blurs in and out, and I don't know where I am, but I hear Ava's voice and I feel Tristan's arms holding me as he runs. I wonder if this is a dream, because I can't imagine them both being here with me.

The running makes me feel like I'm being jostled by rough waves, like the tide is about to pull me under, and suddenly I'm eight again and Tristan is trying to teach me how to swim.

"Ava," I whisper.

"You're safe, Kaye," Tristan says in that solid voice I know so well. He was distant for so long, but now, as he runs through the woods with me and Ava, it feels like he's only been gone a day, a night, the wink of an eye.

I don't know how long we run, but night falls and their steps slow down. I'm no longer jostled by waves, but carried along a slow current. They set me on a pile of leaves, and when I try to sit up, Tristan stops me.

"We need to stop the bleeding," he whispers, and I wonder who's bleeding. I remember that he and I faced a Flame witch together, and I thought we were winning, but . . . my memory goes blank after that.

The silver dagger. I blink, the image reeling through my mind. Am I the one bleeding?

Panic rushes through me and I sit up again, but this time Tristan is too slow to stop me. My head throbs and my vision starts to spin when I see my leg covered in blood as crimson as the leaves below me. Nausea roils through me at the sharp, rusty smell. How am I even alive?

At the edge of this clearing we've come to, Ava is arguing with Tristan as he fumbles bandages in his hands, his face pale with fear.

"I can help, Tristan, just let me try," Ava says in a tremulous tone.

"What if you lose control?" he hisses back. "There's blood everywhere. I trust you, Ava, but—"

"I haven't attacked her yet, have I? If I don't try, there won't be any time for you to save her. More vampires will smell her blood and find us, and they won't be as nice as me."

Tristan must have mumbled in agreement, or maybe Ava just pushed him out of the way, because in the next second, she's leaning over me, her hands splayed and a look of concentration on her face that I recognize in myself when I try to call my magic. But in her hand, she holds a purple flower with long petals and hornlike buds. I vaguely remember it from a page in my mother's journal. Rampion flower.

"Kaye, I'm going to try to stop the bleeding. I'll be honest with you, I've never tried this before, but . . ." She gulps, sweat beading on her forehead, and I don't need her to finish her sentence. If she doesn't try, there will be no hope for me. I'm dying. The thought enters my mind vaguely and uninspiringly, like someone's just told me the weather. I can't even think what it means; it's not important when I have these two here with me. Tristan watches as Ava leans over me.

"Ava, I . . ." I grab her wrist, and though my grip is weak, she pauses, her hair shrouding her face. "Wait."

"I need to heal you or—"

"I'm sorry," I choke out, my vision wavering as I speak.

"That can wait, Kaye, lie down." She pushes me back to the ground and then sets to work on my wound, breaking off one of the buds from the flower and crushing it up. I can't see anything on my leg, but from here, I watch the tears well up in her eyes. She blinks them away and focuses on stopping my blood loss.

Then, as I lose focus and can barely make out what they're saying, they start arguing. Tristan asks Ava something, then buries his face in his hands. The words are a jumbled mess in my mind. But I can read the panic in them, and become slightly more lucid as Ava bends toward me again. Her own wrist is bleeding now, and I frown at her, wondering what happened.

"You've stopped bleeding, Kaye," she whispers, and one of her hands brushes my hair back from my sweat-streaked forehead and neck. "But you're still weak with a fever. Vampire blood can help you heal."

Her hand shakes slightly as she holds it up, and behind her, Tristan swears under his breath.

"If she dies with that blood in her system, you know what will—"

"Of course I know," Ava says through gritted teeth, her hand pausing on my neck, checking my pulse. "She's stable, but she'll be out for days if I don't do this. Kaye?"

She holds her wrist toward me so droplets of blood fall on my neck. My vision swims in and out of focus again, and everything around me is too hot. With my back to the ground and my head resting against it, I hear my own pulse loud and clear. If I don't drink the blood, I'll put us all at risk.

But if I drink it, there's a chance I could turn into a vampire.

I hesitate for another moment, but my thoughts are all a blur and I know I have to make a choice. I give Ava a stiff nod, and she brings her wrist toward my lips. I'm so out of it, the taste of her blood on my tongue doesn't even bother me. I grimace slightly when I swallow it. Then I close my eyes and fade away from it all.

At some point, I register that we're moving again. I don't know how long I'm unconscious, but when I finally open my eyes and look at the world without it spinning, I'm lying on soft, muddy ground. Grass tickles my cheeks and I gasp at the feel of it. It's green and alive, not dead like so much of this forest. Tilting my head to the left, I breathe in the woodsmoke of a small fire a few feet away and let the flames warm my face. Next to the fire is the pillowcase sack with my mother's journal, and the scarf I gave Ava, inside it.

"You're awake!" I turn to see Ava holding her hand to her mouth in shock, like she fully expected me to die.

Beyond her is a lake—my eyes widen in surprise. After seeing all the dry streams in the forest, I'm surprised this lake is here at all.

When I sit up, Ava places her hands around my waist and shoulders to help me. The warmth of her touch brings me completely back to my senses.

"What happened? I know we fought our way out of the camp, and I remember drinking your blood, but not much more."

"I tried to heal you with a flower I saw on the way," Ava says, looking down at my leg. There's a bandage stained the rust color of blood. I feel no pain right now, but when I stand, I know it'll hurt. At the moment, I'm just glad I can't see the wound. "It helped stop the bleeding, but then we heard vampires approaching and had to run. Your wound reopened on the way, and I had to start over. I stopped the bleeding again with the flower, but used my blood to speed up your recovery."

"That's a flower my mother wrote about, isn't it?"

"Yes, rampion. It's a species that only started blooming once vampires made this forest their home. Everyone always thinks of vampires as inherently evil, so they probably thought this flower was evil, too. But Calluna knew differently. It healed you." She swallows hard then. "Casiopea was one of us, but not just a witch. I think she was one of the very first; one of the Arkana who took on a human form to pass down magic."

My mouth falls open. "She's one of the gods? I thought they all left."

"Most did, after they passed on their powers. But I think she stayed and lived as a Root witch. Back when the empire experimented on witches, she was captured. She escaped and tried to re-create the experiments in a way that would amplify a witch's powers. To give them—her mortal descendants—something to fight with and protect themselves. But instead, she created vampires. She turned her son, too. When hunters killed him, she made the Bone Wall herself." Ava shakes her head, and there's a bitter tone to her voice when she says, "She became a vampire to protect her family, but she's hurting them, too."

I fall silent as Ava looks toward the forest, like she's searching for the vengeful vampire lost in those trees.

"My mother . . ." Ava began, her voice halting and frightened. "She has a plan."

"I know," I mutter. "She wants to destroy the Bone Wall, with Liander's help. He killed my mother, Ava, because she found out the truth."

Ava nods slowly, her eyes wide with fright. "While she held me captive, my mother leached my Root witch powers from me. Only a Root witch can bring down the barrier, but they have to destroy the Heart Tree to do it. Casiopea wants the vampires to go free, but not by destroying the tree. It's important to her for some reason. She's cautious of my mother and won't let her near it. My mother wanted to send me to destroy the tree, but now she has to come up with another plan."

Her voice has turned hard by the end, and her hands have curled into fists. I want to reach over and smooth them out, but I don't know where she and I stand now.

"It's good you got away when you did, then," I say slowly.

But Ava shakes her head. "I can't let Casiopea keep taking human sacrifices, and forcing vampires to side with her. But I also can't let my mother ambush them and lead the vampires to attack human cities. So I've been thinking . . . what if I go to Casiopea first?"

A chill passes through me at her words. "What do you mean?"

"She and I are so similar. I'm a Root witch and a vampire,

too. She doesn't want the tree to fall, and neither do I. I'll convince her to stop trying to escape and stop taking sacrifices from my mother. I think her taking these sacrifices is what's making the forest sick. All of it needs to end, and if I can convince her, we'll all be better off for it."

I think of the vampire queen I saw in the field who caused the earth to swallow men whole and choked them with vines.

"I'm not sure she's open to a chat, to be honest," I mutter.

"If she's not, I'll fight her, too," Ava says, her chin jutting out and eyes blazing. "But people do change. What about you, Kaye? Why did you change? Are you going to change again?"

I don't want to just spit out any answer, so I take a long moment to gather my thoughts before speaking—holding her gaze the whole while. Beyond her profile, the lake spreads away. A pang hits my heart at the sight of it; it reminds me so much of the one Mom brought me to when I was little. When will this one dry up, like all the others?

"I know the truth now, Ava. My whole life, I've been told my purpose will be to bring safety to Arborren by getting rid of vampires. But we're not good either. Liander is willing to kill his own people. I can't trust the Flames anymore, even though they're all I know." I gulp then, tasting tears on my tongue. "I'm a hypocrite, like you said. My whole life, I've wanted people to only see me for who I am rather than what they want me to be, or what they've been told I am. I've been trying so long just to be accepted that I stopped thinking what that means."

"I know what you mean," Ava says in a shaking voice. Tears fall from her eyes and land on the back of my hand as she speaks. "I've spent so long trying to be what other people want me to be that I don't know who I am. But I'm only going to make my own choices from now on."

I take her hand in mine. "I'm sorry, Ava. I betrayed you. I know I might never be able to make it up to you, but I'll fight at your side against anyone who comes for us. I promise."

Ava bites her lip as she looks up at me, and I can see the uncertainty warring in her eyes with a spark of hope.

"Well, you and Tristan did save me back there," she says with a shrug. A smile tugs at one side of her lips, and for some reason it makes my heart ache. Her expectations of the people in her life are far too low.

"Don't forgive me that easily, Ava," I whisper. "You deserve more than someone who only comes for you when it's almost too late. That's not good enough, and I won't let you settle for it. Don't forgive me until I prove I deserve it. I think we both need to learn how to trust again."

After a long minute of silence, Ava pulls me into a hug and rests her chin on my shoulder. I tense up, but then I relax into it and wrap my arms around her, too, staring out at the lake beyond.

"I want to forgive you," she says, her lips moving softly against my hair. "But you're right. I'll wait."

We stay like that for a long while, the chill of the night banished with our embrace. Cricket chirps soon fill the air, accompanied by the soft push and pull of waves on the lake. Moonlight pours over it, glistening over the surface like a million fireflies.

"Where is Tristan?" I ask then.

"He went to look for food and check that there are no vampires in the area," she says, leaning back and wiping tears from her face. "He should be back soon. This place seems untouched; I don't think any of Casiopea's army is here."

I nod, my eyes trailing toward the lake. "It looks just like the one my mom and I used to go to in the summer."

While she stares out at the lake, I remove the bandage from my leg to get a good look at the wound. There's a scar, but the wound has closed and no more blood is gushing out.

"Ava, you healed me," I say in awe.

She beams at me over her shoulder. "I thought it would be harder to focus, with all that blood. And it was at first. But when I looked at you, the thirst fell away. You were injured, and you needed help. You were the only thing that mattered, and I stopped thinking about blood at all."

She reaches out a hand and places it over mine. I let out a slow sigh, just grateful for her touch. With a soft smile in return, I nod at the lake. "Let's go in."

Her eyes widen and her mouth falls open in shock. "Kaye, I know you're basically made of fire, but . . . it's cold, if you haven't noticed. I'll freeze to death."

It's such a bizarre statement out of a vampire's mouth that I let out a burst of laughter. She places a finger to her lips to shush me, but there's mirth in her eyes, too.

"I'll keep both of us warm," I say with a wink, and I really wish vampires could blush, because I know she would be blushing right now. She smiles back at me and ducks her head shyly. Then she stands to walk toward the lake, and when she reaches the shore, she tilts her head up to catch the moonlight.

Maybe I don't know how to trust. But I have a feeling I'm beginning to learn what trust looks like.

It looks like the curve of black hair around a soft jaw. Oak-colored eyes gleaming beyond the light of my flames, fierce and bold and beautiful. Like secrets whispered in the night and etched into our skin by morning. Like a long-fingered hand giving me a cloth so I can wipe my tears. Trust looks like a girl who wants to live so badly she forgot she's already dead.

I know now I'll do whatever I can to make her feel alive again.

# CHAPTER
## 29

- AVA -

*The connection the Arkana have to our world is intrinsic, and*
*never leaves us.*
   *Like the forest itself, everything is intertwined.*
   *When one thing dies, another is born.*
                    —ORAL HISTORIES OF ERLANIS EMPIRE

I stand at the shore of the lake, waiting for Kaye to join me, and
breathe in to catch the fresh scent of the water. I notice there's
a salty smell to it, and frown in confusion.

"Does this lake go to the ocean?" I ask Kaye when she comes
up next to me, and search for a sign of the end of the lake. But
I only see a winding body of water leading from the opposite
end of the lake. "Oh, no, it's just a river over there. So why does
it smell like that?"

"I can't see any of that," Kaye says, frowning. Then she goes
silent for half a minute. "But I think this is the same lake my
mom used to take me and Tristan to."

Tears are at the corners of her eyes. I reach over to wipe
them away, and she catches my hand when I lower it. I think

about my time in that cage, this girl who turned me over and then came back to save me. . . . I want more than anything to trust her, to run away with her and have a new life somewhere else. But I know that the anger inside me can only be resolved by stopping my mother's plans to rule with a vampire army behind her. And I know that stopping her is the only way I'll have any room in my heart for trust.

Kaye, though . . . I felt her sincerity in her words earlier. She'd lost so much blood, she'd almost died, while running from the people she'd considered family her whole life—because she wanted to save me. She'd found out the truth of her mother's death and I found out the depth of my mother's deception. I know how much pain she is in.

"You look like hell," Kaye mutters under her breath then. She meets my eyes and I notice the slight amusement in her gaze.

"You smell terrible," I say.

We both burst into laughter at the same time. Then we turn to the lake.

"You're right," I say abruptly. "We should swim. It's been years since I have, and . . . I want to see underwater. It's a whole new world."

"It is," Kaye says softly, her eyes far away like she's lost in a memory. "I'll race you."

With a snort of laughter, I say, "Good luck."

Adrenaline buzzes through me as I face the shimmering water. I don't want to hide my powers, my strength, my speed. My fangs bud at my gums with the familiar dull pain, and I let them rise, but this time, I'm in control—not my mother, not vengeance, not fear. I won't hide me anymore, and this time, it will all be on my terms.

Sprinting away from Kaye, I feel the wind rush in my ears, feel my feet lift off from the ground so fast, it's like I'm flying, and suddenly I'm in the water. The cold shoots through me like a bolt of lightning, and I start shivering. A few moments later, a hand lands on my elbow and warmth spreads through me. The water splashes gently as Kaye comes up next to me, using her magic to bring warmth to us both. A soft glow emanates from under her hand, and from all over her skin.

"You cheated, but I forgive you," she says, brushing her hair back from her shoulders with her other hand. "I liked seeing you run like that. You looked strong and graceful."

I give her a soft smile, then walk with her deeper into the water with her hand still resting on my elbow. The glow of the lake reflects in her eyes, making her look golden and goddess-like. Soon we're deep enough that our feet come off the ground. We let go of each other to swim away from the shore, our movements spreading ripples over the water. It's been years since I've swum, but the technique comes back to me quickly. Once we're a bit farther out, we face each other and tread water in the quiet night.

"It's beautiful here," I say, following the trail of moonlight across the water with my eyes.

"It is," Kaye whispers, but she's not looking at the water. She's staring at me.

My stomach flips at her words. I don't know how to reply, even though everything in me wants to tell her she's more beautiful than any lake, any sunrise, any star in the sky.

I duck underneath the water, letting it envelop me entirely, and open my eyes to try to peer into the depths of the lake. If I were a human, it would be too dark to see anything. But I can make out weeds and pebbles on the bottom of the lake, silver fish swimming together at a distance. It's an entirely different world under here, and I let out a laugh underwater. Water fills my mouth, but I don't need air—I won't drown.

This is the kind of world I've been searching for. Something so new, so far from what I know. So why does my heart still feel empty?

A hand wraps around my upper arm and tugs. Kaye's soft fingers. I rise up out of the water then and throw my head back to get my hair out of my face.

"You were under there so long, I thought you'd drowned," she laughs. "But then I . . ."

"You remembered I'm already dead?" I quip, raising an eyebrow. She blushes, and the tinge on her cheeks brings out the slight copper burnish to her hair, the one I'd noticed in the sun. It's still dry; she hasn't dipped her head underwater yet, and just now, she shivers slightly.

"Are you cold?" I ask. "We can leave the lake."

Kaye shakes her head quickly. "If I go under, I'll get used to the temperature. I'm a little scared, though. I'm not good at holding my breath underwater. My mom and Tristan taught me when I was younger, but I never really got comfortable with it."

Before thinking better of it, I reach for her and place my hands on her shoulders. "We'll go under together."

She bites her lip for a moment, then nods.

"One," I begin.

"Two," Kaye whispers.

"Three." I go under, holding her steady as she follows.

She tenses up as soon as the water covers our heads. Opening my eyes underwater again, I look at her. Her face is scrunched up, not relaxed in the slightest. But her hair drifts around her like something ethereal. Strands of it circle her neck, resting on her fierce features and flowing behind her.

We burst from the water at the same time, and I brush the hair out of my eyes. She's soaked now, her hair sticking to her face and neck, her wide smile turning to me.

And then I draw her toward me. She wraps her arms around my waist and all space disappears between us. I rest one hand under her chin. Her heartbeat races and her cheeks flush in a way that makes her completely captivating. I stare into the dazzling green of her eyes and draw out this moment between us.

Then her eyes soften, and I lean in to kiss her. Her heat floods through me, our lips moving as one, and I press even closer with the swells of the lake crashing around us. There's no hesitation in her movements as she traces a line along my fangs with her tongue and I gasp, not even needing the air but wanting it. I hear her pulse, the vibrations of it against my skin, and the smallest, primal part of me knows there's blood close at hand. But it fades away and I wrap my fingers in her hair, trailing through it like it's the water beneath us. A different kind of hunger takes hold, a steady warmth building in my core, and I want to be even closer to her than seems possible. Even with my eyes closed, the whole world seems brighter; the chill of the lake disappears and only our fire is left.

# CHAPTER 30

## · KAYE ·

*As a spark of fire contains light and energy inside it,*
*so must Flames learn to respect all life.*
——Training Academy for
Young Witches of Arborren

She's warmth and sunlight and ice and stars all at the same time. Her light fingers on the back of my neck, the passion in her kiss . . . I lose myself in it, drawing her to me with the smallest intake of breath. And I don't care when her fangs graze my lips, when the lack of her heartbeat is somehow louder than any other sound. I don't care, I don't care, I don't care.

This is how it's supposed to be. I pull her closer and almost don't notice when the warmth spreading through me isn't just from us, but from the lake itself.

When she pulls away, though, I see it—the spreading circle of light across the lake's surface, like a slow-moving ripple. The entire lake glows as if thousands of fireflies cover the surface.

"What—what is that?" I gasp, pushing wet strands of hair behind my ears.

"It looks like when we were in that burial ground, and we saw the lights there. It might be the same thing," Ava says slowly, trailing a hand through the glittering water. Her eye widen with panic. "This will attract attention."

She looks around as she speaks, like she's already searching for vampires or the Flame witches to come out of the trees at the lake's shore. Her hand splashes in the water, and a ripple spreads outward. I reach for her hand and hold it.

"Okay, let's find Tristan and then leave. I think you're right: we should go to Casiopea before your mother gets the chance to attack the tree."

We swim back to shore, and with my heart lighter than ever, I look toward the trees ahead without fear. Our journey through the woods, miles and miles where we relearned to trust each other, just to take me back to this lake from my childhood . . . it makes me feel like I've stepped out of my past, and I'm that much closer to learning where I want to be in this world.

"I don't know how I'll convince her to side with me," Ava says in a pensive tone. "But I'm ready to stop them, Kaye. We won't let them all control us anymore."

She gives me a wide grin, and I'm reaching over to pull her into another kiss when footsteps reach us from the shore.

"What was that light?" calls Tristan. When I look over, I see he's returned carrying a dead squirrel and a collection of nuts and roots.

I try to think of an explanation, but Ava answers first: "I asked Kaye to show me some of her magic."

Tristan curses under his breath. "You might as well have sent up a flare. The vampires are going to find us."

"We want them to," I say in a grave voice as I wring water out of my hair. "So they can take us to Casiopea."

"I'll wait for them alone," Ava says in a soft but firm voice. When I jerk around to face her, my shock must be obvious, because she adds in a rush, "It's not that I want to separate. I don't want to be apart from you either."

"So don't be," I reply, stepping forward to take her hand and ignoring Tristan's questioning glances. "Why would we need to separate?"

"Um, why do we need to find vampires at all?" Tristan interjects then, his face going pale.

"My mother and Liander are planning to attack the Heart Tree so that they can let vampires loose in Arborren. My mother plans to kill Casiopea somehow and take over as queen to make the vampires fight for her." Ava gulps, brushing back wet strands of hair stuck to her face. "I don't know whether I want them to be free or not . . . but they shouldn't escape one prison just to end up in another."

"I don't know if I want them to be free either," Tristan says haltingly, then looks to me with a beseeching expression. "Some, like you, Ava, are fine. But plenty of others are dangerous. It would be naive to think they won't kill us."

Ava bites her lower lip while she considers what to say. "I've learned it's possible to survive off animal blood instead of human. What if they could learn that, too?"

Tristan, looking thoroughly unconvinced, opens his mouth to argue, but I interject, "We don't have time to debate it. Ava will need to persuade Casiopea to not work with Eugenia anymore; then Eugenia won't be able to get close enough to the tree to do any damage." Then, realizing we truly must separate, I say, "We'll stall Eugenia while you talk to Casiopea. The vampires will be drawn here by that light and you can go with them."

"You two should leave soon," Ava added. "I'll be outnumbered when they come. I won't be able to protect either of you."

I pull her into a hug before she finishes her sentence, wishing there were some way to stay together. "I know you can handle it," I say in a low voice into her ear. "You're stronger than anyone I've ever met, Ava."

She smiles and squeezes my hand once before letting go.

We extinguish the campfire, and I pick up the pillowcase sack and swing it over my shoulders before Tristan and I leave to backtrack our path through the woods. I look over my shoulder at where Ava stands by the lakeshore, her hands folded in front of her and a resolute mask on her face. Then the trees cover my view and I tear my eyes away.

We'll stall Eugenia, but Liander will try to stop us as well. A rush of energy floods my veins at the thought, and I feel my mother's strength coursing through me.

"Kaye," Tristan says with a stony look, "I don't think my father saw us leave. What if he doesn't realize I've deserted?"

Noticing the mischief in his voice, I send him a hesitant glance. "What are you thinking?"

"I'll pretend I got separated somehow and come up with a good excuse. I'll go into the camp to see what's happening, and you should use your invisibility to sneak around and look for Eugenia. We need to stop her from going to the valley with the Heart Tree."

When we reach the edge of the camp an hour later, I'm covered in sweat even though the air is chilly. We pause within the trees to catch our breath and take in what's happening.

Casiopea and her vampires are gone, leaving only the ravaged earth in their wake. There's no sign of the humans who were taken as sacrifices, not even blood on the ground. My heart twists when I picture Ava facing those vampires alone, but she's the only one of us who would stand a chance against them anyway.

The tents are being packed away by the hunters, and the empty cages are hooked together by a long chain. Liander speaks to the Flames in a separate group. Eugenia and Zenos stand behind him.

I can practically feel Tristan shaking with rage next to me, but the tense look in his eyes is like grief—like he already know his father is lost.

Tugging on his sleeve to catch his attention, I say, "You'll be okay, Tristan. If you need to find me, walk up to the tree line and I'll come to you. I won't leave you with him."

He nods, then gives me a tight hug before reentering the camp. As he walks toward the others, the tension in his shoulders drops, and he lifts a hand in a wave.

I hang back in the trees while shooting furtive glances at Tristan. I can't help my heart beating fast for him and hoping he'll be able to fool Liander.

As I place the invisibility over myself, I move closer to the camp and strain my ears to overhear Tristan and Liander ahead. Liander's face is hard as stone as he listens to the excuse Tristan came up with to explain his disappearance and how he didn't know anything about my escape. Eugenia watches them, her brow furrowed as she takes in Tristan's words. I watch her carefully, waiting for her to make any move to leave.

"If you really aren't a traitor, then get in line and shut up." Liander's voice breaks through the quiet, sharp and cutting, but I sense the nerves behind it. As badly as he treats Tristan, he doesn't want his son to be labeled a traitor like I was. It would reflect too badly on him.

Tristan steps away, confusion clear on his face as he and the other Flames begin to line up in front of the trees, about five feet apart from each other. Something's dreadfully wrong. I can feel it in the back of my throat like a sour taste.

Liander directs Tristan to one end of the line. Once Tristan arrives there, his eyes dart toward where he left me, even though I'm probably too far back in the trees for him to see.

I move toward him, blending in seamlessly with the foliage. My footsteps crunch in the leaves as I near Tristan.

"What is it?" I hiss, my eyes darting to the other Flames and hoping none of them will overhear.

Tristan's hands shake as he begins to speak, and I wish I could step forward and hug him now to help him calm down.

"They need to *distract* Casiopea to get her away from the tree," he says, the panic so clear on his face, my heart beats faster. He emphasized the word "distract," and that, plus looking at the ready stance all the Flames have adopted as they've lined up in front of the trees, opens a pit in my stomach.

"No," I breathe, the realization dawning on me. Liander and these Flames want to sow chaos. They want the vampires to run free so that the Flames are more valuable to the empire than ever. So they don't care about the forest, and Liander lied to the human hunters about winning it back for them.

And if they want to draw Casiopea's attention . . .

Vaguely, I notice that Eugenia, Zenos, and the hunters have all slipped away from the camp, but that thought vanishes from my mind when Liander shouts, "Begin!"

His sharp command cuts through the air, and at the opposite

end of the line, one of the witches raises his hands, flames bursting to life on his palms.

I run toward him, but I'm too far—he winds up his arm, then throws a sparking sphere of flame in an arc.

The trees catch, a burning maelstrom of heat at my back. In the span of a breath, the fire races across the forest behind me.

# CHAPTER 31

## - AVA -

*The mines run deep in the earth, and more paths close every year.*
*Only the most determined still seek them out,*
*and cross paths with the roots seeping underground.*
——JOURNAL BY CALLUNA MENTARA

They come one at a time, blotting out the stars behind them.

I watch from the shore, trying to count the vampires as they slink through the trees, perch atop branches, and slither in the grass. As I wait for them to approach me, my panic rises, and I peer through the trees, but I can't make out any sign of Kaye or Tristan. It's been twenty minutes; they must be far away by now.

One of the vampires approaches me with nearly as much ethereal grace as his master. His long legs move like those of a predator, and matted dark hair hangs around his gaunt face. When he stops in front of me, his bare feet hardly make a sound.

After a beat of silence, I say, "Is Casiopea here?"

My voice seems to echo in the silence. The vampire takes me

in for a moment, seeming to judge whether I'm worthy of being spoken to.

"What was the light we saw?" Then he breathes in, his eyes darting around our little camp. I freeze, hoping we haven't left anything here. "I smell blood."

I sniff the air, too, keeping my face as blank as possible. With my eyesight, I would see any specks of blood on the ground, but there's nothing. Then, the sloshing of the lake breaks through my thoughts and it dawns on me: when Kaye and I swam, some of the dried blood on her might have gotten washed away by the water. I try to catch a hint of it in the air, but I only get a faint metallic whiff that doesn't make me think of blood. His senses must still be stronger than mine.

"I drank from a squirrel," I say flatly. "I'm tired of wandering these woods alone. Can you take me to Casiopea? I want to join you all."

After a long pause, he nods and gestures for me to join the rest of them. As we walk toward the tree line, he mutters, "She likes the newly undead. Means she can mold your minds better."

A chill passes through me at his words, and I wonder if Kaye is right, that Casiopea won't listen to anything I have to say. But there's nothing else for it but to try. We quickly fade into the trees.

Even knowing I'm not truly joining them, there's something freeing about moving as swiftly as a wild animal through the trees. Some vampires leap from branch to branch, while others, like me, pass through the wood with quick speed and sharper senses. I've definitely gotten better since my first clumsy days traipsing through the woods.

I've convinced these vampires to take me with them, but now I must convince Casiopea to stop my mother's plans.

But there's more to it than that. She's Arkana, one of the ancient gods, and her power can apparently sway the other vampires to her cause. The barrier she constructed around the forest has only harmed it, and every day vampires, witches, and humans suffer because of it.

I don't know what to do yet, but I know that all of this must be stopped. If only the other Arkana would speak to me . . . That light in the lake seemed like a sign from them, but I don't know what the sign could be for.

Faster than I anticipated, we break through the other side of the trees and come onto a dirt path. It rises and then dips into a fog-cloaked valley. Wild grass prickles at my legs as we descend below the fog into the valley.

The vampires spread out, heading off in different directions. This is their home, I realize with a sinking heart. This is the home I'd wanted, the one I'd dreamed about finding for so long. And now that I'm here, I can't stay for long. There might never be a real home for me.

But instead of crushing me, like that thought once would have, it fades away and I think of Kaye again, her arms around me and her lips touching mine. Her heartbeat at my side as we fall asleep feels more familiar to me than anything else.

Maybe I have found a home, after all.

"Beautiful, isn't it?" The vampire next to me speaks—the same one who came up to me at the lake. Jolting out of my thoughts, I follow the line of his finger as he points toward the tree appearing in the middle of the fog.

Afternoon light breaks through the fog to shine on the silvery leaves that cover the massive branches of the Heart Tree. The trunk itself is nearly black, with hints of crimson through it, and below the silver leaves, in the deeper reaches of the branches, I see gold and emerald, too. Roots break through the ground near the tree and, when I look down, I see lines protruding from the earth and running toward all ends of the valley.

"It is," I breathe. The crimson streaks on the Heart Tree's trunk remind me of blood.

And then a shadow steps out from behind the tree—or more accurately, floats away from it like a ghost. Hair made of gray leaves, skeletal features, and eyes that pierce through me. The vampire next to me falls away with a nod.

"You were recently turned. No more than a few years, I'd wager," Casiopea says then, in a voice like sharp wind and crumbling bones. A smile splits her face, which is somehow ancient and young at once. "And you are still a witch. How did you find me, young one?"

"I came to tell you something," I say in a rushed, low tone. Something darkens in her eyes as she registers my panic. "My name is Ava Serení, Eugenia's daughter. She turned me a year after you saved her. I'm a Root witch, like you."

Casiopea's face goes utterly blank, and I wonder when the last time someone surprised her was.

I'm about to say more when she rushes toward me in a flutter of leaves and wind. One of her bony, skeletal hands reaches forward, just barely brushing my hair. I almost flinch away, but force myself not to.

I can't look weak in front of the vampire queen.

"You're like me, but she is not," Casiopea whispers in a fascinated tone. "My guess is that she siphons power out of you."

I blink, not having expected her to figure that out so quickly. "How did you—"

"Oh, I knew she had to be doing it somehow, or else how would she fool all of Arborren? I did not know she had a daughter. But what she steals from you are small tricks, here and there. She makes one little flower grow and they don't need to see anything else. It is not real."

"I know what you are, Casiopea. You're Arkana, and you want to protect this tree and the forest. But the forest is sick because of this, don't you see?"

She waves a hand dismissively. "I only do what I must. But how do you know what I am?"

I squeeze my fists, trying to hide any emotion from my face. I don't want to reveal that the other Arkana have spoken to me.

"It was obvious," I blurt out. Her eyes narrow at me and I force myself to meet them. "Only an Arkana could be so powerful, and since you're one of the first Root witches to ever live . . . I was able to put it together. But Casiopea, why have you held out this long? In a vampire's body, you're . . . dead. The furthest thing from a Root witch, and your real power as a god. Don't you hate it? Being hunted by the witches you helped create and requiring blood to survive?"

"And what is blood but the life-stream of the body? We are still Root witches no matter what. You control and crave life, Ava Sereni, because life is still a part of you. Does that answer your question?"

The sun fully slices through the fog then, and the valley turns a pale green.

"My mother is planning to attack the Heart Tree," I say in a rush. "It's the only way to tear down the Bone Wall, and I know you want the vampires to be free, but you also don't want the tree to be damaged. You have to stop this alliance you have with my mother or she'll manage it."

A grimace pulls at one side of Casiopea's lips. In a steely timbre, she says, "Your mother will never touch my tree. We will find another way to be free. Your mother and I have a mutually beneficial agreement that—"

"An agreement to kill innocent people and trick more vampires into serving you, yes, I know," I say, cutting through her last words. I'm arguing with a thousand-year-old goddess with hundreds of vampire soldiers on her side, but it's hard to care after I saw what she did to the humans back at the camp.

Her obsidian eyes turn deep and heavy at my words, almost looking alive. "My children need to feed, and they need to be protected within this home I've provided for them. I failed to protect my first child. I won't fail the rest. You have not suffered long enough to understand my pain."

"And perhaps you've suffered so much that you can no longer see reason," I say, trying to keep my voice calm but hearing the desperation claw up my throat. "More children die or lose their parents because of what you and my mother have done, and if she reaches the tree, she'll cause a great deal more destruction. All you have to do is stop her."

The hollows under her eyes deepen as silence falls between us. When she next speaks, a sad tone enters her voice. "As I said, your mother will never touch my tree. She is not a true Root witch. I will remind Eugenia of her place. . . . And Ava, stay here. Speak to my other children. They will watch over you for me."

There's a sinister note to her voice as she departs. She glides away, moving swiftly along the valley and up the hill like a shadow.

The other vampires close in on the path she took. My stomach drops, and I realize what Casiopea meant by them watching over me. If only a Root witch can damage the tree, of course she wants them to watch me and make sure I don't do anything to it.

I used to think she'd protect me if I came to her, another lost Root witch. But maybe she only sees me as a threat.

It might have been a fool's mission to try to sway Casiopea to my side. If I'm going to save the forest and protect both the humans and the vampires, I need to find a way to do it myself.

I wait, imagining Kaye's heartbeat in my ears as I count out the seconds from when Casiopea disappeared. If I can make it out of the valley and around, maybe I can catch up with her.

But before I walk more than ten feet, two vampires speed in front of me.

"You are a guest here," one of them says, mud and blood stains coating his face and torso. The veins under his eyes pulse as he steps closer to me, footsteps soundless as a ghost's. "Where do you think you're running off to?"

Panic shoots through me, and I do the first thing that comes to mind: I fling my hands upward, dragging roots out of the ground to wrap around their ankles. As they try to rip free of the roots, I dart around them and race toward the perimeter of the valley with more vampires closing in on me from behind. I reach the trees at the edge of the valley and quickly kneel down, digging my hands into the mud. Faster than I've ever used Root magic before, I draw the thickest roots I can find up into the air and twist them together so they create a wall over this copse of trees. The first vampire slams into it, and I sprint away before they can tear it apart.

I run through the trees, and whispers rise up around me. The same whispers that have been pulling me here for over a year now.

All the trees around me are bone white, bark peeling off the trunks like sliced skin. The roots protrude from the ground and spread in long, vascular lines over the forest floor.

And then I smell it: a hint of that same metallic scent from the lake. The vampire who'd met me there thought it was blood, but . . .

My foot catches on a root and I trip, flying toward the ground. I manage to hold back a yelp as I crash onto the dry grass and roots. The metallic smell from the lake hits me even harder here, and then I realize . . .

What if it's not blood at all? The silver mines run through the forest, but many of them are abandoned because of the vampires' presence. I dig my hands into the ground, closing my eyes and listening to the earth below. It's hollow, wide, empty . . . like some kind of complicated maze.

The sounds of vampires chasing after me are coming closer, and I lurch to my feet. They'll catch me unless I do something to disappear.

I lift both hands and thrust them upward, coaxing the roots to lift from the ground. The earth creaks and shakes beneath me, and a deep crack splits in front of me. Rocks and dirt tumble down, landing on the mine floor, and the opening becomes visible. Without looking behind me, I jump inside, then urge the earth to cover me again. Dirt and dust fall on my face as I shift it all back into place, and the vampires' shouts become muted once I'm fully underground.

Shoving a spiderweb off my face, I look around this tunnel. This darkness is so complete, it's difficult for me to see. If this tunnel leads me out of the valley, I can follow Casiopea without getting caught.

But after a moment of silence, the whispers reach me again.

*Come to us.*

With each step I take, the whispers speak up, louder than they've ever been before. They grow stronger, rhythmic and insistent, pounding in my eardrums like the steady pulse of blood.

# CHAPTER 32

## · KAYE ·

*The elders of our community are meant to guide*
*and teach young Flames how to burn bright,*
*for they are our future, and though we have not always been*
*respected in these lands,*
*we can still guarantee our place here tomorrow.*
—TRAINING ACADEMY FOR YOUNG
WITCHES OF ARBORREN

Heart pounding in my throat, I race to the end of the line of witches. I have to stop them from burning down the whole forest. The fire spreads from tree to tree behind me, and I'm already soaked in sweat. As I shift behind a tree across from one of the witches, I make sure I'm still invisible and try to figure out what to do, but I don't have much time. The witch in front of me brings a flame to life on her hands. I only have seconds.

I lift my hands above my head and draw them in front of my face, then separate them. Using the same technique as I do for my invisibility, I draw light away from the forest. If it works properly, it will look like the trees have disappeared and there's only a field.

Liander shouts for the witch to attack. The witch blinks rapidly, like she's trying to clear something caught in her eye. She throws the sparking sphere of flame in an arc toward the forest, and at the same time, yelps in confusion. I dart to the next Flame, who stands a few feet to the right of the first. But Liander shouts at him to fire, and he does. I feel my grip on the magic falter, and the trees become visible once more.

Then Liander's voice breaks through the crackling of flames and, with a metallic whistling sound, he withdraws a long silver blade from his belt. "This is your doing," he barks as he comes up behind Tristan, blade raised.

I abandon the witch in front of me as Liander lifts the blade and brings it down in an arc. Tristan dodges at the last second but falls to the ground, his eyes wide in shock at the sight of his father standing over him with a deadly glare.

"No!" I shout, throwing myself the last few feet until I'm standing between them, letting my invisibility drop completely. I raise a silver blade in one hand and bring fire to the other.

Tristan scrambles to stand and withdraws his own weapons.

"You're not killing him, too," I hiss. "You're done, Liander."

He doesn't even blink as he lifts the blade, aims it at me, and throws.

I whip my blade in front of me to knock Liander's aside, a mere breath before it can slice through my neck, but there's a flash of light and the blade is forced out of the way. It skids across the ground, and the bolt of light speeds off and then flickers away.

He comes for us; I block his next strike, but then he vanishes. Tristan and I stand back-to-back, and I look at the grass for some sign of Liander's footsteps. He does know how to use invisibility, like my mother and me. Tristan falls back in shock, a gash appearing below his jaw where Liander must have struck him. Then I notice the grass below pressing down with each step Liander takes.

"There!" I shout, flinging one of my dagger toward where I think Liander is. He grunts, and the invisibility flickers away for an instant; long enough for us to attack. We strike from opposite sides, moving too fast for him to put the invisibility back in place. Together, Tristan and I don't give Liander a second to breathe or recover.

The clashing of silver blades fills the air along with the thunderous cracks of flame devouring the forest behind us. The heat makes sweat pour into my eyes, but I fight back against Liander more fiercely than I've ever fought before.

His eyes widen as we start to drive him backward. The other witches approach, but he shouts at them to leave, and the look in his eyes only grows more murderous.

*He doesn't want them to watch as he tries to kill his son,* I think with a sinking heart as the other witches leave. *He won't stop until we're both dead.*

With a wild snarl, I clip him across the chest. Blood gushes down his white shirt, and he sways, but then thrusts back against us harder.

Liander's blade hits my wrist and I scream at the sudden, sharp pain. My dagger flies out of my hand and Tristan steps in front of me to deal Liander a quick slash across the chest.

"Dad," he pleads, the word choked out like a prayer. I

clutch my shaking wrist, too frightened to look down at the damage for fear it might make me pass out right here. My vision turns spotty and I feel myself leaning forward, slowly falling, but I grind my boots into the mud to push myself upright.

Liander swings his blade and cuts Tristan's collarbone.

"I was never good enough for you, was I?" Tristan gasps out, his face streaked with sweat. "You stopped paying attention, and you missed the moment I became strong enough to face you."

Liander goes still, his face hewn of rough stone. Tristan's hands spark with golden light.

I step behind Liander and lift my undamaged hand. The light Tristan holds is just light; it can be directed, brightened, or extinguished. But it can also be reflected.

"You still have so much to learn, Tristan," Liander says with a dismissive laugh, but I notice the tension in his shoulders. "Are you really going to turn into a traitor like this girl and her mother? The least you could have done was respect me enough to disappear so I don't have to watch that happen."

"Respect?" I say in a flat tone. The sky turns a sinister mix of red and gray above us, and the hot air seems to hold its breath. "You certainly respected my mother enough to stab her face-to-face instead of with her back turned. A small consolation; at least she knew she was right about you before she died. But Liander, I wonder if you're teaching your students a valued, fundamental lesson of controlling light, fire, and all the energy inside it: It never goes away. It just gets redirected. And it will come back to you, too."

Before he can do anything else, I create a screen of light in front of my face. Tristan throws the light from his hands and it reflects off my screen toward Liander. It pierces through him like lightning made into spears, coming out of his chest and his neck. He freezes in place, one last guttural plea leaving his lips, and then he hangs there like the humans Casiopea skewered in the field with her roots.

# CHAPTER 33

- AVA -

*The Arkana formed new families across the world every time they began a new life,*
   *to pass on their knowledge and teach mortals their ways.*
   *When they returned to their plane, they left whole lives here, friends, parents, and children.*
—ORAL HISTORIES OF ERLANIS EMPIRE

The mines are nearly collapsed, but I sense all the souls who passed through here. I smell their sweat, their fear, their exhaustion as they worked to draw silver from the earth. I run a hand along the rock wall as I walk, hoping this path will lead me around the valley so I can follow Casiopea out of it. Roots protrude through the roof of the mine, some tumbling down and swaying along my shoulders as I pass. The whispers grow stronger in my ears, like the buzzing of insects or the crackle of flames.

The light that Kaye and I saw on the lake, and the metallic scent there . . . maybe that was the Arkana's way of telling me to go underground.

At some point, the path levels out. I suppose I must be deeper in the valley now. Cracks in the mine roof let in sunlight, and it gives me an idea.

When I traveled here from the lake with the other vampires, some of them leapt between the tree branches like the distance was nothing. What if I can leap to the roof of this mine, and use my Root magic to break a larger crack in the ceiling so I can look through it to see what's happening in the valley? I need to see where I am.

I run toward the wall and jump feet first. My feet touch the wall and I use it to launch myself to the ceiling and grab the clumps of dirt hanging there, then balance my feet against the wall. With my Root magic, the earth bends around my hands, holding me in place. This is easy, I realize. With my speed and strength as a vampire, and my Root magic, I can do almost anything. Confidence floods me as I rip apart one of the cracks in the ceiling so it's big enough to peer through to the valley ahead. Hanging there like a spider, I look through the crack to check my surroundings.

I've moved closer to the Heart Tree while underground, its massive silver boughs slightly to my left, and I'm facing the valley and the forest I came from. Smoke is rising above the trees in the distance, and I can just make out the crackle of flames miles away. It hits me then. What if the way my mother planned to pull Casiopea away from the Heart Tree was by setting the forest on fire?

I imagine the trees aflame, devouring everything. I look up at the roots around me—the long, curving vines that hold hundreds of years of history. The whispers in the earth rise again, more insistent than before.

Through this crack in the earth, I check the positions of Casiopea's vampire soldiers. All their attention is turned away from me, toward the lip of the valley where Casiopea glided away not long ago. For a moment, I wonder if she's returned, but then I see another figure approaching, this one wearing a high-necked black dress and a ruby pendant at her throat, her head held high and long dark hair whipping behind her with the wind. My whole body goes cold. How did my mother get here without Casiopea stopping her? She's heading straight for the Heart Tree. At some distance behind her, Zenos leads the hunters from Chrysalis, and all of them hold crossbows armed with silver bolts that shine gold in the sun.

As I watch, the other vampires start to close in on my mother, and some spread out toward the approaching hunters.

The whispers pull at me, telling me to go deeper, right to the heart of this valley and the great oak that overlooks it all. The distinct scent of rot reaches me as I peer down the sloping, dark path.

There's a shout from up above, and I look through the crack in the earth again to watch flames and plumes of smoke shoot above the trees in the distance. The whole sky has turned bloodred, and my mother is closing in on the Heart Tree. I can't see Zenos anymore, but the hunters have spread out and are shooting silver bolts into the heads and stomachs of vampires at random. One of them lets out a piercing scream as a vampire lands on his back and then snaps his head to the side.

As my mother approaches the tree, I tear a bigger hole through the crack and reach through it to grab the pale roots of the Heart Tree that snake along the ground. It responds to my touch, recognizing me as a Root witch. More roots wrap around my wrists, pushing me toward the exit. I let out a gasp as I land halfway out of the tunnel and the roots finally let me go. Then I pull myself out the rest of the way.

As several of the vampires close in to stop my mother, she slashes her hand through the air. Roots shoot out of the ground and into the throats of the vampires. I wince at the sight; the powers she took from me are still running strong through her veins. And she's using it to kill the vampires she claims she wants to free and rule over. I can't let her do this. I pull myself out of the crack. I'm very close to the tree now.

With a vicious snarl, my mother wraps the roots around the vampires' bodies and squeezes until their ribs crack and they go limp. I watch them fall as I move toward the tree, reaching it in a few quick strides. She attacked them so easily, it sends a wave of cold fear through me. She won't stop when she sees me— she might attack me, too—but I have to stand against her.

My mother leaves the vampires where they fell, her blood-shot eyes fixed on the towering Heart Tree and nothing else. The fallen vampires' pale limbs stretch out, their hands reaching for the tree and the end of my mother's dress to pull her back, but they're too late.

She comes to an abrupt stop in front of the tree, her eyes wild, her hair a tangled mess behind her as she gazes up at it. My heart sinks at the sight of her, and I finally understand the depth of her belief that everything she's done has been to give us a better life. And so there's nothing I can do that will convince her to stop.

But I can still try.

"Attack it!" my mother shouts. Several hunters abandon their battles and run to her, lifting their crossbows and aiming at the tree.

I flinch as the first silver bolt whistles through the air above me and sends a shudder through the upper branches of the tree. None of them has seen me yet. This grass, the leaves, the tree, the very earth itself . . . After I was turned, I thought they were so far away from me because they were alive and I wasn't. They were pure and I was monstrous. The only time I felt closer to nature was in the autumn and the winter, when it was close to dying and became more like me.

But they're not that different from me at all; they're alive, but they're capable of death. They could lose their lives as easily and quickly as I did, as easily as I still could. We are the same. And in the spring, they are reborn, forever undead. I feel more alive now than I ever have before, and more connected to the ancient magic of this forest. I want to defend it, protect it, and carry it through the danger it faces.

I'm filled with a stunning, bright clarity. I'm not hopeless and lost and dead. I'm more alive than I've ever given myself credit for, right in this moment.

And I'm no longer going to run away from the things that try to take that from me.

I slam one foot into the ground and bring up both arms in a sharp motion. The hunters shout as the land beneath them shakes and cracks, rocks shooting up like knives that knock them backward and send their crossbows flying.

My mother finally lowers her gaze to me.

# CHAPTER 34

## · KAYE ·

*Any Flame that snuffs out their own is no longer one of us,*
*and must continue adrift, lost without a home,*
*as ash on the wind.*

—TRAINING ACADEMY FOR
YOUNG WITCHES OF ARBORREN

Next to me, Tristan trembles, tears streaking down his cheeks. I wrap him in a tight embrace. Tears blur my eyes, too, even though I no longer cared about Liander. He was still the person who taught me from when I was a child; I looked up to him until just a few days ago, and this is the first time I've ever used my powers to kill someone.

But somehow, I feel numb about it; besides the tears, my body isn't reacting or rebelling against it. My mind has gone blank, like it knows that thinking about it too much will paralyze me against surviving the rest of the day. I look toward the burning trees in front of us, the plumes of smoke and flame that streak into the sky and turn the whole world crimson. The only clear thought that enters my mind is that Ava is still alone, and the fire is barreling through the forest so fast, we might not be able to contain it.

The other Flames have fled; to where, I don't know. Perhaps to start more fires, or to help Eugenia attack the Heart Tree.

"We did the right thing, Tristan," I say in a shaky voice. "We finally stood up to him."

He takes a long moment to reply, but when he does, his voice twinges with pain. "He would have killed us, just like he has so many others."

"I'm glad we were together for it. And we'll have Ava, too, once this is over. I'll never push either of you away again."

Tristan touches my shoulder lightly. "Kaye, you're hurt." He lifts my wrist to examine it. I dart my gaze away, still not wanting to see the damage, but the world swims in front of me. "You should wait here. I can stop the fire."

"No," I say fiercely, ripping my hand away. I feel blood streak down my arm but still don't dare to look. "You can't do it alone, and I'm not getting left behind. We're staying together. I'll be fine."

After a moment of hesitation from Tristan, he takes my hand to help me stand, and we face the burning forest. We move through the trees together, sweeping the flames upward and away. Orange flames spiral toward the sky, where they then scatter and turn into golden dust that falls back down to gild the treetops.

As we race through the trees, we narrowly dodge the Flame witches that Liander sent away. They start more fires before running again, south in the direction of Arborren. They'll destroy the entire forest if we don't stop them.

Sweat is pouring down my face and back in the heat, and soon I'm coughing on the endless smoke and running through flames just to put out more. Tristan stays at my side, and when there's a deep groaning noise from the earth that rises above the roar of the flames, I push us both out of the way and grab on to the nearest tree that isn't on fire.

"What was that?" he shouts, his voice barely audible over the flames.

Above us comes a gust of wind, and when I look up, my mouth drops open.

It's Casiopea, the ancient vampire. Arkana, like Ava said. She glides to a rest atop a tree, avoiding the flames herself, and her eyes search the forest floor with a thousand-year fury in them. I press farther into the shadows with Tristan, hoping she doesn't see us, and beckon for him to help dispel more of the flames.

But as we do, there's a bone-chilling scream nearby. Looking between the columns of flame, I see one of the witches, trapped in place by two long vines that have swung down from the trees to wrap around his limbs. They start pulling and he screeches in pain.

Casiopea still perches on the tree above, and with her hands moving in intricate patterns, I know she's the one hurting him. In seconds, the witch is pulled under the earth, like all the others.

She descends on us next, her eyes glowing gold with the remaining flames. Her hands are outstretched to attack us, too, but Tristan and I keep moving and sweeping the flames toward the sky. The vampire queen watches us for a moment and must realize we're trying to save the forest, because she leaves then, in the direction of the valley.

The smoke trickles away in the wake of the flames as we run, and all I hope is that we can reach Ava before the fire does.

I don't know if she managed to talk to Casiopea at all, nor where her mother is. But if we manage to stop Eugenia's and Casiopea's plans, what comes after that? If the vampires stay in the forest, the same war will continue, and this place will be rife with bloodshed for years to come. But if they escape, that puts all other humans at risk. Arborren will no longer be the barrier between the living and the undead.

I don't know what the right choice is. All I know is that as I run to Ava, when I think of her touch and her voice, my heart races fast like it's trying to beat for both of ours and it knows there's not much time left.

# CHAPTER 35

## - AVA -

*I cannot stop my old friend from the harm he wrought with the
vampire woman.*
  *All I can do is try to show a better way, and teach my own
daughter how to be kind,*
    *in a world that will test her.*
                              —JOURNAL BY CALLUNA MENTARA

"Mother," I call to her, and she snaps out of her shock at seeing
me here. "It's not too late to turn back. All you have to do is
stop this."

She flicks her head sharply to the side as if shaking off
a bothersome fly. "Ava, we can put all this behind us and
pretend you never even left home. Don't go down this path,
daughter."

"This path," I scoff. "You are the one who put me here.
You turned me into a vampire. You locked me in that tower.
You knew exactly what Zenos was doing to me and you never
stopped him. You made it so that I had to run from you. So that
I have to stop you."

Her face twists in grief, like I'm hurting her with my words instead of stating the truth. She twists one hand in the air and tugs, and I recognize it as the gesture to call a root toward her. When nothing happens, she lets out a barely audible gasp. I try not to show any reaction to that, but it's clear the powers she's stolen from me are fading away.

"Everything I have done is to protect you," she finally says, her eyes shining, each of her words trembling. Her hands stay open, fingers splayed, as if to grab on to anything that will come to her. For a long moment, my heart aches for her. She's tried everything to gain safety and acceptance for us, but only in a way that hurts people.

"I know," I say, my heart aching for a brief moment, "that you think that."

I've started to turn away when she calls my name.

"Ava," she says, and I slow my steps. I don't know what I want to hear from her, if anything at all. "You are so much stronger than you know."

Her words sear into me, and as I walk away, I do feel pain for her. Losing my father and her own life and having only me left in the world, she'd settled for Zenos and found a way to make a new legacy for herself, one where she was in charge and no one would lay a hand on her again. Something about that feels achingly familiar, because I tried to do the same. I force down those thoughts, though, knowing they won't help me now.

If she still wants to end this, to live with peace instead of terror, all she has to do is walk away.

And if I'm going to be as strong as she believes me to be, as strong as the ancient witches in the stories my parents told me, then I need to choose for myself what I do now.

"What are you waiting for?" she shouts in a strangled voice

behind me, and when I whip around, the hunters have lined up again in front of the tree, their silver weapons gleaming in the fire still raging along the trees and heading straight toward us.

Before they can load their crossbows, I place my hands on the ground and search for the roots of this ancient tree. They shoot out of the ground at my command and twist themselves into a cage that surrounds the tree, a stark gray turned bronze under the red sky. The first silver bolt cracks one of the roots, but then falls to the ground uselessly. I gulp as I return to the crack in the earth and reenter the underbelly of the tree. The roots aren't invincible; I can put up as many as I want, but eventually they'll fail.

I slip back into the crack I made in the ground, landing hard on the mine floor. Then I move down the path that leads directly under the tree. But I don't get more than a few feet before a shape lunges out at me from a corner.

I spot the silver blade in their hand and fling up my arm to catch it. The cut burns and sears along my arm, but I grit my teeth and push the weapon back toward Zenos. He charges again, but I shove him and knock the blade out of his hand. I fling my hand upward, fingers splayed, and roots shoot out of the ground and grab him. They force him to the ceiling, where he screams as he's pinned in place like a fly caught in a spider's web.

"You're pathetic," I hiss at him.

I only have to go a short distance down the sloping hill under the tree until I reach a cavernous chamber with roots hanging down like vines. These roots are black instead of the gray above. Then I see the bodies.

Jerking back with my hand over my mouth, I fight down

my disgust. There's a loud crashing noise above and the creak of broken branches, but I don't even react.

The humans are here, their bodies strung along the cavern's ceiling in the same way I trapped Zenos. Most are unmoving, their corpses gray and in some early state of decomposition.

Dorothea is among the dead humans here, dried blood coating her throat and torso from when the vampire attacked her aboveground. "I'm sorry," I whisper to her body as I pass.

More tunnels branch out from this central one, with humans locked in place on the walls and ceiling. Shimmering shards of bone dust float up from each of them, coming from exposed, disintegrating bones—I imagine it floating all the way up to the Bone Wall, and then it hits me: this is how Casiopea created the Bone Wall. The sacrifices become part of it, their bone dust traveling through the tree and up into the Bone Wall. All the bodies I've seen devoured by the forest floor must also become part of the Bone Wall eventually, forced to feed the barrier that wraps around the woods.

All these people, stolen from their homes simply to build the Bone Wall. It doesn't protect mortals. It kills them, and it traps us vampires. It can't stay. There is no good choice here.

"If you are here," I whisper, hoping the Arkana will heed me, "show me what you want."

There's a slight breeze, and on it I hear the voices again, clearer than I've ever heard before:

*Return our sister to us,* they say, and I know they must be talking about Casiopea. They want her back in their plane, away from the mortal world. But why is she so insistent on staying, and how do I convince her to leave?

A spark of light draws my attention from the center of this cavern. A root is lodged in one of the dead human's throats, and it pulses crimson, like blood. I follow it toward the middle of the room, and . . .

I clench hands into fists, pressing so hard my nails start to cut into the skin. I'd thought it was another human. But this person's alive, and has no heartbeat; his eyes hang half open and dart about the room lazily, like he's not really taking in what he sees. He doesn't seem to notice me at all. No breath leaves his lungs.

She trapped a vampire here, too.

He was a few years younger than me when he was turned. All the other roots lead to him, carrying the blood of the sacrifices. His body is suspended by hundreds of roots that hang down directly under the oak tree. And inside the black mass of them lies a heart.

Pulsing, glowing, ruby red . . . it's locked inside a cage of roots. The roots carrying the humans' blood go to this vampire, poking into different parts of his body. But others still lead to the heart itself, connecting the whole gruesome picture.

"So you've found him," a voice says behind me so suddenly, I jump a foot in the air.

Casiopea stands at the top of the sloping path into this chamber. I look between her and the boy behind me, connecting what I know from the journal and stories to what I see here.

"This is your son," I whisper.

Casiopea's eyes flick once to the boy behind me and then back to my face, like she can't bear to look at him for more than a moment. "Eugenia is stronger than I expected. I've strengthened the cage you placed around the tree, but it won't be enough."

A brief silence falls over us, and I think of how my mother's powers were faltering when I last saw her and she began to rely on the hunters with her to attack the tree. While the hunters can cause some damage, only Root magic can destroy the tree. Casiopea doesn't seem to know that my mother's powers have waned, and thinks my mother still stands a chance to destroy the tree with her Root magic. If I can convince her my mother is actually a threat, maybe she'll listen to me.

"I've kept it intact so long for his sake," she continues, "but my son hasn't said a word in a thousand years. I would cut you down where you stand if it meant I could hear his voice again."

"How did this even happen?" I ask, slowly lowering my hands as another attack pounds on the tree above. Rocks and dust tumble down from the ceiling. One of the dead humans falls from the roots holding them and drops to the ground in a clump. "I thought the hunters killed him a thousand years ago. They cut off his head. And then you used his heart to make this tree and the Bone Wall."

"What kind of mother would cut out her own child's heart?" Her voice turns sharp, and I shrink back, thinking of my own mother and what she's done to me. "No, that's what *they* did. I took the heart they left bleeding and tried to fix him, but nothing ever worked. The disintegration process had already begun for him, and he's been stuck like this, halfway between life and death, ever since. The hunters back then thought removing his heart would kill him, but they didn't understand how vampires worked. They didn't know that silver could hurt us, or that fire and decapitation are the only ways to kill us. When they realized their mistake later and that he must have survived, they revised the records they kept of all their catches and wrote that they had beheaded him. Mortals can't help but take credit and call themselves heroes. My son still lives, but he's never been the same."

"You've kept him alive by killing other people."

"Come, Ava, you should understand." Casiopea gestures to herself as another boom shakes the earth and more rocks crash around us. "We vampires will do anything for life. Join me, and we will defeat Eugenia together."

I shrink back, taking a step toward the cage holding her son and shaking my head. Her eyes harden.

"It doesn't work on you," she says under her breath.

"What doesn't?"

"The pull." At my look of confusion, she smiles a little and says, "You guessed that I am Arkana. The people of your world, both living and undead, can't help but be drawn to me. They crave guidance and a leader. They would feel a pull toward me and hear my voice calling to them. But it doesn't work on you because you want to lead yourself, don't you? It doesn't work on your mother either. Some other vampires manage to avoid the call as well, but most are susceptible to it."

I think of Nuira then, a vampire who had to be captured by my mother to be brought to Casiopea's army.

"So you manipulate them to join you with your powers as a god," I say slowly.

"Oh, they come when I call, and they named me their queen because they long for someone to help them lead their new lives, or else they'd be lost. I can't deny it's been useful to me. Without that pull, I wouldn't have been able to form my army."

"But you still control them once they join you," I spit out. "Just like you try to control the forest and everyone who enters it. You're no different from my mother. Everything living here gets killed because of what you've done."

The earth shakes, splinters, and cracks above me, and I fight to keep my balance.

After a heavy pause, Casiopea says, in the loneliest tone of voice I've ever heard, "All I wanted was to keep him close."

"You must have gone through other human forms before you became this one, didn't you? When the Arkana took on human lives to create the first witches. That's thousands of descendants you must have throughout the world, all using the magic you taught them. All the vampires you've changed as well. They're your family, too, and you're hurting them. And you and my mother want to hurt even more people. Stop hurting this world and go back to your own."

"I have pulled so far away from the Arkana, and all my other lives." Casiopea bares her fangs as she approaches me. "This is the only one I know."

Before I can react, she slashes her hands through the air, and roots from above swing down to wrap around me. They squeeze my chest and legs so hard, I feel like I'm going to split in half. I try to break them, but they're too strong, and my hands are pinned down so I can't use my own Root magic.

The earth continues shaking above us and more humans tumble out of their cages, and Casiopea watches it with trepidation. Roots collapse to the ground and turn to dust that billows out across the floor.

"You didn't believe me before," I blurt out. "About my mother. But she's attacking the tree now with the powers she took from me, and it will fall. If you leave to stop her, I'll destroy it from the inside. You can't stop both of us at once, but you can choose to end this on your terms instead."

The desperation grows deeper on Casiopea's face. The roots around me begin to loosen, and I thrust them off.

"My power is one that can be passed on, like all magic can,"

Casiopea finally says. "It's been a millennium, but my son stays the same. I know my time is over."

The earth shakes so hard then, I nearly fall over. I catch my balance and turn away from Casiopea, toward the heart. My heart aches for her for a moment. All she wanted was to keep her family close. But she ended up poisoning everything around her.

The gods chose me to come here for a reason, maybe because of my connection to both life and death. I used to think it was impossible for both sides of me to coexist, but they are both a part of me. Vampire and Root witch.

I've never wanted to lead before, but I also never recognized my own power. If anyone understands vampires and how difficult it is to lead a new life, it's me. I can guide them, but I won't force them to my side or to fight, like my mother and Casiopea wanted. I will find a way to make all of this right.

There's a sharp gust of wind behind me. Gray leaves settle on my skin and then disintegrate, seeping into me.

I reach the boy and his caged heart. My fingers spread along the roots of the cage, and then I break it open. Bark splinters in my hands with a wailing, creaking noise. A soft sigh emanates from the within the tree. The boy drops to the ground, his eyes shuttering closed. His heart rolls free from the cage and lands a few feet away, its crimson light fading until it's a hard black rock.

In moments, the boy turns to silver dust in front of me, disintegrating one body part at a time and floating away into nothing.

I have to get out of here. I jolt away from this collapsing cavern, narrowly dodging a falling rock. I race up the dirt path—empty now—and past Zenos, who gawks down at me from his cage of roots. As he yells for me to release him, I climb out of the crack in the earth, the roots pushing me along the way as if they know I only have seconds left.

As I race onto the field and pry my way out of the final roots of the cage I placed around the tree, it happens. Light splits the air, golden and blinding. I drop to the earth, covering my head as a fierce, spiraling wind rages behind me. Roots and rock and bark fly away from the Heart Tree and skid across the valley. Wind sweeps over the trees ahead, pushing away the smoke that still hovers above the forest. There's a flash of lightning, but it covers the whole sky, bolts traveling like snakes toward all horizons.

And then, glittering golden dust—bone dust—drifts down. The Bone Wall is collapsing.

The vampires are free.

# CHAPTER 36

## · KAYE ·

*While Flames are known for our brutality and skill in battle, there's one thing people often forget:*
*We always protect the ones we love, and burn brighter at each other's side.*

—TRAINING ACADEMY FOR
YOUNG WITCHES OF ARBORREN

By the time we reach the valley with the Heart Tree, we've extinguished most of the fires. The treetops are still dotted with orange flame and black smoke, but only in scattered places. We did the best we could, and now that we've reached the valley, we're both near collapse. But the battle below reenergizes me. Even the deep cut on my arm and the hint of white bone doesn't deter me, although I almost fainted in the forest when I finally saw it.

"The hunters still think we're on their side," I say, my gaze sweeping across the field—the vampires and hunters engaged in battle while Eugenia stands ahead of them all, not even looking back as the men she's brought to fight are slaughtered.

She stands in front of the silver-boughed Heart Tree, which is locked in a gray cage of some sort, and with her own powers flings heavy rocks and spear-shaped branches at it. I can't see Ava anywhere. "They'll trust us when we tell them to fall back. The hard part will be leading them past the vampires without getting our heads ripped off, but—"

"Not you," Tristan says, and when I scowl at him, adds quickly, "They'll recognize you as the traitor Liander arrested. I'll tell them Liander's calling them off. They won't come with us at all if they see you."

I grumble in frustration. He's right, but I won't just abandon him to do all the hard work. He extends a hand past me and points toward a copse of trees at the crest of one side of the valley. "See there? The humans and vampires they took prisoner. You can free them."

My heart pounds in anticipation when I spot them; they're tied to trees with vines. Vampires guard them, but only two, and they look tense and agitated, like they just want to join the fight and protect their own instead of babysitting the prisoners.

"If you can," I whisper, "bring the hunters in that direction. Vampires will follow to stop you, and I bet the two guards will leave their station to help. They look like they're dying to join the fight."

"Well, they can't do that, Kaye, they're already dead," Tristan says seriously, then laughs when I roll my eyes. "Good plan. I'll meet you there."

I nod, giving him what I hope is an encouraging smile that conceals my nerves. Then he slips down the hill, moving toward different groups of hunters and dodging vampires whenever he gets too close to one. I can't let my fear for him overshadow what I have to do now; those prisoners need my help, and I won't leave someone else locked away if I can free them.

I use the skill of invisibility my mother taught me and hope it will cover me all the way across the valley. As I skirt the edge, I watch the battle from the corner of my eye. Loud crashes sound every few seconds as Eugenia directs her hunters to shoot silver bolts into the cage around the tree. As I round the valley, moving closer to the center of it, I realize the cage is made of knotted gray roots and vines. That's something only a Root witch could do—which means that either Ava or Casiopea is holding off Eugenia alone now.

Soon, I'm crouched in the copse of trees. The humans are tied to trees in the back of the line, while the vampire captives are closer to the front, next to the guards. I recognize the human boy who was in Ava's cage with her, and the vampire Nuira, who attacked me.

Moving as quietly as I can manage, I step in front of the line of seven human prisoners, briefly lift my invisibility, and place a finger on my lips. They gasp when they see me, but I quickly replace the invisibility before the vampires guarding them turn around.

I wait one long minute for the guards to turn back around, then approach the captives. I move behind the closest one to start sawing through the vines that bind their wrists and ankles to the tree trunks. As I work, sweat pouring down my forehead, I check that the guards haven't noticed anything; their focus is entirely fixed on the battle below.

One free. The boy steps down lightly, looks over his shoulder to mouth "thanks" to me, and then tiptoes back toward the trees behind us. Once he's ten feet away, he breaks into a sprint.

I work on the second one, my fingers shaking with the need

to work faster. This prisoner lands slightly heavier, and my heart shoots into my throat. The guards are still distracted, but Nuira cranes her neck around to look behind her, as if she's searching for me. I briefly release my invisibility so she can see me. She strains at the binds on her hands and nods her head at them as if to tell me to hurry up.

I gesture at the remaining five prisoners to show I'm freeing them first, and her answering eye roll could rival one of my own.

Once my invisibility is back on, I cut through the next three prisoners' binds in a trance, my mind focused only on the task I need to do. But a throbbing headache is building at the back of my skull. I can't see Tristan or Ava from here, or any of the battle, but loud crashes and creaking branches tell me Eugenia is making progress with that tree.

I free the last human prisoner, who sprints toward the trees behind us without a backward glance.

The guards finally turn. One of them yells at the other that he should have been paying closer attention. My heart beats so loud I can hardly make out their footsteps as they run to the trees.

"This vine was cut," one of them spits out, then freezes. "Do you hear that pulse? A mortal is still here."

Cursing my racing pulse, I look for a way out of this mess. I walk as quietly as I dare to where Nuira is bound. She strains against the bindings on her wrists again and mouths, "I'll help."

I consider fleeing right now, while the two vampires behind me are still searching through the trees to find me. All the humans have escaped, and the only prisoners left are vampires who've tried to kill me and surely would try again. I can escape; they'll remain trapped here and they won't get to me at all. A bitter taste rises in the back of my throat, telling me to abandon them here, that not all vampires are good like Ava.

*Neither are all Flame witches,* I think, remembering Liander.

As Nuira strains against her bonds, I'm reminded of Ava with silver cuffs around her hands, Ava strung up in a net that burned her at every touch. Ava with a burn mark at her throat. All of that was done to her by humans and witches.

As I shift my weight, a twig cracks under my foot. The two guards turn toward Nuira and race toward us as I feverishly cut through her bonds. I expect my head to be ripped off at any moment, but I keep going.

Then she's free. She shoves me into the mud behind her and takes my dagger, then catches the first guard. With a sharp twist, she cracks his neck. His body drops and she slides her knife into the chest of the second vampire. He collapses, blood spilling from him to coat the forest floor. They'll recover soon enough, but they're definitely incapacitated for now.

Once Nuira finishes freeing the other vampires, she slides the knife toward me as I finally drop my invisibility. "Stay alive."

"You, too," I say as she races down the hill instead of fleeing into the woods. She pulls down a hunter, pierces his throat with her fangs, and drops him after one long swig of blood. Then she leaps for a vampire and twists his neck like she did with the motionless guard behind me.

"At least she's fair about it," I mutter, and then I stand to move farther down the hill, but still in the shade of the trees. Eugenia has nearly broken through the cage surrounding the tree and has dealt significant damage to the trunk and branches. If this were a regular tree, it would have collapsed long ago. I wonder, with a twist of fear in my heart, where Ava is.

Scanning the battlefield, I spot Tristan leading a few hunters toward the lip of the valley, some ways down from where I am, with two vampires chasing after them at a stunning speed. He shouts at the hunters to run, and they abandon him without a second thought. Shaking my head at how foolishly heroic he's being, I race down the hill, bringing flames to my hands.

"Move!" I shout at him as I barrel toward them, and send flames streaking across the grass to curl in a circle around the vampires. The fire catches quickly and rises above their heads, trapping them in place.

Tristan lowers his silver blade, panting from how fast he'd run, and sends me a grateful smile that lights up his whole face. I grin back at him, but we're far from safe right now.

Then, the earth rocks beneath my feet. I nearly fall over, but Tristan catches me. There's an earsplitting metallic shrieking sound that makes me clamp both hands over my ears. A bitingly cold wind sweeps dust and dirt all around us.

Forcing my gaze up, I look toward the Heart Tree just in time to watch it happen: It splits down the middle with a pained wail. The roots, vines, branches, and bark break off and fly through the air like shrapnel after an explosion. Eugenia's too close, and she steps back, but never tears her eyes from the tree. She's not fast enough.

I bite down hard on my lip to stop from screaming as one of the flying fragments rams into her skull. I look away quickly, but I still see the moment her head leaves her body.

But that gruesome thought is swept away when the gusting

wind picks up speed, swirling through the valley like a storm. Tristan and I flatten ourselves to the ground, hands over our heads as we wait for it to pass. Light flashes above, so bright I squeeze my eyes shut. The scent of burning cinders reaches me, and tiny sparks of flame land on my arms as the fire I'd trapped the vampires with is swept away. I expect their fangs at my throat and tense up, one hand going to a silver dagger, but all I hear and feel is the wind.

It dies away after long minutes, and the quiet that settles over the valley is scarier than all the fighting. Heart pounding, my mouth dry with fear, I look up.

The Heart Tree is split in half, as if a giant has sliced an ax through the very center. Smoke rises off it like it's burning. The silvery branches fade to a light brown, and the leaves all fall off, fluttering to the ground in the light wind.

The Heart Tree is dead. Vampires are fleeing in all directions, some east to Arborren, others west, south, north to the mountains and the sea. A golden dust falls from the sky, coating everything like glittering ash. Was this something Eugenia did or is this Ava's doing? Fear for her jolts through me.

"Where are you?" I hiss, willing her to appear in front of me, whole and safe.

"So we've found the traitors," says a deep, gravelly voice behind me. Tristan and I scramble to our feet to face two hunters, some of the ones who were on the front line with Eugenia—I can tell because of the massive, loaded crossbows they wield.

"We were trying to help you all get out of here," Tristan says with his typical charm, and my fear eases a little; he'll be able to talk us out of this, like he always can.

"We'll take you to Liander," one of the hunters finally says, lifting his crossbow and aiming it at me. "You can come dead or alive. Make your choice."

"Liander's dead," I spit out.

"Sounds like someone lying to get out of a punishment," the second hunter says, his crossbow aimed at Tristan. "Well, I'm trying to get paid for catching a pair of traitors."

"Kaye," Tristan whispers in a warning tone, and from the corner of my eye I see the flames building at his hands.

The hunter sees it, too. "I like decisive people."

The screech leaves my throat at the same time the hunter looses his crossbow. A silver bolt flies toward Tristan and I'm a finger's width away, reaching to shove him aside, when something slams through my torso and knocks me back. I drop, hitting my head hard on the ground. Stars explode in front of my eyes. It feels like a wild animal has just knocked me over, and I can't feel anything, I—

My hands land on something long, solid, and metallic. My whole body shakes. I look down. There's a silver bolt pinning me to the ground, and blood blooms from my chest like red star flowers. My next breath comes out as a choked sound, and blood spurts from my mouth.

Tristan is a few feet away. Blood pools underneath him like a lake. He meets my gaze as more blood spills from his lips.

In the distance, Nuria is running toward us and closing in fast. Dust kicks up around her in clouds. There's so much blood pooling around me and Tristan I don't know how either of us has our eyes open. Nuira is too late, but she doesn't stop—she reaches the hunters before they can collect our dying bodies. In two quick thrusts, she breaks their necks.

She's closer to Tristan; dropping to her knees, she speaks with him, but I can't hear very well. As I watch the scene with blurry vision, Tristan lifts a trembling hand and points to me. He tries to say something, but it's like cotton is wedged in my ears and muting all other sound.

My body is shutting down one part at a time. I wonder what'll go last—my brain, my breath, my heart?

As my eyes slide shut, the last thing I see is Tristan's eyes staring unblinkingly at me. Someone's calling my name, but it's coming to me as muffled as if I'm underwater and they're still safely above.

I don't know if it's only in my imagination or if he actually speaks, but I hear Tristan's voice saying *I'm right here. You'll be safe.*

And then the current carries me away.

# CHAPTER 37

## - AVA -

*The emperors of old knew the witches were the descendants of gods,*
  *but fear drove them to try to conquer the witches and steal their powers for themselves,*
    *and out of that pain, vampires were born.*
    *Out of greed, humanity created its own predator.*
      —JOURNAL BY CALLUNA MENTARA

Vampires have fled in all directions, no one staying after it was clear the Bone Wall was gone and there was nothing keeping them in the forest.

Then I see my mother's body and put my fist in my mouth to stop from screaming. Blood streaks across the dirt beyond her. I clamp my eyes shut, not wanting to see any more. Did the hunters turn on her and do this? Or was it from me destroying the Heart Tree?

My whole body starts shaking as the image imprints itself in my mind. She's gone . . . after all that time. Memories sprint through my mind, of her holding me when I was a child, of her locking me inside and ending the life I knew . . . how she wanted to use me again.

But I never wanted her to die. I just wanted her to stop.

I stumble back, toward the opening into the Heart Tree, but it's collapsed now. Dropping to my knees, I grasp at the roots, now brown instead of gray, and the grass, which was yellowing before and now has a slight green tinge at the tips.

Then a scream breaks through my clouded thoughts. Standing and wiping away tears I hadn't noticed, I search for whoever screamed. It was a girl's voice.

"Kaye," I call out, my voice seeming to echo in the deep valley. It's nearly empty, except . . .

Panic shoots through me like lightning. Some hundred feet away, two people lie on the ground with blood spreading around them and silver bolts wedged in their bodies. Someone kneels next to them. At first I think it might be dead vampires, but then I see Kaye's chestnut hair gleaming in the sun.

I'm running so fast, my feet seem to leave the ground. Fifty feet away, twenty feet away—

I can't hear her heartbeat.

I skid to my knees next to Nuira, who's just turned away from Tristan and is trying to shake Kaye awake. I grab Kaye's shoulders, but she's limp. Are her limbs already cold or is that my imagination?

"Kaye—" The word catches in my throat. I can't think or speak. Everything human about me seems to die and fade away alongside this fiery girl who is now cold as ice.

I glance over my shoulder toward Tristan and it feels like a heavy weight is beating me in the chest. I feel myself sinking, losing all sense of where I am, what just happened, why any of it matters at all.

"He's gone," Nuira whispers beside me, and I jump, having forgotten she was there. Then she stands, nodding at Kaye. "There's still a faint pulse—but I won't change someone without their permission. Do what you will."

Her words come to me one at a time, and my brain makes sense of them piece by piece. I can barely manage much else. I lean over Kaye as Nuira vanishes into the trees.

Kaye didn't get another chance, not like me. My tears fall hard and fast as I remember every minute with her in these woods, her vibrant laugh and curious gaze and the expression she got whenever I said something to make her question all she knew. The grief in her voice whenever she spoke of her mother.

*Everyone dies at their time, fair or not,* she'd told me, but even then, I could hear the doubt in her voice. I don't care if it was her time, it's not fair at all. I lean over her, gripping her shoulders as if that will shock some life into her. Tears blur my vision and sobs rack me. If I'd been here, if I'd helped her . . .

"Ava," says a quiet, weak voice. I nearly fall apart at the sound of it. As I turn back to Kaye, my breath stutters as her eyes slide open blearily.

"Kaye, I can help you," I say, then bring my wrist to my mouth and sink my fangs into it. Blood slides down my forearm.

A long beat of silence passes. *Say something!* I want to tell her. But she gulps, her forehead crinkling in thought.

A memory spikes through my jumbled thoughts.

I was sixteen, and it was an hour after my mother told me to drink her blood. Someone had attacked me from behind while I stood at my window. I'd yelled for them to get off me, and then something sharp pierced my throat. Hours later, I'd woken with dried blood on my lips, staring at the domed ceiling of my attic.

Then the fever began, and the pain as my body died and became something else. I can still remember what every inch of death felt like, every painful second of the long march to another kind of existence.

I shake my head to clear the memory, and when I stare down at Kaye, she focuses on me with what little strength she has left.

*Don't go quietly, Kaye,* I think to myself. *Fight, live, claim your own life.*

"Do it," she whispers.

A strange sense of elation flutters through me, but I bite my lip, tamping it down. Should I really turn her into something she's spent most of her life hating?

With a shaking arm, I bring my bleeding wrist over Kaye, and look to her once more.

Noticing my hesitation, she says, "I'm not done yet."

I nod. She's choosing it for herself, and that's what matters most. I tilt my wrist so the blood falls onto her tongue.

She closes her mouth and swallows, her eyes nearly drooping shut. I watch her, hardly daring to blink. At first, I don't notice the shadow coming up behind me and then spreading out ahead of us like a scythe in the dirt.

I barely manage to turn and see a mud-covered, dirt-stained Zenos standing above me before he swings a silver rod at my head.

Three days after my return to Arborren, I stare at the ceiling of the cell they've put me in, my mind blank and calm. My thirst pierces at the back of my throat. I'm more desperate than ever before, but I won't give them the satisfaction of seeing that.

Even as they wave cups of blood in front of the cell bars to taunt me. Even as I fight the urge to strain against the silver cuffs that pin me to a cold table. I'd rather disintegrate to nothing than beg for blood.

I wonder why it's taking them so long to arrange a pyre.

Zenos managed to transport me back to Arborren with the help of some hunters. Regular bashes to the head kept me sound asleep the whole way, I wager, judging from the endless throbbing sensation on my skull. Days later, I woke up in a cell—likely one of the ones underneath the Clarity Council Hall in the middle of the town.

I'm not surprised that I'm back in chains waiting to be burned, but I am surprised Zenos turned me over to the Clarity and didn't just keep me for himself.

The guards like to taunt me, but they also like to whisper, and the spreading rumors fill me with a grim satisfaction.

"She destroyed the Bone Wall and sent the vampires to massacre everyone" was a popular whisper. A quieter one, but one that intrigued me more, was "She's the new vampire queen—yes, it's all real, I'll tell you what Zenos saw."

The table I lie on is cold and grimy, probably with the sweat of other vampires preparing to die a second time. It's also made entirely of silver. But unlike all the other times I've encountered the metal, it doesn't bother me as much as before. I wonder if higher resistance to silver is some of the magic that Casiopea passed onto me.

There's a sliver of my reflection visible if I angle my head just right. Sometimes it's my face, the sharp cut of my hair, eyes that stare back at me questioning if I'll ever get out of this mess. Other times, there's the sway of gray leaves in my hair, or a fissure of skeletal hollows under my cheeks.

They're both me, but one of them has gained the powers of a goddess. I'm not a god myself, but something in between. Casiopea passed on her powers in full before returning to her plane, rather than the small bits of magic the Arkana gave to humans.

I have her strength. I have yet to test my Root magic, but I'm confident that will be stronger, too. I rattle the bonds at my wrists and think how easy they would be to break right now. But it doesn't seem like the right time yet.

I have her instinct. It's telling me to wait for something, but it's in my voice, not hers.

And I have her pull. Now that I have this power, I can tell what she means by the pull she has on people—mortal and immortal alike. The guards here are fascinated by me, even as they wait to lead me to my death. My pull to the vampires . . . that's deeper. It's like there's a warm glow at my heart, one that connects me to my kind. I can extend it and send it pulsing outward, or I can keep it close.

My mother wanted to keep me close . . . but she only did that by hurting me. A heavy grief still weighs on my chest when I think of her. She was trapped in her own way, but no one came to save her. A single tear escapes as I remember her telling me I'm stronger than I think I am. I won't dwell on regrets or what our relationship could have been like if she'd never become a vampire or if my father had never died, because that's not reality.

Now that Casiopea's power has seeped into me, I have to decide what to do with it—what part of her strength to use, and whether I'll attempt to call the vampires to me or not. The only thing I know for sure is that I won't command them.

I'll need to find my own way to commune between life and death, to give the vampires a path that differs from endless bloodshed.

All day and night, I wonder what happened to Kaye after I left. Was she reborn as a vampire, like me? Where is she now?

I doze off imagining Kaye with her arms around me, my hands in her hair. I imagine how things would be between us now if we really are the same. I slip into a dream of falling asleep with her near a flickering campfire, a million stars watching us.

The cell door creaks open hours later, jolting me awake. Although I don't know what time it is, I know that only night can be this still, the very air holding its breath to watch what happens next.

A man slides into the cell, his ratlike face and jerky movements so familiar to me I roll my eyes.

"What are you doing here, Zenos? Other people have appointments to kill me, you'll have to get in line like everyone else."

Two more men slip inside after him and work silently, methodically. They slip different chains onto the bottoms of my bare feet before unlocking the old ones, and quickly move the new ones into place. Then they do the same to my hands. My ankles and wrists are still cuffed, with short chains holding them together. Zenos gestures for me to get up, still without saying a word.

I follow without complaint. If Zenos is stupid enough to take me outside of a secure cell, sneak me away, and convince himself this plan will go perfectly, well . . . I'm not going to ruin his fun just yet.

We go out a back door, marked for employees of the facility, and toward a horse-drawn wagon tucked away in a side street. The predawn, deep autumn chill makes me shiver, but I welcome it. There's a silver cage bolted down in the back of the wagon.

"Where are we going?" I ask in a chipper tone.

Zenos shoots me an exasperated look from the corner of his eye, then sighs. "The capital. My uncle heard about the unfortunate passing of my wife and about the Bone Wall—he no longer thinks this is a suitable place for anyone in the family to live and has offered me my own private quarters in the palace. I'm commissioning it to be turned into a lab—not that he's aware of that. Studying vampires or witches is one thing, but you're something different now. I want to learn more about you."

"Hmm," I say with a dismissive smile. I look beyond him, down the street toward the houses of Arborren, some of which are streaked with the pastel light of early dawn. I spent so many hours staring at those terra-cotta tiles that I know exactly what they look like. I take in the colors of my home now, possibly for the last time—sandstone, and coral, and chestnut.

I stare at those roofs for a long moment, careful not to show any emotion on my face, and then step into the back of the wagon next to the cage. "Well, I'd like to see more of the world. It'll be nice to have a free ride somewhere."

His forehead crinkles as he glares up at me in suspicion, but then he gestures for one of the men with him to unlock my cage. I hear the man's rapid heartbeat as he opens the door for me, and I imagine the sweet taste of his blood.

But a proper queen knows when to strike, and when to wait.

I avert my eyes from the man and step inside the cage without complaint. I even sit on the silver floor, and this time, the burn from it is barely noticeable. I can withstand far more now.

Then I decide to test the pull Casiopea gave me. I don't know how exactly it works, but she said the vampires who sought her out wanted a leader. She used that against them, but I'll let them decide for themselves to follow me. I know how it feels to lose your life and all sense of self, and to feel like all you're capable of is hurting people. I only hope they'll want to listen, and join me in finding new homes, new ways to live . . . a new family.

Under my breath, I say, "I'm waiting for you all. If you want a guide . . . someone to show you a new way . . . I'll be near Arborren."

After Zenos pays the two men who helped him, he takes up the reins, and then the horse starts to pull out of Arborren. The road to the capital is seldom used, almost overgrown with weeds and roots, and the forest runs alongside it, but there is no more barrier. Zenos continues, whistling to himself as the world wakes up around us.

I stare into the trees and imagine eyes looking back at me—waiting for their queen to return.

# CHAPTER 38

## · KAYE ·

A fever consumes me all the way to Arborren. At some point, after I'd lain in the dirt for a few hours, Nuira returned for me. She found a wagon to transport Tristan and me back, muttering the whole while that I'm lucky she likes me and decided to come back for me.

For days I lie staring at the star-speckled sky next to Tristan's body, my thoughts as unstable as wind in a brutal storm. Every time I try to focus on something, my mind floats away, and another wave of pain crashes into me—sharp teeth biting through my skin, a hammer slamming into my bones. All of it, I feel over and over again. And though I can't see the teeth or the swing of the hammer, they are as real to me as the wagon beneath me.

I pass in and out of consciousness, over and over, until one day I wake up in my bedroom in Arborren.

My hands go to my torso, which feels like it's been ripped open and then sewn back together hastily. Pain jolts through me. Under my shirt, I feel mottled skin.

But how? That silver bolt tore right through me. There was blood everywhere.

The back of my throat prickles, like tiny knives stabbing me. I move one hand up to my throat, massaging it to try to get rid of the discomfort.

I made it somehow, but Tristan . . . The tears come in moments, and I don't know how long I lie there sobbing, but eventually I pass out again.

When I wake, my hand resting on my chest, my thoughts are clear, like a deserted hall where everything around me echoes. I can finally hear myself think again.

Where my hand rests, right over my heart . . . there's no beat.

Images slam into my memory. The blood pooling under me and Tristan. Tristan pointing at me when Nuira came to save us. Ava's bleeding wrist over my mouth.

Blood.

The stabbing sensation in my throat hits me again, and my gums ache, like something is trying to push through them.

Panicking, I roll off the side of the bed. I need to get out of here, I need to—

I land next to a sealed jar placed near the head of my bed. The jar is clear, and inside it is a deep red liquid. Sniffing close to the jar, I catch a gamy scent and my mind careens back to when I'd skinned the squirrel for Ava to drink from.

Without pausing to think, I rip off the lid and take long gulps of the blood. If I pause to think, I'll lose my mind or vomit it all up or pass out again until I disintegrate.

When I lower the jar, the stabbing sensation is gone. The fangs growing at my gums stop aching. The whole world is . . .

I can see ants crawling up the hinges of the door, so tiny

I never would have noticed before. Without even straining my ears, I hear the low tones of a conversation in one of the other rooms in the building. I hear footsteps somewhere nearby.

Then I start shaking and haul myself back onto my bed. Drawing my knees to my chest, I stare at the empty jar of blood like it's about to attack me.

I'm alive, but I'm dead. I clench my jaw so hard, my teeth might break, and wrap my arms tighter around my knees.

I just drank blood, and I'll need to often if I want to . . . survive? A derisive laugh escapes me at the thought. Life and death have never seemed so similar until now.

I'll be hunted with silver arrows and blades, and if I'm caught, one of my old Flame brethren will light me on fire.

The walls seem to close around me, both trapping and protecting me in this room, as my thoughts spiral out of control.

Ava. I'll be like . . . Ava. The storm in my mind starts to settle as I think of her kind eyes, the softness of her smile, her fierce voice. Where is she? If there's anyone who can talk me through this, it's Ava.

A knock sounds at my door.

"Kaye, are you awake?"

It's Nuira's voice. "Come in," I call, and the door swings open with a creak.

"How did you get me back here?" I breathe. The vampire strides into my room and wipes blood off the corners of her lips.

She shakes her head in disbelief. "It's been decades since I was turned. I forgot how disorienting it can be. I saw your friend, the vampire, get attacked and taken, and I was going to go after her, but . . . trust me, she's fine. She, uh . . . kind of became the new vampire queen."

I blink rapidly. "What?"

"That's the rumor going around. The old queen passed her powers on to Ava, like how the gods first did. You know witches' power has been diluted over the centuries? Still strong, but not like it first was. Sounds like your friend got a bit of a boost. I think she'll be a better queen than the old one, at least. I stayed when I saw you, because if you woke up alone there with no blood around you and no one to help, you wouldn't make it very far before disintegrating. When we reached the town, you woke up long enough to tell me where you live."

"Someone took her?" I ask, sitting upright. "Who?"

"Some human man," she says with a shrug. "Looks a bit like a rat."

An image of Zenos comes to mind, and I know it must be him. Where is she now?

As if reading my thoughts, Nuira says, "She's in a cell under the Clarity Council Hall. I found the man and overheard his plans—he's going to break her out of that cell and take her for himself. He didn't really have a choice but to hand her over when he reached the city. Vampires were storming in, and the Clarity has locked up a lot of them. They're planning to burn them all, one at a time. I snuck you in while they were busy handling the others."

"When is he planning to take her?" I ask in a rush, already standing.

"I don't know, but he's going to do it soon," Nuira says.

I bite my lip, considering what to do. As Nuira turns to leave, I ask, "Why did you help me?"

The other vampire crosses her arms and leans against my door behind her. "I owe it to you, after helping me get away from those vampires and a lifetime of serving Casiopea. And . . . I admit,

I thought it was strange how close you and the vampire girl were in the forest, when I first saw you there."

"When you tried to kill me," I say in a flat tone.

"Yes, that time." She waves a hand dismissively. "I've been a vampire for fifty years, Kaye Mentara. All I've ever heard is how different we are from mortals, how there is no coexisting between us. But you two proved that wrong, and now . . . I think she'll do great things. You should be at her side."

Nuira leaves shortly after that, and I'm too antsy to stay here. I walk through my house one more time and take in everything with my vampire sight. I take nothing with me—except for the contents of the pillowcase that Ava carried, and which I took once she was captured by the Flames. Inside it are my mother's journal and the blue scarf I once gifted to Ava. The sack itself is completely covered in my own blood, which spilled on it when the hunters attacked me. I place the journal and scarf inside a different pack, and I leave behind everything else, even the gold wrist cuffs I used to love so much. I say goodbye—to my past, to my mortal life, to my mother's ghost. I'll take all the lessons she taught me and use them to forge my own future, with her and Tristan in my heart, and Ava at my side.

I climb the rooftops in the hour before dawn, the wind propelling me along at a speed I've never imagined. The world is clearer up here than ever before. The Clarity Council Hall, and the prison beneath, are just a few blocks away now.

I pause when I hear her voice—clear as a bell, the most beautiful sound I've ever heard. Then I see the horse-drawn wagon in a side street with a silver cage bolted down in the back. Ava looks in my direction for half a second, and for the first time I see the soft glow that hangs over young witches, which they taught us about in Flame witch training, but that only vampires are able to see. I'm stunned by how beautiful she looks with it, even more beautiful than she usually is. If I still needed to breathe, I'm sure I wouldn't be able to right now at the sight of her.

Without a shred of fear on her face, Ava climbs onto the wagon and into the cage, while her stepfather takes up the reins.

With a small laugh, I follow, wanting to test my new speed and my powers before I act.

Out of Arborren and down a weed-choked path, I follow and feel no hesitation. Just like Ava climbed into that cage willingly, I follow them without fear.

For the first time in my life—and this new life—I let go of safety, fear, doubt. I let go of trying to change myself to fit into what other people want me to be.

Plenty of people have tried to control both me and Ava. They've all underestimated us, our voices and our presence and our power. And they all missed the exact moment we grew strong enough to stand on our own.

# CHAPTER 39

## - AVA -

Fog rolls over the path Zenos continues down, and I let the misty feel of it wrap around me. It's noon now, but the sun is only a pale yellow glow above the thick, swirling gray of fog. The trees on either side are rife with crimson foliage, and I take in every color as if I've never seen it before. Watching the forest heal is like a balm for my soul; even damaged, wrecked things can become whole and beautiful again. For the first time in so long, I feel life stretching out ahead of me like a clear forest path rather than a narrow cell.

I watch the trees for one more moment, noting the blur of movement among the ocher-brown trunks.

Letting out an exaggerated sigh, I call to Zenos, "I thought we were friends, Zenos. We spent so much time together the past few years, and now you're carting me off to the capital."

Zenos scoffs, turning his head slightly to look back at me in disgust. "Why would I be friends with a bloodsucker?"

I raise an eyebrow. "You wanted to become one of us for years, didn't you? But my mother never gave you what you wanted because she needed to keep you around. I suppose people always find ways to hate what they can't have. So many years together, Zenos," I say with another dramatic sigh. "All while you fought me and hurt me and used me and thought you were entitled to me. But you do not know me at all."

There's a light tapping on my shoulder as Zenos turns back around with a snarl. I lean into the hand that's reaching through the bars and tilt my head so it rests against her invisible fingers for a moment.

Twisting around in the cage, I reach through it, grasping at air until I land on something solid. Kaye flickers in and out of view—a clip of mischievous green eyes, a fluttering strand of chestnut hair, the edge of her smile. Placing one hand on the back of her head and the other on her shoulder, I draw her toward me and kiss her through the bars of the cage. Her warmth melts into me, banishing the chill around us, even with the cage pressing in on both sides of my face.

As I pull back from her, the carriage slows. Zenos lets out a frightened whimper ahead of me, and I wonder—did they come?

Zenos was right all along; I am the monster. Only now, I love the word, let it wrap around me as I approach the cage bars. I spent so long convincing myself I was weak that I never saw a chance to be anything else until now.

Kaye lets half of her body slide back into view and lifts a hand toward one of the bars of the cage, a questioning look in her eyes.

"Allow me," I whisper, and she vanishes once more.

When I turn and stand, I see them—so many vampires I can't count, gathered on the path ahead. Zenos has stopped the carriage some fifty feet away from them, and I watch as sweat trickles down the back of his neck.

I walk up to the edge of the cage right behind Zenos, and wrap my hands into fists around two of the bars to pull.

The metal comes apart easily, with a shrieking noise that sends birds flying from the trees in panic. I shove through the bars in a breath, and as my shadow falls over Zenos, he jerks his head around.

I don't give him a chance to beg. I force his neck to the side and sink my fangs into his throat. The warm blood rushes through me as he jerks and convulses uselessly under my iron grip. I drink for a few long seconds, then stand and wipe the blood off my chin. Kaye stands next to me now, fully visible with a hungry gleam in her eyes and fangs extending past her lips.

"Breakfast," I say, handing him over. Then I lift a hand to wave at the vampires ahead.

Kaye dives for Zenos instantly. While she drinks, I stare out at the path ahead, leading to new towns, forests, lakes, and mountains.

*Why are you alone? You could have an army at your command, with those powers.* One of the vampires that attacked me and Kaye had said that with awe in their voice.

But I'm not alone. I have Kaye, and now this whole family of vampires. They won't be my army, and I'll never command any of them. I'll show these vampires different ways to live, so the thirst doesn't consume them and truly turn them into monsters. There's no escaping what we are, and maybe it's naive of me to think there's a way to coexist among mortals. But I'm determined to try.

Then, I notice the ring my mother gave me is still tight on my finger even after all this time. The ruby's shine is duller now. For a moment, I wonder if I should keep it. But I've entered a new life, and the woman who ended my old one and imprisoned me is no longer in it. It hurts a little, to get rid of this final memory of her. But I have to move on. I remove the ring with one sharp tug, and let it fall to the grass outside the wagon.

I touch Kaye's shoulder once she finishes drinking. Dropping Zenos's body, she stands next to me with blood coating her chin, neck, and torso. She wipes away some of it, but misses most. With a wild grin, she takes my hand and whispers, "Let's go."

Together, we jump off the wagon, and the other vampires are fast behind us. We run across the dirt path, past the weeds and roots and reaching branches, and we vanish into the trees.

# ACKNOWLEDGMENTS

My amazing publishing team deserves all the praise and thanks. I am forever grateful to my agent, Peter Knapp of Park & Fine Literary, and my editor, Eileen Rothschild, at St. Martin's Press/ Wednesday Books. This book wouldn't be possible without both of you: Pete for your tenacity, passion, encouragement, and drive; Eileen for your endless enthusiasm, kindness, and stellar editing skills and attention to detail. Thank you both for your hard work getting this book into the world. Thank you to the team at Park & Fine, especially Stuti Telidevara and Abigail Koons.

Thank you to everyone at Wednesday Books who works incredibly hard to make books come to life: Lisa Bonvissuto, Rivka Holler, Brant Janeway, Meghan Harrington, Alyssa Gammello, Tiffany Shelton, Alexis Neuville, and Melanie Sanders. Thank you so much to Noa Wheeler for helping this book come together with your thoughtful, nuanced notes. A huge thank-you to Olga Grlic, the cover designer, and Colin Verdi, the illustrator, for the cover of *The Witch and the Vampire*. You've given this book the most beautiful cover I could have asked for. And thank you to Denise and Biondo Studios for crafting a beautiful author website.

Thank you as always to my mother, without whom I would never have been a writer. She became disabled when I was a child, and although we didn't have much money growing up, she made sure I never missed out on experiences and opportunities. Thanks to her, I got involved in sports, art clubs, dance, Girl Scouts, and plenty of other activities that helped me stay focused and passionate about my interests. She gave everything she had and never asked for anything in return or for help, and never did anything for herself, making my happiness and future her priority. She's an example of what all mothers should be. Thank you for everything, Mom.

Thank you to my friends, who have been the best people to experience this journey with; I can't imagine my life without any of you. Thank you to Las Musas for always being a solid community to find support, calm voices, and a safe space. Thank you to Michelle for always being the most wonderful friend I could ask for. Here's to another decade of friendship!

I hope this book finds its way to those who need it, to those who feel cast aside and like they don't belong, in whatever way that may be.